GUARDIAN OF WHISPERS

Diminishing Magic
Book Three

CAT COLLINS

For more information or to book an event, contact: Web@catcollinsbooks.com

Cover images via Canva by Dramatic Tuba Designs, a division of Dramatic Tuba Books by Cat Collins

ISBN – Paperback: 979-8-9870363-4-1

First edition 2023

GUARDIAN OF WHISPERS

Diminishing Magic
Book Three

CAT COLLINS

OTHER BOOKS BY CAT COLLINS

Diminishing Magic Series – series complete

Jewels of Clay
Flames of Gold
Guardian of Whispers
Ripples of Glass

Reindeer Games Series

A paranormal Christmas WHY CHOOSE series of standalones
Fixin' Vixen
Not So Stupid Cupid

Curse of Between Series

An Urban Fantasy Romance novella series featuring two
overlapping stories in each novella

Read Between the Grinds
Between the Sheets

Re-membering Series

An 'unhinged' spicy novella series featuring Dr. Frankenpeen who
"re-members" those poor male souls who have tragic accidents with
their…eggplants.

Book 1, Wood, is based on Pinocchio.
Book 2 coming soon

For the two teachers who inspired my love of words.

Dianna Denton, my ninth-grade English teacher

Dean Duncan, my college journalism professor & friend

Without your enthusiasm for storytelling, I wouldn't be here.

Thank you both.

"The origin of magic lies deep within the aethereal realms, where dreams intertwine with the limitless possibilities of imagination, sparking an energy that awakens the enchantment hidden within all the creatures I created. In other words, I dreamed of magic and it was born. You're welcome."

- The Mage

WELLS

She spoke to me in my dreams. I knew otherwise, but I pretended her voice was real, wrapping myself in the soft words of reassurance falling from those plump lips I loved to take between my teeth. It was enough to convince me that reality was fucking overrated. Every night I woke up growling, aching, and grasping onto the idea of her, but finding nothing but shadows in my clenched fists.

That was why morning was my favorite time of day. The sunrise meant there were more things to occupy my mind than the nightmare of being without Terra. Daytime, I could do. It was the night that brought out the beast in me.

"Are you sure about this?" Gideon asked. For the third time. My answer was apparent in the glare I gave him. "Okay. We're with you." He glanced at the couch where Ren usually sat when we met in my office. That fucker may not have said a lot audibly but his absence in the room was deafening.

I had to get them back.

Then we had another task—rid the worlds of Tristan.

Slowly.

Painfully.

Unmercifully.

I'd imagined stabbing him with the knife Terra had created when she first made gold. It would've been so much more fitting than using it as a letter opener like I'd been doing. Even opening my mail reminded me of her, thanks to the masochistic bastard that was me.

It was Tristan's fault we were here. Yeah, he and his fae buddies had opened the Conduit in their attempt to take all the magic—magic that belonged to us in this realm according to the Mage—but we could've handled that threat. It was his arrogance, his lack of faith in Terra, and in me, that caused her to do the unthinkable and shut the Conduit for good. No matter how often I went over it in my head, I couldn't understand or justify how he'd fooled us all along. She'd once said it had been a fluke that she'd captured him in the first place. She was going for the first fairy she could find. It was random.

Unless it wasn't. And if that was the case, then someone had sent Tristan to our world to lie in wait for twenty-two years before she met up with him. That was a long time to linger and do nothing.

There had to be something more to him than any of us ever knew. He was on the other side of the sealed Conduit, and I couldn't get near him to ask. Or rip his throat out.

Mace snapped his fingers, dragging my attention back to the present. "You're looking pretty murderous there, Hannibal. Might want to take it down a notch before you step out."

I rolled my shoulders. He was right. I had to be able to control my emotions better if I was going to make it through this ordeal and remain the alpha my pack deserved. I had to bring them in on everything and they'd need me more than ever. I couldn't lose my shit over Tristan or Terra. I had to reign it in. "Right. You go on down. I'll be out in a few minutes." Gideon and Mace left me to it. They knew me better than anyone and probably guessed what I was about to do. Still, they allowed it because they understood what was raging inside my heart and mind.

The second the door clicked shut, I shucked my clothes and shifted. The crunch of my bones morphing into my wolf was comforting. Most wolves would have felt caged locked up in an office, but I had control that others didn't, thanks to my phoenix blood. I stayed aware enough to keep my office in relative tact, but when I brought my wolf to the surface my thoughts were less formed, and I reveled in the dullness of it. I was more predator, less me when I was 'wolfing out,' as Terra always put it, There was deep comfort in it, even though it was fleeting.

I paced around my desk, stretching my muscles and growling the rage out of my system. When that wasn't enough, I trotted over to my leather chair and ran my claws over the back of it, shredding the leather apart, and making it look like my heart felt. When didn't settle my soul, I tore into the arms with my teeth, growling and salivating as I freed it from the chair.

I'd have to get another one. Again. Gideon was going to start asking questions when the bills rolled in.

After a few minutes, I shifted into human form and threw my clothes back on. The anger and hurt were still there, but I was slightly calmer and my mind sharper than it had been before.

I took a deep breath and exited my office which overlooked the open expanse of the lodge. The rest of the pack was gathered. Spencer, my newest beta and pretty much my right-hand for day-to-day operations had let them know I was making an announcement.

She was down there somewhere too. Autumn, my fated mate. I didn't have to lay eyes on her flaming red hair to know she was in the building. I could feel her heartbeat along with my own, thumping out of time and sending undulating waves of nausea through me.

It would get worse too. Denying the mating bond was like giving yourself a terminal illness. It would result in a slow agonizing death for both of us. I could've stopped it, severed the bond, but if I had, neither of us would ever love anyone again and I couldn't do that. Not because I was some noble creature who always did the right thing, no. Because it would rip Terra from my heart, and I just couldn't fucking handle that.

So instead, I allowed us both to suffer for the sake of my fragility.

My mother would've been so disappointed.

Terra too. For some unknown reason, she thought I was a good guy. I hadn't felt like a good guy in weeks. Three of them, to be exact.

The pack settled as I stared down at them. Normally I'd go down to the same level as they were, address them as more of an equal. But today I had to let my alpha flag fly. There were empty seats now, a symptom of sending pack members with pups into Illusion Hill for their safety. Add in the guards we'd stationed there to help quell the magic-stealing attacks too—they'd gotten worse—and it seemed like all Magicals were on our way into a dark oblivion.

I couldn't let that happen. Not on my watch. So, I steeled myself, ready to make the announcement that might send even more of our numbers running for the hills. Even so, I couldn't—wouldn't—let festering secrets ruin us. I signaled Spencer and she held up her hand.

Those still murmuring quieted down and there was nothing left but haunting silence and the faint thump of a heartbeat.

Next to the last row. Third seat in from the right.

Mage did I hate how accurately I could feel her.

"Thanks for being here. I know there are rumors and suppositions and all kinds of nonsense being spread about what happened a few weeks ago. First, let me assure you that nothing that happened will affect how this pack runs. Our job is the same as it was before the Conduit closed. Even though it's presumed to be permanently blocked, given the remnants of gold that burst through after the golems were stopped, make no mistake, our task is more important now than ever."

There were scattered mumbles among the group. Mace, Gideon, and Spencer had been fielding questions for twenty-one days, essentially giving the lines I'd asked them to say: 'Everything is fine, stay the course, we have it under control.'

All of it, bullshit.

We had nothing under control and if I didn't get Terra back, everything would *not* be okay. I had a plan for that though. Specifically, a person. He was waiting for me and as soon as I finished addressing the pack, I was going to use my wolf speed to get to him as fast as I could.

"Our pack is no longer just guarding the Conduit. We're protecting Illusion Hill and the Magicals within it. We're going to step up and step in during attacks and make sure all the innocents in our area are protected. Yes, the magic is running out."

More muttering. This time louder. I spoke over it. "Some of the species that held little to begin with are tapped out and dying. I hate it, but it's the way it is. And with some Magicals dying off, the Ambient magic the humans depend on is waning too. There will be chaos in the streets soon. I say this, not to scare you, but to prepare you."

They didn't even try to keep it quiet after that.

Mace yelled a quick "shut the fuck up" to get their attention back for me to go on.

"No, we don't have a solution to getting more magic yet. But if you know Terra like I do…" I paused. I hated looking weak in front of my pack, but the truth was that I was weak without her. Without Ren. "I believe Terra and Ren will find a way to open another Conduit. Or maybe we will. It doesn't matter who or how, but things will get worse before they get better. Now is the time for us to buckle down and do what this pack was meant to do."

I growled, making my position clear to them.

"I know I'm asking a lot of you, but I also know what this pack is capable of, and I believe…" I thumped my chest with my fist. The dull pain inside me echoed. "…in here, that we'll be more than enough to protect Illusion Hill and the camp from threats. We have to do this. No one else will."

A voice carried from the back. One of the lazy troublemakers, Micah. He was a problem. I should've kicked him out of the pack a long time ago, but I didn't want to be like Mateo, playing Mage with everyone's lives. I wanted the pack to have a say in how things were run. Nobody had complained about Micah, so I let things lie. I was starting to regret that. "How are we supposed to protect ourselves if you've got us doing double duty here and Illusion Hill? You can't make us guard the whole damn world, Wells. It's not a fair ask."

I'd told Mace and Gideon to post up in the back of the crowd for security purposes. I'd hoped I wouldn't need them to step in, but I'd learned hope is a fickle bitch sometimes. They shifted silently toward Micah. Those in seats around him scooted away, making room for their approach, knowing shit was about to go down. But the dumb fucker was so busy channeling his anger at me, he didn't even notice. I noticed. I also observed a few heads bobbing in agreement with Micah.

Not wanting things to get out of hand, I leaped off the balcony, landing softly on my feet in front of the pack. Though most wolves could do that jump as well as I could, something was intimidating in seeing your alpha hurl himself off a balcony in human form, just so he could skulk forward and face his adversary eye-to-eye.

It had the intended effect.

"What in the fuck makes you think life is fair, Micah? Newsflash, it's not. Am I going to have a problem with you shirking the duties I, *as your alpha*, assign you? Or do you want to challenge me right now? Up to you. Spence, maybe get the torches ready. He looks like he's dumb enough to do it."

Spencer scurried out of the lodge, her boots echoing across the hardwood floor as Gideon laid a hand on Micah's shoulder. Not hard. Just enough to make him aware he was there. Micah craned his neck in the other direction and found Mace grinning at him like a madman. He had a gift for that, Mace. Normally, he was Mr. Happy-Go-Lucky and the life of the party. But there was a subtle difference between his joyful smile and the one he was leveling on Micah at that moment. This one was downright maniacal and scary as fuck.

I stalked forward and leaned down in Micah's face, allowing my white fur to ripple over my arms. With the annoyance I was feeling, I was sure my purple eyes were flashing near magenta too. I'd been told it was intimidating. I added a growl just so he understood what was happening. "What's it going to be?" He made a move to stand up, but Gideon kept him in his seat. I towered over him and while I was probably a sadistic asshole, I enjoyed seeing his upper lip coated in sweat.

"Uh, I, yeah, I'm good. Just asking rhetorically. Let me know what you need me to do, alpha." Rhetorically? I doubt he knew what the word meant.

"That's what I thought." I stood up to my full height again and he shrank in his seat. "I won't trust a coward to protect anyone's life. You get Conduit guard duty until I tell you differently. And I promise you this: one little slip-up or negative thing out of your piehole, I'll kick you out. Capiche?"

He nodded.

I glanced at Mace. "Did you hear that?"

"Nope. If you're unable to speak, do it in sign language, Helen Keller."

Gideon laughed. The rest of the pack had the good sense to stay silent. They recognized a ticking time bomb when they saw it.

It was me. I was the bomb.

And my heart was ticking a treacherous tune.

Micah finally woke up. "Yes sir, alpha."

I didn't give him the courtesy of another glance in his direction. Instead, I strolled to the front of the room, whizzing by Autumn like she wasn't there, and faced the crowd. "I get it. This is tough. But if you have any doubts about what I'm asking you to do, now's the time to leave. I won't hold it against you, nor will I retaliate in any way. I need my pack strong. I'll even turn my back now so you can go without my judgment. If you leave, know I appreciate that you were here for a time, but don't expect to come strolling back in when this shit is done."

I swallowed, closing my eyes at the finality that swirled inside me, not just for those who were about to leave, but for Terra and Ren. Then, as a man of my word, I turned my back. There was some screeching of chairs and mumbling that put my nerves on edge. I didn't want any of them to go, but I understood why they might have that desire. After a few minutes, Gideon called for me to turn back around.

Every single wolf in the pack had taken a knee. Not one of them had fled. Not one of them looked scared. They were united. And ready to go into battle if they had to do so. I was man enough to admit it choked me up. "Thank you. Now let's get to work."

It had taken Ren and me the better part of a week to go from the Conduit, which I'd permanently sealed with a shiny gold cap, to the castle. Or fortress. Citadel, maybe? I had no clue. All I knew was that it was a big shiny square building. It looked like it had been plunked on the top of a peak. And the Conduit appeared to be in the backyard. *Way* in the back.

In the time it took Ren and I to trudge anywhere near the building, we saw zero people or creatures. Not even a bird flying overhead. It was like we were invisible people walking in an unseen world. I mean, a massive tizzy of fae had attacked us, yet they'd disappeared the second I closed the Conduit and their golem giants turned to gold dust. They never came back.

Reply hazy. Try again.

We'd gotten up early to make the last leg of our trek as the sun peeped over the horizon beyond the building. I hoped when we got to the shiny square building, our questions would be answered. I wasn't even sure what we were doing, other than looking for Trickstan, my former friend and the one who betrayed us. Sad that I'd wanted to come to Aetheria for so long, but now that I was standing in my birthplace, there was a hollowness in me that nothing could fill.

Yeah, that was a golem reference. I'd spent a lot of time thinking about my nature as I slogged through the remains of the golem army I'd destroyed. That was me—killing my people.

I snapped my fingers at Ren. "Hair tie me."

He dutifully dug in his pocket and produced an elastic. "Are you eating these damn things?"

"Sorry, my hair isn't as full and luxurious as yours. I can't help it if they fall out and I lose them. I'm on a mission here, you know. Don't have the brain power to keep a watch on hair ties right now."

"I don't have an unlimited supply. Keep up with that one." He pulled his hair down and redid it. He was on the same hair tie he came with. "Your hair is fine, by the way. Good even."

I fanned myself. "Oh please, stop. You're embarrassing me with your compliments." I shoved him in the arm, he faltered for just a second, then steadied himself again, looking over and giving me a rare smile. He seemed to do that when I needed it most. Like as I was coming to terms with the reality that didn't include Wells or the rest of the pack. At least for the moment. "Thank you, by the way."

"I'm keeping a list. You owe me four hair ties and a new shirt."

"I didn't mean thanks for the hair ties. By the way, I don't drool in my sleep." He grinned again, then raised his eyebrow. "Okay, whatever. I mean to say thanks for being here for me."

"It's not like I had a choice."

He *had*. I didn't know if he realized I knew what he'd done. Probably not. But he could've made it to the Conduit after Autumn dragged Wells through after he'd died to protect her. Ren had plenty of time to follow them, but he chose to stay with me anyway. I'd never be able to express my gratitude to him. Having someone with me meant everything. I couldn't have done this alone. "Thank you anyway."

Something whizzed past my head. I reached up to swat it, but Ren used his wolf speed and grabbed it out of the air before I could connect. He laughed, then held up his prize. A tiny little bluecap was buzzing between his fingers. Finally. Another living being other than the two of us. I leaned in and got his attention. "Hi. Can you tell me what this building is?" We kind of needed to know before we waltzed up into it. We only had about three hundred yards to go, and the bluecap had been the only breathing thing in sight.

The bluecap tried to get free, but Ren kept his grip tight. His voice was tiny and thin but carried enough for us to hear his response. "Uncapture. Uncapture."

"Not happening until you answer her question." Ren's growl wasn't as fierce and panty-melting as Wells' growl was, but it did the trick to get the bluecap talking. If you could count his language as words. "Ruler. Unhome. Magicals unharmony, unfreedom. Undishonor."

"What does that mean?" Ren shook his hand, jarring the little thing, but it didn't help. He just said it again, this time louder.

"It seems like they speak in opposites when they use the 'un' prefix. What would the opposite of a home be? An office?"

"Maybe. And unharmony would be chaos. Unfreedom, would be caged, I guess?"

"And undishonor would be honor. So, it's an office for chaos, caging, and honor?"

"That makes no fucking sense." We stared at the bluecap, but he wasn't giving any clues that we'd figured it out. "Shit!" Ren flinched and the bluecap flew out of his grasp. "You know they have stingers?"

"Nope."

Ren lunged for him, and his fist hit an invisible wall and bounced back. The sound was horrific, and he let loose a string of words that made me blush and laugh at the same time. The bluecap, though, sailed right past the barrier and out of our reach.

What in the Infinite Chasm was that?

Ren reared back and kicked the general area where his knuckles hit. The barrier didn't budge. He pounded a few more times with his fist, but it was useless. "We're not getting in this way."

I wasn't sure if I wanted to go to the Office of Chaos, Caging, and Honor, but it was the only place we had to go, other than through the shiny gold trees which led to…Mage knew where. Something in my gut told me the building was the place to be. Call it a hunch or a feeling, but I had to get in there.

My wrist warmed and I knew I was right. I glanced down at the amethyst bracelet and for the first time in hours, I thought of Wells. *Really* thought of him. My heart seized and I would've sworn I felt him in my mind through our connection. But just like every time I tried to send him thoughts in the past week, all I got was static. He wasn't there. No matter how badly I wanted him to be.

"Hey." Ren tucked a stray hair behind my ear. The stupid hair ties didn't work. "Look at me. What are we going to do?" He was good at that. Sensing when I was spiraling and bringing me back to the present with a question or a goal. I loved him for it.

I blew out my breath and focused on the barrier, which was hard, with invisibility being a key factor in its existence. I truly didn't care that we weren't supposed to be going through it. All I cared about was revenge and survival. Everything else was too painful.

Raising my hand, I angled my bracelet at the wall. At first, nothing happened, but the bracelet began to glow, so I pressed on the wall with my hand, and it slipped through. It felt the same as when I manipulated glass. Though this wall wasn't glass. Ren would've shattered glass with his kicking. I pushed further and my whole arm went through. Ren pressed against the wall in the exact place I had been, but he didn't get through.

There was no way I would be leaving him behind. None. "Pick me up."

"Getting lazy on me?"

"No. I have a theory."

He grumbled a bit like he didn't want to, but he finally lifted me off my feet and cradled me in his arms, honeymooner, over-the-threshold style. I wrapped one arm around his neck and used my other to breach the wall. "Walk slowly. I think I can keep it open enough for us both to get through as long as you're touching me. Don't let me go, okay?"

He bit his lower lip and sighed. It was a strange reaction. I knew he wasn't scared—he didn't get scared about anything—but there was something in his expression I'd never seen before. There was no time to figure it out though, because he stepped right through the barrier like it wasn't there.

REN

on't let me go, okay?

D If she'd only known how far I would've been willing to carry her. Pretty much to the ends of Aetheria. But it wasn't the time to let her know just how far underneath my skin she was. I still had a while to figure out how I was going to get the memory of Wells out of my head before I laid a finger on her. Other than the fingers that were dangerously close to her ass at that moment.

Her ass was like a fucking magnet.

I adjusted my grip, making the hold a little more acceptable. Something that wouldn't have offended one of my best friends if he'd seen it. Wells was more than that, though. He was my brother, and I was in love with his Magedamned girlfriend. Even though he had a fated mate at home with him, he loved Terra too. That's what made everything so fucking complicated.

One step at a time, Renfield.

That line was the first thing our foster mother taught us on day one of homeschooling. Bash and I were scared and confused, werewolves living in a vampire house, but when Bash complained about not being allowed to attend school during normal daytime hours, she told us everything was a process. Things had to be taken one step at a time. The first step was to prove we were capable of learning. From her.

We never made it to regular school.

"I think you can put me down now."

Oh yeah. Right. I set her down in front of me and the immediate loss of her warmth settled on my skin and in my bones.

Shit. I had a problem.

One step at a time. Step one: help her figure out what this building is. Step two: track down the fairy. Steps three through infinity: make her love me.

I focused on her chocolate eyes. She was drowning again, lost in thoughts that overwhelmed her. She needed a purpose; my own was to give her one. "Should we just walk up and ring the doorbell?"

Her head swung around and screeched. "There's a doorbell?" I loved taking her by surprise like that. Her face was so fucking readable. I doubt she knew that, but it was one of the best things about her.

I took a look around to assess the situation. There were no people around that I could see, but I heard distant voices, so we weren't completely alone. That, in and of itself, was progress. I didn't mind being alone with her, but it had been an eerie feeling to be surrounded by nothing but shiny golden trees with no signs of life anywhere. I'd watched her as we made our way toward the building. She was drawn to the trees, but too smart to veer off among them without knowing where they led or what was in them. She'd even joked about finding a map like the ones in malls. There were no maps.

When we breached the barrier, there'd been a definite change in the atmosphere. Where we'd been the air was stale, stagnant even. Beyond the wall, the air smelled crisp and sweet, like apples in the fall.

Several birds were swooping around the building. It was like we went from dark inky midnight to bright daylight in one step.

We were close enough to the building to see a glass door set inside the gold panels of the frame. It was pristine and cold and the sense of foreboding it gave off was high. "I was joking about the doorbell. But I'm with you. How do you want to play this?"

She squinted at the door like she might have been able to see something special about it or a way in. For all I knew, she could. She was made from the clay at our feet and her magic had grown exponentially from the first day I'd met her. "I guess we just go inside and see what's up."

The direct approach. I expected nothing less.

I took her hand because it seemed like she needed it. I'd been careful with how often I held her hand. I didn't want her to feel like I was pitying her or that I thought she wasn't capable on her own. She was more than capable. But at times she needed a boost, and I was more than happy to provide it for her. She looked down at our entangled hands and smiled. I felt that smile right down to my balls.

I *really* had a problem.

We walked along in silence. The grass had turned from shiny gold to green. That soon gave way to cobbled stones of brown and gray, with flecks of gold between them. The closer we got to the building, the bigger it loomed, which made sense, of course, but it was far wider and taller than it appeared from far away. I wondered if it were a trick of the eye or maybe a touch of magic. As we inched along, I used my wolf senses to get my bearings. There were walls, actual ones made of gray bricks, on both sides of us, effectively trapping us in. Unless we scaled one of them or went back through the invisible barrier, the only way forward was the glass door.

Terra dropped my hand and edged ahead of me. I was content to take up her rear. Not because of her magnificent ass, but to protect her. I could see more around us that way. She was practically jogging to get the last few steps to the door. When I caught up with her, she was standing with her hands on her hips peering inside. "This is weird. I can't see anything."

I leaned in, bringing my wolf forward, just a bit, to use the eyes. "It's a double pane. There's swirling air inside the glass." The view wasn't obstructed, exactly, but blurry enough that it was hard to see more than a few feet. All I got was the floor was white and there appeared to be sunlight coming in through some windows. There was a gold handle with a huge keyhole on the outside of the door. It looked ancient, though the building itself was modern. Way too modern to have been built eons ago when the Mage was alive and ruling. "Think it's locked?"

Turning the knob, she glanced over her shoulder with a mischievous grin. It flattened me. "One good way to find out."

WELLS

The abandoned gas station was four miles from Boulderbrook. It was good for me to stretch my legs and run the whole way at my wolf speed. Even in human form, we were fast. It had taken just a few minutes to get there, not even enough to break a sweat.

That would come later when I worked out in my cabin until I passed out from exhaustion.

My leprechaun contact wanted to meet at Boulderbrook, but I couldn't risk any of the pack knowing what I was doing. Gideon, Mace, and Spencer were up to speed, but the rest of the pack were clueless. So, Liam used his leprechaun magic to locate a suitable space for our meeting.

Leprechauns could find anything you wanted as long as you paid them. And I'd paid this one well. Ironically, he didn't want gold though. I could've had Diggs handle that, but the thought of gold-making of any kind made my stomach swirl. Thank the ever-loving Mage Liam was good with cold, hard cash and a stock tip from Gideon.

The location he'd wanted us to use was bizarre though. "We're just going to do this in the parking lot of an abandoned gas station?" I asked as he slid out of his green Volkswagen. There was someone in the passenger seat, but the windows were tinted enough that I couldn't make out any features.

He laughed and his long red beard swished across his chest. Most Magicals tried to blend in with humans. Liam embodied the image of a movie leprechaun: red hair and beard, short with a round gut. He even wore green joggers and a sweatshirt. He was a walking, talking green neon sign that said leprechaun. "No. Just waiting for my security to arrive. Can't be too careful these days."

As I nodded my agreement, a beat-up old truck swerved off the road and peeled into the lot, narrowly missing Liam's ride. A big guy with lots of dark hair and a beard rolled out. He had a wild look on his face and didn't want to be near anyone. He growled as he fished a set of keys from the pocket of his dirty jeans. I recognized the sound. He was a bear shifter. He opened the door and held it open for us. Liam leaned back inside his car and spoke to a person sitting in the passenger seat, then shut the door and strolled into the building.

When I passed in after him, the bear shifter mumbled something that sounded like 'wolf asshole.' I whipped around and got right up in his face. "Say that again, motherfucker."

I had no beef with the guy, but I was in just the right state of mind to take him out. In other words, itching to fight with anyone or anything. And it was going to feel good to take that meaty son of a bitch out.

The bear shifter bumped his chest against mine, a clear sign of a challenge. I shoved him back and lunged for him. We tangled for a second, knocking one of the empty metal shelves on the floor in the process. Behind me, Liam cursed, and then he jumped out of the way as I rolled the bear into another shelf. This one had a few tampon boxes still on it. They tumbled down around us. He scrambled away, throwing a box, and hitting me in the head. It lit a fire in my veins that burned to get out. I dove for him, but before I could get there, an ethereal voice echoed through my head. It said one word. "Stop."

I fell to the ground beside the bear. My limbs dropped to my side and when I tried to roll over or get up, I couldn't. I was frozen in place. I shifted my eyes—because Mage be damned, I couldn't move my head—and confirmed the bear was in the same state. Before I could formulate a plan, my head started swirling with a vision of a flowing brook breaking off into a meadow of yellow flowers. It was so vivid that I smelled the light scent of the daffodils and experienced the coolness of the brook splashing on my face.

"I don't know you well enough to send you precise thoughts yet, but next time I promise to be way more specific with my dream casting. You two need to stand down. Especially you, Alec." There was a swish of wind, and my body was under my own control again.

The bear shifter, Alec I assumed, stood up and swung his head toward the door, anger dripping off him. My gaze followed and landed on the creature who'd been controlling us. He drifted inside the building as if he were gliding on air, not his feet. He wore a long white duster with white wool pants and a turtleneck. It looked like Winter had become a person and stepped inside the abandoned gas station.

He gingerly stepped over one of the fallen shelves. As he got closer to us, the features on his pale face morphed. It wasn't a significant change but enough that was no longer certain he was male. He, or she, ran a hand over his white hair and it went from being slicked back off his forehead, to swooping down over his eyes. Her silver eyes crinkled with amusement. "Since we're being so aggressive, I figured you'd be more comfortable with my female form. I'm Annigan. I'm with him." She jutted her head toward Liam, who beamed at her with pride and affection.

Annigan stuck her hand out, I took it. "I'm Wells. And I'm fine with whatever form you want to take, that's up to you. What did you do to us?"

She morphed back into a man, and I decided on the they pronoun, at least in my head. They slicked their hair back with two hands, then lifted a pale eyebrow at the bear shifter. He didn't respond. Unless you counted staring with a gaping mouth as a response. Annigan shrugged. "I was told to stay in the car, but Liam should've known I wasn't going to do that, especially with an alpha wolf in the mix." Liam coughed, confirming what they'd said. "To answer your question, I simply cast a daydream into your minds to keep you from slaughtering each other. Alec, for one, knew better. I told you he'd be a problem, Liam." They lowered their eyes on the bear, who had the sense to look embarrassed.

I still had the urge to rush at him and put him in his place, but I tucked it down so I could focus on what I was there to do. I turned to Annigan. "You're a dream nymph."

I had a sea nymph friend on the Illusion Hill police force. He'd once told me that dream nymphs were rare but very powerful. It said a lot about Liam that he had one in his employ or his bed. Or both. Hadn't quite worked out their dynamic yet. But I'd taken his number from the journal Terra kept about her Gram. As painful as it was to look at the journal, it seemed to have been a good call.

Annigan turned their eyes on me. Their gaze was unsettling. It was like they were looking into my soul and finding me lacking. It was an awful feeling. "Yes, I'm a dream nymph. If you two promise to play nice I won't cast any nightmares."

"I can behave if he can. I'm here for one reason."

The sound of screeching tires drew our attention. Liam opened the door in time for us to catch a midnight black Bugatti spinning into the parking lot. It was a ridiculous contrast to the Volkswagen and beat-up truck. When the person unfolded from the car, I knew immediately he was a vampire, which made a lot of sense.

Covered, literally, from head to toe in black, the man strolled inside the building kept walking past us and turned to exit a door. We dutifully followed him and discovered the door led to a small garage out back. The scent of gasoline and oil permeated my nose. I glanced back at Annigan who was trying desperately to step anywhere they could to keep their pristine white clothes from getting smudged. By the look on their face, Liam was going to hear about the location as soon as they got back in the car.

Alec slammed the door behind us and stayed on the other side of it. Thank fuck. I was starting to get twitchy with all the new folks and anticipation wasn't doing me any favors either. I wasn't acquainted with that feeling and I hated it. "Can we do this now? I need to get back to my pack."

The man in black pulled off his gloves and hood, then he took his time peeling off his sunglasses and ski mask. When he was finally done undressing, I shook my head. "Nope. I'm out."

I swirled around to exit the garage as fast as I could, but another daydream lodged in my brain. This time it was a mountain steeped in snow, with lots of fluffy white clouds bouncing in a turquoise sky. It did what Annigan intended: shut me up and calmed me down. At least a little.

Not enough to work with *that* vampire though. Once Annigan's hold on me dissolved, I pounded toward Liam. "This is the only vampire you could get. Him?"

"Leprechaun magic never fails. You said you needed a vampire you could trust who had skill and knowledge of Dark Magic. He's the person my magic conjured. I take it you two have history."

The vampire huffed. "Barely. All he knows about me is my girlfriend and I are trying to get pregnant, and his best friend Renny hates me for no good reason. That's the total of our relationship. If he doesn't want to work with me, fine. I'll head on out."

He put his shades back on and was in the process of redressing to go out in the sunlight. In those moments all I could do was think about Terra and Ren being stuck in Aetheria with no one to help them or no hope at all. Sure, they'd probably meet people, but could they be trusted? It's where Tristan was from after all. Thoughts of the two of them lost and alone prevented me from making this decision based on emotion. "His name is Ren," I growled. Fitz paused his redressing. "I'll work with you as long as Liam swears you can be trusted. No one in the pack can know. Neither can Heidi. I mean it. I'll have no problem dragging you into the daylight and letting you sizzle to death."

"The only way you can know if I'm trustworthy is to trust me."

Damn, his logic. He wasn't wrong.

Liam stepped in between us. "The magic is solid. He'll keep this to himself."

Annigan added, "If he doesn't, you can be certain he'll never have another peaceful night of sleep in his life. It would be nothing for me to put him in a night terror loop. I get a thrill delving into minds and finding just the right threads of fear to pluck from brains. I consider it art."

Fitz visibly shuddered at their macabre threat, but in the next moment, he focused back on me. "Off with your clothes, wolf. Everything."

"Why the fuck would I take my clothes off? Especially for you."

He shrugged. "You could walk away now, but if you want Blood magic, your blood has to flow."

I'd expected some weird shit to happen—Blood magic is the darkest kind of magic there is—but things were going off the rails fast. But if I wanted to be able to get to Terra and Ren, the only way out was through.

Liam and Annigan had the decency to turn their backs while I peeled out of my clothes. Fitz didn't give me the same courtesy. He simply stood there with his arms crossed, watching me. He wasn't sneaking a peek at the goods or anything like that. It was more of a show of dominance, a power play to show me I was under his mercy.

And fuck it if he wasn't completely right about it. I was drowning in a pool of misery, and he was my only life preserver. But he didn't know how vulnerable I already felt, so I locked my gaze on him and stepped out of my clothes, layer by layer. As soon as my shorts hit the floor, his fangs flicked out.

Ren was right on my heels when I pushed the heavy glass door with the swirling wind open and stepped inside the Office of Chaos, Caging, and Honor. Already I'd shortened it to OoCCH, ooch, in my head. But I couldn't wait to find out what it was. My anticipation was on level eleven and my skin prickled with goosebumps as I took a few steps inside the short hallway.

The floors and walls were white with gold marbling that made it seem cold and lifeless. Ren put his hand on the small of my back, guiding me forward as he leaned in and whispered, "Feels like a mausoleum."

"Yeah." It was the closest comparison I could think of too. I scooted closer to him, angling for his warmth. He tucked me under his arm, and I instantly relaxed. I couldn't fathom what I would be doing at that moment if he weren't with me. Pissing my pants came to mind.

After a few tense feet, we'd breached the hallway and stepped into what appeared to be the main room which was flooded with bright sunlight. There were gold concentric circles inlaid on the floor, but the most breathtaking part was that the space was open and topped with glass. Near the top of the room were three large cages. They were suspended from gold chains that attached to the underside of the glass.

Due to the height and the angle, I couldn't tell what, if anything, was in them, though they were swaying, so I had to believe something was inside.

Ren gripped my waist with his fingers. "Sixteen floors. Four doors that I can see on each level, one for each element if you look at what's between the glass panels. We came through the Wind door. Guards beside each door but that one. They're the only ones carrying rods."

Thank the Mage Ren had enough wits to figure that all out in seconds. I hadn't even noticed the people in the room or the balconies opening up on each floor, I was so busy gawking upward to see what was in the cages. I tore my gaze back down and peeked around. The guards were staring straight ahead, not acknowledging anyone in the room. They seemed more like statues than living Magicals. The other people in the room appeared to know where they were going because none of them even so much as glanced at us, even though we had to stick out in the cavernous room doing nothing.

I raised a hand at a woman walking by. She was carrying a huge wicker trunk that appeared to weigh her down. "Excuse me, could you tell me where we are? We're here to…" I trailed off, not knowing where the end of that sentence was going. Ren grumbled at my back, angry that I hadn't planned what to do or say. He was cautious and meticulous when it came to security. That had ramped up since we'd gotten to Aetheria and survived the onslaught of the fae golem army. So yeah, it was warranted.

The woman paused. She sounded more pissed than Ren. "I hate it when towns change tributes every other week. It slows up the whole process if you ask me. You don't look like you've got much to offer the emperor, just saying. The more you bring, the fewer times you have to come back, so really, it's just common sense to bring as much as you can when you come. You'll learn." She patted her chest like she was proud of its contents, then sneered down her nose at us.

She thought we were newbs at the tribute thing. I gave her a shrug and a smile, and she marched to the hall across from us, heaving her trunk toward the first door. "Are you coming or not? I won't wait for you. You know once the door closes..." She stepped inside and the door slammed behind her.

Ren smirked. "Wonder what happens when the door shuts?"

"The world may never know."

I took several steps in that direction, intending to find out exactly where she'd gone with her super heavy trunk with unknown contents, but Ren held me back by gripping my hip tighter. "We can't just jump in the ocean without knowing if there's sharks in the water. Let's get our bearings, first."

We were standing near the middle of the room, right on top of the middle gold circle. As we glanced around to get some kind of clue about what to do next, I heard something. I wasn't sure if it was in my ears or my head. It was faint, definitely not loud enough to have been Ren, and it carried a tone of longing in it that matched my own. I put a death grip on his bicep. "Did you hear that? It sounded like someone calling for help."

He stood still, using his wolf ears to try and pick up the sound. It was faint, but it was still present. He frowned. "I've got nothing other than the people in the room with us, but the sounds are bouncing all over the floor and walls. Maybe I missed something." More people were streaming through the doors, most of whom headed straight for where the woman with the trunk went. I sighed, resigning myself to the fact that I was hearing things.

He leveled his emerald eyes on me, and his brow wrinkled with concern. Great. The last thing I wanted was for him to feel like he had to protect me or watch out for the wackadoodle gnome-slash-golem-slash-phoenix blood hybrid monster cocktail that was me. "It was probably nothing."

Yet I heard it again. Or rather, I felt it.

It was familiar.

Like when Wells would slide into my mind through our phoenix blood connection.

My heart cartwheeled and my blood started pumping so fast that I became dizzy. I tried to send some thoughts through our connection. *"Are you there, Wells? Please please be there."* It was a futile idea that after a week he'd somehow be able to communicate with me in a completely different realm, for lack of a better word. But a tiny thread of hope wove through me. Again and again, I tried the connection as desperation clawed its way from my belly to my throat, finally erupting in a deep guttural grunt of frustration when he didn't answer.

Hope was the most painful emotion because sometimes it lied. I'd take anger or fear over hope any day. At least they were honest.

As if my grief was manifesting into reality, something below us rumbled and the ground began to rise under our feet. Ren jumped away, pulling me out of the circle with him. We stood huddled together, our mouths gaping open as the circle continued to ascend. Within a few seconds, a person popped into view, riding underneath the circle like it was a tube. His back was to us, but he was carrying another cage like the ones suspended from the ceiling above us. We gawked as the gold platform rose, inching the man with the cage up toward the top where the others were suspended.

Okay, I gawked. Ren's eyes were darting from the man to the ceiling, trying to determine how the whole thing worked. "I guess that's an Aetherian elevator to get that guy to the top to hang the cage?" I mused as Ren darted over to get a closer look.

He peered down into the hole in the floor, his eyes widening. "It goes farther than you'd expect. Way fucking down there."

"Hey, what are you doing? Get away from there." A guard had stepped a couple of feet away from the Fire entrance she was guarding. She'd pulled her rod off her back but wasn't brandishing it. Not really. "Authorized personnel only on the inner circle. You know that."

Did we though?

Ren shot the woman a curt salute, then backed away from the circle as screeching squawks pierced through the building.

The cages had birds in them.

A flame shot out of the cage the man was trying to fasten into a hook. He ducked, cursing and wobbling, but managed to stay out of the way of the flame and kept from falling out of the support rails and tumbling to his death at the same time. The other cages rattled with excitement until their agitated cries permeated the space, filling it with what sounded like anguish. I wilted onto the floor and slammed my hands over my ears to keep the sound from bursting my eardrums. I couldn't even begin to imagine what it was like for Ren and his wolf ears.

Glancing up, I found him staring at me with a trademark raised eyebrow, confusion written on his handsome face. "Wait. Can you not hear that awful cawing?"

"Nope." He lifted the gold earmuffs that had materialized over my ears, then pulled me up from the crouched position I'd taken in the corner of the room. Embarrassment flooded my veins. Not only had I inadvertently created another useless gold item, but I seemed to be the only person in the building reacting to the sound of the screeching birds.

Over Ren's shoulder, the circle platform the man was on was settling against the floor with a soft hiss. He used his toe to press a button—maybe to lock it in place—then trailed over to the Wind door mumbling something about needing a smoke break after that shit.

Again, that faint whisper tickled my brain. *"I can't see you, but I know you. Can you help us?"*

Someone was calling out to me, and they were doing it internally. Another image of Wells crept into my brain, unbidden, and vivid. I'd just woken up from my little trip to Netheria. He was sitting in a chair, asleep and shirtless, a book resting on his thighs. I remember thinking—feeling—at the time that no one would ever be as beautiful to me. I didn't know it, but he'd used his blood to save me. And I had a sneaking suspicion that very blood was reaching out to me again.

"Can you hear me?" I said it in my mind, and honestly, I felt a little silly, like I was doing a cellphone commercial, but the response I got was immediate. One of the cages started swinging violently, then the others followed as flames shot out of the cages above us.

"Yes. Who are you?"

"I can damn well hear those noisy birds now," Ren spat out.

The cawing grew louder and louder, bouncing around the building. The guards and other people in the room either stopped to gape up at them or ran out of the exits. I pulled Ren down so he could hear me through the cacophony. "I'm going to need a distraction."

His hand snaked around my waist, pulling me up to hear his response. "Bigger than this one? Why?"

"Because those aren't just any birds up there squawking. It's the phoenixes and they need me to help them."

The implication of what she was saying was huge. Wells had told me a lot about phoenixes over the years. The main thing is that there were only four of them ever born. Or made. Whatever. If those cages contained them, there was some serious shit happening here. They were the Mage's first creations and I doubt he'd be down with them being caged in this building.

We still didn't even know where we were. It looked like a place to pay tithes or taxes or homage to the emperor of Aetheria, but the building was steeped in wrongness. There was more going on than that.

Most importantly, since when did Aetheria have a fucking emperor? Each element had a court with royalty, but I'd never heard one syllable about an emperor.

Terra's eyes were pleading with me to help her free the phoenixes. A twinge of annoyance rocketed through me. I hated that she thought she needed to beg. Of course, I would help her do whatever she wanted. I just had to figure out a way to do it that didn't end with one of us being caught.

The guards had reposted now that the man had hung the fourth cage. Everyone was staring up, checking out the phoenixes, but if I understood her—and I think I did—that was exactly where she wanted to go.

I'd have to take them elsewhere.

And the best way to do that was in a form I could move fast in.

I pulled my shirt over my head and toed out of my shoes. "Here. Might want to keep these in your bag."

She took my stuff and her eyes widened. "Are you wolfing out?"

"You said you wanted a distraction." I wiggled my eyebrows at her. "Here I am." I rolled off my socks and started unbuckling my belt. Did she take a cursory glance at my chest as I did so? I'd like to think she did, but it could've been wishful thinking on my end. "If you can use the vines inside the Earth door to handle the guard there, and bust the glass so the Wind releases, I'll take care of the rest."

Both tasks would be easy for her. Her magic had grown, and she'd been practicing wielding it since she snapped out of her stupor at the Conduit. I just had to do my part and make sure she was okay at the end of this.

Dropping my jeans, I hooked my fingers in the waistband of my boxer briefs. She gripped my wrist to stop me from going any further. "Wait a minute, Cowboy." We both froze, catching each other's eye and knowing we were thinking the same thing: Mace.

I'd never admit it to him, but Magedamn, I missed his fucking sense of humor and the ridiculous nicknames he always used. He'd been the light and brevity I needed when Bash and I arrived at Boulderbook. Gideon had been calm in the storm. And Wells had been the stability I craved. Facing a future without them and Bash at my side was hard. It had only been a week, but the finality of where we were made these unpredictable moments of loss creep up on me at most random times. It was like a match striking suddenly, then fire spreading through my whole being, even if it was for only a few blips of time.

I couldn't dwell on it though, I had shit to do. I pulled her fingers away from my wrist, then gripped her hand. "I'll be fine. I'm going to lead them away and I don't know where I'll end up." Her face was pure terror, and it ate a small piece of my soul. "As soon as you do what you need to do in here, go out the Earth door and tunnel. Stay hidden until sundown. I'll meet you at the biggest tree in your line of vision when you step outside."

It wasn't the best plan, but it was all I could give her without knowing what was outside the building. At least I hope there were trees on the other side of the door. I should've done an immediate sweep before I wolfed out, as Terra put it, but we'd already been clocked by the guards and had been in there too long doing nothing. Time was running out. She squeezed my hand. "Okay. Just be careful. I can't lose you too, Ren. I wouldn't survive it."

Her expression was so earnest that I believed her. "You won't have to survive. I'll meet you at sundown." I pressed a kiss against her temple. She gripped my bicep, holding me there a moment longer than I intended. The feel of her hand on my skin was searing. It made my heart flutter like I was a lovesick teenager.

Not to mention what it did to my cock. It was currently at half-mast just from her touch alone.

I had to get myself under control. Especially before I dropped my underwear.

"You're going to have to recite the elders, in proper order mind you, before I will allow you to see your so-called brother, Renfield."

I screamed at my 'so-called' foster mother. "My name is not Renfield!"

"It is now."

"Whatever. I don't see the point in me having to name vampire elders. I'm not a fucking vampire!"

"You are now. Begin."

I growled my displeasure and she laughed. The hold she had over us was unbreakable. And I knew if I wanted to see Bash, I'd have to give her what she wanted. "Augustus I, Cyria, Fantasia, Augustus II, Davina, Leopold, Benedict, Augustus III, Alessandro, Virgil, Leonardo, Helene, Samanthia, Crystal, Benton, Samuel."

It did the trick. I was as flaccid as a piece of lettuce.

I hated that I could still name them all. In proper order.

Terra went to work on the vines, releasing them from the Earth door. The vines began slithering, inching toward the guard. So much power from one small frame. I could watch her all day, but I turned my back to her and stripped, throwing my underwear in her bag while she was preoccupied. We had to time it right or we'd be caught. I wasn't going to let that happen.

Just as one of the vines wrapped around the guard's rod, I threw my Earth magic to break the glass, releasing the Fire from inside the door. Flames flared, sputtering drops of fire everywhere. When the Fire guard turned to see what was happening, I shifted and took off, bolting straight for the Wind guard as he raised his rod. I connected with his chest and threw him down on the ground. Terra coiled vines around his wrists and feet. They wouldn't hold long, so I took it upon myself to use my troll-fused blood and wrapped a vine around his neck. I made it tight enough to knock him out, but not enough to kill him. He was just doing his damn job. Besides, Terra would've wanted it that way.

That done, I turned around and was hit in the face with a stream of water from the Water guard. She came at me full force, sending pulsing bursts of water as I darted away from the guard I'd knocked out. Pausing long enough to send a menacing growl at a poor woman who'd just walked in with a basket. She dropped her goods and raced right back out the door. Two other people followed her outside. That left me alone with three guards to handle.

Terra took one look at the guard I'd incapacitated and did the same thing to the Earth guard, and we were down to two. I yelped at her to get her moving. When I confirmed she'd run over to the gold circle pad and pressed some buttons at her feet, I shot toward the Fire guard. He'd contained the fire in the candles and was marching toward me with his thin copper rod brandished in my direction.

Snarling, I shot away with my wolf speed, just as the stream of fire went over my head. *Missed me, fucker.*

The Water guard joined him, and they banded together to shoot magic at me. Which was so amateur it made me laugh. Well, if I'd been in my other form, I would've guffawed out loud. These Magicals had never been in a real fight. I almost felt sorry for them.

People were coming out of rooms on the upper levels. Some of them went right back inside, slamming the doors behind them. Others, though, were hanging on in curiosity, gawking at the scene below them or up at the phoenixes. Those folks were going to be my unwitting helpers.

My senses were overloaded. It happened when I was in my wolf form. I could smell Terra's adrenaline and her soft rain scent wafting around me. I also got a whiff of the guards' fear. They truly had no idea what they were doing. I might as well have a little fun with it.

I darted toward them, forcing them to part. Naturally, both of them stopped firing magic for fear of hitting the other one. In their moment of stunned recognition, I ran back through them and leaped at the Water wall, using my strong hindlegs to catapult me up. I scaled the wall quickly, and jumped over the railing, landing on the second level, weaving in and out of the idiots who were still standing there gaping.

Now the guards couldn't shoot at me without putting them in danger. One of them yelled in frustration. The other shouted up for some help. "Catch him!"

The man who's legs I was currently running between grunted. "I'm a merman. How am I supposed to stop a werewolf?"

Good question. The answer: he wasn't.

I turned back and growled, sending a message to everyone who was still foolish enough to be on the balcony. *Back inside the doors, you go.* Every single one of them complied. I was a scary motherfucker when I wanted to be.

Meanwhile, the two guards—I was calling them Dumb and Dumber in my head in honor of Mace—finally got the bright idea to separate. Dumb got on the outer rim of the circles and stomped on the button to make it rise. Dumber stayed down below with her rod trained on me as I bounded up another level. It had been a long time since I'd stretched my legs like that. I was enjoying it. A peel of laughter came from above me as Terra's platform finally reached the top. That made me enjoy my little game even more. Her laugh was like sunshine.

I allowed Dumb to get close enough to step off the outer circle platform and onto the third-floor balcony with me. He raised his rod and I shot at him, wrenching it from his grip with my teeth. Then I used the platform as a stepping stone as I bounded back down to the second floor with his rod. The second I got to the bottom again, I spat the rod out, laying it at an angle over the gap in the floor. Then I pawed at the buttons until the thing started descending. Seconds later, the rod was wedged in the gap and the whole contraption ground to a halt.

All I could do was hope that it didn't mess up Terra's way down too. That left me with only Dumber to contend with.

Time to take this outside.

Dumber was right on my tail, sputtering and cursing as she shot water at me and missed over half her shots. It was harder when I was in wolf form, but I managed to pull on the Earth magic I had as I pressed a paw to the glass door in the Fire hall. The glass melted against me, and I pushed my wolf form outside and drew the guard away from Terra. What I saw there made me stop in my tracks.

We had not even begun to scratch the surface of the real Aetheria. Where we'd been with the Conduit, the meadow of golden grass and trees with no other life at all? That was the ass end of Aetheria. This was the fucking front.

I peered down, watching my blood drip into the gold chalice under my feet. Since I'd refused his attempt to vampire the shit out of me, Fitz had unceremoniously used a knife to slice my neck, wrists, and one vein in my thigh that too fucking close to cock for my liking. Then I'd been strung up by chains in the middle of the garage, using the supports they used on cars. I was currently glaring at the mixture of blood and oil at the bottom of the bay where they worked on vehicles.

It had been twenty minutes, and my head was starting to swim. "I'm assuming when this thing is full, I'm done. How long will it take before the spell is ready to use?" Probably should've asked that before I was hung up like a side of beef, but his answer wouldn't have mattered. I was going to see this through to the end. My question had been more of a curiosity than anything.

Fitz slid out of the chair he'd dragged to be at the best vantage point to watch my blood drain like it was a sporting event strolled over to his bag and removed a second chalice. And a third. Then a fourth. They were ancient-looking, likely belonging to the wealthy family he'd been droning on about while I dangled before him. "Think of this as the warmup. I need all the blood in your body. To do that without killing you, I have to train your system to handle it. It usually takes a few months to be able to drain successfully without succumbing."

"That makes no sense. If you take all my blood, I'll have no magic. There's no fucking point in doing this if I'm dead."

He switched the full chalice for another empty one, dipping his finger in and moving to stick it in his mouth and take a little taste. Fire surged within me, and I raised my legs, thumping him in the chest and knocking back on his ass. "You will suffer and die if you even think about tasting one single drop of my blood," I growled, and I knew my eyes were flaming deep purple. "Test me on it."

I didn't threaten him out of compassion for his well-being. Nope, I needed the asshole to help me. I wasn't going to go through the hassle of finding another unscrupulous vampire. Plus, the phoenix thing was for family and friends only. He was neither.

He scrambled from the floor, gazing down at my spilled blood like it was the tastiest snack on the buffet. This time when I growled, fur rippled over my arms and chest. I was not playing with that fool. Not at all. He finally got the message, going back to where he was sitting and leaving the spilled blood on the grimy concrete. "Fine. I won't drink your blood. No need to get testy about it." I'd know the next time we met if he was true to his word or if my phoenix blood burned him from the inside out.

Over an hour later I'd lost count of the number of chalices. I was close to blacking out, so I tried to focus on the items around me, keeping my senses alert. If I could stay sharp maybe it would speed up the process and I'd get results faster. But no matter how long you stare at an oily rag on a shelf, trying to make objects out of it, it is still just an oily rag on a shelf.

"What's the point of the gold chalices if you're just going to throw away the blood?" I asked, my words slurring more than I wanted. Hell, my head was slurring too.

"Who said I was throwing it away?"

My shoulders were starting to burn from being suspended. I tried to rotate them to ease the pain, but it only made my body spin. I growled in frustration, trying to spin myself back around. He snickered as he watched me spiral. "I told you this was a process. I'll keep what you give me today, add it all up, spin it around, throw in some spices, say a few magic words, then boom, you've got your Dark Blood magic."

"You make it sound like a recipe."

"Isn't it?"

"I wouldn't know. That's why you're here, asshole." The guy was starting to grate on my last nerve. So much so that I was wondering how many fucks I had to give about taking him down a peg once he freed me from my chains.

He skulked over to me, spinning me to face him so he could look up and gauge my eyes. "Why are you doing this? I can guess, but I'm going to need to know everything before I make the spell. The darkness is in the details."

"What is your guess, Mr. Know-It-All?"

My eyes crossed under his intense scrutiny. It was like he could see inside there to my brain and that gave me a vulnerability I didn't much like.

Or maybe that was the loss of blood.

"You want to think you're doing this for the most noble reason of all. But love isn't your motivation." The way he said the word made me cringe. I doubted he knew what it meant, even though he claimed to love Heidi. I had a firm grip on the emotions and feelings that went with love. Felt them to my core. He sneered, "Love is just a byproduct of your real reason."

The edges of my vision started to sparkle. It would've been cool if it hadn't meant I was seconds away from passing out. "What are you getting at?"

"You're being selfish, if you ask me. Love is just the band-aid to your loneliness. You're trying to reach her in Aetheria because you can't stand to be alone with yourself."

I wasn't alone. I had my pack. My friends and brothers. I had Terra. He didn't know what he was talking about. "You're full of shit."

"Am I? Think about it. Why do you want her back? Is her pussy that good or are you telling yourself you love her to justify the danger you put her in with the trials? I mean, what if she leaves you when she realizes you aren't going to give up your fated mate? Or are you expecting a three-way scenario because I might want to be around for that." He chuckled to himself, amused at the thought. I did not chuckle. I glared.

It didn't shut him up though. "What do you think your pack is saying behind your back about your situation? You're rejecting a bond that was handed down directly from the Mage and has been preserving werewolf existence for millennia. How long before someone challenges your position as alpha for that very reason?"

He was actively trying to provoke me, and it was working. The fact that I realized that made it even worse. "Why are you asking me all these fucking questions? You don't know anything about me or my situation." I struggled, hoisting myself up so I could release the chains binding me. I fiddled with them for a few seconds but failed to get free.

Fitz tutted at me like a freaking grandma hen, then finally, thank the Mage's puckered asshole, let me down. My shoulders groaned as I rolled them, trying to get the feeling back in my fingertips.

I reached down to redress, but all I had to wipe the blood off was that oily rag. Fitz was unhelpful. "Next time bring a towel."

That was it. I snapped. Like a shitting twig. I lunged at him—completely fucking naked—smacking into his chest and knocking him back. He hissed, then rolled out of my grasp as I clawed a gash onto his cheek. I'd spent all my energy on the attack, and I had none left to use to go after him again. Though I was burning with the desire to rip at least one of his limbs off. I was betting on him being able to do the magic spells with one hand.

He wiped the blood from his face, jumped off the ground, and went over to an ice chest he'd placed in the corner earlier, pouring the contents of the chalices into it. All I could do was drag myself up and throw my clothes back on.

After the chalices were empty, he threw them back in his bag and strolled toward the door. "You'll need some time to recover. I'll see you in two days. This time, we'll meet at midnight." I followed him out of the garage and watched as he climbed into his Bugatti and sped off.

Annigan appeared at my side, whispering in my ear in their female voice. "That guy's a jerkoff. I'll be sure to send him scary werewolf nightmares in his sleep tonight."

I laughed. It was the first time in hours I felt like myself. Turns out a jackass hanging you with chains and draining your blood drop by drop takes something out of you. "Thanks. Remind me to stay on your good side."

"I've no doubt you will. Liam and I have another appointment soon. You can be on your way while we lock up."

Alec, the bear shifter, sent me a menacing snarl as he shoved the keys into the lock. I was at my bullshit tolerance limit for the day after dealing with Fitz. "What's your problem with me, Bear? I haven't done anything to you."

He locked the door, then strolled over to me. "Because of your pack, I was dismissed from my sleuth. If you would've just shared your magic like your last alpha did, I'd still be alpha of mine."

My head nearly exploded. Mateo was sharing magic with the sleuth of bears that lived near Boulderbrook. I had no idea. At this revelation, I wondered how much other shit Mateo was involved in that I didn't know about. "Look, I hate to break it to you, but everyone is running out of magic, so sharing with you would've been impossible. Not that I would've. I wouldn't. And I won't stand for my pack being attacked again, so stay away from Boulderbrook. I might not be able to kill the vampire, but I don't *need* you."

Ren was a sight to behold. He was running the guards in circles, making fools out of them as he bounded around the room in his wolf form. He was smaller than Wells' wolf but had almost as much power. I wasn't worried about him getting caught as much as I was myself.

Most of the people had left the building or gone back inside the doors. Some though, were eyeing me with curiosity. Probably wondering why a person they didn't know was inching toward the phoenixes on the weird circle platform. I did my best to look official, but nonchalant.

Don't mind me, I'm just here having a little peek.

When the platform finally stopped, I was standing in between the four phoenix cages. I could reach out and touch them if I wanted to, but I didn't know how they'd take that. Plus, there was the flame factor.

They didn't exactly look the same, as far as their appearances were concerned, but all four of them had iridescent red feathers with tiny wisps of colored fire on the tips. And they were all dealing with the chaos of mine and Ren's distraction in different ways.

The one with fierce red eyes was standing in the middle of its cage, still and rugged. The only movement was that of its eyes as it tracked every move or gesture I made. On the other hand, the gold-eyed phoenix was straining against the cage, trying to get to the one with bright blue eyes beside it.

It was the one who'd been freshly hung, and from the looks of it, it had also been freshly reborn. It was much smaller and wobbling like it had trouble standing and the fires on the tips of its wings weren't burning as bright. The blueness of the eyes was even duller than the others.

It had been through some stuff, that was obvious. It made my heart clench to see something that should look so majestic, struggling to stand.

"She'll be alright in time. Don't worry."

"She?" I said it aloud before I'd even realized the voice had been in my head. I swiveled on the platform to face the silver-eyed phoenix. The one whose blood I *knew* was pumping through my body. He or she was the most imposing of the bunch. With a puffed-out chest and sharp eyes, he spread his wings, and my breath got caught in my throat. So beautiful.

I don't know why—not that I would've touched it, because flames—I offered the phoenix an open hand and sent my thoughts out to it. *"It's nice to meet you. Your blood saved the life of someone I care about very much. Thank you."*

"It would seem I saved your life too. I wouldn't be able to communicate with you otherwise. I'm Andras. Our blue-eyed sister is Alienor. The phoenix with stoic red eyes is Abira. And the one who bears shining gold eyes is Alaric. And I must thank you. It has been so very long since I have been able to communicate with anyone but these. I do love them, but it's nice to hear a fresh voice."

Andras. I had the deepest urge to run tell Wells. Then I was blasted with a surge of sorrow and regret that I couldn't.

"You're parted from your loved one? How did this come to be?"

Just like Wells had been able to do, Andras could sense my feelings as well as my thoughts.

"Long story, but to sum it up, the Conduit between here and my world is closed. I closed it. Don't even know how really, but he's there and I'm here, hoping to find another way back to him."

Alienor squawked, flapping and as she did, the blue fire flared to life on the tips of her wings. She took a few steps toward me, and a single blue tear dripped from her eye. I almost reached out to catch it because I'd read human stories about phoenix tears, but I stopped myself. Figured it would be rude.

"It's okay. Alienor embodies empathy, one of the four qualities the Mage found most important. She wants me to tell you she can feel your pain and loss. She wants to offer you a gift. Take her tear."

"Um, what?"

"Go on now, she offers this freely. She's recovered enough from what they did to her. She's my mate and I promise you I wouldn't offer if it wasn't safe for both of you."

The word 'mate' opened up a fresh wound in my gut, but I wasn't going to mention the fated mate thing to the phoenixes. Especially when one was offering me a gift of some sort. So, I tucked that hellscape into my mind. I'd cry over it later when I was alone. Which was hard with Ren around, but not impossible. Andras could probably sense it anyway.

I reached inside Alienor's cage and extended a finger. I wasn't sure how to collect a phoenix tear, nor did I know what to do with it once I had it, but I figured details would come. She bounced over to me and angled her head. A single blue teardrop fell from her eye. It was warm on my finger but didn't burn. I turned to Andras, questioning him with a raised eyebrow.

"You may wish to sit first. Place the tear in your own eye, then allow yourself a few moments for the experience as it unfolds. We'll wait. It's not as if we have anywhere to go."

He spread his wings and the flaming tips jutted out of his cage. I experienced the melancholy in his thoughts as he projected them to me. They were caged against their will and being used for something. They didn't even know what, but I wasn't going to stand for it. And as soon as I was finished with the phoenix tear thing, I was going to get them out. Consequences be damned. Ren would understand if I was delayed.

I plunked down on the platform, leaving my legs swinging over the side. Then I used a finger to open my eye as wide as I could and rubbed the tear along my lower lid. The effect was immediate. It was like the entire room had whooshed away and I was back in Wells' cabin. I could smell his sandalwood smoke wafting all around me. I could taste the salt of his skin. Feel his warmth.

"What are you thinking about, Precious?"

I swallowed as the sound all but consumed me. He wasn't physically with me, but his voice was *right there*. I had to answer him. I had no choice in the matter, not when he was searching me with his flaming lilac eyes. "I'm thinking about you."

An honest answer. He was with me, in my thoughts, in my heart, every second of every wretched day that I'd been in Aetheria.

But I wasn't in Aetheria. Not at that moment. I was impossibly with him in his cabin.

"Do you mean how I just curled your toes with my tongue alone, or how you'd like for me to do it again? I need specifics."

I molded my body around him. We were both naked in his bed. I didn't know how I could feel his marble chest or sense his heart thumping because I knew—*knew*—I was sitting on a platform in a strange building in Aetheria, talking to phoenixes. Yet his thigh was brushing against mine and his fingers were trailing up and down my spine, sending shivers of pleasure rocketing through me.

Phoenix tears were the bomb.

His hand slid over my hip, inching toward my core. "I suppose I could feel those specifics out for myself," he breathed, leaning close and nipping on my ear. I could tell by the rasp of his voice that he was a man on a fiery mission and that mission was me. Specifically, my next powerful orgasm.

It felt like it had been so long since I felt like this, reveling in his heat and passion, tangling with his sinfully artful mouth. My breaths came quickly. All I could do was pant his name. "Wells."

He hummed against my neck as he made his way down, kissing and licking my neck and collarbone until I was squirming and shifting in his grip, opening my thighs for him so his hand could reach where we both wanted it to be. "Lie back so I can watch you come undone," he growled.

Loving the sound of that, I turned so I was on my back. He loomed over me, smirking as he dropped his fingers between my legs, dragging them along my seam to wet them before he moved up and began circling my clit. Arching my back, a guttural moan escaped me. And Wells leaned down to kiss me, stealing the sound from my lips.

Reaching for his shoulders, I pulled him closer and opened my mouth for him. His tongue invaded and began a sensual dance, moving in time with his fingers. As I ran my nails softly down his back, he groaned. *"I'm so fucking enraptured with you. You know that, right? There will never be another woman for me. End of."*

I gasped. It sounded like something he would say, but I knew he'd never said that to me before. Not in those words. And he'd touched me like this—many times—but not exactly like this.

The feel of him, of this, was so familiar, yet this wasn't a memory. Nor was it real communication between us. It was something else entirely. Because of the phoenix tear. I didn't know if I wanted it to continue or not.

I mean, yeah, I did. It didn't erase the thought that I was sitting with my legs dangling from a gold platform mind orgasming, but at the same time, it seemed too damn real. *He* seemed real.

Wells sucked on my lower lip, then pulled away. "Tell me what you want with that pouty mouth. My only wish is to get you off."

So *so* many things came to mind. One of which was getting back to him, but that wasn't what he was talking about. Even though I was aware of the falseness of the situation, my mind, and my heart were tripping on him, and I chose to give in to his demand, no matter how fake it was. I reached down between us, taking his hard cock in my hand. "I want to make you come. And I want your fingers inside me."

As I ran my hand down his thickness and back up again, I kissed him, sucking his full lips in mine and then thrusting my tongue inside.

He groaned in response, then gave me what I'd asked for, driving his fingers inside me. "You're dripping for me, aren't you? Just like I like it."

The sound I made was a whimpering mm-hm. He echoed the sentiment and then we were lost together, frantic, panting, pulling at each other like magnets. I moaned at the pleasure of his hands, his mouth, his flesh on my body, and at the pain of knowing it was a hazy dream.

After a few more intense minutes, I exploded for him, the release escaping at terminal velocity. I saw stars and flames in my vision as I floated back into myself. And into the square room in the square building in a realm so very far away from him.

I couldn't open my eyes for a long time. I didn't know what the phoenixes saw or heard during my little trip, but as grateful as I was for the experience, if I had a chance to do it again, I knew without a doubt, I wouldn't. Because now that it was over, the pain of losing him all over again was too astronomical to bear. Tears of my own washed away everything I'd just experienced.

After I regained my composure, I stood back up. Alienor flapped in her cage, having grown a little bit bigger and stronger than before. Andras reached out and touched the flaming wing of the gold phoenix, Alaric, who in turn, reached out to Alienor. There was an obvious connection, a communication between them that wasn't meant for me.

The phoenixes all settled after a moment, and I fired off the questions I had in my head. "How did you get to be in these cages? Do you want out? Can you help me get to where I need to go? And this may be none of my business, but did someone purposely hang you away from your mate so you couldn't be close to her? Because, if so, that's a bitch move."

Andras ruffled his feathers, then settled them back behind him. As he did so, the flames withered. *"To start, yes, we were hung this way on purpose. Abira and Alaric are mates too. We've been here for many years, and it never gets easier."*

I could understand that. I'd only been away from Wells for a week. Imagining more…well, I couldn't imagine more. My brain shut it down. "We can solve that problem right here and now." I reached out to unlock Andras' cage but stopped midway through when I didn't see a lock to undo. Whipping my head around, I found the other cages were similar.

I concentrated hard, eyeing the cages to see what the best way to get them out would be. Then I closed my eyes and allowed myself to remember the terror that had flooded my veins when I thought Wells was in danger. And envisioned Autumn rolling his burned body through the Conduit without me. And I thought of Ren, imagining him running out the door into the hands of waiting guards. For all I knew, it could've happened.

Panic, pure and vile, steeped within me. A second later, I had a shiny gold crowbar in my hands. It kind of sucked I had to put myself in such torment to get it, but it did the trick I'd hoped it would.

I tried to shove the crowbar between the slats of Andras' cage, preparing to pry him out, but as soon as the bar touched the golden cage, it vibrated, whizzing out of my hand as if someone had jerked it away. It plummeted to the ground below, clattering across the cold marble floor when it hit.

At the sound, a door on the uppermost level creaked open. Two wide-eyed Magicals peered up at me, sneering at the noise.

Andras squawked to get my attention. *"Thank you, but it's useless to attempt to rescue us. Magic holds us here, old, and powerful magic. There's no escape for us, but you really should get on your way. You're in danger here."*

"How? Why? Where are we? And I'm sorry about all the questions. I tend to ramble when I'm nervous." I sucked in a breath to steady myself. "I want to help you."

"Maybe, in time, you can. But we're used to the treatment we receive here. They can take our blood, our fire, our magic, but it always grows back. I'm not sure yours would. This place, everyone and everything in it belongs to the emperor of Aetheria."

The number of people in the upper balconies had tripled. And some of them were making their way closer. "Just tell me who put you here?"

"The emperor, Magnus. He fooled this entire land into thinking he'd make Aetheria better with his 'Square Logic.' He's got more magic than any fae I've ever known, but his claims are false and his reign over the courts has been nothing but a terror-filled manipulation. It's an abomination of what the Mage wanted, yet now that he's positioned himself, none can overcome him."

Fresh shivers ran down to my toes and back to the ends of my hair. The square is what Trickstan had mentioned, the sole reason for his awful betrayal. He'd said it had something to do with his sister, but how could I trust his word after what he'd done?

"We haven't figured out how Magnus uses our magic, blood, and fire, but don't fear for us. You must leave now. If they catch someone with your power and find you're from the other side, you'll be tortured, used, or even killed. You must get away. Don't worry about us."

"How do you know I have great power?"

"I feel it inside you. You're meant for things greater than us. You must hurry. They're coming."

Sure enough, another group of guards had been brought in. Three of them were currently strolling toward me from the top floor and a fourth was waiting on the ground below. I had to take my chances on the one guard.

I stomped on the button to lower the platform, hating myself for not being able to help the phoenixes. They all began flapping and squawking at the same time. It hurt my soul. "I promise you; I'll come back for you. Next time, I'll bring a friend. We'll set you free."

I meant every word of it.

The platform sunk toward the ground. I lost sight of the phoenixes before I wanted to. In my head, Andras whispered. *"I can't project as far as I could because my magic is weakened, but I'll try to reach out and check on you when I can. Be safe. Stay away from Magnus and the Square. And one more thing. I believe you'll see him again. We all do. The kind of magic that binds you goes beyond mere spells and elements. Beyond fate."*

I wanted to believe that more than I wanted to believe anything in my whole life. I just hoped they held some sort of Seer properties that meant it would be true, but I didn't have time to dwell on that or the overwhelming helplessness that came with leaving the phoenixes behind in cages, fighting for their magic and their lives. I had to deal with a very angry guard pointing a platinum rod at my face.

Platinum rods meant she was Wind elemental. She didn't appear to be elven, meaning she didn't resemble an animal of any kind that I could tell. She did resemble a pissed-off individual, however. She wasted no time lowering her rod and shooting a blast of Wind at me.

I threw myself on the ground, ducking away from the Wind. She grimaced and lowered her rod. Using my hands to gather my Earth magic, I picked up a terra cotta pot with a big plant in it, leveling it at her and smashing her over the head. She fell to the floor just as several people jumped down off the balconies above me.

I didn't even have time to stop and enjoy the fact that I'd thrown something so huge with little effort at all. I had to get out of there.

Scrambling onto my feet and hauling my bag over my shoulder, I took off toward the Earth door. There were several people close to me. Simply going through it wasn't going to keep me from getting caught. I had to think of a way to keep them inside the building.

I used my magic to slip through the glass door, which was surprisingly easy for me. I just started running and poof, I was on the other side. It was crazy, but so much had happened—mainly Wells-wise—since gnomes got in the Conclave, I hadn't had much time to explore what I could do with that extra boost. And now that I was in Aetheria, my magic seemed to come unbidden.

Using that same magic, I reached beyond the glass and moved all the vines in the building around, securing them over every door in the place and growing more. It took about half a minute, but when I finished all the doors were blocked. Not even a shimmer of light was getting through. *"Clever."* A voice whispered.

I turned around, hoping to see Ren, but found no one there. I thought maybe the voice had been Andras speaking in my mind, but he couldn't see what I'd done. A sickly sense of dread filled my brain. Who was talking to me? I simply didn't have time to stick around and find out.

Once I was sure that the vines were in place, I raised my arm and angled my wrist, so the bracelet was touching the glass. I had no clue where that idea had come from or what I was doing, but the sentient thing inside the stone seemed to think for me.

It flashed to life, shooting a stream of purple electric magic at the door, fusing it with the vines. It wouldn't hold forever, but maybe it would stay until I was underground.

I put my back to the door, preparing to look around for the biggest tree in my eyeline like Ren had said to do. And I was stunned into motionless silence.

Aetheria was nothing like I'd imagined.

I was halfway up the stairs to my office, my mind racing. I tried, unsuccessfully, to imagine buying a nice new chair, but my head didn't stay there for long. Nope, it went straight to the ordeal I'd just been through with Fitz. There was a tingling sensation in my fingers and toes, and I don't think it had anything to do with my blood being drained.

It was utter guilt racing through me. It was so fucking wrong to use Blood magic. And I knew Fitz hadn't told me everything about the procedure. From my extensive reading on it, there was a final component to it that would be revealed at the very last second and that was the thing rattling around my brain.

It was the one aspect I couldn't control because I didn't know what it was.

The rest, I was sure I could handle. I had phoenix blood. I'd come back from anything. Sure, it would hurt like I was rolling around in the Eternal Flame, but I'd come back from that. I had no idea if I'd recover from whatever the last step of the Blood magic spell.

"Wells, there you are. I've been looking everywhere for you."

I paused on the stairs, attempting to unclench my jaw before I turned around to face Autumn. "Yeah. What do you need? I've got some work to do." I tipped my head up toward my office, hoping she'd get the message: I wanted to be alone.

Being close to her was a big problem for me.

"Can we talk?" Her voice was like silk, and I hated it. Besides that, though she'd phrased it as a question, she wasn't waiting for my answer. Taking my non-response as a yes, she sashayed up the stairs, touching my chest as she skirted around me. Sometimes—most of the time— that was all it took to light the spark that I worked so hard to bury in me.

My nostrils flared and I got a whiff of her perfume. I didn't even like it—too sweet for my taste—but the fucking pecker in my pants surely did. By the time I'd made it to my office, I was fighting a hard-on and looking anywhere in the room that wasn't her tight sweater.

Hm. Never noticed the base of that globe over there was made of glass. I wonder if it would break if I threw it across the room.

"...so I was thinking maybe if we got away from the camp, perhaps had a date in Illusion Hill, it would help us to, I don't know, get closer."

Zoned out on the first part of her discourse. Hated the last part. "Leaving camp right now isn't the best idea."

"I feel safe with you. I know you wouldn't let anyone get near me." She perched on the edge of the desk, crossing her legs so that her skirt rode up. Who wears a skirt in the dead middle of Winter in Vancouver? Autumn Quartermaine, apparently. She kicked her foot out, drawing my attention up her long leg to the place where it joined the other.

Fuck.

I need to water that plant over there.

I crossed my arms, trying to keep my thwacking heart from jumping out of my chest. "You're right, I wouldn't let anyone hurt you or anyone really, but the pack needs me to stay close. Maybe we could…"

I had no idea where the end of that sentence was going. None.

She did. "Oh, yes! That's a great idea. We can do something here. Maybe at the stables. I'll get with the fae in the kitchen. Set it all up for us. You don't have to do anything but show up. Say eight o'clock tonight. Bring your appetite."

She wasn't talking about whatever meal she was planning to serve. Her eyes danced over my body, and chills followed in their wake. She wanted us to get naked and roll around in the literal hay. Mace had mentioned that fantasy to me once, in passing, but that wasn't my idea of a good naked time.

Nope. My idea of a good naked time involved less scratchy hay, the distinct absence of the aroma of horse manure, and someone else.

She ran her tongue over her lower lip, cocking her head and lowering her lashes. AKA, her power move for seduction.

Damn, that window should be cleaned. I need to make a to-do list.

She crossed her arms over her chest, mocking my stance, in a sense. All it did was push her tits up. She probably knew this was going to happen. She probably practiced the move at night when she was alone in her cabin, and I was alone in mine tossing off or tangling in the covers over nightmares.

The worst thing was that I couldn't hold her off forever. That bright gold band around her ring finger was like a fucking neon sign. She was my mate and I needed to either give into the bond or sever it.

I couldn't do either.

Instead, I held her off as best I could and planned to keep it that way until I finished my business with Fitz. I opened my mouth to agree to her little date, but blaring music outside shut me up.

Autumn jumped off the desk and ran over to the window. "What is that?"

I joined her at the window but put a respectable distance between us so she wouldn't grab my hand like she so often tried to do.

I had to shake my head at what I saw outside. Mace was standing there next to a tree with a freaking eighties-style boom box over his head. Just like from that old movie. Mage only knew where he'd gotten the thing. He was looking up at us in the window like this was a completely normal thing for him to do.

Autumn giggled at the sight of him. "Is he just out there playing music to entertain the camp?"

Not likely. This was a calculated move. I'd told the guys and Spencer to help me avoid Autumn if it seemed like I was getting too close to her. This was Mace's way of doing that. Idiot. Couldn't tell Autumn that though. "I wouldn't put it past him. He's in charge of morale and the morale around here sucks right now."

I'd successfully stamped out Micah and the nay-sayers and things were running as smoothly as they could under the circumstances, but I was getting daily reports from my contact at Illusion Hill. Magic stealing was at an all-time high and things were getting worse out there. I felt that pressure in my chest on the daily. Enough to snap my damned ribs.

Autumn cracked the window so she could hear better. "Is that Billie Eilish?"

Yep, it was. The song was "All Good Girls Go to Hell."

Maybe he wasn't an idiot after all. That was one of the tunes he'd put on the playlist he curated for Terra when she was in the Netherian coma situation before I gave her my phoenix blood and brought her back.

Not that I needed his help to think of her, but it was the kick in the balls I needed to fortify myself against Autumn's advances. At least in that moment. He was a good fucking friend.

I threw my hand in the crack Autumn had made and shot a stream of silver phoenix fire at his feet. From where we stood in my office, Autumn couldn't have made out what I burned into the grass. But he'd see it and know I appreciated him. It was one word: thanks.

And a set of big tits. Just like he liked.

I slammed the window closed and turned to Autumn. She took a step closer to me and I responded by pulling out my chewed-up chair and sitting down at my desk, forcing her to walk around to the other side of it so she could look at me. "I do have work to do. But you're right. Some time together would be nice. But make it at nine, okay?" I patted my laptop to demonstrate I had a lot on my plate. She leaned down over the top of it, giving me a stellar view to ponder.

Laptop. Yeah, I needed to clean out my inbox. So much junk mail.

She bounced on her toes—hugging herself because Mage knew I wasn't going to hug her—and guilt threaded through me. I hated stringing her along, but I couldn't do what she desperately wanted or deserved. I was too much of a coward to go on with my life without Terra. So, I'd try to be nice, but I'd have an important conversation with Mace before I did it. I was going to need more than a boom box tonight.

Terra

I completely forgot I was being chased by people out to get me. All I could do was stare at the vision before me. What we'd previously seen as Aetheria was nothing. It was trash. Garbage. In an instant, it occurred to me that the Conduit had been placed in a dead part of Aetheria. In front of me though, there was nothing but life.

It was bursting from everywhere.

A large courtyard loomed ahead. People were starting to mill about as the sun was rising in the sky, scuttling around to one place or another under the hazy orange glow. I was reminded of Dorothy when she set foot in Oz, but the courtyard was more colorful than that. The cobblestone paths they crossed looked like brightly colored stones that signified something, though I couldn't see a real pattern to any of it.

But it wasn't just the cobblestones that were popping with technicolor madness. Very few of the trees I could see were green like the trees in our world. Nope. The foliage was splattered in pinks and reds and blues, all growing beside each other as if the weather or the soil they were planted in made no difference. They were as breathtaking as they were baffling. Did they not have chlorophyll like the trees in our world?

My eyes widened as I turned in each direction, trying to make my brain accept what I was seeing. On one side a mountain range rose, etching into the sky. On the other, a river with deep blue rushing water. From what I could tell, it would've been hard to breach either one of those things. Maybe there was a path or a bridge over the river, but being that close, made me feel closed in, but at the same time, gave me a sense of hugeness. Like I had internalized the fact that it was just a tiny portion of the whole of Aetheria.

I had the urge to run and scale the mountain that was sitting *right there,* but I gave myself a little slack on it. I'd only been in the area a few minutes. No need to go exploring. Not until I found Ren anyway.

I needed him. And I needed my bearings to be straight, so I squared up and turned my gaze forward, searching for the biggest tree. Which led me to the most insane sight. Not far away, plunked right there in the middle of the cobblestone street was a castle. This time there was no mistaking it for anything else.

And cage the Mage, it was made of sand.

Like some giant child had been at a beach and used a mold to create a building with battlements, turrets, and even a drawbridge, though I didn't spot a moat. It was ridiculous. And beautiful. And I was drawn to it, despite myself.

Anxious to get my feet going, I scrambled down the dirt slope, using my Earth magic to guide me like a surfer, heading for the cobblestones. I didn't have time to take the winding path etched into the dirt. I was certain the guards were going to pour out of the gold building any second and I didn't want to be standing there gawking at the awe of the Aetherian terrain when they did.

When I landed at the bottom of the rise, I turned back to check it out. It was like it was sitting on a dirt mound of dead and decay. There was a well-worn trail to the door that I'd come through, but there were still no signs of life around it. It was the exact opposite of the glistening castle beyond.

I set one foot on the cobblestone, and I swear, they called out to me, singing some chorus I neither recognized nor understood. Was this because I was made of the same stuff as these stones?

"Ask again later."

Had that been in my head?

It seemed like they were speaking to me, but stones don't talk, right? Although glancing at my bracelet, it wouldn't be absurd to assume they had a sentience of some kind. Arlo had said as much. Before Trickstan had killed him.

"Andras, was that you?"

With no reply from the phoenix, I pushed the sense of eeriness inside me and started walking. I wasn't hearing voices in my head. It was just the overwhelming sense of being in Aetheria. The biggest tree I could see happened to be a turquoise one—*turquoise*—with big puffy leaves. It was nestled among a patch of other colorful trees and flowers near one side of the castle.

As I made my way, I tried to look like I belonged. I didn't. For one thing, my clothes didn't blend in with those the Aetherians were wearing. Another thing, I was eyeballing everything and everyone. My slack-jawed wonder at the things around me was so bad that I slammed right into a man's back who'd stopped to retrieve something in his pocket.

I pressed my hand to my chest, rubbing it as if the action would dislodge the feeling of utter longing I felt for Wells at the moment. How many times had I bumped into the solid wall of muscle that was his back? Too many to count.

Not nearly enough.

Never again.

"I apologize. I wasn't looking where I was going," I whispered to the man. There was no way my voice wasn't going to break if I'd been any louder. I was choking on memories of Wells.

I'd discovered in the past week that sometimes it was the tiniest of things that punctured my heart, like nails being driven into wood. I wish my heart would've been made of brick instead. It would've made things much easier when the nail of Wells came at me.

"Unless you've got a rammer in that bag, back off," he huffed. I'd never heard of a rammer and was fairly certain I didn't want a further explanation either. He stared down his humped nose at me—like I was vermin— then mumbled something about swearing on the square, then moved on.

Weird. Disconcerting even.

Shaking it off, I resumed my trek to the turquoise tree, this time focusing on the people around me instead of gaping at the lush colorful setting.

I quickly fell in stride behind a woman who wore a flowing pink dress with a gauzy train. All of the women were wearing dresses. Some of said women were eyeing my jeans and hoodie like I was a freaking clown. And I guess to them I was. I made an internal note to get a dress somewhere as soon as I met back up with Ren. I was already nervous. Fitting in would be the best play. Of course, that meant Ren had to get him some neon-hued, wide-legged ninja-esque pants like the men were wearing.

He would hate them. Especially because I hadn't seen a black pair at all. The most subdued color I'd spied so far was buttery yellow.

It made me giggle to think of him in something like that. Though I supposed he'd like their tight open-weave tunics with no sleeves. Most of them were brown or gray, which would be more his style. And they'd show off his tats too. They were *hawt* with a 'aw.' I'd always wondered about the meaning behind them but never asked. I supposed there would be plenty of time to talk about it now that we were stuck here together for the foreseeable…forever.

The woman I'd been following veered off to the left, so I made a big show of slowing to check out the flowers planted along the edge of the castle as I made my way around it, inching toward the tree. There were no barriers of any kind, though the people had all gone off in other directions, which left me strolling around the castle into a stunning garden all alone. It seemed wrong to be there somehow, but there weren't any signs forbidding it, so I ambled over like I was supposed to be there checking out the flowers, not eluding potential guards who could be on my tail.

The turquoise tree was the focal point of the garden, with soft blues and purples of the bushes and flowers planted around it. The bark was white, just like the smooth bench that sat underneath it. The bench itself was covered in turquoise pillows and throws and made from the same type of white bark. It was cool and cozy, like a place you'd want to sit and just be in. The entire area gave off the same vibe as Wells' mom's garden—serene, secluded, and peaceful.

All in the middle of the courtyard.

The spot called out to me, and I was aching to lounge on the bench and hide away from the rest of Aetheria, waiting for Ren. I intended to do just that, but a resounding crack of a heavy door slamming kept me from it. I whirled in the direction of the sound and discovered a woman with bouncing blonde curls, wearing a shimmery yellow dress advancing straight for me.

Or rather for the sitting garden.

From the grim look on her face, she'd been the one who'd slammed the castle door. Girlfriend was pissed. I almost felt sorry for the person she was angry at.

Two guards wearing head-to-toe white leather skulked behind her. Seriously. White leather pants, white leather tunics, and white leather helmets covered most of their faces and the backs of their necks.

Ren would've probably dug their outfits.

If they'd been black.

"Ma'am. My lady, perhaps you should—" one of the guards started, but the other one shut him up with a look that said, *'If you value your life, you'll keep your pie-hole shut.'*

The blonde woman stalled, then spun on them giving them a glare that told them all they needed to know about getting the fuck away from her. The first guard shrugged and stalked back into the castle with a resolute *'not my problem'* face. The other one stood at the edge of the garden, looking at her with eyes full of fear.

I was so enthralled by the whole scene I almost forgot I was standing there in her path. It didn't seem like this was the right moment to introduce myself, so I took Ren's advice and ran to the back side of the huge turquoise tree and dove into the soil, hugging my bag and burying myself as shallow as I could be without being detected.

The dirt around me hummed as much as the vial around my neck. There was no doubt in my mind that this was the earth I was made from. I'd known that even had it confirmed when I first arrived in Aetheria really, but it still amazed me on a level that not much ever had before.

Because I'd made a point to stay shallow, I detected the pounding of feet above my head as the woman and the remaining guard walked to the bench. I did my best to estimate where the bench was and as carefully as I could, I inched toward the surface, angling to hear what they were saying.

Admittedly, eavesdropping.

Gram would've been disappointed in me—using my gnome skills for inappropriate things, like trying to get the tea—but I shrugged that off. I needed intel if I was going to keep evading the guards, blend in, and survive in Aetheria. This woman came from the huge sand castle in the middle of the courtyard. She was important.

I peeked through the dirt, hoping I was hidden by the bench, and saw the backs of her shoes.

Score! I was under the bench, hidden, but I could see and hear everything they were saying.

And dang, that tea was spicy.

I've got you." Mace wrapped his arm around my neck. "You're going to love it."

"I'm failing to see how you've got me when you're walking with me right now. You said you had to set something up. What, exactly, do you have planned?" Was I nervous that Mace had agreed to help me divert Autumn on our, quote, unquote date? Honestly, a little. But he'd come through for me. He always did.

I was more bothered by the fact that I'd asked him.

"If I told you, you'd be expecting it. I need this to be organic." He ruffled my hair, which I immediately de-ruffled by running a hand through it. "I promise you're going to love it, Romeo."

I huffed. "I don't think that's your best nickname." Pausing and running it around in my head, I had to admit a certain amount of nervousness was prickling through me. "Shit. Are you going to poison her?"

He stopped walking and I had to turn around to read his face. "Let's call that plan B."

"Let's call it off the table. I don't think that's the way to handle the situation."

"Fine. How about this for a plan B? I—because I'm such a good friend—am offering to take her out of your hands, so to speak. Put her directly in these hands, if you get my drift." He squeezed some imaginary tits, then rolled his tongue around to drive it home. He had a rep with the women in the camp, hell, in Illusion Hill, but I surely hoped his game didn't include those moves. "I mean, I'd hate it, but I'd do it if it would help you out."

Fuck me if I wave of jealousy didn't wash through me. I didn't want to touch her, but I damn well didn't want Mace to touch her either. Magedamn things were complicated. "So, you'd take one for the team and screw the sexiest woman at the camp, just so I didn't have to? So chivalrous of you. Let's label that one plan X. Maybe Y or Z."

"Fair enough. It's a standing offer, just so you know. I feel the need to point out you just called her the sexiest woman in the camp."

A growl came out of my throat without my permission. I was doing that a lot. Trouble was, I wasn't sure if I was growling at him for pointing it out, or myself for saying it. "Terra's no longer at the camp, so…"

He nodded, content with my explanation, and then he pulled his phone out to check the time. "Bro, you're seven minutes late. Autumn will be worried."

Exhaling, I shook my head. He was right. I needed to go. I hugged him, slapping his back, and then I thrust myself into a high-speed run.

A few seconds later, I arrived outside the stables that I hadn't visited in years. Candlelight was flickering through the open door and the soft sound of jazz music wafted through the air.

She was setting the mood.

While the fresh air in my lungs helped to clear my head for the task at hand, I found my feet trudging over the dirt instead of strolling in like I was the alpha of my pack.

I hated that feeling. The uncertainty. The hesitation.

It occurred in that moment what was troubling me the most about this. Missing Terra was a punch to the gut, sure, and wanting and alternately not wanting Autumn sucked beyond reason. But the triggering event for all of this—specifically, the mate bond—didn't just rip Terra out of my grasp. It was taking my alpha away piece by piece with its taunting.

I was weak for loving so much, so completely. There was no other conclusion to make about it. If I'd kept Terra at arm's length, like I'd planned to do in the first place, maybe I'd have some semblance of myself as I dealt with this shit.

Too fucking late for that.

Not that I regretted one millisecond with Terra.

I didn't.

Instead of coming apart at the thought of her, I stuffed the unsettling thoughts inside my thumping heart and strolled into the stables like the alpha I was. One solid step at a time.

The scent of manure was fitting. I felt like shit.

"There you are! I was getting worried you were going to be held up with pack duties." Her eyes were earnest. And her chest was heaving with desire just from looking at me. The mate bond was alive and well and thrumming between us.

She was wearing what I'd call a summer dress. Light blue, the exact shade of her eyes, with spaghetti straps, fitted to her feminine form and with a hemline I had no idea how she was keeping from showing her pert ass.

Magedamn. She was not playing fair. One glance and my brain went right to how easy it would be to rip that sexy dress off of her. That particular thought went straight to my dick at lightning speed. My mouth dried, but I managed to squeak a response. "Sorry. Something came up. You look nice."

Nice? She looked completely and utterly, no-getting-around it, fuckable. And she was looking at me like I did too. And I was the asshole who was about to deny us both.

"I don't think I have long. I just got an email from Lore in Illusion Hill." Truth. Not that I could do anything about the contents of the email until the morning, but she didn't need to know that. I needed an exit strategy in the worst way. Especially if Mace's plan A didn't pan out.

"We should eat then. I just fed Moonbeam, so she won't bother us." She strutted over to the first stall inside the building where she'd laid out a complete spread for us. This is where the candlelight had come from. Because there were at least ten thousand candles in there. Total fire hazard. I stood there gaping at her, so she managed to seductively curl into a sitting position and patted the blanket. "Come sit."

Since when did sitting down become alluring?

I took myself over—I had no choice—averting my eyes and noticing the rusty rake hanging on the wall.

To do: buy new rakes for the stables.

After I'd sat as far away as I could, she scooted toward me, unsuccessfully keeping that hem in check.

How did she fucking know I liked nude panties?

Oh yeah, she was made for me, so of course, her natural inclination would be to do things I liked. Which meant I did things she liked.

Was the key to keep her from wanting me? To act like someone else? I could probably borrow some of Mace's loud clothes, though they'd be a bit snug on my shoulders. And maybe I should walk around saying things like 'amortization, return-on-investment, aggregating' like Gideon did all the time. Or drink myself into a stupor like Bash.

Maybe that one.

Her horse neighed from a distant stall. It served to help me out of my brain spiral. I couldn't stomach wearing Mace's shirts. What had I been thinking?

Autumn grinned at the sound, then literally tucked a napkin in my collar like she was going to feed me too. Her hand trailed down my chest, my stomach, finally hovering *just* over my cock, which had started to swell at the sight of her. Fucking traitor. She lowered her lashes again, basically asking for permission to touch me. Permission I would never give. I grabbed her hand and kissed the back of it.

Not her palm. That, I only did for Terra.

"Thanks for doing this. I'm famished. What are we eating?"

Not her. Not her. Not her.

I was going to need a very frigid shower after this.

Undeterred by my self cock-blocking, she started removing items from the picnic basket at the corner of the blanket. "I went for food that wouldn't be messy and quick to eat, in case we wanted to..." Pause heard and understood. Also, rejected. "...do other things. There are finger sandwiches, veggies, and fruit, some yummy croissants, and strawberries with melted chocolate for dessert."

"Sounds good." I reached for a finger sandwich, cramming it in my mouth. I was going to need a dozen of them to satisfy my hunger. After the third one, I stopped eating long enough to have an actual conversation with her. The mate thing wasn't her fault. I owed her something for all her efforts. And I respected her as a person. I just didn't want her. "Have you made any progress on a possible new Conduit?" I'd asked her to check it out. She was intrigued because ancient ruins, myths, and legends were her passion. Another bothersome thing that told me she was made for me. She'd borrowed a half dozen of my books to research.

"Yes and no." She slipped a pineapple—Mage help me—into her mouth seductively before she finished her discourse. "You know that phrase that goes 'when one door closes another one opens?' It seems the Mage was keen on that philosophy. I've found evidence that indicates when the Mage was alive, he'd always open a new Conduit to our world when he closed one. The trouble is, there was never any discernable pattern to these new Conduits. It could pop up anywhere in the world."

I shoved a croissant in my mouth. It was drier than the ones I made from scratch, but it was decent enough to eat and good enough to keep my mouth occupied and not wanting to kiss her. After I swallowed, I posed a question that had plagued me in the depths of the night. "I've been checking closely. The magic hasn't increased in the hangar. So, it feels like there's not a new Conduit, since it was the sole function of the thing in the first place—to get the magic here for us. Maybe it's a lost cause."

Voicing it hurt like a son of a bitch.

"Maybe. But who's to say that people in Aetheria know how to shove the magic through the new Conduit anyway? Maybe the Mage didn't make plans for that before he died and went to his resting place. It could be a simple matter of someone over there directing it through the new Conduit once they know about it."

Someone over there.

Terra. Ren.

If anyone over there could do it, they were the people. I knew that in the deepest recesses of my troubled heart. But it wasn't as simple as it sounded.

"If that tracks, we need to find a way to communicate with them." I didn't specify names, but from the look on her face, she knew exactly who I referred to.

"Yes, but I wouldn't know how to do that without using Blood magic."

Neither did I Which is why I was working with Fitz.

A squealing neigh interrupted the silence. She jumped up in a heartbeat, panic in her expression. I didn't blame her. The horse sounded distressed. "Moonbeam?!"

She tore off out of the stall and toward her prized possession. I followed her, arriving just in time to catch the startled horse bucking out of the stall and bursting into the dark.

After a few panicked moments, Autumn lifted her dress over her head.

Hay's looking a little low. I bet Gideon could find a cheap hay source.

When I turned back toward her, she'd shifted into her red wolf form and was running toward the horse. "Should I come help you?" I

93

yelled at her, but she didn't respond. She just galloped off into the night.

I decided I wouldn't be of much help, seeing as the horse had no idea who I was, in either form, so I went into her stall to see if I could see what spooked her, expecting to see a snake or some other animal. I had no clue what scared horses into bolting.

It occurred to me it was probably Mace. The horse escape was his plan A. When I got inside the stall, I found no snake and no Mace. I found someone I didn't expect.

The woman's exhale was audible, but the guard facing her was undeterred. "Joy. Please, give it more time before you do something you can't take back. If I lost you…" he trailed off. Like someone else I knew. It was like a stab in my heart. I didn't have time to fully appreciate the thought of Wells as her name was another kind of stab entirely.

I'm sure there were lots of people named Joy in the realms, but if I factored in the blonde mess of curls, and simmering blue eyes, it had to be her—Trickstan's sister. He'd said she was his reason for the square nonsense, and it appeared that I stumbled right into her without trying.

Though, it hadn't been hard to stumble into a massive sand castle in the middle of the courtyard.

"What do you expect me to do, sit around being doted on by a lunatic when I know my brother is out there suffering because of me?"

"You have no choice if you want to live. If the emperor found out you truly don't follow the tenants of the square, I don't care how much he thinks he loves you, he'd send you to the Forge for your betrayal."

The Forge? Was that the official name of the Ooch? Possibly.

She shifted on the bench, pulling her legs underneath her, I guessed, since I lost sight of her shoes. "What would he say about our other betrayal, hm Fox? Or have you forgotten how I screamed your name just last night?"

Sleeping with her guard? The scandal!

His voice immediately softened. He stepped close to the bench. Too close for a guard, but he wasn't just any guard. "I haven't forgotten a second I've spent with you, nor do I regret any of them. I'm just saying we need to be cautious. Until we find Trickstan and formulate a plan to get you out of here, you need to keep playing the good little empress, no matter how difficult. Just bat those eyelashes and lean forward so he can see your bouncy tits a few more times and he'll give you anything you want. Just a little longer."

There was a rustling sound above me. I imagined her swatting at him and him grabbing her hand to kiss it. Or maybe I was projecting my relationship onto theirs. The palm of my hand tingled as I thought of how Wells used to kiss it. I clenched my fist to stop the sensation as Joy groaned. "I know you're right. I was just in the dark for so long and now that you've shined light on reality, I can't live in the shadows like this. I need to find Trickstan—he did what he did for me—then we need to end the emperor's dominance over the court royalty and this realm."

"You know I'd slit his throat right now if he didn't have his protections in place."

"I know. One problem at a time. We can't get rid of Magnus until we know what's in my boneheaded brother's head. We need to find him first and learn Magnus' secret."

The sadness in Joy's voice was palpable. She knew what Trickstan had done by joining the square and now she was stuck in a bad marriage to the emperor, because of it. So far, Aetheria—or at least the part of it we were in—seemed more like a weird cult than a kingdom. They were afraid of the emperor and Trickstan was at the center of it, somehow.

While I'd never forgive Trickstan for his betrayal, it was hard not to feel for Joy and Fox. They were in love and trapped and most importantly, they were fearful. The emperor was the problem. Though, if that problem could be solved, maybe I could get the Conduit open and magic flowing again.

Back to Wells and Bouldebrook.

For the first time since Ren and I had found ourselves there, I experienced a glimmer of real hope. Though I knew enough to listen to it fully.

I needed to know more about Emperor Magnus, but it was hard to do it from underneath the ground. I wondered if I should risk it with the two of them, come out and introduce myself, and see if they could give me answers. Or at the very least, shed some needed light on the situation. I weighed it in my mind. What was the worst thing they could do to me?

"Reply hazy. Wait."

I whipped my head around, searching for the source of the voice that appeared to have read my damn mind and given me an answer to my question. I found no one. Which was a good thing considering I was buried in the dirt.

I sent a thought to Andras through the blood link we shared and still got no response, so I ruled him out. I was likely too far from them. It wasn't Ren. There didn't appear to be any bluecaps or other creatures in the dirt with me either. The voice was not as intimate as Wells' thoughts always were. It was more mechanical, with no emotion.

Maybe I was cracking up because that had definitely been a Magic 8-Ball answer. I dug mine out of the bag and checked it out. "Are you talking to me Magic 8-Ball?" I shook it up.

My reply is no.

Figured not, still on the off chance I wasn't losing my mind and some whispering voice was helping me, I decided to stay put.

Joy and the guard both gasped and moved suddenly. "There you are, my love," a large booming voice said. "I was searching everywhere for you. Everything square out here, Blevins?"

"Yes, Emperor. The empress just wanted to take in some fresh air."

"Good. Now that I'm here, you can go back to your regular duties. Thank you, as always, for making sure my wife is content." Ha, he had no idea. It secretly made me chuckle that the two of them were pulling one over on him. Even the sound of the emperor's voice was unnerving. It screamed of pompous overconfidence.

Fox had no choice but to leave. The emperor wasted no time going in for the kiss. Man, it sounded sloppy. No wonder she sought out another guy. You should not be able to hear a kiss. Not from several feet underground. Just, no.

After a few excruciating seconds of more tongue, Joy must have pulled away from him. "We can't. Not out here in the garden where everyone will see, Magnus."

"That's precisely why I made these gardens, for everyone to enjoy their beauty. You, my love, are my most beautiful flower. Why shouldn't they look while I give you rapturous pleasure? We're married and there's nothing wrong with it."

She sighed. "Maybe not, but I have told you repeatedly that it makes me uncomfortable. We should go inside if you insist on manhandling me."

Magnus bristled. I could hear it in his words. "You like it when I manhandle you, do you not? Or is there something I should know?"

"Of course, I do. I apologize. I was feeling melancholy, and it must have affected me. Yes, let's go inside so you can make love to me."

Gag.

"Sire, there's been a disturbance at the Forge. Someone has used magic to lock the doors. Your presence is requested."

The Ooch—trademark pending—was the Forge. It didn't seem like the place where things were being made or beaten into shape, but we'd only seen one room.

The emperor grunted. "Is there not anyone competent enough to handle it?"

"That's the problem, sire. All of the most powerful of the Magicals you had assigned to the Forge are trapped inside and can't get out. Tributes are going unmade as we speak. There's quite the disruption there."

That got his attention.

If those were his most powerful people, how had they captured and contained the phoenixes? I was missing something.

"Fine. I'll take care of it. Thank you, Gilbert."

He said a few words to Joy, then dismissed himself, going back inside the castle with the guard. That left Joy alone. Maybe it was time for me to make my appearance.

"*Signs point to yes,*" the creepy whisper confirmed.

I wasn't sure if I could trust this disembodied voice or Joy for that matter, but I had a feeling about her. Besides, she could give me intel on the situation, and I could use my friendship with Trickstan to my advantage.

Former friendship.

Not that I would tell her that.

I decided to trust the wayward whisper for now, so I dug deeper, heading for the other side of the tree so I wouldn't spook her when I crawled out of the ground. After I'd wiped as much dirt from me as possible, I went around to the other side and found her curled onto the bench, her fingers twisting in the low-lying branches of turquoise leaves. "Um, hi there."

Way to go, me. I still sucked at introductions.

Her eyes widened. I don't think it was the surprise of seeing me suddenly, but the surprise that anyone would dare to speak to her. She *was* the empress. I didn't know how royalty worked in Aetheria, but I'd seen movies where people were beheaded for less.

I kind of liked my head.

Maybe it was a bad idea to speak to her.

"Hello." She gave my outfit a once over, scowling at my jeans, but correcting herself like the good empress she appeared to be. "Who are you?"

"My name's Terra. I'm not from around here."

"Obviously." At the sight of me approaching, two guards piled out of the doors to the garden. The first one whom Fox had dismissed and another. She held up her hand to stop them. "It's fine. I called her over here." Lie. I'd take it. She shooed them back inside with a wave of her hand.

"Nice trick. Can you teach me how to do that? I'd love to be able to make people scatter when I wanted."

There were a few perilous seconds of awkward silence, then she burst into laughter, her voice breezing through the trees like bells. Joy was a good name for her. At least the sound of her laugh was joyous. There was that undercurrent of immense sadness that carried through too. "Nice to meet you, Terra. I'm Empress Joy and if you call me Empress even once, I'll flick my hand again and this time they'll make *you* scatter."

The look on her face told me she wasn't serious at all. She seemed downright giddy at the thought of talking to me. That's when I realized it wasn't sadness in her voice, it was intense loneliness. And it spread to her big blue eyes.

The empress may have had a side piece, but she needed a friend.

And while I loathed the thought of doing anything that might seem kind to Trickstan, I made a point to separate them in my mind. At least for the time being. I liked her already.

"Come inside now, Terra. Let's get you out of those hideous clothes and into something that could disguise where you came from." I cocked my head, wondering what her angle was. She gave it to me without me asking. "I have a dress that would look great on you and besides, if you're who I think you are, you and I can help each other."

D iggs? What are you doing here?"

"I appear to be helping you."

"Mace talked you into his crazy plans to keep me from forgetting Terra. I can see Kelsey maybe getting on board. Or Gideon, but you?"

He crawled all of the way out of the ground and brushed the loose dirt from his clothes. "I'm as surprised as you are. I know you don't need help remembering Terra and I know you're doing everything in your power to get back to Aetheria. I was persuaded by his effervescent charm. Plus, I wanted to speak to you about something, so I agreed to surprise Moonbeam so that he, Gideon, and Kelsey could be out there in the night making sure it doesn't come to actual harm. He only wanted a distraction, but I feel I have to point out that could change at any time. He's very determined."

He was. Mace was not a halfway kind of guy. None of us were. Which is why he should've known that I didn't need reminders. Although when I thought about Autumn's dress riding up over her thighs and that lacy little thong meant to resemble panties, maybe I needed to thank Mace again. "What did you want to discuss? I'm all ears."

We walked out of the barn, toward my cabin. "When you mentioned the special jewels Terra's Gram was guarding, I went to my donsey to see if any of the other gnomes knew anything about them."

That sounded like a little bit of good news. It sure felt like we'd earned that. "Did you find anything out?"

"Yes and no. I have a story passed from gnome to gnome over generations, so I don't know how reliable it is, so please temper your excitement." I nodded, hating to admit that the ship had sailed. "A gnome I know said his grandmother used to tell the tale of some jewels belonging to the first Queen of the Winter Court. He said she called them the origin stones and while she didn't understand why they bore such a moniker; she knew they'd gone missing in mysterious circumstances. The tales handed down say the gnome who locates these stones will have wealth and luck untold."

"I didn't think gnomes could have wealth."

"True. That's why we must take this spin with a grain or two, however, it does give me a direction to look when doing research. I'll dig up what I can on these origin stones. If we can confirm with pictures or illustrations, we'll be one step closer to understanding how Terra's bracelet works and maybe that will roll over into some actionable intel on how to use it to open the Conduit."

Diggs was a good guy. And smart. I slapped his back, drawing him for a hug. "Go for it. Let me know what, if anything, you find."

I didn't want to get my hopes up like he'd said, but I let his calm positivity flow through me as I followed the path to my cabin.

I was an hour and a half into my nightly wear-myself-out workout when someone pounded on my cabin door. Even though I was a sweaty garbage pile, the blood in my veins turned to ice as the tell-tale thump of her heartbeat beyond my door.

The very last person I wanted, needed, to see. Still, my feet were carrying me to the door like they were attached to someone else's body. On the way, I swiped my face with a towel threw a t-shirt over my head, and hitched up my sweatpants, trying to look more put together than I felt. Not to impress her. To guard myself against her. As soon as I got the door open, I realized it was a big mistake to turn that knob.

Gargantuan.

She was wearing white yoga pants and a neon green sports bra that shouted for me to look at her tits.

How many fucking clothes did she have that said that for her? Too damn many.

Her hair was tied up in a messy bun and her eyes were lighting all over my body like she didn't know where to make them land.

I imagined I was doing the same to her.

Fuck me.

"Autumn. Hey. Did you get Moonbeam back safely?"

"Yeah, all good. I don't know what spooked her, but luckily, Kelsey, Mace, and Gideon were out for a run in the woods and helped me track her down and get her back in the stall."

"Mm." Did I feel a little guilty knowing what they'd done and why? Yeah. Didn't come clean though.

She barged in, uninvited, but the asshole I was didn't stop her. Or maybe my stopping her would've been the asshole move. I had no fucking idea.

The second I closed the door behind her, she pounced.

When I say pounced, what I mean is she pushed me across the room until my ass hit the chair by the fireplace, then climbed on top of me like a leopard in green lycra. She moved to kiss me, but I grabbed her wrists and held them in front of my face as a barrier to my mouth. "What are you doing, Autumn?"

"Nothing fucking wrong, that's for sure." She struggled against hold and ground against me in the process. The big bad wolf between my legs woke up and started howling.

The moment I thought about what Terra had named my cock, my eyes shut, and I groaned. Not the good kind. But she mistook that sound as permission to continue her gyrations against my groin. It felt like a bomb exploded inside me. "Wells, I get why you think this is wrong. I understand your feelings for her and for me are all tangled up in your mind, but we're mates. And I can't keep waiting on you to get your head out of your ass. I'm mad with desire for you and it's not wrong for us to give into it. You're the alpha and your denial of this bond between us isn't just hurting me, it's affecting the pack too. We have to give this a chance."

That seemed extreme. No one in the pack had said anything to me about her or Terra. However, when I thought about it for a few more seconds, I realized they wouldn't have. I told them not to and I was alpha. They'd obey.

Fuck, maybe she was right.

She bit her lip, clearly getting into the feel of my hard cock against her pussy. Her breath hitched before she spoke again. It sounded like a speech she'd rehearsed on the way over, but the whole time she kept on grinding. "Before the giant golems attacked, you and Terra had already gone your separate ways. You were trying with me and making progress. I get that you're suffering from extreme guilt over leaving her there, but I had no choice, and neither did she. Can't you just let her go and be thankful for your time together? I need all of you here with me, with the pack, not some of you with her in Aetheria."

She wasn't wrong about that either. I had tried to break things off with Terra and find my way to our mate bond, but what Autumn didn't know was the night before the golem attack that changed everything, Terra and I had concluded we couldn't stay away from each other. I loved her and she loved me, even if she wouldn't admit it. We were the stronger bond. I knew that in my deepest soul. I just didn't know what to do about it or how to erase the bond with Autumn.

The salacious moan that left her throat seemed to bounce in between my ears on volume eleven. I was going to need a five-hour cold shower after this. "Okay, we need to take a beat here. Let's talk about this."

"We've done that for weeks. I don't want to talk anymore. I want to fuck you." She demonstrated her desire by rolling her hips as she bucked against me. Throwing her head back, all her hair tumbled down from its tie, and it may have been one the hottest things I'd ever seen.

Or felt. Magedamn she was riding me so fucking hard.

"I'm sorry, but I can't. I won't let this get physical with you."

I finally released her wrists, and she gripped my shoulders, slowly lifting her head and narrowing her blue gaze on me. She let out a breathy laugh. "Your erection would disagree." Couldn't argue with that. Nor could I argue with the plea in her voice. "Please, Wells. If I can't have your heart, give me your body, just for now. I'm so close. I need to come. I've held off for so long, waiting on you to decide."

It took a few more torturous moments for me to make the decision and give her the smallest part of myself I could.

Okay, there was nothing small about it, but it was something I could reconcile giving her at that moment with her hips bucking and her eyes begging, her panting moans echoing in my head. She wasn't forcing me, she was asking. So, I shifted my hips to give her a better angle and let her take what she needed from me. It was an offering, a reconciliation for the awful mess I'd put her in and the rest that would come after this.

For the eventual choice I would make.

I did it because she deserved it. And I knew one day she'd finally see the truth of my heart and what Terra meant to me.

Maybe that made me the bad guy in this. Or maybe it would make me the bad guy to Terra when we eventually found our way back to each other and I told her about this night.

Making certain not to touch her or move, I averted my eyes as she moaned, "Fuck, yes. Your cock feels so good."

I need to chop some more firewood tomorrow.

Oh, and do a load of whites. My towels are running low.

My knuckles were white as I clutched the armrests, refusing to move, to give in to the burning raging desire I had for her. She came hard, fast, shuddering as she fell apart. The ache in my cock was more painful than I'd ever imagined. I think it would've been more pleasant to whack my dick with a sledgehammer.

But I still didn't look at her.

I still didn't move against her.

It would have to do.

She collapsed against my chest, and I was thankful for that thin layer of white fabric that stood as a barrier between us.

There would always be a barrier between us.

Terra.

"Thank you," she whispered.

I chanced it, running my hand over her hair for a few seconds, then dropping it back on the armrest. "I'm sorry."

"I know."

I admit, I was a little wary about entering a sand castle, but since the river was far enough away that it wouldn't encroach, I decided I could do it. I mean, I could've tunneled out if it collapsed, but it would've been a bitch and I'd have sand in my crack for days.

The white-clad guards all side-eyed me as I followed Joy inside and through the winding corridors. None of them spoke, but I gathered a visitor was a rare occurrence. "So, how long have you been empress?"

"Not long," she said as we passed by a set of guards at the bottom of a huge staircase.

In a sand castle.

I would never get used to that.

When we'd gotten to the top and started our second flight, she glanced back, her eyes alight with mischief as she whispered. "Too long."

Did she just come right out and say that? Yes, she did. You go, girl. The emperor seemed like a real asshole.

At the top of the third floor, we veered left until we got to a massive set of white doors with two guards posted on each side. She nodded at them, doing her little wavey thing and they parted, both declaring in perfect unison, "Control, order, restraint, devotion. We swear on the square."

Well, *that* wasn't creepy at all.

She pulled me into the room and addressed the guards. "Go to the other end of the hall. I need some time alone for girl talk." She didn't even wait to see if they complied. She just shut the door in their faces. Their clacking footsteps signaled they'd done what she asked.

I whistled. "Wow. I want to be an empress."

She walked over to her bed piled high in pillows and bright yellow bedding, falling flat on her back. "No, you don't. Trust me. It's not as fun as it first seems."

Sitting beside her, I pulled a pillow to my chest. "Nothing rarely is. I mean, all I ever wanted was to come to Aetheria, and now that I'm here, all I can do is think about going back home."

"What's his name?"

"That obvious?"

"No. I've seen that look in the mirror way too many times not to recognize it."

"His name is Wells. He's my werewolf. Though, you have Fox, don't you?" I arched my eyebrow, and she sat straight up.

"I assume your brains are as sharp as your eavesdropping skills and if they are, we can help each other. But we don't have time. The guards won't leave me alone long. And the bottom line is that outside of Fox, I can't trust a soul in this sandy cage my husband calls a castle. I hate it here."

There was that loneliness again. I felt it this time, beating in my chest. I wanted to help her. No matter who she was. I was seconds away from confessing when she bolted off the bed and swung open the closet. The one that was bigger than my cabin at Boulderbrook.

So many clothes.

She began pulling things off hangers and throwing them on the bed. "I'm going to say one word to you. If you react correctly to this word, then you and I will be friends for life. I must know I can trust you and this is the only way to prove I can. Got it?"

"Yep. What if I react in the wrong way?"

"Then you get your pick of dresses and be on your way."

Sounded like a good deal to me.

If I could trust her.

I trusted Trickstan and look where it got me. 'What's your word?"

She set a teal dress on the bed on top of the pink, purple, orange, and red ones. A fair amount of nerves were currently eating at my gut. It all seemed very ominous, and I worried about landing the right response. Because in all fairness, she could've easily thrown me in a dungeon as help me and I was still there in her room combing through dresses.

This one is for a luxury cruise in the Bahamas and a lifetime supply of lasagna, Bob. The magic word is...

"Babycakes."

I gasped. I should've guessed, knowing who she was, but I hadn't been prepared for the onslaught of emotion that would come from hearing it uttered out loud again. Traitorous tears welled in my eyes. And I clenched my fists.

Guess it was the right reaction.

"Okay, here's what you need to know—"

"Wait. Hold it. We need to talk about Trickstan. He is, he was…I don't know how to say it."

"You don't have to. After you sealed the Conduit and the golems my dumbass emperor of a husband forced him to make disintegrated, he came to me secretly. It was a risk for him because if Magnus discovered him, he would've been executed.

"I don't expect you to forgive him, but I hope you'll help me find him. He's the only person in all of Aetheria that could help us take out Magnus and restore fae rule in the realm like the Mage intended."

Say what now?

"I don't get it Tristan, *Trickstan*, was a lot of things, but I seriously doubt he'd hold the key to anything. He simply wasn't powerful enough or, dare I say, smart enough. No offense."

She started holding dresses up in front of me. All of them, beautiful. "None taken. He was always a joker and played the fool well. It's why his name is Trickstan. When I joined the square and brought Trickstan in with me, Magnus took one look at his power and started grooming him to help with his plans. I'm not surprised you didn't know the real him."

Sadness swept through me. I'd liked, loved, the man I knew as Tristan. I hated that he was a whole different person. Though maybe it would make it easier to separate him from what he did to us. The Tristan I knew was gone, just like Arlo. They'd both been casualties of a war I knew nothing about. "Why did he come to my realm?"

She threw the red dress on the floor, then the orange one, pulling the purple one back out and forcing me to stand in front of the mirror so we could look at it together. It was a good color for me. No shocker there.

"I don't know his real purpose—why Magnus sent him and the others specifically—but I know Trickstan regrets his part in it. He's determined to make up for it and that's why I need to find him before Magnus does. The answers are in his brain. If Magnus finds Trickstan and learns he faked his swearing on the square, I know in my soul if he I'll never see my brother again."

That would've been awful for her, but I was failing to see what I had to do with any of it. "I hate to put it like this, but since you and I are new friends, I have to ask. What do you want me to do and what's in this for me?"

She took the yellow and gold dresses ad folded them neatly and stuffed them into my bag with Ren's clothes. "It's okay. I get why you asked. Trickstan told me about your magic, what you are, and how you've got all this magical blood inside you. If you help me find him and unlock the secret in his mind, I swear on our mother's beating heart, we'll be able to open the Conduit and get you back to your werewolf."

I t was no surprise that I'd evaded the guards all day. Honestly, I didn't think they'd even come out of the building. Which was all Terra. She was a badass.

I was nervous being apart from her though. Not that she couldn't take care of herself, but because I didn't have an accurate picture of our surroundings. Did not like surprises. At all. So, I'd spent most of the afternoon making myself useful and scoping out the lay of the land, sticking my wolf nose into places it probably didn't belong.

Though the locals didn't even blink at a werewolf strolling around their central marketplace, I stayed shifted to blend in. Didn't have my own clothes and I damn sure wasn't about to step into the ones like the men were walking around wearing. No, thank you, batshit neon yellow wide-legged trousers.

However, their mesh shirts were alright.

In my intel gathering, I stumbled upon several key things happening. The first of which was the dumbass square swearing. Even in my wolf form, I could tell most of it was sarcastic bullshit. These people didn't believe in it, whatever it was. They were afraid of the person making them say it.

That was no way to rule. I knew that thanks to Mateo. That emperor character, Magnus, had them fearing for their lives or livelihoods, either would work and beyond that, what we'd seen in the building we entered, the Forge, was exactly as I'd thought: he was making them all pay tithes to him and the square cause. Whether that was financial, magical, or some combination of both, I wasn't sure. There were dire consequences for not complying and the people didn't dare refuse.

This was all for the greater good, according to Magnus, of course.

Asshole. I didn't know how he got into the elevated position of emperor over the four fae kings and queens of court, but he was taking their offerings and using them for his own purposes. I was sure of it. And he'd tried to get magic from our realm on top of it.

The second thing I'd learned was the Spring Equinox was approaching. Made no sense since we'd arrived in Aetheria in early January. That led me to believe time was different in the two places. This is not something I'd ever heard anyone—not even Wells, the scholar, or Arlo, the guy who'd been here for years—mention before.

Along with the Spring Equinox came a huge festival called the 'frolic' and many people made mention of the barriers between the courts dropping for twelve hours. Aetherians were forbidden to travel from one elemental court to another whenever they pleased. They stayed in their own lanes until the equinoxes and solstices. They'd thrown around the words 'planting seeds' so many times concerning this frolic it made me believe it was probably a free-for-all fuckfest of epic proportions.

I didn't even want to go, which said a whole lot about me and my damned crush on Terra.

Mage, help me. I was despicable.

"We're running a special leading up to the equinox. I mean, if you'd like to get your kicks at Aetheria's most popular brothel before the big night."

I spun my head at the word brothel. A sexy woman, I'd bet my life she was a nymph of some kind, was speaking to a large beast of a guy, thrusting a card in his hand.

The stories of fae brothels were legendary. According the Arlo anyway. It wasn't illegal in Aetheria, and they didn't even charge money, just magic, which was easy to replenish. It was a big part of their culture and while I'd always been interested when he told us about them, I found myself strolling past the discarded card the guy chucked seconds after the nymph went on to her next mark.

Nosing my way into a few more conversations and noting how everyone was alluding to the empress in hushed whispers—apparently, they loved her and had sympathy for her situation—I made my way over to the sand castle as the sky began to purple above me. Didn't care for the emperor's taste in architecture, but that's where the biggest tree was, so that's where I headed.

I didn't see Terra, but it took less than two seconds for me to smell she'd been there. No mistaking the scent of dewy grass and rain that I'd come to relish. Once I'd busted into Wells' cabin a few minutes after they'd fucked, and I almost went feral at the aroma coming off him. She was all over him, and it made me want to punch him, so I got out of there fast. I loved him and I didn't want to be that guy.

Not that I'd ever stood a chance with her back home.

Here, though...

After I'd scented her trail leading into the castle, the rest of my senses went on high alert. I wasn't going to panic because there was a high probability she'd just strolled right in to say hey, but if I found out she'd been taken in there unwillingly, someone was going to have a problem. If that meant tearing out the throat of the emperor, so be it.

Maybe the people of Aetheria would love me for it.

"What have we got here? Shoo, puppy." I did an about-face, growling and prowling toward the asshole in the white guard uniform. He had his rod slung over his back, so he didn't consider me a real threat. Not yet anyway. I snapped at him, letting him know I didn't dig that he'd called me a puppy. He frowned. "I said, leave wolf. Nothing for you to see here."

Oh, there was plenty for me to see. I wasn't going anywhere.

Unfortunately, I had my back to the door as I faced down the guard and when a second guard came out and threw a blanket over my head, I couldn't defend myself. I growled and bucked, but all I got was a snoutful of fuzz as he dragged me into the door.

Dumb fucker.

As soon as I got the blanket off, I was going to do some damage. You don't just trap a wolf like that and expect to get away with it.

Another set of hands grappled with the blanket, effectively subduing me, or at least keeping me from shooting out from underneath it, and then I felt a sting in my back like I never had before.

Violent tremors rocketed through me and couldn't keep from shifting back into my human form, even though I was trying hard to stay wolf. The whole thing was so sudden and any control I thought I had was nowhere to be found.

I landed on my ass with a thud, then the blanket ripped off my body, leaving me writhing naked against the cold marble floor. "The fuck was that?"

The guard who'd come outside to get me looked at me like I was crazy for not knowing what his little Insta-change tool in his hand was. It was a small cylinder, like an ink pen, but it packed a punch like a jolt of electricity. Beyond the pain, I'd had zero control over my shift, which was a first. I had more control than any wolf I'd ever known outside of Wells. "Never had a dose of sunstone, wolf? I feel privileged to have popped your cherry."

"I'm going to pop your skull, asshole," I lunged at him, but whatever was in that sunstone had also robbed me of my strength and made my knee wobble as I took the step.

The other guard sneered at me. "Who are you and what were you doing in the garden? You know it's off-limits to all but our emperor and empress."

"I don't fucking know that because I've never been here. Would it kill you to put up a sign or two?" Wouldn't have followed them, but it *was* a good point.

They closed ranks on me, and several other guards came from Mage knew where to help them. What did they think I was going to do buck-ass naked? I guess I could've shot Fire magic at them—they knew I was a wolf and had it —but I was thinking more along the lines of using the Earth magic they had no idea I had. Burying them in the sand sounded like fun.

One of the fuckers whacked my back with his rod and I landed on my knees. I raised my hand to dislodge some of the sand in the ceiling three or four stories above us, but a swath of purple descending the staircase caught my eye.

Didn't just catch my eye. It nearly blinded me. She tore down the stairs toward me, panic lighting in her eyes. "Ren? What's going on?"

I stood up, not giving two shits about the guards and what they'd do to me. I wasn't going to let her see me on my knees. Not unless it was in a vastly different arrangement that involved my tongue and her pussy.

She was dressed like the locals now, in a purple gauzy dress that hugged her body and flared out in the waist. The hem was shorter in front, just over her knees and near the ground at the back. The best part was the black combat boots she still wore. I'll be fucked if it didn't make the feminine dress look hotter. It was so her—soft and tough all at the same time—and it was the kind of purple that made her olive skin glow and her deep dark eyes shimmer.

It probably reminded her of Wells.

"Magedamn, you look mouthwatering." As soon as it came out of my mouth, I wanted to stuff it back in.

We think before we speak, Renfield.

Not this time.

She was too fucking beautiful for me to hide that from her. Though I did need to hide my rising cock. I ripped the blanket out of the guard's hand and wrapped it around my waist. She rolled her eyes like it was an insane thing for me to have said. "I'm not going to take it back."

She laughed as she approached me, throwing her arms around my neck. "Thank the Mage, you made it. I've got a lot to tell you." I had to angle away from her as she whispered in my ear for fear of my hard-on poking her in the stomach and giving me away. Thankfully, she didn't seem to notice. She turned around, pushing me behind her like she needed to protect me. It was so damned adorable; I almost dropped the blanket so I could grab her. "He's with me," she said, challenge laced in her voice as she faced down the now-dozens of guards that had come in due to the commotion.

A petite woman whose curls were eating her alive sailed down the rest of the staircase. "Everyone calm down. They're here with my permission and about to leave anyway." We were? I took a step so I could see Terra's expression. Yep, we were.

"And who are these people, my love? I don't recall permitting anyone to enter the castle today, let alone a naked man. I could behead him for that alone." A man had strolled in the other entrance. His presence seemed to loom larger than the foyer and he wasn't looking at my head with the brain in it when he spoke about beheading.

Terra's posture changed, as well as the person I was now starting to understand was the empress. "Oh, hello Magnus."

The emperor strolled over and took Terra's bag right off her shoulder. His wife shot Terra a warning look that he didn't see since he was too busy dumping all the contents out on the floor. When it was empty, he picked up my clothes and the ones Terra had changed out of, examining them and concluding that we weren't from Aetheria. He dug deeper, coming up with two other dresses clutched in his hands. Terra snarled. "I didn't steal those if that's what your expression means."

The empress put herself between Terra and Magnus. That's when I picked up the rusty-haired buff guard who'd sunstoned me stiffening. His eyes were glued on the empress. Interesting. "Magnus, you know I believe we should do what we can to help others."

The emperor dumped the last of the bag out on the floor. Terra gasped as her Gram's 8-Ball went rolling across the room and landed at the feet of the red-haired guard. He picked it up and examined it like it was a nuclear bomb while the emperor huffed his displeasure.

Magnus recognized where we'd come from, and the empress was diffusing his anger before he could let it loose. "Think of how you'd feel if I got stuck on the other side with no one to help me, love. I wanted to give them some clothes and food and point them in the direction of the correct court. That's all."

He softened. At least a little. "Of course, you're being charitable, but you don't understand the implications of what's at stake here. If anyone knew what you'd done, I'd have to punish you for it. Remember the tenants: control, order, restraint, devotion. This isn't showing restraint or control on your part. You know we can't give them anything until they've sworn to the square that keeps Aetheria working as it does."

I'd stick a fucking triangle up my ass before I swore on any square.

Terra put her hand behind her back, reaching for me, gripping the blanket, and pulling me close so her back was flush against my chest. For a second it seemed like she was trying to take the blanket off, but I knew she wasn't. She was trying to get me to follow her lead when she responded to Magnus. "Of course, we understand. What do we need to do?"

Terra

We were ushered back into the Forge for the swearing ceremony. I was allowed to keep the dresses and Ren had been forced into a kelly green pair of Aetherian pants with a black mesh top. I hated to tell him it looked amazing on him.

Nah, I didn't hate to tell him. I told him the second I saw him and laughed the whole way back to the Forge. The outfit was sexy, but he wouldn't hear it because he thought the whole look was hideous.

Though he loved wiggling his fingers at the guards he'd evaded when we were there last. Everyone in the building straightened up at the sight of Magnus strolling in for the second time in one day. It didn't take a genius to see he hardly ever set foot in here. Our little commotion earlier had already brought him out, which was probably the key factor in figuring out where Ren and I had come from.

What I wasn't sure about was if he'd discovered our direct connection to Trickstan. It was likely. A man doesn't just become emperor without being smart.

I lowered my head, keeping myself from glancing up at the phoenix cages as the guards positioned us on the platform. I didn't want to cause any suspicion. Instead, I projected to Andras as the platform started to descend this time. *"Hey, I'm back. Everything okay up there?"*

"Terra? I was just reborn so I'm not as strong as before. I'll be back to full strength in a while. We're fine though. Why are you here?"

"We got caught by the emperor. He's making us swear on the square before we're let go. No big. We're just going to do that, then he said we'll be able to walk around Aetheria. Then I'll figure out how to free you."

Ren grabbed my hand as the platform moved fully underground and the light faded. Fires were burning in torches on the walls but gone were the pretty marble and gold tiles. We were in a carved rock tube that led Mage to know where.

"No, no, you can't do that. Please don't swear on the square."

"What? Why not?"

I got no response from him. Either we were too far down, or he wasn't strong enough to project. Great.

Outlook not so good.

I squeezed Ren's hand, and he stepped closer to me. "What's wrong?" I wanted to tell him I was now more nervous than I had been, but I couldn't say anything in front of the emperor or guards, so I just shrugged, hoping I hadn't just doomed us to something we couldn't get out of. He didn't deserve that fate. Not my Ren.

"You're protected from the square."

"What did you just say?" I asked him.

"I just asked what was wrong."

"No, after that."

"Nothing."

"You didn't hear anything?"

"Nope." His posture changed as he tried to listen more closely. Because I'd alarmed him. I'd joked about turning unstable like Gram many times before, but deep down, I never really thought I was. There was always some hidden—or buried—thing inside me that made me feel and think the way I did at the time.

This time though, I had no idea why I'd heard the freaky whisper.

Maybe it was the soil of Aetheria itself calling to me. Or maybe it was my bracelet. I shook my arm. Just to see if it pissed the bracelet off.

Got nothing.

The strange whisper that seemed to know what was going on at all times would have to be a mystery for another time. The platform jolted as it hit the bottom of the tube. I wasn't ready for it, so I toppled, only for Ren to pull me to his chest. It was a weird time and place to do it, but I'd never noticed how great he smelled. I couldn't even describe it with words like Wells always smelling like sandalwood and the warm smoke of a campfire. I just got an overwhelming feeling of sunshine in the moment. Which was awesome considering we were in a cavernous dark hole underneath the Forge.

"Oh, my Mage, you smell fantastic." One of the guards grabbed a torch and swung it in our direction just in time for me to register the shock on Ren's face. "Not taking it back either."

"I wouldn't let you." He poked my ribs to get me walking, then put his hand on the small of my back as we followed behind the guards as they veered into one of five identical arches carved into the walls around us. How they knew which to use was beyond me. There were no markings of any kind.

We went down the long winding dirt path which led to another open chamber that gave me the full 'aha' moment. This room was made entirely of rock, and it was square. Like it had been sliced out of the rock with the straightest edge possible. The dimensions appeared to be the same all around us, so I couldn't help but feel boxed in from the low ceiling. "This is more like a cube than a square if I'm honest."

Ren snorted, but the emperor was not amused. "Each of you put your hand on a wall. It doesn't matter where."

No sense dragging out the inevitable because even if I wanted to back out, there was no way he'd allow me. And hey, if the haunting whisper voice was to be believed, I was protected. I just hope that extended to Ren. I dragged him over to the wall and placed his hand before putting my own beside it. He slid his thumb over mine, connecting us and grounding me for a moment. "You sure about this?" he mumbled.

"No."

"Okay good, as long as you're certain."

I laughed in response and the emperor's booming voice echoed against the granite. "Repeat after me. Control, order, restraint, devotion."

"Control, order, restraint—"

"You too wolf, or I'll have to lock you up down here and lose the key. You wouldn't be the first."

Ren shuddered as he released a deep breath. He didn't like it down in the dungeon-like cavern. The only one who seemed comfortable was the emperor. I smiled at Ren, giving him a nod, and we started over together. "Control, order, restraint, devotion."

The wall groaned. There was no other way to put it. It made a sound, and then without me using any earth magic, my hand pushed through, and we were both up to our elbows in the granite. Ren growled, trying to break free. Magnus just laughed and watched as we both tugged. It seemed like there was nothing but air on the other side where our hands were, but I couldn't be certain without using my magic. I cast a wave of magic, blasting it from my hand.

There was no mistaking the tug. It was like something beyond the wall was shaking my hand in a formal greeting. "Do you feel that?"

"Yep." He whipped around to face Magnus. "Who is that and what are they doing?"

As soon as I heard Ren yelp like he'd been hurt, I channeled everything in me through my bracelet on the other side of the wall. If I needed to blast the whole thing down to get us out, I would.

"As I see it, you may rely on me to see you through to the end."

Not the time, disembodied whisper. Not the time. And no fair quoting the 8-Ball.

The magic shot from my hand and there didn't appear to be any effects from it. At least on our side of the wall. Had I blasted someone back there? Done structural damage? No clue.

The next movement, the wall released our arms. Ren jerked his out, inspecting his fingers. There was a drip of blood coming from his index finger. "Did you just take our blood?"

"Yes. All part of the ritual. Now all that's left is to receive your task of devotion. Once you complete it, you may settle wherever you like and do as you please."

Doing as I pleased sounded great. The other stuff? Not so much. "What do you mean?"

"Everyone in this realm was assigned a task of devotion to the square, its tenants, and me who has the Mage-given right to rule over all of Aetheria. I've decided to make your task mutually beneficial, being the benevolent leader I am."

Ren scoffed and I grabbed his hand to keep him from saying anything further. Or, you know, punching him. "I know where you're from and how you got here. With that in mind, your task will be to find Trickstan and bring him back to me. For punishment. I assume that would be something you could get behind since he closed the Conduit to your world and cut you off forever."

Ren ran his hands through his hair. "If you're the all-powerful leader you claim to be, why not just open the Conduit again? It must be simple for you, right?"

Magnus puffed out his chest. He looked ridiculous. "I'm not the Mage. I can only access what he laid out at the beginning of time. There may be a new Conduit somewhere between our worlds, but it isn't like it's going to jump up and wave us down when we pass it. So no, at the moment, I can't do that. Once I get Trickstan back though, it may be possible."

It didn't compute in my head how Trickstan could be the key to opening the Conduit, yet here is the second person we'd come across in Aetheria saying it was true. I didn't want to believe it. I didn't want to find him at all, but if there was one shred of truth in it, I'd be a fool not to hunt him to the ends of Aetheria.

Though, I'd do it for us and Joy. Not Magnus.

He was asking me to do what Joy had anyway and I *did* have a great tracker with me. "Fine. We'll do it, but we don't know anything about this realm. Got any maps or suggestions on where he might be?"

He nodded at the platform, indicating we should get on it. It reminded me of Wells, so I spiraled for a second before recovering enough to step on it and grab at Ren like the lifeboat he was. The emperor paid no attention to it, stepping on and getting right up in my face. "I've got something better than a map. I'll send my most trusted guard to guide you. Right, Fox?"

I'd gone into Illusion Hill in the guise of speaking to my friend and contact on the police force, Lorian. I was avoiding another encounter with Autumn. Since she'd come on my lap we'd had a few conversations with others around, but I'd avoided her for four days without another incident.

Fuck, did I hate to call it that, especially when I'd actively allowed her to get off on me. I was just as complicit as she was, but the whole thing was wrong in my mind and worse than that, I'd thought about it more than I'd wanted since that night. I didn't know if I could trust myself if there was another repeat performance.

I strolled into the small police station, taking a seat until Lore called me back to an interrogation room at the end of the hall. He shut the door behind me, and I took a seat, glancing into the corner of the room. "I made sure the cameras were off. We'll have privacy."

"Good. I've got a favor to ask you."

"Anything. You know I've got your back because you've got mine."

"Man, I hate to drag you into this because I know you're in shit up to your eyeballs with increased Magical attacks, but I need someone I can trust to take the Water position on The Five. Jael, the former member betrayed us and went through the Conduit before T—" I paused, thinking better of uttering her name from my lips. I needed to keep my mind on the subject at hand, not her. "—before it closed permanently. Not only is the position vacant, but I need to fill it with someone strong enough to handle the rest of the group when I'm not there. You fit that bill, my friend."

"First tell me what I'm supposed to handle and add on when and why you'll be gone while you're at it."

I rubbed my jaw, trying to decide the right angle to take here. Yeah, I trusted him as much as I trusted my pack, but a part of me was ashamed of what I was planning to do to get Terra and Ren back. Lore was a stickler for human law enforcement. I had no idea how he felt about Dark Magic. Probably not good.

"You know the magic is diminishing. I've decided to ration what we have. My pack seems to be okay with it, but some of the other members of The Five don't like it. Specifically, the Earth member, Heidi. She's a troll trying to have a kid, so she wants all she can get. Guster, our Wind elf is having a hard time after losing Arlo. I think it's just a matter of time before he leaves us. I've got a line on a new Wind elemental that may be able to take his place, but I'll need you to call the shots in my place."

He put his feet on the table and leaned back in his chair, rocking as he looked at me. Being a Water elemental, he was used to moving his body around a lot. He very rarely sat still. "Okay, so where are you going then?" I hesitated, just for a moment. Long enough for him to question me. "What are you planning to get Terra back? Don't tell me it's something I'd disapprove of."

"Alright. I won't tell you."

"Wells. Come on—"

"Are you in or out Lore? I need to know."

"Of course, I'm in. I'll do whatever you need. Including kicking your ass if you try something dangerous." He put his chair back on all four legs. "Look, I'm a nymph. I understand how love sex and relationships drive people. I just don't want you to get hurt or do something you'll regret later."

Screw that. Regret was a whisper in your ear trying to tell you secrets after they'd been spilled. I didn't intend to listen to that motherfucker.

"Noted. Thank you, friend. I owe you a drink."

"I'd say you owe me several, but while I have you here, I'd settle on some advice." I nodded for him to continue. "There's been a string of murders in town that the chief thinks are ritual satanic cults—I know, right—but I recognize it as the remnants of wendigo ceremonies. Found a mask left behind one of the scenes.

"You're sure it's wendigo?"

"Positive. It was the stench that helped me find it. At any rate, I have it in the bed of my truck, you know, in case anyone were to go looking for it. Don't bother trying to deny you're working with the leprechaun. I've spotted him and his dream nymph heading toward Boulderbrook a few times. I won't ask why. I just thought maybe he could help us find the wendigos before they killed more innocent people."

I wasn't surprised to learn Lore had discovered Liam and Annigan. I didn't care either. Lore was a good guy and if I could help him, I would. "I'll take care of it. Just make sure the Magicals in town know to steer clear of any wendigo haunts."

He sat on the edge of the table in front of me. "That's the thing. Most of the people killed were humans, though they had their hearts removed and the arteries around them frozen, just like wendigos do when they steal magic. So, maybe I'm off and it really is some human satanic nonsense they get up to, but I'd like to be sure."

"That's fucked up. Let me get with Liam and I'll have something for you tomorrow morning when you come to release the magic."

He held out his hand for me to shake. "Sounds good, Man. I've got to get out on my beat before long. I'll talk to you later."

We left the room and, on my way to my SUV, I stopped and collected the mask from under a tarp in Lore's truck. The stench was so awful, I stole the tarp to wrap it in. I was gagging by the time I arrived at the gas station for my third session with Fitz.

I grabbed my duffle bag of supplies, then as quickly as I could took the mask from the car and shoved it, tarp and all, at Liam. "I need you to locate the person this belongs to. I'll cash-app you as soon as I'm done here." I didn't give him any time to refuse. Not that he would have.

As soon as Alec opened the door, I went straight to the garage without speaking to him. Why would I? He hated me and the feeling was mutual.

Fitz was already hoisting the chain down from above the bay. I took that opportunity to pull a second chain from my duffle bag. "If you insist on stringing me up each time, I want one chain for each arm." He huffed but took the chain from me and hung it while I took off my clothes.

Once again, he got a little too close to my dick for my liking, but after he'd strung me up, at least I wasn't twisting around in a circle like I had the first two times. Still didn't enjoy the process. After an hour or so, I broke the silence. "If I took a blood thinner before I came next time, would this be any quicker?"

"Maybe, but it would taint the spell to have anything in your system."

I couldn't tell him why I thought I could handle more due to my phoenix blood, so I kept mum on that part. I was troubled by something else though. "Why do you need so much blood for the spell? Or are you getting a supply to put in baby bottles later, assuming a child born to a vampire and another species would need to drink blood?"

"Why don't you stick to growling and pissing on trees? Let the vampire vamp."

His mood was even more foul than the other times. It had been the same with Heidi in the cafeteria earlier. She'd come close to biting my head off when I asked her to step aside so I could get into the kitchen, "Heidi was off earlier. Trouble in paradise?"

He stood up, advancing on me so fast another Magical without increased speed might have missed it. "You have no idea what we're going through so you should shut the fuck up. All we ever dreamed about—"

"What do you dream about?" Annigan stepped into the garage. They'd been smart enough to wear all black this time, though their skin was pale and hair ghostly white.

Fitz hissed in my direction, then slumped back into his chair. "Nothing. Forget it."

Annigan stepped around my body, avoiding me and narrowing on Fitz. "One really should avoid telling a dream nymph to forget dreams. It isn't possible."

"I didn't mean a sleeping dream. I meant a goal or deep desire for something you want kind of dream." I didn't like the guy, but the way he spoke did soften a little part of me. I had a dream too. To get Terra and Ren back. I could feel the anguish emanating from him as he spoke. I'd be damned if it didn't make me choke up a little. *Had* to be blood loss.

Fitz shook his head, trying to dismiss his thoughts. "Sometimes you need to forget those kinds of dreams because they cause you nothing but heartache when you can't achieve them."

"Are you sure they're not the same, Mr. Huntington?"

"Yeah, unless one of you dream fuckers planted the idea to have a child in both my fiancé and me."

Annigan shooed Fitz, making him stand up and offer them the only chair in the room. Bold move, but he got up and gave them the chair. "It's best explained as a chicken-and-egg scenario. Who knows which came first? I can honestly say that your nocturnal dreams influence your waking ones. For instance, I could plant an idea in your head right now to prove my point. Or yours, Mr. Payne."

They'd proven they could project thoughts already. I didn't need to see more evidence of that. "No thanks, I'm good. I have enough nightmares to deal with right now. Maybe plant an idea in Fitz's brain that he wants to hurry this process up and not dangle me from chains next time."

"I told you, it's part of the process. Anyway, no thanks to the dream implants. I'm with Wells on that."

"Suit yourself, boys. I could give you some real scorching dreams that will make you come faster than you ever have. Or ones that help you speak to the dead."

Fitz swapped out the chalice under my feet. "You might be able to simulate a conversation with a dead person, but there's no way you can make my grandpa Ernie reach up from Netheria to speak with me. Not a dream nymph."

Annigan shrugged. They strolled out of the garage without saying another word. They had the mysterious vibe down. I peered down at Fitz, who was watching them go. He shuddered. "I don't know if they were trying to fuck with us or all dream nymphs are like that, but I'm not sure I want to go to sleep tonight."

"Welcome to my world."

Terra

We sat in what appeared to be an office on the second floor of the Forge. Waiting. We had four guards on us. We hadn't completed the emperor's task of devotion yet, so I guess we weren't completely trustworthy. I'd done a full inspection of my hand and didn't find any remnant of blood like Ren had, nor had I felt the prick of a poking device either. We'd surmised—via whispers of course because the guards were not trustworthy for certain—that my bracelet may have prevented it. It made me feel better about what happened, but fearful for Ren.

The emperor strutted in the door, pushing my duffle bag at me. "You have until the Spring Frolic. If you aren't back with Trickstan by then, your devotion will be found lacking and I'll revoke your status."

"What would happen then? We'd have to return the lovely tote bags and square-encrusted ink pens we're getting as a signing incentive?"

Ren chuckled. "I'll never stop appreciating your sense of humor."

Meanwhile, Magnus was confused AF. I didn't feel inclined to enlighten him on the joke. He cleared his throat. "You'll be outside of the square's protection, forced into the fringe, unprotected from all manner of creatures and other physical threats."

Reading between the lines and glancing at his face, I got what he didn't say out loud: we were goners if we didn't produce Trickstan. I wrapped my arms around my waist so he wouldn't see my trembling hands. This fae wasn't messing around.

"I suggest you employ due diligence and find him in seven days. I've packed you some supplies. My man will meet you in the garden by the castle. He had to retrieve something first."

I tore my bag open because I wasn't going anywhere without my Magic 8-Ball and the last time I'd seen it; Fox was looking at it like it was a biohazard.

It wasn't in the bag.

I did my best wolf impersonation. "Where is it?" I growled. Ren went on immediate red alert, jumping up out of his chair.

"What?" the emperor spat out. He knew what. He was playing with me. Ren took a step toward him. The guards advanced in response. There were a few tense seconds before Magnus huffed. "Blevins has it with him. I told him to make sure to give it back and since he is a firm believer in the square, he will."

If he only knew. I surely wasn't going to be the one who told him. I kept my mouth shut as he led us out of the room into the main chamber of the building.

As soon as we got there, I knew something was off. It took seconds to realize none of the phoenix cages were hanging above us. Panic clawed in my chest, and I tried to contact Andras but got no response.

Magnus looked over his shoulder at me, noticing my steps had faltered, but Ren was there in a heartbeat, taking my arm and guiding me along with him and distracting the emperor with questions. "This is a big fucking place. How are we supposed to find him without intel?"

Thank the Mage for Ren. He truly was one in a million.

"I've heard whispers. Blevins will lead you to his last known whereabouts. You'll have to use your intelligence and charm to get further." He sneered at the word charm, and I was certain it was the moment Ren decided to come back and rip his throat out later.

Fine by me.

As long as we got a new Conduit first.

Magnus practically kicked us out of the building, then scurried back inside like a cockroach, taking his guards with him. I released a deep sigh of relief. "I guess we're on our own now."

Ren pulled his hair tie out. "Thank fuck. Is there anyone in this Mageforsaken place that isn't an asshole?"

I couldn't help it. I wrapped my arms around him and jumped up making him catch me and dropping his hair tie in the process. I was just so overwhelmed with appreciation and love for the guy. We could handle anything together. "I'll never stop appreciating your sense of humor either. Promise me you won't change."

He stood there dumbfounded, being respectful of where he put his hands. I mean, he could've been groping my ass, but he wasn't. "I don't think I can change anything about me. Trust me, I've tried."

"Don't. I love you just the way you are." He smiled and warmth seeped into my soul. Beyond that, it was the first time I'd stopped to look at him with his hair down since the Christmas party. I ran my fingers through it, getting out the tangles. "Why don't you wear your hair down sometimes?"

An expression I couldn't read crossed his emerald eyes. It was so fleeting I almost missed it. "If you keep that up, maybe I will."

I tousled his hair and jumped out of his arms. "I guess we should go find Fox and hit the road." He bent down to pick up the hair tie and a brown card lying on the ground beside it. "What's that?"

"Nothing. Just an ad for the Spring Frolic." He shoved it in his back pocket and slid the hair tie on his wrist before taking my hand and walking beside me back to the castle.

We waited on the bench under the blue tree for half an hour. The guards at the door told us Joy was busy and we should stay put until Fox was ready. It was annoying, but I was able to catch Ren up on everything I'd learned about Joy, Trickstan, and the phoenixes. Most importantly, the fact that this search could ultimately lead to ending Magnus' reign of terror and get us a way home.

The news didn't seem to get his tail wagging, so to speak. "Don't get your hopes up."

"You're right. I know. I just think I need some kind of carrot dangling in front of me to keep my feet moving, you know?"

He went to retie his bun but realized he wasn't wearing it, so instead he ran his hands through his hair. He looked like a cover model getting ready to smize for the camera. "Carrot in front of you? Did you just call yourself an ass?"

"Ha. Ha. Very funny. I'm just—" I struggled with what I wanted to say. I'd kept a lot of stuff inside, purposefully, but as things started to stack up, it all got very heavy. Though, if anyone could help me bear the load in this world, it was Ren. "I'm struggling. Seeing the phoenix cages gone earlier has me on edge because I had a connection to Wells through Andras. What if Magnus does something awful to them?"

He pulled me close, sensing I needed it. "They're phoenixes. They'll come back from whatever he does to them. We need to focus on our goal now. We'll handle the phoenix problem after. They've lived millennia. They aren't going anywhere."

He was right, but it still felt like I was abandoning them, but I didn't have time to dwell on it because Fox strolled out of the castle wearing red pants and a white mesh shirt. Ren jumped up, pulling me with him. "About fucking time. Where is her 8-Ball?"

Fox fished it out of his bag. "This? Before I give it back, tell me what it is. Is it magic from your realm?"

Ren smirked. "It's complicated technology. You wouldn't understand."

"What does it do?"

He seemed truly curious, so I had a good feeling he wasn't lying. "It guides me."

"That's what I'm here for, to help you find the fairy who destroyed the Conduit."

Ren bristled beside me. I was the one who'd closed it. No need to take credit for that little stunt. If he thought Trickstan had done it, then I wasn't going to share the truth. Besides, I still had to fully understand everyone's motivations at this point. Because of Joy, I thought I could trust Fox, but there was no way of knowing for sure until we got to know him.

"Not in the geographic sense. In the advice sense. Ren's right though, you wouldn't get it. Just know it's important to me and please don't take it again." He huffed and handed it back to me. I instantly calmed, clutching it to my chest for a few seconds before whispering, "Magic 8-Ball, are we going to find Trickstan?"

A voice in my head echoed the words on the 8-Ball.

Better not tell you now.

That voice in my head was starting to get on my last nerve, but I wasn't going to let on to Fox that something was off. "Alright, let's go. Does Aetheria have a bus we could take to wherever we're going?"

Fox cocked his head. "What's a bus?"

After Fox had asked a million questions about transportation in our world, Ren stopped answering. Who knew an innocuous throwaway line would open up such a huge can of worms?

It had taken most of the day to travel to the edge of the central province of Aetheria where the castle and courtyard were. That's what the locals called it. Everyone was welcome there at all times, but the castle was forbidden. None of the people even gave us a second glance on the way thanks to the clothes. I mentioned to Ren several times that he was being checked out to the fullest, but he just shrugged and shook his head.

Had no one ever told him how hot he was?

I knew he'd slept with Kelsey but that was a friends-with-benefits situation. When I started thinking about it, I'd never even seen him look twice at a woman. Though I convinced myself I just hadn't noticed it back at Boulderbrook. He wasn't all 'I'm hot and I know it' like Wells. He had to *know* though.

He tugged on my sleeve, gesturing to two huge trees that branched together, forming an arch similar to our Conduit, only the trees were blooming with blue, green, and purple leaves. Nestled in the trees were flags of all shapes and sizes, each of them emblazoned with the word

Summerlands. Giant windchimes hung from the branches, tolling softly as the wind blew between the trees.

This was the entrance to the Summer Court where Trickstan had grown up. It made sense he'd return to his home, though if he was trying to evade capture, it was the last place he should've gone.

"Okay, I think I get subways, but at least tell me you have flying mats in your world."

I put on the brakes, turning to Fox. "Wait, what?"

"Flying mats." Fox pointed a little way up the cobblestone path under the tree arch where a group of people were standing in a line. Just beyond them were attendants organizing things. Just beyond that? People sitting flying carpets and taking off like damned Aladdin.

"Flying fucking carpets." Ren ran his hand through his hair. I couldn't improve on that statement.

"No, we don't have flying carpets, or mats, in our world. Please tell me we're going to get on one."

Fox led us over and shuffled us to the back of the line, hoisting his bag over his shoulder, then lowering his voice so nobody would hear him explaining this to us like we were tourists. "The wind element guides the Summer court, so the only way to travel there other than walking is by flying mat. The attendant uses Etching magic to inscribe the destination in the threads, then you get on and it takes you there. Pretty simple really, though you'll probably have to get used to the feel of it."

I couldn't wait to try it. I couldn't wait to hear more about how to travel in the other courts, but I didn't have time to ask because an attendant grabbed me by the arm. "Next. Destination, please."

"Uh." I looked up at Fox.

"We're going to Midsummer. Outskirts is fine." He plopped down on the red mat—which looked exactly like one of those fancy antique tapestries, or you know, flying freaking carpets—and held out his hand. "Maybe you should ride with me. I don't want you to fall off."

He seemed polite and sincere, but Ren was not having it. "Nope. She's with me." He threw himself on his knees, pulling me down with him on the green carpet laced with purple stripes. As soon as I'd crossed my legs, he wrapped his arms around me and barked at the attendant. "Where he said."

The attendant placed his hand on the mat and *Midsummer outskirt* formed in shiny gold letters, then disappeared.

I shrugged an apology to Fox but was grateful for Ren's overprotective nature anyway. I felt safer with him. Always.

Before I could do or say anything else, the flying carpet—I refused to call it anything else—levitated about six feet off the ground, and then it took off. I squealed, falling back into Ren's chest, laughing at the way my stomach dropped when the carpet arched over the colorful trees and back down again, falling behind Fox's red carpet ahead of us.

The ride was surprisingly solid like I'd imagined a surfboard felt under your feet. Not like riding on puffs of air like I expected. I leaned over the edge, trying to get a better view of the ground below as we sailed over the dense trees. The dizzying swirl of colors made me giggle. "This is so cool."

Ren's breath tickled my ear. "I figured you for a roller coaster girl."

"I wouldn't know. Never been on one, but if it feels like this, I'm down. Let's go to an amusement park when we get home."

"I'll go anywhere you want."

I whipped my head around. The serious tone of his voice had caught me off guard. He took me in with the same thoughtful expression and I couldn't help but feel like the air stopped rushing around us. "I bet Wells could make someone close a park down for you." He tucked some of my flying hair behind my ears. "And the pack, I mean."

"Yeah." I turned back to catch my breath, then tried to figure out why I'd lost it in the first place. It had to be both of us missing the pack.

Reply hazy. Try again.

We were out in the open now. Most of the other flying carpets had veered off in other directions leaving us together with Fox on his.

Ren shouted ahead to Fox. "Are we there yet?"

Not getting the joke, Fox turned around. "We'll land when we arrive. It could be a few hours. I'm going to nap." He laid back on the carpet like it was a normal thing to do.

No way I was going to miss any of this flight.

Ren repositioned himself, leaning back on his hands and opening his legs so I could squeeze between them. Keeping me safe once more. It took a second to get up the nerve, but I turned around so I could face him, crossing my legs. "You don't talk about them much."

"Who?"

"The people back home. The pack. Bash." I still didn't know much about his mysterious foster brother who kept to himself like the lone wolf everyone said he was. Hadn't even met him yet, but as soon as I said the name, Ren's eyes darkened.

He took the hair tie from his wrist and secured his man bun. His hair was a defense mechanism of sorts. Like me clutching the Magic 8-

Ball or Wells rubbing his hand over his jaw. "Not much to say. We're here. They're there."

"Yeah, but it may help to talk about that. I know you miss them as much as I do. More probably. You've known them longer and Bash is your brother." Apprehension spread across his face. I didn't want to hurt him, but I knew he was being strong for me, especially when I needed it. I wanted to do that for him. "What's he like?"

"He's a dick."

"I don't believe that. One, you grew up together and you're not a dick. And two, Wells wouldn't have allowed him free reign of the camp. He's exempt from all the pack activities but is there to fly them anywhere they want to go. He's just as much pack as you are. Tell me something about him, a story from your childhood. Anything."

He reached up to do his hair tie but stopped himself, leaning back on his hands instead, taking a moment before he spoke, a wave of sadness passing his eyes first. "Our foster parents didn't like physically touching us wolves. They saw us as dirty vermin in need of rescue and cast themselves as our saviors. Not long after we arrived, I was told I needed a haircut. They made Bash give it to me. He was a few years older than me and had no clue how to use scissors. He tried, but he butchered my hair to the point I couldn't even look in the mirror."

I could picture a little Ren huffing as he checked out his reflection. "So, you stopped getting haircuts?"

"Not then. It wouldn't have been suitable to walk around with long hair, so they forced Bash to use clippers to shave our heads down to fuzz all the time. As soon as we got out of there, I swore I'd never get another haircut. Went years before I even considered a trim."

I clenched my fists in my lap to tamp down the urge to run my fingers through his hair. It's not like it would've been the first time, but it felt intrusive in that moment, wrong on some level. Besides, he had it back up in a bun anyway. "I know it was tortuous, but the results speak for themselves. Your hair looks amazing. All the time."

He grunted. It reminded me so much of Wells, that my brain went into overdrive. I had to swallow over and over to stop the tears from bursting from my eyes.

"You good?"

I took a deep breath. "Yeah, these thoughts pop up from nowhere all the time. One second, I think about Wells and I'm fine, then the next second, I'm overwhelmed. I just miss him so much. I know when we make it back to them, he'll be with Autumn, so I try to make myself remember that and it feels like trying to peel my skin from my body like I'm ripping a part of myself out."

"That sucks."

It is decidedly so.

"Have you ever been in love, Ren?" I didn't know where the question came from, but as soon as I asked it, regret washed over me. He turned his head away from me and peered off in the distance so long that I thought he wasn't going to answer.

"Yeah. It sucks too."

"Being in love doesn't suck."

He turned back to me and the look in his eyes gutted me. It was like he was staring right into my soul, "Being in love with the wrong person does."

Nailed it.

Leave it up to Ren, to tell the truth of it all. Being in love with Wells—not that I wanted to admit that, even to myself—did, in a way, suck. He wasn't mine to love. He was Autumn's. Flashes of white blurred my vision as those thoughts began to settle inside me.

I'd planned to come to Aetheria to escape the awful truth of their bond, but I'd changed my mind at the last second when he appeared and talked me out of it with his desperate kisses alone. Then the giant golem army had disrupted the entire camp, uprooting our lives forever.

Leaving had been my only way to escape the terror of watching him and Autumn grow closer.

Now I was in Aetheria, and he wasn't. I *knew* our being apart was for the best. I just had to keep telling myself that until I believed it.

Yeah, we still needed to open the Conduit to save magic in our realm, but once that was done, where did that leave me and Wells? And Autumn?

Nowhere good.

"Come here."

In my mind-spinning panic, I'd forgotten Ren was there. Though, that was dumb. He'd always be there for me. I folded myself into his arms and he let me cry it out like he always did, saying nothing. Doing nothing save for the soft stroke of his hand on my back.

I'd never been more thankful for anyone in my life.

I was playing the most dangerous game with myself.

One I was certain to lose.

She was in my arms crying over my best friend and I was sitting there getting hard. I shouldn't have let her get close. I should've been the bigger man and kept my feelings in check. I managed to do it when I was a Magedamned child, yet I couldn't do it as an adult, not with her in my arms, the sweet rain scent of her wafting into my nose.

I would be damned if I was going to let her suffer alone.

Even if she was crying over Wells and Autumn's mate bond.

She'd work through it. She was strong.

All I needed to do was be patient and resist the pull of her.

Which was easier said than done, considering how every second I grew harder for her. I positioned myself, shifting her so that she wasn't so close to my groin. She squeezed me, then sat upright, which was the last thing I wanted. "You were good where you were."

She took a second to collect herself, squaring her shoulders and swishing her hair off her face. "Thanks. I'm okay now. Besides, it's not every day you get a bird's eye view of the Summer Court of Aetheria."

She had a point.

I scooted as close as I thought I could get without falling over the edge, checking out what was below. The trees were more sporadic, and the colors were muted compared to the ones in the central province. In the distance, I spotted some buildings. I tapped Terra on the shoulder. "Town over there."

A flying mat took to the sky as we got closer. Within minutes our mat veered to the left to avoid the oncoming traffic, toppling Terra back into me. "I don't remember Aladdin and Jasmine falling to their deaths in a flying carpet collision."

The thought unsettled me. I locked my arms around her just to make myself feel better. The way she settled back into my hold told me she didn't mind. "If you start singing, I will hurl you off this thing myself."

She laughed and the wind left my lungs. "It *is* a whole new worrr—"

I picked her up, throwing her back down behind me. The mat didn't even wiggle a little bit. My cock did. There she was lying underneath me, hair splayed out all around her, cheeks pink from the wind, smiling. I had her right where I'd pictured her. More times than I could count or remember.

That was my moment.

The thing is, I was certain she would've let me kiss her. It was in her eyes, the way she gripped my bicep, the slight part of her lips as she looked up at me.

Pick your moments, Renfield. Don't go charging into every situation like a bull.

I let the tension coiling between us slip by like a gust of wind.

Not yet.

"We've adjusted to the carpet flying." I pulled her up, letting her grip me to get her bearings.

'Yeah, I barely feel it now. I'm not even nervous about falling." She peered over her shoulder. "I know you'd dive right off and catch me if I did."

She meant it as a joke, but no truer words had ever been uttered.

The flying carpet in front of us took a turn, passing over another small town. Fox was still asleep. "Some tour guide he is."

"Yeah, I guess this is mundane to him, but I don't think I could ever fall asleep on a flying carpet." She paused for a second. "Do you think we can trust him?"

"Gut instinct? No, but we don't have many choices other than ditching him. It might come to that, but for now, we need him."

She agreed, humming that stupid song as she settled into me again. Despite her big declaration earlier, she fell asleep against my chest, and I watched the gentle rise and fall of her breasts until I got distracted by the way her eyelashes touched her cheeks, and how her mouth curved into an almost smile as she slept. For a few treasured moments, I allowed myself to believe her dreams were of me, not him.

Terra and Fox woke at the same time, as the carpets descended into the trees, The way they swerved to miss them was a wonder, for sure, but I couldn't let myself get caught up by the passing blurs. However, I noted the trees had turned from all the colors of the rainbow to bright yellows, aqua blues, and sandy beige. It was like a beach had exploded onto the leaves. Guess that made sense for the Summer court.

"Oh, my Mage, did I drool on you again?"

So damn cute. "No. You're good."

She stretched, peering down over the edge of the mat. We were barely five feet off the ground at this point. The trees were still thick, but I'd seen buildings rising on the horizon before we dipped down. Why we didn't go directly into the town was a mystery. One I'd solve as soon as we landed. "It's warmer here," she mused.

"Summer court."

"I wonder if the King of the Summer court is the same as when Tristan—Trickstan—grew up. He said he and Joy used to play pranks on him."

"Don't worry. Fox will be answering my questions before we take one step toward that town." She nodded her agreement as the mats sailed softly down until they landed in a clearing of dirt between a copse of trees. It looked old and worn, like mats had been flying there for years. There were even a few there waiting for people to use. Though there were no workers there to etch their destinations.

As we stepped off the mats, I glanced around to get my bearings. From ground level, the trees seemed much older and larger than those in the central province. Beyond that, we were being watched.

I pulled Terra close, whispering in her ear. "We've got eyes on us."

"Yep. I can feel them. I don't like it."

I grunted my agreement.

Fox strolled over, pulling his bag over his shoulder. Before I could get my question out, he nodded toward the trees. "We need to get some cover. This area is prime real estate for fae pirates."

Terra's eyes widened. Not with fear, with amusement. Fae pirates sounded like something from one of those romance books she complained that she didn't have with her. One of the multiple things she'd put on her list of things she missed. Wells was first, bacon second and romance novels were somewhere after those.

I took Fox by the elbow. "You're fae, right? How do we know you haven't led us into a trap by putting us on the outskirts instead of directly in the town?"

Fox jerked. "Damn it. Because they've already got me."

He hit the dirt right before a sting pricked my neck. I clasped my hand and found a tiny dart buried in my skin. I turned to Terra, shouting. "Run! They've got darts." She took off, but I didn't get to see if she made it or not before everything around me went white and I hit the ground next to Fox.

M y mind was whirling when I approached the Conduit. Sometimes it helped me to sit there and think. Other times, it made that simmering rage inside me boil. I was hoping for the former but when I got to the Conduit, the latter is what came out.

Micah was nowhere to be found.

I paced for ten minutes, then sat on the bench devising punishments for him, including but not limited to throwing him out of the pack on his ass or making him scrub all the toilets in the camp. I was leaning toward throwing his ass out, but the toilets did need scrubbing.

"We need to go to Siberia."

Autumn had snuck up on me and I hated my weakness in that moment. Should've heard her but I was too preoccupied.

She was clutching a book to her chest, panting from having run from wherever she was. The excitement in her eyes was catching. I was about to ask why when she slid next to me, flipping open a book. One that she'd taken from my shelf. *Magic and the Stars.* Mateo had given it to me when I was around ten. I know now he was trying to get into my mother's pants. I shuddered at the thought, but I remembered flipping through the book and attempting to draw star maps for a while. Gave it up in favor of inventing my own super hero, Super Wolf Boy.

Never said I was creative. I was ten.

"Have you ever heard of the constellation, Allura?"

I remembered quite a few constellations, but not that one. "I'm not an astronomer."

"Look." Undeterred by my smart-ass mouth, she flipped some pages and pointed to a constellation with connecting lines that made it look like a five-petal flower. "According to this book, the Allura constellation is hidden from humans with magic, which tells us that it's important to Magicals for some reason. I got to thinking, why would the Mage create a constellation just for us? It made no sense unless it does make sense and we just don't realize it."

She looked at me like we were waiting for some confirmation that I understood her, but I didn't. "I'm not following."

"What are constellations? Recognizable patterns in the stars, so I figured the Allura constellation was important in some way. It could be guiding Magicals to something, like a map." She took out a world map she'd stuck in the back of the book. "My Aunt Tia was in a movie once where she played a professor of mythology and symbology. Her character was called in to consult and found an important clue to solve a string of murders by a serial killer. The police couldn't find the pattern for his kills until she came in and correlated the locations with the Orion constellation. He'd called himself 'the hunter' and she figured out he was talking about the Orion constellation. They caught him because the police were waiting at his next location based on the Orion star map."

"How does this pertain to Siberia?" I asked. My curiosity was starting to peak. It could've been the way she was presenting her case, so excited. So desperate to make me understand. I bet she'd be eager like that in the sack.

Nope.

Make Micah sweep all the dead and fallen leaves out of the camp.

I tried to focus on her words instead of her. It wasn't easy. "I was growing frustrated by looking for Conduit information, so I decided to give my brain a break and started flipping the pages of the star book, saw the Orion and remembered that movie and it gave me the idea to mark each Conduit location that I knew on this map. I don't have them all, you know, but there's enough here to see a correlation. The Conduits form the Allura flower, Wells. I'm certain of it."

I zeroed in on the marks she'd made. There were some missing points, but it was hard to deny it looked very close to the constellation sprawling across most of the continents. Still, it was a huge leap to think nobody had thought of this in the past twenty-two years since the Conduit closed. Or ever, to my knowledge. I crossed my arms over my chest, nodding for her to continue. "Siberia is one of the only places I didn't mark as a known Conduit. We're talking about Siberia, so it's likely no one is near enough to discover it. Another Conduit could be sitting there waiting. It can't hurt to look, right?"

My gut clenched. It was hard not to jump on her enthusiasm.

Hard not to jump on her, literally, when she was standing there smirking and looking like a wet dream in a tight blue sweater and those fucking white yoga pants. To make things worse, she set the book down and straddled me, wrapping her arms around my neck. "Come on, I can see you're interested."

I took her arms and moved them so she was touching her thighs instead of me. It didn't faze her. At least not visibly. "Yeah, it's a good lead, but Siberia is a huge place, not to mention a tundra. When you add in the political ramifications of flying into Russia without permission, it would be damn near impossible to get there. On top of that, if there is a Conduit there, it's not open. We'd know because the magic would be increasing. It's not." She pouted and it made my cock twitch. "I'm not saying it's a bad plan. I'm saying don't pack your bags yet. We need to know the exact coordinates; do more research before I make Bash sober up enough to fly us to Siberia."

Her eyes softened. "He's not doing well without Ren, is he?"

"He doesn't do well on good days. Bad days are nightmares for him. We're checking in on him constantly, but as a lone wolf, Ren is the only touchstone he has. Pack means very little to him, so it does no good to try and support him. I've got to get them back."

She slid off my lap. "Them."

"Yes, them."

I steeled myself, waiting for the argument, the discourse, the fumes of confusion I usually got from her when we talked about Terra.

This time, it didn't come.

"That's why you want the Conduit open, isn't it? Not the magic, not Ren, you want Terra more than anything."

"It's not just one thing I want, Autumn. I want everything: the magic for our realm, Ren, *and* Terra. Nothing is right here anymore, and I won't stop until I have all of it back. What's the fucking point of my life if I can't get this done? I'm alpha of the strongest pack in the

Magedamn world, and I have this fucking fire in my blood. It has to be for something."

I released a ragged breath, feeling somewhat better that I'd let all my anguish tumble out of my mouth. Instead of arguing or disagreeing or even trying to talk me into giving in to the mate bond, she stroked my hair.

And I closed my eyes and let her.

Terra

Before my eyes fluttered open, the sweet scent of earth permeated my nose. We were underground and while that gave me some comfort, I knew I needed to take immediate stock of the situation.

Outlook not so good.

We were lying on cots in a cavernous room carved from earth with the only light source being a few lanterns hanging sporadically. There were some stairs that led to a cellar-like metal door an Earth elemental must have created. I could see with my gnome vision, but I doubted Fox, who was facing me on another cot, could detect much of anything in the low light.

Ren could probably discern what was happening, but he was at my back, facing the other direction. Our hands were bound with rope and when I tried to free mine, I got nowhere fast.

Beyond Fox, two people were speaking in hushed tones. Well, one was speaking, and one was listening and pacing back and forth, clearly distraught about something. The woman talking finally grabbed him by the shoulders to stop him. "For the love of the Mage, Louie. You're going to wear a hole in the ground if you don't stop."

He put his hands on his thin hips. His whole body was lithe and lean, and the way he moved was graceful. "We're already in a hole in the ground and you know I'm like this when I'm on land for too long. It's been this way since the day you found me floundering in the Fringe, Bex. Don't act so surprised when I act like myself."

Bex huffed at him, then let him go back to his pacing while she clambered up the dirt stairs to the rusted metal door above them, opening it to peer outside. I could tell by the way she moved quickly and easily over the bumpy soil surface that she was some kind of Earth elemental. "You're right. He should've been here by now."

Ren wiggled, brushing his ass against mine, telling me he'd woken up and asking the same of me. I wiggled back and gave him the report I knew he would want, whispering, "Two people, third incoming. They've dumped out our bags, but I can't tell if they took anything. One rusty metal door above some carved stairs. Don't know where it leads."

"I can shift and get out of the rope, take them by surprise. Be ready to get up and run." Unsurprisingly Ren had a plan and was wasting no time enacting it. I didn't want to leave our things, especially my 8-Ball, but we didn't know what we were in for, and it was probably the best course of action. As soon as we got out of there and knew where we were, we could always backtrack.

Fox stirred, flopping over on his back. "I demand to be released this instant."

So much for the element of surprise.

The woman, Bex, strolled over to his cot, looking down at him. She was short with big dark eyes and long strawberry hair that reached her waist. "You do? Imagine my shock at this moment."

Her sarcasm didn't work on Fox. He just kept on yammering. "I work for Emperor Magnus. If he finds out you pirates have taken one of his elite guards, he'll send you to the Fringe." Louie shuddered visibly. Wherever the Fringe was, it didn't seem or sound pleasant.

"I couldn't care less what Magnus thought or did, moron. We're not fae pirates. We're not even fae. He's a merman and I'm a troll, as if it mattered. We're not going to rob you."

I sat up, rolling my shoulders to get the stiffness out. We must have been there for hours. "Why are we here, then?"

Ren popped off the bed. Even with his hands still tied, he was menacing as he prowled toward the two strangers. They both backed up against the wall near the stairs, getting a good look at him as he stepped into the light. "Good fucking question, Terra. One of you, start talking now." The 'or I'll rip you to shreds' part was implied. Why did I find veiled death threats so hot? The world may never know.

The door creaked open before Bex or Louie could answer him. Their friend peered down into the room and before I could get a word out, Ren lunged at him, hands still tied, bounding up the stairs and using a foot to thwap his chest, sending him sailing up the rest of the way and back outside the door above him.

The move had been swift, but not so fast that I didn't catch a glimpse of him.

Trickstan.

My legs gave way and I fell back onto the cot. Yes, we were looking for him, but I wasn't ready to face him yet. Seeing him stroll into the cavern was like looking directly at the sun on a bright day.

It hurt.

Ren managed to loosen the rope around his wrists enough to snap it off, which gave him the ability to pull Trickstan back inside. He threw him down the stairs, picked him up, and slammed him against the wall, placing his hand around his throat. "Tell me why you took us—and it better be good, motherfucker—or I will end you this second and not blink an eye."

"Hold your ponies, Ren," Trickstan rasped. "I wouldn't hurt you or Terra."

His misuse of a common phrase made my throat squeeze with emotion. He glanced at me, begging with his eyes and I caved. I felt weak and vulnerable and hated myself for it. "Let him go. Let's hear him out."

Though I wasn't sure he would, Ren finally released Trickstan, who predictably coughed like he was dying. Ren shoved him before coming over to untie my rope. "I didn't even choke you that hard. You could still speak."

Trickstan crossed the floor, eyeing Fox the whole way. Fox gave it right back to him too. I wasn't sure if Joy had told him about her affair with Fox or if Fox even knew who Trickstan was. Surely, he and Joy would've discussed it. The way they looked at each other though told me there was animosity and suspicion from both sides. Before he addressed Ren and me, he turned to Bex. "Get him some food and water, two packs for their journey. Keep him occupied."

Both Fox and Ren huffed like there was no way Bex and Louie would be able to drag Fox anywhere he didn't want to go and contain him. But in the next second, a flame appeared out of thin air, ripping across the low ceiling. Next came a body with two heads, a lion and goat, and the tail of a serpent to boot.

Chimera.

It shifted from its creature form into a woman with shiny black hair, a sweet face, and a timid posture. The juxtaposition was incredible. She peered down at Fox, her eyes disappearing as she smiled. "Are you going to give me trouble, Mister?"

Fox was smart enough to shake his head no and be led out of the bunker without saying a word. Chimera were some of the fiercest Magicals there were. She didn't look like she could hurt a fly in her human form, but she could take anything out with either of her heads or that nasty tail.

A chimera can make you purr, bleat, and hiss, all at once if you're lucky. Just don't let them light your post-coital cigarette with their flame. It'll ruin the experience.

"Nice security," Ren sneered.

"She comes in handsy when I need it, but she's not my security guard, she's my friend."

I couldn't stop the lava of emotion spewing out of me. "We were your friends and you played us. And now our world is running out of magic, we're stuck here and Wells is over there. I don't understand any of this. Why? How could you do this, TristanI mean, Trickstan?"

His big blue eyes softened, but he didn't answer me. Instead, he turned to Ren. "What would you do if Bash was being held against his will and in so much danger, he was certain to die?"

"Anything, but I wouldn't betray my friends in the process. I'd trust them and find another fucking way, you coward."

"I'm not a coward and I'm deeply sorry for all the hurt I caused, but when I met you all, I had no idea what I was doing. You have to believe me on that if nothing else."

I wanted to believe him, but he'd caused too much pain and suffering for me to forgive him. "I'm not sure I can, but I don't want to talk about that. I want to know why you captured us." It was mind-blowing that he seemed to be in charge of this group. There was so much I didn't know about him.

He started pacing, just like Louie had done, only faster. "Long story, sport, I wanted to warn you not to trust anyone."

"You mean, like you?"

This time he ignored Ren in favor of me. "Anyone. Everyone. Nothing here is what it seems. That's why I had to go to extreme measures to get you back, Babycakes."

I leaped off the bed. "What do you mean get me back? Do you know who made me—please don't say it was you—and don't ever call me Babycakes again."

"No, it wasn't me. I'm not sure who created you, exactly, that's been locked out of my mind by Binding magic, but I know you're the key to getting everything back like it's supposed to be. The magic in your realm and the fae magic in mine. I just need some more time to figure out how to use you. It's all in here." He thumped his head three times. "It comes out in waves. When I have the whole picture, you'll see. Until then though, we can't be seen together. It's not safe for either of us.

"I just wanted you to know how sorry I was and make sure you understand not to put faith in anything you see or hear. I'm looking out for you, Bab—Terra. You too, Ren even if you don't believe me."

"I don't," Ren grunted.

Trickstan dug in his pocket, pulling something out. "Before you ask, I don't know what this goes to. I just know it's important and if I'm caught with it, my moose will be cooked."

Ren snatched the small object out of his hand. "Oh, so you want to give it to Terra so her *goose* will be cooked instead. Nice, asshole."

"No, it's safe with her. I can't tell you why I know. It's all up here somewhere." He pointed to his head again, clearly frustrated he didn't have all the answers. I felt a moment of compassion for him. Been there, done that.

I grabbed Ren's wrist, making him open his hand. The item in question was a shiny gold key. Sort of. It had a big gold circle on top, then at the end where the little bumpy parts that go into locks usually were, it had a smaller circle with four prongs sticking out. When I took it from Ren's hand, the smaller circle spun around. I couldn't imagine the kind of lock it went to.

I looked over at Ren. "I don't know why, but I feel like I should keep it."

In my head, I heard a whispering voice. *"Yes, definitely."* I closed my hand over the key, and the decision was made. Nobody would know I had it but Ren, so I wasn't worried about my goose being cooked.

Trickstan smiled when he saw I was keeping the key. He looked so much like my Tristan, I had to look down at my feet to keep from getting emotional about losing that version of him.

He headed toward the door. I couldn't help it; I ran after him. "Wait. I talked to Joy. She says you have the key to taking the emperor out for good. Do you think this key is part of that?"

He shrugged. "You're lurking up the wrong tree when you ask me. Maybe."

Hearing his sister's name changed his posture completely. I thought I might have found the angle to get him to come cooperatively. "Once we take care of the emperor, we can get the Conduit open, and everything goes back to the way it was. We all want the same things. Just come back with us now. It'll all be over."

My chest was heaving. Yes, I wanted to end things in Aetheria and get back to Wells, but damn it, I wanted my friend back too. I didn't want him to be a traitor or a coward or someone who'd hurt me so much. "What do you know about Magnus?"

He backed away from me. I hadn't even realized I'd closed in on him enough to touch him. "I don't know yet. The Binding magic is fucking with me. When I know something, I'll track you down. Just be careful out there and don't come looking for me. That's all I have for now. Sorry."

"Trickstan. Tristan, please—"

"Fox will be waiting outside. The door spell will last two hours, so don't freak out." He swung the door open and miniaturized. His crystal blue wings shimmered against the purple dusk of nightfall. Before I could take a step forward, the door slammed shut and locked. I jerked on the knob, but it wouldn't give.

I raised my hands and banged on it over and over and over, sobbing and shouting for him to come back, half of me begging him and the other half relieved he was gone. Not my most mature moment, but I was beyond my limit. We'd had him in our grasp, and he'd escaped. "Stupid son of a bitch, why did you do this?" I hit the door harder, pain rocketing down my arms until Ren pulled me down the stairs, wrapping me against his chest and sliding down the wall until we hit the floor in a crumpled heap.

He brushed my hair away from my face. "Sh. It's okay."

"It's not, Ren. There was no point to his kidnapping stunt, and I bet he goes somewhere we can't find him. I should've explained it better. Maybe he would've come willingly, and we could've taken down the emperor and gotten back to normal."

"Stop. He wouldn't have come. Right or wrong, he had an agenda in his head. The door will open in two hours. Let's just chill and talk about something that has nothing to do with him or the emperor."

My sobs subsided at the feel of him stroking my hair, when he wrapped his fingers inside, brushing my scalp as he stroked, an illicit chill ran through me. "There's nothing else to talk about here."

"Sure, there is. Did you see that huge yellow tree on the way here? You think Big Bird lives there?"

I had to keep myself from snorting. I managed it, but I don't think he would've cared either way. He was awesome like that, just letting me be me with no judgment. I leaned back so I could look at his handsome face. "You're ridiculous and I love you for it."

He swallowed. "Yeah, I'm a real clown."

"No, Ren. Mace is a clown. You are a caring, thoughtful guy who says little but misses nothing. You make me believe everything will be okay just because you're here with me. You get me and you let me take the lead when I need it and you protect me when I need that too. No other person in this world or any other could do that like you."

I didn't miss his sharp intake of breath. He was not used to anyone talking like this to him, that much was clear. But I had to tell him because it was true and more than that, there was something else brewing in my head. Something I didn't want to let out, so I figured if I told him how much I valued him as a friend, that little niggle of an idea would go away. His gaze fell to my lips, just for a second, before he looked into my eyes. "Not even Wells."

There was a question in his words. I'd considered it many times: what it would've been like if Wells hadn't gotten fried by the golems because he jumped in front of Autumn to save her. If he'd stayed with me.

"It would be different if he was here. He would've barreled through this whole realm fighting and burning it down to get to Trickstan and going after the emperor with phoenix fire blazing. No telling how many people would've died. And he would've done it for me despite his mate bond with Autumn."

"You don't think I'm willing to do that?" A pause. "For you." He would. I knew that, but I also knew what he was asking me. What I was starting to realize was happening. What I was afraid of happening. More than anything else I was dealing with if I was honest. His voice was barely audible. "They're mates, Terra."

"I know."

"Do you?"

I bit my lip, unsure, unsteady, un-fucking-ready to deal with this, but knowing I had to. "I'm not sure."

He leaned down and I was certain he was going to kiss me. As certain as I was I was going to let him. My heart was banging against my ribcage like a hummingbird at the thought of it, but he pulled back at the last minute, mumbling under his breath. "Not the right moment." He pressed a quick kiss to my temple, then held out his hand to help me up. Once we were both upright, he started throwing all of our belongings around, rummaging around until he found what he was looking for under the cot where Fox had been.

Fishing it out, he spun around to hand me my Magic 8-Ball. "Ren. I—"

His smile was full of sadness. "Nah. We're good. Let's get our shit together and get ready to go."

"I think we should talk ab—"

"About how we're going to find Trickstan, yes. Everything else will have another moment."

He went back to shoving things in our bags and I leaned against the wall, asking the 8-Ball a question in my mind, then shaking it to get my answer.

Cannot predict now.

The whispering voice in my head came through loud and clear again. It was something else entirely. *"As I see it, you must find me."*

She'd been shaking the shit out of that 8-Ball as I distracted myself by packing up our gear. I had to turn my back on her, so I didn't lunge at her, throw her down on one of the cots, and get inside her like I wanted.

I'd been one fucking breath away from it.

Because in the deep recesses of my heart, I got the feeling she wanted me as much as I did her.

The sudden stillness in the room caught my attention. She'd stopped shaking and had her head cocked sideways, listening intently for something. "Did you hear that?"

I turned. "What?"

"I don't know. I keep hearing these whispers. It's not Andras and I don't think it's in my head. It's faint, yet when I hear them, I feel them too. Like they've physical presence." She shuddered, shoving the 8-ball in her bag. "Maybe I'm cracking up."

The thought of her losing her mind didn't feel good. "You want me to shift and use my wolf ears?"

"No. Next time maybe. I just want to get out of here."

"I hate to break it to you, but it's only been half an hour at most."

She climbed up the stairs, touching the dirt around the cellar door. "Yeah, but we have Earth magic. We don't have to use the door."

Of course, Trickstan would've been too dumb to think of that. He was supposedly the boss of the operation, and if that was the case, I had no doubt we could track him down. The odds were better if there was a fresh trail anyway. I gathered the rest of the stuff and met her at the top of the stairs. "It'll be fun to tunnel with you again."

"Yeah. Give me a boost." She steadied herself by putting her hand on my shoulder as I cupped my hands for her to use as a step. It took no time for her to sail up into the soil above us. When I was sure she was good and anchored, I jumped up and joined her in the dirt.

We made it through faster than I expected. I had a hunch that her magic was increasing in Aetheria. Or maybe it was the bracelet we still knew nothing about. Whatever it was, she was like dynamite in the earth, blasting her way up and out in no time.

I brushed the dirt off my clothes, then retied my hair, glancing around for Fox or some kind of landmark. We found him sitting against a beige tree, stuffing his face and humming. The sight of him like that didn't sit well with me. He wasn't troubled by our kidnapping. And yeah, it turned out to be nothing, but he didn't know Trickstan like we did. He should've been alarmed or at the very least tried to get us out of the ground. Or he should've gone off after them.

I sailed over to him, pulling him up. He was way heavier than I expected him to be. Probably because he'd eaten his face off while we were down in the hole. "Dude. Where did they go?"

He finished off what looked like a funky turkey leg. It made my stomach roll. "That way. Toward Mystia would be my guess. The place is rife with fae and popular due to its proximity to the largest fae brothel."

Terra folded her arms. I wondered if she had any idea how often she did that. Wells was in her head, always. "What are we waiting for then? Let's eat and carpet at the same time."

"No flying mats in this area. They brought us miles away from Midsummer. Luckily, your friend left us two packs of supplies, including tents we can sleep in tonight. But we don't have to leave until morning, honestly. We're only three or four hours away, at best."

Now that we'd bumped into Trickstan, this guy didn't seem that keen on catching him at all. That raised my hackles. "No, we go now. I'm not losing him because you're too lazy to care."

He stood up, wiping his hands on a towel he had folded in his lap. "I'm not lazy, I'm just saying it'll be easier in the daytime, but if you want to go now, we can. But it'll be best to wait until morning to go into Mystia. If we take one wrong turn and accidentally get lost in the Moaning Mist, it could be deadly."

I grabbed the other pack, strapping it to my back and Terra fell in beside me. I could see the wariness in her eyes. Not over what we were doing, over Fox. He was a mystery that needed solving. "Okay, you can't just drop a term like Moaning Mist without explaining it. And go." Fox shot her a bewildered look. He didn't get her sense of humor. At all.

"I suppose I can use this time to educate you on how Aetheria works." Finally, we were getting somewhere. We'd been there too long to know relatively nothing. "Each court is its own entity, with a king or queen and it's surrounded by different impenetrable obstacles. Magicals who live in these courts are confined there except for the Spring and Fall Equinoxes and Summer and Winter Solstices. During those times, the central province has frolics, all courts are open and we're free to roam as we please, but as soon as the time passes, the borders close again thanks to the magic placed in them.

"There are some who traverse across the divides, but it isn't wise. Death is most often the reward for being foolish enough to attempt it."

It occurred to me that this guy had a very strange way of speaking. He didn't sound like a person who looked as young as we did. It was hard to say with Magicals though. He had an air about him that screamed experience and privilege and was yet another thing that had my guard up. How did a guy like that get to be in the guard? It was a lowly position, all things considered. But maybe I was projecting our world onto his.

Terra ran ahead, then turned around to walk backward so she could see him. She'd dug a lantern out of our pack, so we weren't stumbling like Fox had predicted. "So, the Moaning Mist is one of the barriers?"

"Yes, between the Summer and Spring courts. I've never been inside the Mist, but I'm from Wysteria on the North side of the Summer Court, far from it."

"What happens in the mist? If it isn't moaning, I'm going to be disappointed." Terra was into the romance of Aetheria, and it was exciting to see the beauty of it from her eyes.

"It was designed by dream nymphs and water nymphs, so when you enter the mist and the droplets absorb into your skin, you begin to hallucinate your dream lover. The mist becomes a corporeal version of that person, and you can imagine now where the moaning part comes from."

That got my interest. "I'm not seeing a downside to sex mist."

"I've been told it's great to start, but the mist can trap you in a loop and get you turned around so that you don't know which way is out. Then you're tempted by your lover, so you don't want to leave anyway. People have starved to death or succumbed to dehydration in the Moaning Mist."

I laughed "I guess if you're going to die, that's the way to do it."

Terra turned back around, watching where she was walking. "Yeah, but I'd rather know I was with the real thing, not a misty version of him."

Fox stopped walking, looking at the compass he'd dug out of his pack. "We're about a mile from Mystia. The Moaning Mist is in that direction. We should camp here and go into town in the morning when we have light."

I was still picking up Trickstan's scent in the air, so I knew we were on the right track. Besides, the sun would wake me up early anyway. So, I let Fox act like he was in control of this op and set up camp among the trees. Terra wanted to light a fire, but he insisted he didn't need it. Neither of us did, her with Wells' phoenix fire and me with my wolf blood. It was on him if he wanted to refuse warmth.

The tents we'd been given were woven from some kind of magical cloth and camouflaged to our surroundings. Once we set them up, I couldn't even see them with my wolf eyes, so once we got inside, we'd be there for the night. There would be no finding them otherwise. "What kind of creatures are out here in the woods at night that would cause us to need camo?"

"All manner, but we're okay in the tents. I swear." Terra and I both paused, waiting for the "on the square, but it never came.

Fox crawled into his tent soon after he'd set it up, and then Terra and I squeezed into the other one. I could've—should've—slept outside, but I didn't. When she curled into my arms facing me, I knew I'd made the right call. The position was more intimate than our usual spooning and I couldn't help but trace my hands down her spine, over the curve of her hip and back again.

She didn't stop me.

I didn't stop myself.

"Ren?"

"Yeah."

She waited a long damn time to speak again. In those moments I could nearly feel her thoughts twirling in her head. She was moving closer, inch by inch. "Never mind. I mean, goodnight."

"Night." She fell asleep against my chest, and it took no time for me to drift off, breathing in her sweet scent and loving how her body melded against mine.

I woke hours later with the most painful hard-on I'd ever experienced.

Something wasn't right.

I was aware that I was in bed. I could feel the sheet over my body and the pillow under my head, but when I opened my eyes instead of seeing the wooden beams above my bed or my mom's paintings on the walls, I saw only white.

I blinked.

It did no good.

So, I tried to get up, but my body wasn't having it.

"Wells? What are you...where are we?" A flash of white light shot across my vision, and I was standing in front of Fitz in a white room.

No, that's not an accurate description. It wasn't a room because it had no walls or ceiling, no floors. It was just white space and somehow, we were in it. He was panicking. I could feel it rolling off him as if it were my own emotions. He waved his arms in front of him like he was reaching for something. "The fuck is going on?"

I took a tentative step, though I couldn't feel the ground beneath me. I managed to get closer to him, so I could move around the space. "No clue."

He lunged at me, connecting with my chest and knocking me off-kilter—only because he surprised me—but I righted myself and grabbed him by the shoulders. "Calm down, capiche? Panic never helps any situation."

"What have you done to me? I was asleep. Are we dreaming?"

"Dude, if I was dreaming, it sure wouldn't be about you."

As soon as the words left my mouth, something flickered in my periphery. Both of us whipped our heads in that direction. My heart leaped out of my chest when a vision of Terra appeared in front of me. I reached out to touch her and she faded as quickly as she'd come. The gut-wrenching pain that always came when I thought of her was a hundred times worse than usual. "Did you see her?"

"Terra? Yeah. She was there, then she floated away. Man, I feel so desolate now that she's gone. Like I want to claw out my heart and stomp on it to make it stop hurting. I barely even spoke to her when she was here at the camp. What are you doing to me?"

A growl left my throat, and I almost pounded the shit out of him. Not only was he seeing into my head and experiencing the torment I had over losing her, but he was being stupid about it. "It's not me, Asshole. But I'll give you one guess who it is."

It took him a second, but he finally got it. "Annigan."

"Yeah. They told us they could do this. Seems like they wanted to make believers out of us."

He started pacing, walking right through the spot where Terra had been. I clenched my fists, the desire to see her so overwhelming I could barely handle it. With that thought, she appeared again. This time a little more corporeal than the first. She was wearing a purple dress I'd never seen her wear before along with her black boots, and though I couldn't hear her, she was calling out to me, her pouty kissable lips forming my name.

I couldn't stop myself from reaching out to her, but there was nothing there to touch.

She was a dream.

While I didn't want to share her with Fitz, the idea of waking up with her still in Aetheria sent waves of panic sailing through me. I didn't have time to deal with it because the cry of a baby robbed my attention. I looked over and found Fitz with his hands over his ears, trying to keep from hearing it.

The cries just got louder and louder until he crouched down to a kneeling position and started rocking back and forth. Which was better than him opening his eyes and seeing what I saw beyond him. A wiggling blanket covered in yellow stars.

Why would Annigan send him dreams of a crying child when he and Heidi were trying unsuccessfully to have a baby?

It was so fucking cruel.

I managed to get him to stand upright and removed his hands from his head. "We're in some kind of dream space. It's not real."

"It feels real. Somehow that baby is mine."

There was a rumbling growl from somewhere far away. I ignored it in favor of keeping Fitz looking at me instead of turning around and seeing the baby. "I know. I think we just have to ride this dream out. We have to wake up sometime, right?"

"Okay, but how are we able to talk to each other?"

"That's going to be question number two that I ask Annigan."

The growl was getting closer. "What's question one?"

"Why the fuck?"

He nodded. Finally hearing the growl, he did an about-face just in time to see little wiggling toes poke out of the blanket and a massive white wolf jumping in from nowhere.

It was my wolf.

And it was separate from me. Meaning, I couldn't control it. Mage knows I tried. Even though I knew—I fully *knew*—none of it was real, my muscles locked tight in preparation for the inevitable.

Fitz screamed and shot toward the baby, rolling and absorbing the bite of my wolf as its teeth clamped into his arm.

I tasted blood in my own mouth.

When he stood up, the baby was gone, but his arm was a mangled mess with blood dripping down his forearm and fingers onto the whiteness underneath us. He shot toward me, leaving a trail of red as his fangs descended. "That was your wolf. I've seen it before. Why would you do that?"

"I didn't. It's not real."

"Then why is my arm hurting like a son-of-a-bitch?"

"Don't know. We need to find a way to wake up from this nightmare." That's what it was, a true nightmare, but I'll be damned if the thought of waking up didn't activate some kind of mechanism in my brain to make Terra appear again. I didn't want to leave the place if it brought glimpses of her to me.

This time, she was crying, and I couldn't wrap my arms around her to comfort her. It was the worst I'd felt since I came back to life in our world without her. My hands shook and then suddenly, the Christmas present I'd made for her—a glass orb made from my mom's sea glass with my phoenix fire inside—appeared in my hand. I was so overwhelmed with emotion and angst, that I threw it as hard as I could.

It crashed against some unseen surface, the shattering pieces shearing my heart in the process.

I woke up, gasping and kicking the sheets off like a rabid dog. It took a few weighted seconds for me to feel my body again. It was a lot like when I died and was reborn again—heaviness, followed by a rush of adrenaline that made my mouth taste like metal. Then the burning fire usually finished it up. This time, there was no burning, just a vague sense of cold dread weaving through me.

I rolled out of bed, running my hands through my hair as I paced the room. It wasn't enough to dislodge the thoughts in my head though, so I threw myself onto the floor and started push-ups as I went through it in my mind.

Annigan had done something to Fitz and me. That was obvious. The reason why would be answered as soon as I got near the nymph. The thought that nagged me as I pushed past the two-hundredth push-up was how they'd done it.

And more importantly, could they do it again?

REN

Needing to rid myself of my hard dick, I made the difficult decision to unwedge myself from Terra and crawl out of the tent. She was sleeping so soundly, she didn't move.

My feelings for her were going to come spilling out if I wasn't careful. Literally and figuratively. I had to find a way to get control over them. At least until the right time.

Deciding that jerking off right there in the camp was a bad idea, I peeled out of my clothes and shifted into my wolf form. I still wanted her with a raging abandon I could barely contain, but shifting dulled my lust into a general need to run wild instead focused desire for her and her alone.

The moon was filtering through the brightly colored trees, causing fractal patterns of light on the ground. I stifled my urge to howl at the near-full moon, instead choosing to bolt into the woods, scenting Trickstan on the wind. It was so much easier to follow in wolf form, so I let my senses guide me as I ran through the trees away from the thing causing me so much torment.

His scent was strong, so I knew he was close. I'd imagined he and the chimera would move quickly, but the merman and troll were going to slow them down some. I might be able to catch them and save us all some trouble in the morning.

I wasn't going to let him go the next time we met. Not with so much at stake.

Putting my snout in the air, I raced through the dense woods, stopping every so often to make sure I was still on the trail. I was able to scent the merman's fear in the air as I bounded along. Trickstan had some fear, but I'd spent a lot of time with him, and I could tell it was more deeply rooted. He wasn't worried about something jumping out of the woods to get them. He was afraid of something else entirely.

I didn't give two fucks about it.

I just kept running, chasing him down like the prey he'd become to me. I was certain I'd caught up to him when the scent vanished. Pausing my run, I sniffed the air, catching a whiff of rain and soil, the smell was so overwhelming and familiar, that I yelped into the night.

Whipping around, I looked for her but found nothing but a hazy darkness around me. The moon had disappeared, as well as the trees, and I was enveloped in a feeling so overwhelming I couldn't even name it. It was there inside me like a weight, pulling me down into something I couldn't understand. I snorted, trying to snuff wetness from my nose, but all it did was make me breathe in deeper, taking in more and more of her.

Had she followed me? I had to know, so I shifted back into my human form, searching for her in the fog I'd apparently run into. "Terra?"

"I'm right here."

The fog swirled, revealing her like a curtain had been pulled back to reveal a goddess on a stage. She was wearing nothing but the short black dress I loved on her. I hadn't even realized she'd brought it with her to Aetheria, but I was thanking the fucking Mage she had. If she'd known how many times I'd fantasized about peeling it off her…she probably would've been embarrassed, but she didn't look embarrassed as she crept toward me.

Nope. She looked turned on.

"Terra." I noted the rasp in my voice when I spoke. A sure sign this was going to end in a way I wasn't going to like at all. I should've tried to get away from her, but I couldn't. Didn't want to. I was naked and hungry for her and for some unbelievable reason, she looked just as eager as me. "What are you doing?"

She ran her hand over my shoulders as she trailed in a circle around me. The second her fingertips touched my skin, my dick woke like it was a sleeping giant. I clenched as she made her way around to my front. There was no hiding my desire from her at that point. She trailed her hand down my chest, glancing down at the hardness in front of her, then licking her fucking lips. "I'm doing what you want. What we both want."

I groaned when she ran a single finger down my shaft. "Terra. Don't."

She stepped close, so close I could feel her breath on my neck as she went up on her toes. "Why not?"

Honesty tripped out of my mouth before I could stop it. "Because if you regret it, I won't live through it."

"I won't regret it," she whispered in my ear. Then she bit my earlobe, sending chills down to my toes. How did she know how much I liked that? "I want this, Ren. I want you." Another nibble. "Please."

It was all I needed. I snapped. Like a fucking rubber band. I grabbed her wrists and guided her back. I couldn't see for shit, but I seemed to have sensed a tree behind her. She gasped as her back hit it and I threw her hands up above her head, pinning them beneath me. "Are you begging for me, Beautiful?"

Didn't mean for that name to slip out. Oh well. It was true. She bit her lip. "Yes. Please. I need—"

I didn't let her finish. Every fucking need she had, I was going to fulfill and then some. I crashed my mouth into hers, kissing her like I'd spent a lifetime waiting for it. She opened her mouth for me, the good fucking girl she was, meeting my tongue stroke for stroke and panting her need as we kissed.

She struggled to free her wrists, but I wasn't ready for that. I wanted her in the same state that I was—aching. It would only make the release better when I got around to giving it to her. "Not yet. Not until I say."

Her pupils dilated as she wiggled beneath me. It was the best thing I'd ever seen. Her, wanting, needing me, arching her back to get closer. I gave her a little, stepping in and rolling my hips as I pressed my cock against her core. Her dress and panties were still between us, but it got my point across. "Is this what you want?" She nodded, lifting her hips to meet me and my veins filled with liquid lightning. "Tell me what you want me to do to you."

"I want you inside me. Please, Ren, fuck me now. I can't wait."

I released her wrists, and she tugged me toward her as I kissed her again, savoring the sweet taste of her, but that wasn't what I wanted. There would be time for slow kisses in the dark. My desire ran further south. If I didn't taste her pussy soon, I would turn feral. It was a very real concern. Dropping to my knees, I ran my hands along her thighs, pushing up the skirt of her dress. I moaned at the sight of her white lacy panties, the scent of her arousal.

Running my nose against the fabric between us, she twitched. "You're so wet, aren't you Beautiful?"

"Yes, yes. Please, Ren. Don't make me wait."

It was too much. I wanted to draw this out, but all my senses were drowning in her, and I couldn't hold back another millisecond. I hooked my finger on her panties, pushing them aside and licking up the center of her.

She buckled.

I moaned.

She tasted exactly like I'd expected, and I could not get enough, lapping at her as she rocked against my face and groaned in pleasure. "More. Mage, give me more please."

I fucking loved how she begged. As a reward, I pushed two fingers inside her, pumping as I sucked on her clit. The sounds she made in response were *my* reward. Nothing would ever mean more to me. If it was wrong to feel this way about her, I didn't care. I needed her and I wanted to hear her release like I'd wanted nothing else in my life outside of getting out of my foster home. "Are you going to come for me like a good girl?"

She didn't answer. Don't think she could. Instead, she grabbed my hair, pulling in time with the thrust of my fingers, setting the pace the way she wanted it. "That's it. Come on my fingers. I want to feel it."

The next second she exploded, her warm wet pussy pulsating around my fingers. As soon as she stopped bucking her hips, a soft sigh escaped her mouth. I didn't even let her get another breath, standing up and lifting her so I could thrust my hard cock into her depths.

She threw her head back, groaning as she adjusted to the feel of me inside her. When she lifted her head and looked directly into my eyes, I pulled all the way out of her, then drove back in. She took my thrusting, meeting me with the same groaning fervor I had for her. I gave her all my strength, my speed, never taking my gaze off the warm depth of her big brown eyes as she murmured in that breathy way that told me exactly what I was doing to her. "You feel so fucking good, Ren. Give it to me just like this."

I would give it to her. I would give her everything.

Grabbing her thigh so I could angle her better, I shifted my hips, hitting that spot that made her scream my name. "Look at me when you come again, Beautiful."

She raised her head and the smile on her lips brought me to a place I never knew existed. She came hard, pulsing around my cock as I tried to go as deep as I could. "Fuck, yes." I kept my eyes on her as I came too. I stayed inside her, riding it out as long as I could until we were both sweating and panting.

"Ren, you've got to come with me now." Her hand trailed along my spine, gently, the barest whisper of a touch.

I shook my head. Her hands were around my neck.

Yet so was the cool touch of her fingers on my back too.

How?

"Ren, come on. We have to hurry or we're both going to be stuck. Brace yourself."

Ice-cold water hit me, flowing over my head, down my shoulders, in my ass crack. "The fuck?"

I looked down, searching for her, but the only thing in front of me were gauzy tendrils of mist in my clenched fists. "Terra?"

"I'm right here." Another dump of cold water. My brain raced back to Boulderbrook when Terra had dumped a cooler of water on her own head before she joined us for our poker night. I remembered what the chilly water had done to her tits. Even then my eyes were riveted to her. "You've got to get out of the Moaning Mist. Please, Ren, come with me."

The shock of her words—and maybe the third dose of water— helped me get my senses back. At least some. I turned and found her, fully dressed in her jeans and hoodie covering the top half of her face. She had a t-shirt tied around her mouth and even her sleeves covered her hands as she gripped a bucket in her hand. I couldn't find an inch of her skin in all of that.

For a second, I didn't understand.

Then I did.

"Oh shit. I was in the… Fuck. Oh, fuck. I was—" The back of my neck started to tingle. I was fucking her in the Moaning Mist. Terra.

None of it had been real.

I wanted to hurl. Sheer will kept me from it. Because if she'd heard me say her name when I… "Terra." I couldn't fathom another word or string of words to fix the situation. There was a sum total of nothing in my head.

"Don't be embarrassed. I didn't see, well, I didn't see *everything*. We need to get out of here before I succumb to it too. Come on." She grabbed my hand, pulling me toward her, then shoving me as she trailed behind.

When we cleared the mist, I looked behind me. Mage knew I wasn't going to look at her. Maybe never again. I don't know how I'd missed it the night before. I should've been able to detect the mist in my wolf form, but nope, I went straight in like it wasn't even there.

Part of me wondered if it was a subconscious move on my part.

Because being with her had been a dream.

But I'd just woken to a nightmare.

I spent the most awkward minute of my life waiting for Ren to dress after I shoved his clothes at him. Yeah, I'd heard the end of his experience when I approached to get him out of the Moaning Mist.

All I could think about was what Kelsey had said about him being able to go all night and by the time I got to him, I smelled the most delicious smell ever to grace my nose. I knew he gave off a scent when he was turned on, thanks to his fused troll blood, but I wasn't prepared to experience it like that.

It was better than any cologne or natural musk or fragrance. I stood there for precious seconds trying to decide what to call it and how I could capture it and make candles. The only word I came up with was sexscence.

Trademark, pending.

While I wished I could bathe in the stuff, I was troubled by one singular fact: I'd smelled it before.

When we were huddled on the floor of the bunker. When I thought he was seconds away from kissing me.

So, if I followed logic, it meant he was aroused then.

Aroused.

By me.

I had to have misread it. Or missmelled it. Something. Maybe he'd been thinking about someone else at the time.

He was my friend, and he didn't want ... I mean, he wouldn't…

Would he?

Fuck. Did he?

"It happened. It's over. Hope you got a good look." He rolled his mesh shirt over his head, trouncing away with his back to me. He had no idea where to go, but I could tell by the way he focused on the ground, his only goal was to get away from me. "Where's Fox?"

And yep, I got a pretty good look at his ass. I'd shut my eyes, but still. I had to own the fact that I'd seen it. He knew it too, which is why he'd asked.

I ran to catch up with him, dragging the pack I'd brought with me along with my bag. He may have been unwilling to deal with what had happened, but his mind was definitely not in the moment. There's no way he would've allowed me to carry both heavy things if he'd been in his normal headspace. I'd barely lifted a finger since we'd been there.

I needed to make him deal with this embarrassment or regret or whatever it was. "Ren, wait."

He waved his hand, grunting and dismissing me as he trudged forward. "We need to move. I picked up Trickstan's trail last night before…" his breath stuttered. "Did Fox not come with you to get me? I don't trust him and if he doesn't answer the questions I'm about to ask, we're ditching him."

"Hold up." He kept walking, increasing his stride as I yelled out for him several more times. I cared too much about him for things to get weird between us. We could deal with it like adults. Like the good friends we were. "Renfield Whatever-your-middle-name-is Cavanaugh, stop right now so we can talk about this."

I put my hands on my hips and gave him a very pointed look. When he turned, he tried his best to suppress a grin but failed. It was there half a second before he scowled at me. "I don't have a fucking middle name, and do you really want to talk about how you just saw me jizz on a tree?"

I took a few steps toward him. He met me halfway, staring down at me with an expression that seemed full of challenge. Not aggressive, just daring. He'd said he didn't want to talk about it, but it was right there between us anyway, like a maze with invisible walls trapping us in together. Maybe I should've let it go like he wanted, but my gut told me we needed to talk about it.

Without a doubt, you should.

There was that haunting whisper again. I caught on to the Magic 8-Ball answer in it. They'd all been like that, but I hadn't realized it until that moment. I fished through my bag, grabbing the ball and inspecting it. "I don't suppose you heard that whisper, did you?"

He leaned close, wrinkling his brow in concern. It did the trick to get him to stop running from me. "You're still hearing things?"

"Yeah. It's using the Magic 8-Ball responses, but this thing isn't actually talking." I handed it over and he shook it and put it up to his ear. "It's more internal than a voice coming from the ball. I don't know how to describe it. I just feel it and it's starting to freak me out a little if I'm honest."

"So, something or someone is communicating with you in a language you understand, in a way that's important to you specifically?"

"Guess so, though nobody in Aetheria knows about the 8-Ball but you and Trickstan. He does know how to throw his voice into my head. He's done it a bunch, so I guess it could be him, but I don't know why he'd be telling me these things."

Ren grabbed the pack from me and then shoved the 8-Ball inside. "I want to carry it for a while and see what happens. What's the voice saying?"

"It's different each time, but usually it gives me guidance. For example, it thinks we should talk about what happened in the Moaning Mist."

He hitched the pack over his shoulder, grunting at the mention of it. "Fine. You win, but no good can come of this. Did you see or hear anything specific when you found me?"

"Um, the end, I guess? I'm sorry, I know this is uncomfortable, but I really couldn't tell much of what was going on other than your moaning. Didn't catch any names or see a vision of a person. What was it like?"

"Fucking epic. Like the real thing. I would've given up the rest of my life to stay there like that, if that's what you want to know. I have no trouble believing people die there. Good call on the water, by the way. It shocked me back into reality. I can't believe I was so fucking dumb."

That was the root of it. He wasn't embarrassed about me seeing and hearing him have imaginary sex. He was upset because he'd stumbled into a dangerous situation without knowing it. He'd appointed himself as protector and he'd blown it. Not in my eyes, but in his.

I shrugged. "There were a dozen buckets by the well near the edge of the mist, and I put two and two together and figured out what they were for. Obviously, you weren't the only one to succumb. I'm just glad I found you before I got sucked in too."

Bad choice of words. He winced, irritated at me for forcing him to keep talking. At this point, I was going beyond what the voice had said, beyond what would have been normal for me to ask. Now, it was my curiosity that drove my questions. "You really couldn't tell a difference between the mist and the real thing?"

Part of me regretted opening this discussion up. The rest of me was traveling down a slippery slope in which I had to know everything about his experience. He clenched his fists at his side, trying to reel his anger in "Do you want me to describe how her pussy felt? What she said, what move she made that sent me over the edge? Is that what you want to know?"

"No. I don't know. Never mind. Let's just go find Fox in Mystia."

I moved to leave, but he grabbed my elbow, spinning me around to face him. "I was content to leave it alone, but you started this. The question is, can you finish it?" He glanced at my lips, then flicked his eyes back up. I was certain he was seeing a deep hidden part of me that I'd buried, even from myself. "Ask me what you really want to ask me, Terra."

There was the Ren I had grown to know and love. Staring down with those piercing green eyes that seemed to be able to read my thoughts before I had them. Speaking the truth of things without saying the words.

"I can't."

He released a deep breath. "Didn't think so. Let me know when you can."

My thoughts were a jumbled mess as we trekked the short distance to the town. I couldn't ask what my mind was screaming. *Was it me?* Instead of confronting that issue head-on like I should have, I went to a more comfortable space. The reason why I'd woken up and known Ren was gone in the first place.

"I dreamed about Wells last night."

"Makes sense."

"I guess so, but it was more real than any dream I've ever had. He was right there like I could reach out and touch him. I woke up crying because I was speaking to him, and he couldn't hear me."

He grabbed my bag and slung it over his shoulder. I tried to wrestle it back from him, but he wasn't having it. "Seems pretty straightforward to me. Don't think you need Freud on this interpretation."

He was probably right about that. It was a far assumption, but I couldn't shake the feeling it was somehow more real than a dream. Nor could I shake the image of Fitz and a crying baby that randomly appeared in my dream too.

I'd almost gotten caught. Worse than that was when she needed me, I was off in the Moaning Mist fucking an imaginary version of her while she cried over Wells.

My life was a shitshow. One that I had to get it under control before it wrecked me. Though there was little hope for that because I'd gone too far and dared her to admit there was something between us. It had been right there trying to escape her parted lips, but she'd stopped herself before she let it slip. And I stopped myself from outright explaining what I knew: she still loved him, but she'd come to a point where she looked at me differently.

Fuck.

I'd hoped we'd left the perilous situation behind us like we'd left the Moaning Mist. We were on a mission, which is how we worked best—together. I was determined to keep the rest of it buried in my heart until I could get a grip and make sure we were truly *there* before I did anything else stupid.

I trudged ahead, muttering under my breath, "Augustus I, Cyria, Fantasia, Augustus II, Davina, Leopold, Benedict, Augustus III, Alessandro, Virgil, Leonardo, Helene, Samanthia, Crystal, Benton, Samuel."

She caught up with me faster than I wanted. "Why are you randomly mumbling names? Was it an orgy?"

Leave it up to her to try and diffuse the weird tension with humor.

"It's nothing. My foster parents used to make us recite the names of the vampire elders when we'd done something wrong."

"The Moaning Mist wasn't wrong, Ren."

"I know. Just forget it. What did Fox say when he let you wander off in the woods by yourself?" She turned around, cocking her eyebrow. "I mean when you chose to do what you were absolutely capable of doing and came to find me alone."

"Better. He told me if we got separated, we'd meet in the open market right inside Mystia. He said there's a park and food vendors we'd be able to easily see."

We were already coming out of the dense forest area and had found a road, of sorts. There had been dozens of flying mats overhead, and most of the riders hadn't even looked down when we turned onto the road, which was just a worn path where people had walked. Mystia was looming on the horizon as the sun rose beyond it. There were many buildings, though none of them too tall. I likened it to a town about the size of Illusion Hill.

A pang of longing hit me. I missed home.

Looking back points you in the wrong direction, Renfield. One must always keep an eye on the forward path.

"We can agree there's something off about Fox, right?"

She nodded. "Yep. He's not acting like someone who wants to truly find Trickstan or help us in any way. I say you were right. We should ditch him." She raised her voice and angled her face toward the sky.

"Right magical, mysterious voice who speaks in my head?" She paused, before she said, "It is as certain as the sun on the horizon."

"Going off script this time?"

"Apparently. I think it's right though. We can't trust Fox. Let's lose him here."

She was taking the strange whisper better than most. It wasn't every day a disembodied voice spoke in your head. Though, I guess it was an everyday occurrence in her world. Trickstan had thrown his voice, Wells had given her his phoenix blood, so they read each other's minds, then the phoenixes. "It must be very crowded in your head."

She laughed. "You have no idea."

We walked the rest of the way, about a half-mile, in silence. I just enjoyed walking next to her without the distraction of Fox. Things had gotten back to normal quickly, thank the Mage. I could tell she was determined to make it that way and I loved her even more for it.

As soon as we hit the border of the town, the path veered in three directions. We went straight into the heart of the Mystia where we easily spotted the area Fox had been talking about. It was a park with bright blue grass instead of green. There were some of the same trees we'd seen everywhere in the Summer court, but they were flanked with flowers and bushes that were shaped into all kinds of animals and creatures. It took a few seconds, but I even spotted a werewolf with its head back howling. People were everywhere, talking, milling about. Kids were running around. It all seemed like a Saturday in the park from our world.

"Which one of those food carts looks the most likely to serve bacon? I'm starving."

"I could eat. We need to get a feel of how it works first." I pulled her over to a bench that was close to one of the carts. Aetheria's version of food trucks, I guessed. They were enclosed spaces with just two wheels in the middle. Easily pullable, but big enough for one person to get inside and fix the food.

A woman walked up to the bright pink cart near us. She had a long face and gangly arms and legs. Elf, I'd bet. "I'll take a dark flapper sandwich and a peach, please."

The man started making a sandwich, using what looked like pita bread. As he was pulling meat from a steaming pan, he asked. "What drink?"

"Mm, give me a nut milk, no bubbles."

"Sure thing."

Terra and I exchanged a look. So far the peach was the only thing I was willing to try. And there was no mention of bacon.

The man finished up her meal, stuffing it into a paper sack, and then he pulled out a black box with a long cord attached to it. He lifted the top off. The woman placed her hand inside as he asked her. "Earth, wind, fire, or water?"

"Wind." Elf. Nailed it.

The cart guy closed the lid and pressed a button on the back of the box. "Release your magic now." The woman nodded and I assume she sent some magic from her hand. It lasted a few seconds and then he opened the lid, and she pulled her hand out and went on her way. It reminded me of when we had to swear on the square, though that took my blood along with my magic. There was no indication of the woman's finger being pricked in this process.

I knew there was no currency in Aetheria, but things weren't free. "We pay with magic."

"Okay, cool. At least we have that. I wonder what a flapper sandwich is, but if nut milk tastes like almond milk, I'm not drinking that. Gross."

She stood up, but I pulled her back down, bringing her closer so I could whisper in her ear. "I'll pay for everything." She frowned and along with that came her signature pout that always made my cock stir in my damned ugly pants. "I'm not being chivalrous. I don't want anyone to know about your special magic with the golem and phoenix blood. It's too risky. Just tell me what you want, and I'll get it."

Resigning herself to my request, we circled the perimeter of the carts, listening to people's orders for a while longer. When someone asked for an oinker sandwich, the code unraveled for us. Oinker was pork, flapper was chicken, and planter was some kind of vegetarian thing that smelled awful. Fruits were like our fruits, but there was one weird one called a lura. It was the size of an apple, but it had curls in a rainbow of colors all over it, like petals. We watched a kid buy one, then pull the curls off one by one, sticking them in her mouth and giggling. "I want to try one."

Of course, she did. That girl was so baller sometimes.

She gave me the rest of her order and I strolled over to the sunshine yellow cart. "Two oinker sandwiches, a lura, and an apple. Two waters." The cart attendant nodded and got to work on our food. As she did, I scanned the area, trying to see what we had to work with. I wasn't looking for Fox but kept my eye out anyway. Didn't want him sneaking up on us.

I held my breath when the attendant pulled out the black box for payment. "Earth, Wind, Fire, or Water."

It was a tricky question for me, but it would've been worse for Terra. I decided to go with my trueborn magic in favor of pulling out the Earth magic I'd been fused with. "Fire." She popped the lid down and nodded. I released a bit of magic, feeling it flow from my fingertips. Glancing down, I followed the cord with my eyes and found it attached to a bigger box at the bottom of the cart. So, they were storing magic, but for whom? Was this something they took with them as payment, or did it go somewhere else?

I'd bet my life it all went to Magnus by way of the Forge. Like in those trunks all the people had carried in.

When she was satisfied I'd given her enough, she popped the lid open and thanked me. I took a chance that I wasn't sure I wanted to take for security's sake, but I decided it might be worth it. More than that, I'd figured out how we might find Trickstan without Fox interfering. "Hey, this is our first time in Mystia. We're visiting an old friend, a leprechaun. Is there a place where they normally hang out?"

The attendant cocked her head. It was a weird question, and I knew it. She eventually shrugged. "I've seen some leprechauns going into the Golden Arches. That's really where everyone goes in this Mageforsaken town. Horndogs, all of them. I'd start there. Can't miss it." She pointed behind us and I could not believe what I saw on the horizon.

Ren

Ren was more mysterious than usual. "Where are we going?"

After we'd scarfed down our oinker sandwiches—which amounted to the best ham sandwich I'd ever eaten in my life—he'd told me we were going to eat our fruit on the way to a place we might be able to either find Trickstan or find someone who could help us find Trickstan.

"Don't want to spoil it."

Cryptic Ren was not my favorite Ren. Though the look of amusement in his eyes was a nice change from the brooding he'd been doing all morning.

As we walked, I took out my lura fruit, examining the colorful tendrils sprouting from it. I'd seen a girl pull one off, so I plucked a bright green tendril off and popped it in my mouth. It was sweet, like caramel just before it burned. As soon as I identified the taste, there was a vibration, a tickle, that made me laugh, and then the tendril melted on my tongue like cotton candy. "Oh, my Mage, Ren. You have to try this."

"No thanks. Exotic fruits are not my thing." He bit into his apple to prove his point.

I plucked a red curl off, and it gave me the same effect, only this time the taste was a bit saltier. The blue tendril was sour, but when I mixed it with a green, it tasted a bit like those sour gummy candies in our world. The yellow was bitter, so I had to add it with red or green. The purple curl was the strongest. It tasted savory, like mushrooms or meat, but it wasn't off-putting. Especially when you pair it with a salty red or sweet green. The combinations were endless really.

"Come on. It's delicious. What do you like, sweet, salty, sour, bitter or savory?"

He glanced down and a smile crept across his face. "I like salty with a touch of sweetness. Kind of like you." For a second it seemed like he wanted to take it back, but he didn't. He just stood there waiting for my response.

I had none. His words were intimate or maybe it was the look on his face. Whatever it was, the heat of a blush painted my cheeks as I plucked two reds and a green off the fruit. "Open up."

Surprisingly, he did what I asked. I placed the tendrils in his open mouth. The look on his face when he experienced that tingle was everything.

"Damn. That's good."

"Told you so. You should listen to me." He snatched a few more curls off my lura and led me around some buildings, his eyes sweeping as we walked. When we got to our destination I was gobsmacked.

There were buildings all around us like we were in the business center of Mystia. No homes that I could detect, just buildings made of brick or metal, pretty nondescript outside of the colorful signs next to the doors. There was a barbershop, a healer, and an herbalist on this street. But it was hard to ignore the huge golden arches looming over the building in front of us. It looked like a fast food restaurant chain with its red and yellow color scheme, but the arches that I'd seen billions of times in our world were turned into huge breasts with nipples on the top.

"Wait. Is this a—"

"McBrothel."

My mouth dropped open. No way. Nope. "I'm not seeing what I'm seeing."

"Yep, you are. Look." I'd been gaping up at the huge arches—tits—but Ren was pointing at the door.

My Mage, I was going to need therapy after this.

There was a man with bright red hair handing out flyers. He was wearing a yellow overall jumpsuit, so it showed off his smoking body, bulging arms, and nice chest. When he turned around you got the full view of his ass since the cheeks were cut out of his suit.

He even had on comically big red shoes.

Next to him was a woman with the same bright red hair. Hers was long and in braids, but her red and white striped dress was cut down to her navel, showing off the girls, and she was covered in that signature yellow paint. There were two of them. "My eyes, my eyes. I'm never going to be able to unsee this, am I?"

"Nope. Wait until you start thinking about what happens if you order a Happy Meal." I slugged his hard bicep. "Why did you put that in my head, Assdick?"

"If I have to think it, so do you. Let's get a good look at how this works."

"Oh, you want to go in and order you up a Roni McSexDoll like her?" A prickling feeling fluttered through me. I didn't know what it was, but it was uncomfortable.

Ren dragged me to a bench in the grass to be closer to the drive-through window—my Mage there was a drive-through—so we could see how it operated. He huffed. "You should know better than that by now. I'm not trying to get laid again. We need help and this is how I think we can get it. Watch."

It didn't take long for a man to pull up on his flying carpet. He leaned into the window and asked the near-naked attendant for "a water nymph with blonde hair who was okay with foot stuff."

I had to put my hand over my mouth. Did not want to hear about his order. Nor did I want to hear about the woman who strolled up to the window on foot asking for a "troll who liked to go down."

Ren shifted next to me, clearly amused that the second person asked for someone who had his type of blood. He shrugged and something close to anger rose in my chest, unbidden. "Go on then, if that's what you want. I'm sure you could take care of her."

Why was I provoking him like that? It had to be seeing him the night before. He peered at me with a dare dancing in his eyes. "I think you know what I want."

Did I?

Concentrate and ask again.

If I'd been a bit sooner rescuing him from the Moaning Mist, I might have seen who he was with before the body evaporated. Then I'd know for sure.

I bit my lip, telling myself I was insane for letting my thoughts travel that direction. I needed to focus on how to get into the brothel, not Ren's sexy times night adventures in the Moaning Mist.

Each time after they'd placed their order, the people were directed to the next window. We couldn't hear what was being said, but the attendant had brought out the same black cube the food carts had used. So, even in a brothel, you paid in magic.

The third person in line brought a friend. The two men were already drunk based on the way they were wobbling and holding on to each other. "We're celebrating our anniversary, and we want a third, don't care what species or sex is. Surprise us!"

I stifled the urge to congratulate them. They did look happy.

Satisfied that he knew what he needed to do right, Ren grabbed my hand, pulling me along until we were at the window. "We want a leprechaun. Don't care what sex."

She glanced at me, and I nodded. I understood the plan and was fully on board. Leprechauns could find anything using their magic. It occurred to me the plan was so simple, yet Fox nor Emperor Magnus had considered it. Or maybe they had and they were playing us.

The attendant unrolled a paper scroll, etching something onto it. "You're in luck. We do have a leprechaun working today. Don't get too many requests for them. Would you like a sprite with that?"

Oh, if there was Sprite in Aetheria, I knew what I'd be ordering from the next cart. "I'm sorry, what? Like a drink?"

"No, a sprite. You could have a water sprite or a wind sprite with the leprechaun. Two-for-one combo order. They aren't completely corporeal, but when they touch your parts, they give a fluttery sensation most find very enjoyable. We throw them in with leprechauns since they don't last very long."

Ren cleared his throat. "No, just the leprechaun, thanks."

"Okay, go to the next window for payment."

We started making our way forward and I had to let my thoughts out. "Did she just offer us a sex sprite like it was a side of fries?"

"Yep."

Cage the Mage. This was insane.

When we got to the next window, Ren was asked to provide his magic again. It was just like it had been for the food. After it had been collected, we were given threaded green bracelets with black and purple strands woven through them. They were meant to direct us to the right room with our leprechaun.

I examined mine. "They look like friendship bracelets. I guess that means we're besties now." I grabbed his arm, pressing it against mine to show our matching bracelets.

He grunted. "Is that what we are?"

My answer was quick. And forced. And even I didn't believe myself. "Yeah, best friends."

Surging ahead of him—to get away from the look he was giving me—I rounded the corner, past the McSexworkers, and went inside the building, anxious to see how it all worked. Because I did not want to be in the room with the dude with the foot fetish.

The design was just like I expected, but where the counter would've been in our world, there was a gate with another sexy, barely dressed attendant standing by. She was checking bracelets and sending people to tables.

I went up and offered her my bracelet. She cocked her eyebrow—I guess leprechauns were rare—and directed me to a table in the corner with a booth. "It may be a while. Feel free to order a drink from the menu on the table. Just wave your hand over the item you want and disperse your magic. Someone will bring it out. When your bracelets vibrate, go through this gate and look for the matching door. Thank you for coming to the Gold Arches, over three billion served!"

My head was going to explode. I was certain of it.

Ren had caught up to me and slid into the booth, draping his arm over the back of it. He patted the seat next to him. "You look like shit. You need rest." To him, that was friendship. Truthbombing all over me.

He wasn't wrong though. It had been a bad night and stressful time after it and while we were back to normal, I couldn't shake this wonky feeling I had where he was concerned. On top of that, I'd been going over Trickstan's actions in my head and finding no sense in it or in Fox being there with us to find him.

My brain was overloaded.

So, I crawled into the booth and laid down next to Ren. He smoothed my hair until my body relaxed enough to fall asleep. I awoke to a white room with no walls or doors, with a familiar warm feeling in my chest that meant one thing to me: Wells.

Spencer had done me a solid and helped me avoid Autumn all day. Once I'd explained how little sleep I got after the dream I'd had about Terra, she was happy to volunteer herself and Kelsey for a girls' day in Illusion Hill. They were going to check in with Lore and do their nails or something. I just couldn't face her after seeing Terra.

I had *seen* Terra.

She'd been as real as Fitz and I were, and there was a chance it could happen again. I felt it as strongly as the fluttering of my belly as I pulled into the garage at midnight. Fitz was already there pacing back and forth in front of the door. I jumped out of the SUV and went right up to him. He was paler than normal. Being terrified in your dreams would do that to a person, I guessed. "You remember it too, right?"

"Yeah."

We didn't discuss it further. What more could be said? We'd had a shared experience that fucked with us both, but I was going to turn it into something good. Something perfect.

As soon as Annigan stepped out of Liam's car, I went over to them. They raised an eyebrow in amusement, preparing to mock us for what they'd done. I didn't give them a chance. "This is how it's going to go. You're going to connect me to my girl in Aetheria in your dreamscape—don't bother saying you can't—and if you don't, I won't hesitate to kill the leprechaun."

It wasn't an idle threat. I would've done it and not experienced a drop of remorse over it either. This was about Terra and nothing else. I'd kill for her. End of.

They didn't seem to care I'd just threatened their lover or partner, whatever he was. "I can't," I growled at them, letting the fur ripple over my arms. "Don't get testy with me, Mr. Payne. You think you'd do it, but I know you won't harm Liam, just like I know Fitz won't ever drink your blood. I've been in your subconscious minds. I know things."

I backed them against the dusty metal door. "Then you know how I feel. I'm not going to ask you again."

They sighed, stepping forward and wiping the dust from their ass. "Even if I could project my dreamscape to Aetheria—that's a big if—I was only able to connect your dreams because you share blood. It wouldn't work otherwise."

I whipped around to face Fitz. He was already advancing. "I didn't drink your blood, Wells. You have to believe me."

Annigan shook their head. "That's true, but when you fought that first day there were cuts on both of you. Your blood mingled, so was able to manipulate it as I liked in the dreamscape."

I didn't know or care how it worked. I just needed it to work again. Ignoring the fact that Fitz now had some small amount of phoenix blood, I smiled. It felt like it had been months since I'd done it so easily. "If all you need is blood, then we're on. We're going to dream up a beautiful woman with a mouth too sassy for her own damn good. We're doing it now."

Mace and Fitz were entertaining Liam, meaning they were making sure he didn't go anywhere and holding him as leverage while Annigan was in my cabin with me. I had Gideon in the living room on standby because I needed someone I fully trusted to be there in case things went sideways. I was warming to the idea of trusting Fitz, but not fully there yet. Gideon would take care of anything wily, and he had the good sense to know when to step in and when to let it play out.

I'd already stopped by Diggs' cabin to get a sleeping potion made of ground jade rabbit's foot. The creatures were tied directly to the moon and held special sleeping properties. Like, a natural Magical sleep aid. Diggs swore I'd sleep soundly if I shot the powder up my nose.

Didn't care I was seconds away from snorting that shit like I was in an eighties movie.

Also absconded his entire supply for future nights and dreams.

Annigan slid into the chair next to the bed as I lined the powder up on the nightstand and took the dose of jade rabbit. They crossed their legs. "I don't think it will do any good, but I feel like I should warn you. Doing this could be very addictive. I've seen people put themselves in comas just to be inside a dreamscape like you are now. I'll do this for you, but it's under duress."

"Noted." I fluffed my pillow and then hit the bed. "If it's a big concern for you, maybe you shouldn't have fucked with me and Fitz last night."

"I was proving my point. Nothing more."

"Point proven. Let's do this. I can feel myself getting drowsy. What do I do?"

"Just think of her and the connection you share. I'll do the driving."

"Fine," I grunted. "Then you get out of my head when she shows up. I'm not doing this so you can get your rocks off on what we do or say."

They huffed. "Whatever you want. You'll have to get yourself out then. You'll need to conjure an object—like you did before—and destroy it. That will bring you out safely. And Mr. Payne, be aware if you stay too long and I have to pull you out, it won't be pleasant. For either of you."

I was done with the talking, the rules, the condescending tone Annigan was taking. I wanted to hate them for what they'd done, but how could I when they'd given me a way to Terra, something I could hold onto until I could get to Aetheria? I nodded at them, then closed my eyes, letting the powder take me under.

Unlike before when I simply appeared in a white room, this time I found myself at the top of a spiral staircase. It was mostly dark around me with the only light coming from a few torches on the rock walls. I checked to see how far down it went, but I couldn't tell. It was dizzying to even try.

Having no other options, I started down the gray marble stairs, my hands gripping the gold rails, my palms sweaty and trembling with anticipation as I descended.

The staircase seemed to go on forever, so I picked up my pace, taking the stairs two at a time and using my speed, needing to get to her as fast as possible. Finally, I hit the last step, placing my foot on the marble floor. There was a flash of bright light that made me squeeze my eyes shut. When I opened them I was in the white space again, like I'd been with Fitz. "Hello?" My voice echoed across whatever surface that surrounded me.

Terra didn't answer and my chest tightened, my limbs tingled. I wanted to see her more than anything but facing her with the mate bond hanging around my neck was going to be tricky. If she asked, I'd have to tell her I hadn't found a way out of it yet. Nor had I found a concrete way to get to her. Or restore the magic in our world.

I was a failure on all counts.

Glancing down at my finger, I checked to make sure the gold band was still covered with a bandage in the dreamscape. It was, thank the Mage's long dong.

"Wells?"

The sound of her voice was music and laughter and all the good things in each world. I whipped around and all my breath left my body in one big whoosh.

She was wearing a purple dress I'd never seen before, long whisps of her hair falling out of her hair tie, framing her big, beautiful eyes. They were lit with surprise as she gaped at me. "Am I dreaming?"

I used my amped-up speed to get to her. There was so much I wanted to say, to do, but I couldn't bring myself to do those things. I just stared at her, absorbing her presence in bits and pieces. The soft dew of her skin, the curves I knew by heart, the way she chewed on that bottom lip of hers. I was knocked on my knees, helpless for her alone, so I wrapped my arms around her waist pulling her close and murmuring, "We're both dreaming, Precious."

"Remind me not to wake up then." She stroked my cheek and the feel of her fingertips rushed through me and I couldn't wait any longer. My love, my desire, my utter ache from missing her burst out of me as I stood up again, picking her up so I could kiss her.

The familiar slant of her mouth, as we kissed, was like fuel to the fire already raging in my heart. Somewhere in the back of my head, I tried to warn myself it wasn't exactly real, but I didn't fucking listen. She tasted real, felt real, *was* real. And the way she threaded her fingers into my hair as she wrapped her legs around me told me she felt it too.

Kissing her pouty lips wasn't enough. I pulled away, pressing soft, slow kisses along her jaw before running my nose along her neck, just so I could breathe in the rich scent of rainfall I'd fallen in love with. She released a shuddering breath. "How is this possible?"

A thought flashed in my mind—the day at the lake when I finally broke through the Binding spell enough to tell her about Mateo. When I'd thrown the stone in the lake and the ancient nymph spell conjured a phoenix feather. I'd been so afraid my blood would hurt her, but I'd given her that same blood and now it was bridging us together.

Over her shoulder, the bench and lake formed in the whiteness. I understood then. The dreamscape was ours and we could manipulate it however we liked. "I could stop to tell you, or we could..." I angled my head sideways, showing her that I'd conjured. It *was* one of the many locations on my list of places I would have her.

She jumped down, grabbing my hand and pulling me toward the bench. "Talk later."

"That's my girl."

I wasn't sure what I was thinking would work, but I decided to give it a shot. I put my hand on her chest, pressing her onto the bench while

224

I used my memory to picture her body, naked and sexy with soft curves and golden skin. Her dress disappeared in a puff of purple smoke. "Oh, that's a cool trick," she said giggling. In the next second, my clothes were gone.

Definitely my girl.

"I miss you, Wells. So much I think I might drown in the tears I won't let myself cry."

I missed her too and it was more than just physical. Sure, I wanted her on every level there was, but being with her went beyond sex. She was my anchor, and I was drifting without her.

"I don't want you to cry for me. I want you to scream and moan and come apart. Let me show you how much I miss you."

Her eager nod was enough to boil my blood. I dropped to my knees and spread her legs. We locked eyes and my heart practically leaped out of my chest as I lowered myself. I made my way up her thigh, kissing, licking, enjoying the way she squirmed as I neared my target.

By the time I got to her pussy, she was soaked and ready. "Lift your hips so I can devour you." She did what I'd commanded and I lowered myself, teasing my tongue over the folds of slick skin, inching my way to her clit. It was hard to hold back, I wanted her so much, but the way she responded to the slow crawl of my tongue was worth it.

"Magedamn it, Wells. Please."

It didn't seem right to make her wait any longer, not when we'd been apart for what seemed like centuries.

Taking her swollen clit into my mouth, I sucked and nibbled as she moaned my name. Knowing she wanted more, I pushed a finger inside her wet depths, making her buck with delight. "Is this what you want?"

I pulled my mouth off her so I could see her answer me. As hard as my cock was, I was more interested in her release than my own. I'd stay hard all day and night if it meant I was giving her every little salacious thing she wanted of me.

She nodded, biting her lip. I added a second finger and flipped my hand over so I could reach her G-spot. That put my thumb right over her clit, so I doubled down, circling it with speed as I pumped inside her wetness.

Cursing, she grabbed my hair and pulled me up to her for a kiss that was more tongue than anything. It didn't last long because she couldn't maintain it due to her panting. She was so fucking beautiful like this. Wild, riveting, free.

I put my other hand between her tits, inching my way up until I had it wrapped around her throat. She leaned her head back, giving me full access, trusting me with everything she was. I squeezed her throat, just a little pressure, nothing life-threatening. She gripped my wrist, holding me there as she moaned. She liked it and I loved her for it.

We were in sync in a way I'd never been with anyone else. It was like our hearts truly were entwined.

"I'm so close," she groaned.

Her muscles tightened, inside and out, as she ramped up to that peak. "That's it. Come for me, Precious." Her release was immediate and intense, and it ripped through me like it had been my own.

Using my hand that was around her throat, I slid my fingers into her hair, pulling her to me and kissing her until she was moaning again. "I want you inside me, Wells."

Sounded perfect. I stood, towering over her on the bench. Her eyes tracked down my body, from my chest to the hard cock waiting eagerly to give her what she wanted. The fire in her eyes was enough to undo me.

She stood, tracing the lines of my chest with her fingers, the lightest of touches and it hit me like a Mack truck. I needed her. I wanted her. I had to have her. So, I took her hand, placing a kiss on her palm. "Turn around. I'm going to give you this hard cock from behind."

Eager, she turned around and put her hands on the back of the bench, then positioned her knees on the seat, sticking her ass in the air for me. Ready. When she looked over her shoulder with an invitation in her eyes, I stepped forward, ran my cock against her slick pussy as I fondled her tits and she moaned. She leaned into me, telling me to get going. "Good girl. Are you ready?"

She nodded.

I shoved inside her, relishing the guttural moan she gave me in response. Giving her a second to adjust, I ran my hand over her spine, around her neck, turning her head toward me so I could see her eyes when I pulled all the way out slowly, then drove in again. She huffed as she leaned back into my thrusting, taking all of me inside her like we were made for each other.

We weren't.

But we were.

Keeping my hand in her hair, dislodging the hair tie somewhere along the way, I held on to her as I pumped. She gripped the back of the bench with white knuckles, and we fucked to the sounds of our moaning and grunting and the slap of my pelvis against her ass.

It was perfect and I didn't want it to end.

Though in the back of my head, I knew it would have to. Eventually.

Not yet.

I pulled out of her and swung her around. She yelped in surprise, but when I sat down on the bench, patting my legs, she got my intention. "I want to look at those soulful eyes when you come again." She crawled onto my lap and took my cock in her hand, pumping a few times with a smirk on her face, then lowering herself onto me. Within seconds we were writhing together again.

"Feels amazing," she panted.

"Yeah, you know how to ride me good, don't you?"

I ran my hands over her body. We were both slick with sweat and the heat of it made it even better. Fuck me, if she didn't start rocking her hips so my cock was buried as far as it would go. So, I bore my weight on my feet and lifted my ass off the bench to meet her.

This was more than great sex.

This was us needing to fill that void where the other one wasn't. And the insane thing—besides the way she was into this—was that I could only hear her heartbeat in the dream space. It was like Autumn never existed.

The thought was so euphoric to me, I came in the next instant, spilling inside her with a primal grunt as her pussy clenched and she came with me, huffing and puffing her release. The echo across the white space was music.

She collapsed onto my chest, fingers threading in my hair. "Mage, I needed you, Wells. I'll never *not* need you. I know this wasn't real, but I don't care right now."

Neither did I.

Nor did I care the next three times we fucked.

Though, I wasn't ready for what happened after.

Terra

Even if I'd wanted to—I did want to—we couldn't do it again. Never in my life had I heard of anyone having sex so many times and for so long. I knew it wasn't real, but I didn't care about that. I was with Wells, and everything was perfect.

I was curled against his chest on his bed, and he had his hands in my hair, stroking while he spoke. "It's not what I wanted, but I'm working on getting to Aetheria. I don't think it'll be long now, but we have this until I can make it happen."

"How are we here? What is this?"

"I met a dream nymph and insulted them. It turned out to be a good thing because they tried to mock me by giving me a nightmare scenario in a dreamscape, but in doing that, I found a way to get to you. It's because we share the same blood, so don't get Ren all excited about seeing Bash or anyone. It's just us, the way it should be." He paused, wrapping a long strand of my hair around his finger. "How is he?"

Talking about Ren to him seemed wrong on one level, but I convinced myself it was silly. They were best friends, of course, he'd want to know about him. It wasn't like I was gossiping or talking behind his back. Not really. He'd want Wells to know he was okay.

"He's Ren. He's looking out for me, being the watchdog, helping me cope when I get sad. I don't know where I'd be without him."

It was the truth. Maybe not all of it, but most.

Wells squeezed me. "Good. I know you're in good hands. What are you doing every day? Sitting at the Conduit waiting for me?"

I rose, smacking playfully on the chest. "You wish. We're looking for Trickstan. His sister Joy is married to the emperor of Aetheria. He sucks, but it looks like Trickstan holds the key to taking the emperor out and getting the magic going in our world again. We're working on using a leprechaun to find him."

I left out the McBrothel because it was a lot to unpack, and I got the feeling we didn't have long. We'd already spent what seemed like hours in the dreamscape.

"First of all, *Trick*stan?"

"Yeah. Fae don't get names when they're born. They try out a bunch until one sticks. It's weird but it turns out Trickstan's his real name, which fits him considering how he tricked us all. We found him for a bit, and he apologized, saying it was all some elaborate plan, but while he remembers some of what brought him to our world, Binding magic has hidden the important stuff from him. So, it's a bit like working with, well Tristan. It's a big mystery but both Joy and Emperor Magnus are saying he's the key to everything. We're going to find him and figure it out."

"I'm sure you will. You two are capable of anything. Tell me about the emperor. Everything I've ever read or heard says there are four elemental kings or queens of court. Nothing about an emperor."

"He's the one who started the square stuff. I can't get a line on how he came to be in power or how Joy got involved with him, but we're going to have to either overthrow him or use him to get the Conduit open again or obtain a new one. So, you know, another day, another save the world situation. I wouldn't be worried if everyone were here with me.

"How is it there? Everyone at Boulderbrook okay?"

He switched positions, pulling me into his lap, which was dangerous considering how we were both still unclothed. Still, though, it was nice to feel his familiar warmth, to bask in his smoky sandalwood scent. "Everyone's good. Things are heating magic-wise, but I'm handling it. Everything will be better when you're back with me."

"About that. How can we do this again? Be here like this, I mean."

"I'm going to force the nymph to stay with me, but I don't think it'll work unless we both happen to be asleep, so it'll be hard to coordinate. What time is it there?"

"Lunch? But it's coming up on the Spring Equinox, so time doesn't work the same for sure. What's the date back home?" The word was weightier saying it to him. He was my home and while I'd always dreamed of living in Aetheria, I was certain I wouldn't stay if Wells wasn't there with me.

"It's February second. You've been gone a little over a month and it's been excruciating."

I leaped to my feet. "Your birthday is in a week!"

He chuckled, giving me that smirk I'd loved from the very beginning, even though I said I hated it. "I hadn't even thought about that. I guess so." He shrugged, holding his hands out. My eye caught the flash of white on his finger. It was like suddenly being buried under a stone wall.

Autumn. I'd forgotten about her in the dreamscape.

But there she was glaring at me. Their bond was still wrapped around them like that bandage. I pointed at his finger. "What about her?"

He frowned. "Can we not talk about her?"

I ignored his request. Sure, I wanted to forget about her, but I knew I couldn't. "I assume she's still there at Boulderbrook?"

"Yes, but we haven't gotten close like you're thinking. I'm keeping her at arm's length." He stood up, towering over me in a way that usually made my pulse flutter, but there was hurt in his glowing magenta eyes. And sadness. He hadn't figured out what to do about her yet. I opened my mouth, but he put a finger over it. "Don't you dare stand there and tell me I need to give into the mate bond. Just don't. I won't, no matter what you say. You're full of shit if you think I can forget you and how much I—"

A horrendous ripping sound reverberated across the space. We both froze. He instinctively put his arms around me, even though he'd been arguing with me two seconds before. Yeah, he'd been mad at me, but for good reason. I knew he wanted out of the mate bond, and he knew I wanted him to do what was best for him, which was to give into it. It was our usual stand-off and neither one of us wanted to change our positions.

Well, I did, but I couldn't be that selfish.

"What is that?"

"Not sure. From what I experienced the first time, anything could be in here. I think they use what's in our heads to create this world and everything in it."

Great. I had at least a dozen voices in my head.

Okay, I had one that I couldn't identify. And Andras. And the voice of my Gram occasionally revealed more than I wanted to know about Magical species.

The sound grew closer, setting my teeth on edge like the scraping of nails on a chalkboard. When it sounded —felt—like it was right on top of us, a shadow grew from the ground, forming a giant figure. It was humanoid in form, but I couldn't tell if it was male or female. It had no features other than the outline and misty black smoke making it up. "Find me before it's too late."

Wells put himself between me and the shadow thing. "Is it talking to you or me?"

"Me, I think. I've been hearing a voice in my head since we started moving in Aetheria. It doesn't feel threatening, but I haven't been able to discern who or what it is."

He turned to me, alarm on his face. "That's not something I wanted to hear."

The shadow thing screamed, like bloody murder. As it did, the ground opened up into a gaping dark hole and swallowed it up. The hole grew bigger and bigger. We ran in the other direction, but it took no time for it to catch up to us. I gasped as Wells was jerked away from me.

I turned in time to see him fall through the hole. He reached out, grabbing for me but as soon as I took his hand, he fell away, slipping out of my grasp as flames shot around his body. I wasn't worried about the flames hurting him, not with his Fire magic and phoenix blood, but it was such a surprise to see them that I jumped out of the way, hoping not to get burned.

Not a moment later, I fell through the same hole, screaming as pain wracked my head.

The fall seemed eternal, and my limbs grew as heavy as tree trunks. It felt like the moment you first wake up and will yourself to go back to sleep because you don't want to get up yet. I couldn't move or brace myself for the inevitable bottom of the chasm.

Chasm.

It occurred to me then. Even though I'd been in a dreamscape with Wells, magicked up by a dream nymph, I was somehow now falling into the Infinite Chasm. The Magical place nobody could truly define or explain. The concept had been expressed in so many ways and forms over the millennia, that it simply stopped being an object in favor of an idea.

I forced my eyes open. Dirt was all around me, ancient, and unending, giving me a sense of calmness amid my panic.

My body hit the ground with a thud. So, the Infinite Chasm is not so infinite. All the air rushed out of my lungs, leaving me gasping and in deep distress. "Sh, it's me. You were sleeping hard." I scrambled up, thankful to the Mage that my limbs had started working. My back hit the smooth leather seat and Ren was staring at me, blinking and running his hand over my hair. "You good?"

My reply is no.

A sharp sting prickled the nerves all over my body like I'd been ripped apart limb by limb. Everything ached and burned. I shook my head and the pain wracked through it like a tornado in my brain. The dreamscape had been so amazing, things there were perfect, but coming out of it tore me to shreds, physically and mentally. Still, I had a burst of desire for Wells so strong it nearly took my breath away.

He'd said it was real.

We had an actual conversation.

We had actual sex.

Many times.

It was outstanding, as it always was.

That wasn't even the best part. Just being with him had done so much for my psyche.

I wanted to go back. Enough to conk myself over the head to make me pass out, but Ren was staring at me with so much concern that I wouldn't dare do it. He would've stopped me anyway. His voice was soft, and he never stopped stroking my hair. I leaned in, soaking in his comfort as I tried to calm my body down. "Bad dream?"

"You won't believe it."

The green, purple, and black bracelet buzzed on my wrist. Right. We were going to see a leprechaun about a fairy. Ren pushed me, scooting toward the opening. "Save it for later. We've got a leprechaun prostitute to meet."

We went through the gate which put us in a short hallway leading to an atrium space with conveniently colored markers. The room itself was carved by an Earth elemental, possibly a gnome. It was nice and tidy, straight, but undeniably earthen. The only other things in there were the wooden doors. Even the floors were made of dirt.

The atrium had four doors: red, black, blue, and white. We went through the black door since we had a black thread in our friendship—I was calling them that. I didn't care what Ren said—bracelets.

Once inside another hall, we were faced with four more doors: pink, yellow, green, and orange. We took the green and found yet another set of colored doors. Bypassing the others, we took the purple door, which led to a long hallway.

Each set of doors led us further down into the earth as we went. It was getting cooler and denser as we traveled. This hall had many doors, each of them with multiple colors. We had to go all the way to the end to find the one with black, green, and purple. We stood there staring at it. "Do you think we should knock?" I asked.

Ren turned the knob, barging straight in. I guess it made sense because we had paid for this.

The room was small but nice. There were rugs all over the floor, covering up the dirt and it smelled of lavender and vanilla. On one side, there was a large bed with white sheets and a comforter. Sprawled on top of said bed, was a sexy woman with long red hair. She had a white nightie that left nothing to the imagination. Which made sense for a brothel, I supposed.

She sat up and crossed her legs seductively, eyeing Ren, then sliding her gaze to me. "Three *is* my lucky number."

I glanced at Ren, catching him swallow. Like me, I think he was expecting a short, round old lady wearing a green top hat, but that was the leprechaun version in our world. It was different in Aetheria. Obviously. This woman looked like she earned her place as a sex worker. "Hello there. I'm Fiona. Who's first or are we doing this together? Either is fine with me. Just know if you want the magic touch that the Golden Arches is famous for, I'll probably run out of magic before I get to both of you." She waved her hand at the wall opposite the bed. "We can find other ways to make it work though. Make yourself at home while I freshen up."

She disappeared behind a door, and I turned to see what was on the wall. It was never going to stop. "Oh, my Mage." There was a small cabinet, just like you find at fast-food places. In the bottom was a trash can and on top, three different containers with those little paper cups beside them. One was red, one yellow, one white. "Is that ketchup?"

Ren walked over and took a cup, placing it under the red container and squirting liquid into it. He held it up for me to see. It was clear. He smelled it, then stuck his finger in. Just when he'd almost gotten it to his mouth, he pulled away. "Fuck me. It's cinnamon-flavored lube."

He squirted out some of the 'mustard' dispenser and shook his head. "This one's grape. I'm not touching the white one." He threw the cup away and grabbed a napkin—you bet they were right there too—

and wiped his hands as the leprechaun strolled back into the room looking exactly as she had before.

"Oh, good, You must have been here before. The toys are on the other side of the cabinet." All I could do was think of Happy Meals, but I got the feeling if we opened the cabinet, we would not find a Spongebob or Squishmellows toy in there.

I went over to the bed where she'd sat. "We're not here for sex. We need your help."

"I don't understand. Did you not pay for sex with a leprechaun?"

Ren joined us, sitting on the bed as far away from her as he could get. "We paid, but the service we're asking for isn't your normal business here. We need you to find someone for us using your magic. Then we'll be on our way, and you can have the rest of our time to…play with your toys or whatever you like."

She waffled between us, looking like it was the strangest thing she'd ever been asked to do. I doubted that was the case, but whatever. "I don't think it's allowed. I can't do it."

She needed convincing, so I went with the true story, just not all of it. "Okay, Fiona. We're not from Aetheria. We came through the Conduit, which had been locked for twenty-two years, but briefly opened after a battle with fae-driven golem giants. It's shut for good now, but if you find this person for us using your magic, it'll not only help us, it'll help all of Aetheria. This man has secrets that could topple the emperor."

Her eyes widened and she swiveled her head like she was making sure nobody heard me. Maybe the room was bugged, I didn't know how Aetherian brothels worked. "I swear on the square," she whispered.

Ren huffed. "No, you don't. Just help us."

He was right. She didn't like the emperor any more than we did. Her disgust was clearly on her face when she fake swore. It did the trick to get her on our side. "Okay. I'll do it, but you can't tell anyone, and you need to get out as soon as I give you the information."

She jumped off the bed and bent over, pulling something from underneath. A cauldron, possibly once filled with gold. I wasn't sure about that either. She set it on the chest at the end of the bed. "I'll need as much info about him that you can give me, and something belonging to him."

Ren slung the bag off, handing it to me as he answered. "His name is Trickstan. He's fae, originally from the Summer Court, but had been with us in our world since the Conduit closed. Last seen near the outskirts of Midsummer about a day ago, but he could be anywhere by now. He's traveling with a chimera, troll, and merman."

I dug the key he'd given me out of the bag. "He gave this to me, but I don't know if it was his." She didn't react to the strange key, but I was going to make sure to keep an eye on it anyway.

"If he touched it, that'll do." She plunked it into the cauldron and held her hands above it. "Do you have a map of Aetheria?"

"Sadly, no."

"Okay, just go grab one over there in the closet. Middle shelf."

Ren went over to the closet, swinging the small door open and laughing hysterically at something. He came out carrying one of those brown trays with a map liner. "The fuck are the trays for?"

She cocked an eyebrow, "All sorts of things. You can spank with them or use them to carry toys around the room. Mostly I eat from them during my downtime."

He shook his head. "I can't. I have to ask before I go insane. Why did you model your brothel after McDonald's in our world? It's disturbing."

He wasn't wrong.

"When the Conduit was opened and there was free travel back and forth, most Aetherians became obsessed with your culture. There was a big influx of businesses looking like yours. This one was one of the first and we'd kept it maintained as best we could since we could no longer get there. I thought someone from your world would like it."

He handed her the map. "It's where we eat cheap food, not fuck. It doesn't turn me on in any way."

She glanced up and down, getting her eyes full of his hotness. "Shame."

"Yep, can we get on with it?"

Nodding, she placed the map in the cauldron next to the key. Then she waved her hands over the cauldron and said the spell. "Faigh an duine atá á lorg agam, tabhair chugam é. Ná folaigh siad níos mó ónár súile. Is léir go bhfuil a suíomh."

White smoke billowed from the cauldron, hitting Fiona in the face, but she kept on chanting the spell, saying it four times. The smoke dissipated and we peered inside the cauldron.

There was a clover symbol on the map, not far from the dot indicating Mystia. She handed it over, pointing to the clover and clicking her tongue. "I guess he followed the chimera to their home. I don't envy you having to go to Crestwyn. The Cinders are the most dangerous boundary between lands."

Ren saddled up, checking out the map, noting how far the clover was from us—across into the Autumnlands at the base of a volcano. I know because it was labeled 'Fire Volcano.' The Cinders ran from the volcano to the central province. I supposed it was a huge lava flow. Nothing I'd want to go near, for sure.

I snagged the key from her cauldron. "It's not like we have a choice." I turned to Ren. "This time, let's stay out of the boundary, okay?"

He smirked. "Bite me."

"I would, but you'd like it."

Fiona giggled. "Are you two sure you don't want to join me now? We've got plenty of time left on your clock." She slid across the bed, laying out and patting it in invitation.

"No, thanks. We need to get going."

"Fair enough. If he moves the clover will follow him but be sure to catch him within a day. The magic will be less reliable as it wears off. When you leave, turn left and go through the white door. That's the exit. Come back when you have time to play."

Ren grabbed my elbow, ushering me quickly through the door as he murmured, "We will." I raised an eyebrow at his statement. "What? I was being nice."

"You're not nice, Ren."

"Maybe I'm trying something new."

"Maybe you should stay exactly as you are."

"I'll see what I can do. Now, tell me about your dream."

Sickening dread flowed through me. I had a feeling he wasn't going to enjoy hearing what I had to say. And for the life of me, I didn't know why, but I didn't want to tell him all of it.

Trickstan

The heat of the Cinders was roasting my back. We were inside a pod at the base of Fire Volcano and even though we weren't close enough to feel it, the presence of it was so large, I was sweating. I hated being anywhere near that thing, but I loved Kiko, and she was right about bringing us here. Nobody would dare come to look for us this close to Fire Volcano. Only chimera and other obscure Fire species dared to live near it. Kiko always kept hidden when we traveled, so we were safe. At least for a while.

I needed somewhere to think. I couldn't remember everything I needed and if the emperor or one of his people found me, I would be in pot water.

The worst part was I knew enough to be a danger to myself, Kiko, Bex, and Louie, but they wouldn't leave me. Not like Jack had.

The five of us had been inseparable for years, but something happened on the day we were to go to the other world through the Conduit. Jack and I were supposed to go through. I recalled us making it though the others with us that day never did. When my memories came flooding in that night at Boulderbrook and I remembered being a part of the square, of the job the emperor had sent me to complete— prep the way for the giant golems I'd made before I left, I remembered

Jack too. Only he and the other three Magnus sent never came to meet me, so I assumed something went wrong with his memory recovery.

I didn't know the others well, but I didn't think Jack would trench me, but it was a possibility.

Whatever the case, it was just me and my three besties now. And we were going pogue.

No wait, rogue. Going rogue.

We were going to take down the emperor.

As soon as I remembered how.

Louie was cooking up something to help me do just that. Bex was in another pod, helping him. I'd been told to stay away so the experience would be organic. "How long do I have to wait?" I asked Kiko.

"He said two hours, so not long now. Pacing doesn't help, Mister."

No matter how many times I'd told her over the years, she still referred to me as Mister. She did that to anyone she saw as superior to her, which was a load of scrap. I wasn't her superior at all. There was hardly anyone in Aetheria who was her superior. "I know, it just makes me feel better to have something to do."

She pulled up a pillow, hugging it to her chest. "So then tell me about your other friends—the girl and the wolf."

It sounded like a human fairy tale, the ones that never got our species right. Terra and Ren were so much more than just a girl and a wolf though. They were true friends and meant enough to me that as I came out of my Binding Magic, I didn't feel the same as when I went into it. My heart could barely take thinking about how I'd betrayed them. I didn't know what I was doing at the time, but they didn't care. I could see why.

If only I could see the hole in the picture.

"I can't talk about them. It stings too much. I was Tristan to them, a completely different person from the real me, but the same too."

I stopped pacing. Something snagged in my mind. 'Different person' or maybe it was 'real me.' I wasn't sure, but it was important, and I tried to figure out what and why, but it slipped away as soon as I'd thought it.

It was like cracking an egg and finding a bit of eggshell in it. No matter what you do to fish it out, as soon as you stick your finger or fork in, it moves away, and you can't get it.

"Oh, do we have any eggs?"

"How would I know? You and Louie do the cooking, Mister."

I resumed my pacing, grasping at sticks—no straws— in my head and coming up with nothing. Finally, Bex lifted the pod door. "We're ready. Close your eyes and take a big sniff when Louie comes in."

I didn't hear him come in—he was silent, like most merpeople on land—but I smelled the evidence. It wafted into my nose, and I nearly lost the contents of my stomach. "What is that stench? It smells like the Boiling Swamps of the Autumnlands." I gagged as I spoke.

"That's exactly what I was going for. It's where you said the emperor used to take you when he had important private matters to discuss with you. Bex said a familiar scent could unlock hidden memories. Here."

He must have shoved his concoction right under my nose. The smell got even more intense. And more disgusting. I opened my eyes to push the bowl away. "Get it away from me."

"Give it a try, Mister."

Bex wrapped her arms around me from behind. "Suck it up for a good cause. You need to remember, and I heard this method from a very good source."

I did need to remember. Badly. "Okay. Bring it back. I'll give it a shoot."

Louie handed me the bowl and I took another big whiff. A flash of memory burst through my head. Me and Emperor Magnus standing on the banks of the Boiling Swamp. He had his arm wrapped around my neck, telling me I was the key to his whole plan.

I didn't want to be the key to anything. I wanted my sister back. He'd taken a liking to her after visiting King Ronas of the Summer Court. She'd served him lemon water and made him laugh and he was under her spell. She'd had no control from the very start.

The idea dissolved as soon as I'd had it.

Sticking my nose in the bowl, I gagged again. "I got something, but it's gone now."

"You could drink it."

Kiko and I swirled around. "What in the Neverending Wind are you saying? I'm not drinking Boiling Swamp water. I'm desperate, not stupid."

"It's not boiling. I just put some carbonation in it to give it that effect. All the ingredients are one hundred percent edible. Try it. I had some. It wasn't that bad."

I didn't hesitate. I tipped the bowl to my mouth, drinking a big chug of the stuff, then spitting it out all over Louie. "This is not edible."

Louie calmly stepped out of the pod and used his Water Magic to clean himself off. Once he did, I shot a blast of Wind in his direction to dry him. He looked at me hopefully. "Did it work?"

"Not really. I remember being at the Boiling Swamp with Magnus, but not anything he told me, other than being the key to his plan."

"Hey Mister, do you think maybe you should've kept that key you gave the girl? If you're the key, maybe you should have the key."

I paced around the pod, which was hard to do considering it was nothing more than an egg-shaped trailer, barely big enough for all four of us with the bed and shower stall. "No, that was a different key. It didn't come from the emperor. It came from…" I paused, curling my fingers like I still had the key in my hand. "…it was a man, I think. One with long hair."

Bex settled on the bed next to Kiko. "Oh, the wolf had long hair. He was hot." Kiko shook her head in agreement.

"You don't even know half of it. I've seen him without a shirt. And don't get me started on all his friends. Seriously, the wolves at that camp are all beautiful and sexy and they didn't even care much that I told them that all the time."

Sadness took over my whole being. I knew none of them would ever forgive me and it hurt so much. That's why I needed to know what I didn't remember. It was the only way to get my life back. Because I wasn't Tristan anymore, but I wasn't Trickstan either. As I stood there looking at my childhood friends, I knew they loved me and respected what I'd gone through, but I didn't feel like I belonged with them any more than I did with the Boulderbrook pack and Terra.

I was a man without a county.

I needed all of my memories back. Maybe then, I would feel whole.

There was one thing I hadn't tried yet. It was dangerous, but I didn't have a choice. I just prayed to the Mage my friends would forgive me for it.

Annigan was smirking at me when I woke. My limbs were numb, my head tingling like it was going to buzz right off my shoulders, and a dreary sense of dread crawled in my chest. I couldn't even take a breath.

They were amused by all of it. "Hurts like a bitch, doesn't it?"

"What did you do to me?"

"I told you not to stay too long. You didn't listen. This is the consequence of being ripped from the dreamscape. Next time get out on your own." They strolled to the door. "You'll be fine in a few minutes."

Gideon appeared on the other side, ready to act if I needed him. "Where are you going, nymph?"

"To collect my leprechaun and go home." Gideon put his hand to their chest, eyeing me for direction. I nodded to let them go. I knew Terra was awake now too, so there'd be no sense in trying to go back into the dreamscape, though I craved her more than ever.

"You'll come back tomorrow night. No wait. Gideon, get them a cabin set up. You two can stay here until Fitz gets done with the Blood Magic. We can visit Terra every night." Annigan rolled their eyes. They might protest, but dream nymphs wouldn't resist the pull of dream magic any more than I could resist the urge to shift under a full moon.

I just had to get through another day until I could get back into the dreamscape.

Things had turned upside down so damn fast. I'd been dreading nights and now I was looking forward to the next one with so much anticipation, despite my aching limbs, I jumped out of bed like I was five and Mom had made pancakes.

After I had a shower, needing to rub one out as I remembered all the things Terra and I had gotten up to in the dreamscape, I went to the kitchen to make those pancakes. Gideon and Mace arrived just as I flipped the first one, so I grabbed the supplies to make more for them. "Everything go without a hitch?"

Mace yawned. "Yep. The leprechaun wasn't keen on staying here, but after Gideon told him we'd pay him for their services, he was cool with it. Greedy little fucker."

"Thanks. All I can do right now is pay you in pancakes." I owed them more than that. One day I hoped I could make it up to them. They'd had my back at the worst of times, and I was grateful for their support and friendship. No, brotherhood.

Though we were down one and he cast a long fucking shadow all the way from Aetheria. Having spoken to Terra in the dreamscape, I was more hopeful than ever that we'd have him back soon.

I slammed my phone down on the desk. Lore had called to say there was a robbery at a bank in Illusion Hill. All of the tellers had mysteriously gotten ill at the same time, having to leave their windows to hit the bathroom. The people in line had gone berserk, taking all the money from the tills and strolling out.

It was one of those freak occurrences that meant one thing: what we feared was already happening. Much sooner than anticipated. As magic ran out, things like this would trickle into the world and soon it would be chaos. We'd have no way of predicting how what or when these things would occur, especially when it came to human involvement. It would be a crapshoot.

I had to get more magic. I'd already rationed as much as I could, using The Five to distribute it every other day instead of daily. Lore and the pack spread the word to us magic only when necessary, but you couldn't police those things. Most Magicals used their magic as a means to make a living. It was a big ask and I hated to be the one to do it. I had no other choice though.

Well, I had one other option, but I didn't want to use it. The Blood Magic spell was already cooking. I would get anything I wanted at the end of it, no holds barred. The one thing I wanted was Terra and Ren back, but if I used the spell to get more magic somehow, where would that leave us? I wasn't sure, but I was damn well certain, I didn't want to leave Terra and Ren alone in Aetheria.

It was a real conundrum. I hated that it even occurred to me.

Would the greater good—enough magic in our world—be enough to somehow get Terra and Ren back too? Or were the two things mutually exclusive? One or the other? Everyone's needs versus my own.

My thoughts spiraled as I weighed it all out in my head, but thankfully hearing Mace's signature knock on my door helped me back to the present. "Come on in."

He, Gideon, and Spencer shut the door behind them. Gideon slapped a piece of paper on my desk. "We need to go to Missouri."

I crossed my arms over my chest. "Why?"

"Check this out."

The paper was a copy of an old newspaper clipping. I scanned the date. September twenty-first, nineteen-twenty-eight. "Why am I looking at news from a hundred years ago? Today's shit is plenty."

He pointed to the grainy photo of a blues band standing outside of a dive called *The Cobalt Fairy*. The name of the club caught my attention for sure. Could be a coincidence, but it was likely Magical. I read the headline aloud. "Missouri Joe Packs Another House With His Unique Instrument."

Mace laughed. "I've got a unique instrument right here." I didn't have to look up to know he was grabbing his crotch. Spencer groaned and punched him in the ribs.

"You're going to have to help me out. I don't think the dreamscape counts as sleep and I'm fucking tired. What do you want me to see here?"

He pointed to a man in the photo. He stood out for multiple reasons: first, he was the only Caucasian in the band. His clothing was a step up from homeless, but the others in the band were dressed in nice suits and ties. He didn't even have on shoes. Finally, unlike anything I'd ever heard or read about blues music in the Depression era, he was holding a violin and cheesing at the camera with a crooked smile. "This is Missouri Joe. Famous musician of this era, birth name, Joseph Houseman."

That rang a bell. "So, he has the same name as the man who owns Terra's Gram's house. It isn't the same person. Are you saying he's a descendant or something?"

Mace slapped my back. "Wait for it."

Gideon laid a second paper down on my desk. This one was dated January first, nineteen, fifty-nine. Headline: *Joe Man and the House Band Ring In The New Year.* "Look at the photo."

I squinted. The band was different this time, dressed for the occasion and year, but the guy in the center was the same. Like he hadn't aged a day. The same man, holding the same violin, wearing the same grungy clothes. However, I was failing to see Gideon's point.

I was going to have to schedule a nap soon.

The third paper was from the eighties. Same guy, same violin, same crooked smile. The only differences were the new band members and the band name: Houseman. I stacked the papers in a neat pile. "So, he's a Magical species that live a long time—like us—and reinvents himself every thirty years or so? What's the big deal?"

Finally, Gideon pulled out his trump card, in the form of his phone. Flashing on the screen was an ad for a concert in Columbia, Missouri, headlined by Joseph H. Mann. There he was holding his violin, same clothes, same crooked smile and bare feet. "His show's in a few days. I know it's not the highest priority right now, but if this Magical guy who's been around for so long knows anything about Terra and her genetic makeup—who made her and why—it could help to not only get them back but maybe find a way to more magic. We can all agree she's special and since she closed the Conduit, maybe she can open it if she can learn how. It's worth a shot to question him, at least. I'm sure you'd love to find out his connection to Terra's grandmother."

I knew he'd continued researching Joe Houseman when he could. I never dreamed he'd find something like this. I thought he was likely an old lover of Gram's and nothing more, but Gideon had made a good point.

I turned to Spencer, needing her level head. I didn't trust my heart at the moment. It was beating far too hard at the thought of discovering more about Terra and getting to her.

She gave me a reassuring smile. "It can't hurt to try if you can spare one of us. Bash will go along and fly us if it has any possibility of getting Ren back."

She wasn't wrong about that, and I decided I wasn't going to reject any option to get Terra home. "Yeah, alright. You guys can decide who goes." I scrubbed my hand over my jaw. "First we need to go to Siberia, then Missouri, where next?"

"I've always wanted to go to Bora Bora."

This time I punched Mace in the gut. He doubled over, coughing. "Why are we going to Siberia?"

"Autumn thinks there could be a hidden Conduit there. I'm not convinced, but things are getting dicey so it might be worth a trip to investigate. She wants me to go with her to check it out." The three of them exchanged glances, cluing me into the fact they'd discussed something behind my back. "Okay, out with it. Why are you looking at each other like that?"

Spencer pulled the chair closer and sat down to face me. She didn't hesitate to dive in, which is why I chose her to be my fourth beta. No sugar-coating with that one. "We just think you should be careful with Autumn. She's confided in me and she's getting desperate for you to finalize the mate bond. I think—we all think—she'll eventually do something drastic. I like her, but we're Team Terra and we know you are too. The thing is, we know you're spread thin and stressed and getting no real sleep, even before the dream nymph. We just want you to be careful how you deal with her. That's all."

Of course, I knew all those things, but something about hearing it from another person's mouth made it sink in. I had to find a way to deal with the mate bond. The only way I could think of would be to use the Blood Magic spell to break the bond. I was as desperate as she was, just in the other direction.

That made three things vying for the Blood Magic spell. Terra or magic or severing the bond. All of them were necessary, all with consequences. What good would it do to get Terra back if I couldn't break the mate bond? But breaking the bond would ensure I'd never be able to love Terra like I did. And getting magic back would save the world, but would I want to live in it without Terra?

I'd need to think about it more. Maybe there was a way to get everything I wanted. I stood up. "Thanks, guys. I appreciate it and I'll take it under advisement. Now—"

The door flew open banging against the wall as Autumn burst into my office, hyperventilating. Naturally, my gaze shot down to her heaving chest, which was only covered with a white tank top, perk nipples visible.

Those pictures on the wall are crooked AF. I should straighten them.

"Please tell me the bathrooms work here." She shifted her weight from one foot to the other. "Mine's overflowing, along with everyone else's on that side of camp. It's going to be a plumbing nightmare, but if

I don't find a bathroom soon, you're going to have a wet spot on your floor, Wells."

Mace shot off the chair, sailing into my bathroom to check it out. "Uh. Someone call Mario and Luigi."

I closed my eyes, hoping to shut out everything else, but knowing it wouldn't work. After taking a few deep breaths and wishing for Terra's gentle touch on my face, I let reality back in. "Autumn, go use my cabin to piss. Spence, call Lore and get a Magical plumber's number. Get them out as soon as they can. Mace, go sober up Bash and prep for Missouri. Gideon, see what you can do to find and organize functioning bathrooms for people."

They all shot out of my office without hesitation. I shifted and tore the chair to shreds again.

It had taken most of the day to handle the problem. The pack came up with the solution to just shift and do the bathroom business in the woods, but that wasn't going to help when it was time to shower. Gideon was able to use his fused Water magic to help the plumbers, but we were down from two to one working water tank for the camp.

Beyond that, the plumbers had reported that water supplies were being affected up and down the western coast of Canada and into the U.S. They were using Water elementals to help, but the supply and demand of it was going to be a problem. Especially when humans started seeing patterns of water movement and increase in areas of need. They'd need to be stealthy about their plans to fix it. So, I told them not to bother with Boulderbrook—we could fend for ourselves— and focus on the greater issue.

They left and I stood in the kitchen scarfing down a sandwich that Mona had forced on me. I didn't want to eat. I wanted to sleep.

No, I wanted Terra.

Needed her.

Shooting to my cabin and up the stairs, I burst into my door, shucking my shirt on the way in. I'd planned to nap a few hours, making sure to set an alarm so I could wake up and get Annigan in to visit Terra.

I strolled to the fridge, downed a bottle of water, and was on my way to the bathroom when a figure in my bedroom caught my eye.

Autumn was standing on the far side of the bed; the bottom drawer of the nightstand was open. I surged over to her just as she was fastening the clasp of the ruby pendant I'd found in Terra's Gram's tree around her neck. She gasped at my sudden presence.

Fur rippled over my arms and chest as my most vicious growl rumbled out of my throat. The audacity of this woman to come here uninvited and go through my stuff. "The fuck are you doing in my drawers? You can't touch *her* things."

I didn't need to define it further. She knew I was referring to Terra, even though she knew this had been my mother's room first. Hurt flickered on her face. "I didn't mean to..." She reached behind her neck. "Here, I'll take it off."

"Yes, you fucking will." She fumbled for a few seconds. Not fast enough for me, so I swung her around and tried to take the necklace off for her, but it wouldn't budge. I moved her into the light, but it did nothing to help. The necklace wasn't coming off just like the amethyst bracelet Terra wore. "What have you done?" I roared, unable to keep my voice steady. "Why are you even here?"

She sat on the bed. "I came to use your bathroom again. When I was done I heard something in the bedroom, and I thought maybe you were home. I don't know how to explain it, but I was drawn over here by a strange whisper like something was calling me. I opened the drawer and found these jewels. Mage, I hope you believe me—I know it's going to sound absurd—the ruby glowed and before I knew what I was doing, I had it in my hand. The voice told me to put it on. I figured it wouldn't hurt to try it, just for a second. I'm sorry. Why won't it come off?"

She was panicking. It made my fury subside, at least a little. Still, I tried to pry it off her neck again, but it wasn't going to budge. I scrubbed my hand over my face. "Fuck. I don't know how I'm going to explain this to her."

"If she manages to come back, I'll explain it. This is on me, not you."

"*When* she comes back."

I wanted to tell her that I had a way to communicate with Terra now, but that seemed like even more of an invasion of Terra's privacy, of our intimate business. I didn't want her near the dreamscape. When she reached up and touched my hand which was still rubbing my jaw like I was trying to erase my stubble, I flinched in response. "Can you at least tell me what the jewels are? They're magic."

We barely knew anything about them other than they seemed to help Terra when she needed it. Like when she passed the trials I'd given her or when she took out the first giant golem. Diggs was looking into a theory but hadn't come up with anything yet.

I could detect Autumn trying to pull the information out of me by sheer desire alone. I could at least give her a history.

"They belonged to Terra's grandmother. She was guarding them with her gnome magic, but the person they belonged to died. Then she did. She left them for Terra to guard with strict instructions not to keep them herself because of the gnome magic preventing it. Terra gave them to me, and I asked her to guard the bracelet for me so she could have it without owning it. We don't know what they are or how they work other than Arlo telling us there was a non-sentient life force or spark of someone's magic in the amethyst in her bracelet. I guess there's one in the ruby too."

I reached down, fingering the dark stone that hung dangerously close to her tits. Her lips parted at my touch and when the ruby glowed, Autumn's need blossomed inside me as if it were my own.

She trailed her hand over my chest and before she'd gotten where she was going—my waistband— all control left my body like a train leaving a station. I was full steam ahead and I could think of nothing but her. I threw her back on the bed, vibrating as I prowled over her body.

Her.

I wanted her.

Needed her.

Had to fucking have her.

I crushed my mouth against her moaning as she grabbed the back of my hair to press me down, making me give her more. I'd never experienced something so all-consuming in my life. I was on the precipice of giving her every inch of me when something in my head snapped, forcing me to pull away from her. My heartbeat was erratic. Every part of me was screaming this was wrong.

The ruby against her chest glowed and scrambled off the bed at the sight of it. "What just happened? That was…" I put my hand over my mouth. The shock of the line I'd crossed settled in and made me want to hurl. "I didn't—I don't—want to kiss you."

Yet I had.

"Tell me what you just fucking did to me."

She jumped up, moving toward me, but I held my arms out, not letting her get close. Our mate bond always made me low-key want her, but whatever had just happened was different. It was dark and unreal and the feel of it sliding in my veins reminded me of sludge. "I don't know, Wells. I swear. I was just thinking about how hot you look without a shirt and how badly I need you to give in to the mate bond. The ruby warmed up, and then you just pounced. I didn't do it on purpose. I thought you—"

"Wanted you? No. I don't know how else to get it across to you. I'm not giving up on Terra. Yeah, the magic makes me feel things for you, but I don't *want* to want you, capiche?"

I was hurting her and feeling like shit for it, but it was time to make it clear. She was not my mate and never would be. "The bracelet jewels helped Terra with her trials. You just said you thought about how much you needed me. Maybe the magic in the jewels gives you what you need. If that's the case, maybe you can learn to control it and open the Conduit."

She touched the necklace. "I don't know, maybe. It wasn't a conscious thing."

"Go practice, try to figure it out. Get Spence or Gideon to help you, whatever it takes. Try it before we run off to Siberia, but Autumn?" She was already backing toward the door, knowing what I was going to say. I still had to say it. "I don't know how this will end, but I can positively say it won't be with us."

"I know."

She didn't stick around, thank the Mage's sweaty ass crack.

There was a huge wall in front of me and I had hit it. Something was going to have to give. At that moment I needed Terra more than I needed anything. More than magic or breath or life. But before I even got near her in the dreamscape, I was going to have to come clean about what I had just done.

On the mat ride to the edge of the Summerlands, Terra told me about meeting Wells in the nymph dreamscape. She was careful not to mention anything specific about their conversations or what happened, but I knew Wells and was certain he boned her the entire time.

Even though the thought of them together again made my toes cramp with rage, a small part of me experienced hope that I'd see Bash and my friends again. If Wells discovered a way to communicate with her, it was just a matter of time before he found a way to get to her.

It was a true double-edged sword for me.

Wanting to avoid thinking of the inevitability of them together again, I laid back on the carpet, studying the Aetherian map and eyeing the shamrock in case it budged an inch. Before long, Terra nestled beside me and dozed off within minutes. Even though it was a risk, I allowed myself a few moments to stroke her hair, loving how the thick strands slipped through my fingers like silk.

Don't fight battles you know you can't win, Renfield.

Magedamn, I hated when the voice *she* put in my head was right.

Didn't mean I would listen to it though.

Terra woke when our carpet began to float downward. I knew she was awake because her breathing changed, and her body tensed. Despite the danger it posed, I kept my hand in her hair. My days with her were numbered and I wasn't going to lose a single second. To my shock, she arched into my touch and a small moan escaped her throat.

Her eyes popped open. We shared a charged look, one full of heat that ramped my pulse. Instead of acknowledging it, she jumped off the carpet, scrambling away.

I would take that sound and lock it in the deepest recesses of my heart for all eternity. She wasn't thinking of him then. I was sure of it.

"Where are we? Close to Trickstan?" She made quick work of surveying the area, looking for threats or things we could use as I'd taught her.

We were still in the Summerlands, but it looked like we were on a different planet. Instead of the colorful trees and foliage, the area was dry and covered in rock, dirt, and brittle hay-colored grass, with abandoned magic mats strewn across it. There was a town rising on the horizon, but the unavoidable difference in terrain was the volcano. It wasn't even that big, more of a large hill than anything. It looked scalable, if not for the steady stream of lava that churned into a boiling river in front of us. We were close enough that her cheeks were starting to flush in the lava's heat.

It was fucking beautiful on her.

I stepped up next to her. "I told the carpet to take us to Crestwyn, but it isn't going to fly over that barrier. We're going to have to find another way across the lava to get to Trickstan."

Wavy lines of heat emanated from the river of lava, telling me it was far hotter just inches away from where we stood, making it possible to walk close to it but not go through it. Fire magic, but not the regular kind. If it were, any Fire elemental could stroll through it without being hurt. This Fire was meant to be an impenetrable barrier to the Autumnlands, like the Moaning Mist between the Summerlands and Springlands.

Terra stuck her arm out, leaning over the lava. I gasped and used my wolf speed to jerk it away. "The fuck, Terra? Are you trying to melt your skin off?"

Shrugging like it was no big deal, she waved her bracelet at me. "This has helped me too many times to discount. I might be able to sail right through it like the barrier behind the Forge."

"Yeah, but you might not. I'm not letting you take that chance. We'll find another way."

Her face crumpled like I'd denied her bacon, and then she stilled. "The whispering voice just told me to look up to find him."

We both raised our heads, peering up at the top of the volcano. It had a very low profile, probably three hundred feet to the top and a white figure was scaling around the side, nearing the rim. No one in their right mind would attempt to scale an active volcano that was meant to be a barrier.

Which told me exactly who it was.

I glanced down at the map. The shamrock was making its way up the side of the volcano. "What in the name of the Eternal Flame is he doing?"

She grabbed the map, eyeing the moving shamrock as it inched up. "I couldn't begin to guess, but the voice is adamant that we stop him. In fact, it's whisper-shouting at me to save him. I think we need to do it." She threw her bag over her shoulder and proceeded to start climbing right up the side of the volcano like it was nothing.

Shit. I didn't trust this mysterious voice anymore and I trusted that bracelet. If I thought about it too hard, I'd have to admit I probably had trust issues. A werewolf being brought up by vampires who hated him would do that to a guy.

Though I *did* trust her.

And I sure as shit wasn't going to let her fry herself on the edge of a volcano. "Stay here. I can use my speed to get him."

She put her hands on her hips. "Pretty sure the phoenix blood or the bracelet would protect me. You'll need help." She took another step, and I pulled her back, slamming her into my chest and putting my arms around her to pin her in. Maybe I allowed myself a moment or two to breathe in her sweet rainfall scent too.

"You're probably right, but he'd never forgive me if I let something happen to you. I can do this faster without you. I'll have Trickstan down before you can get halfway up. Let me do this."

It was all kinds of wrong to play the Wells card against her, but I didn't give a single shit if it kept her safe. It took her a few seconds to decide, but as soon as her body melted against mine, I knew I had her. "Be right back."

Not waiting for her protest, I shucked my clothes, tossing them behind me. Another second later I'd shifted into my wolf form, shaking my fur and settling into the primal side of me.

Being back in my wolf skin was a welcome change, one that blurred my feelings for her long enough to leave her there and tear up the volcano. The pads of my paws warmed as I surged forward, but I separated my Fire magic—something I was able to do after I'd been fused with Earth magic—pushing it down into my legs to protect them from the intense heat.

How Trickstan, a simple fae with only Wind magic was coping with the temperature was beyond me. Though, he'd proven there was more to him than he'd ever let on. I, for one, wasn't letting him out of my sight again until I got answers on all of it.

The wind—regular, not magic—was stronger at the top of the volcano. Sparks and debris were flying as I neared the top. I almost missed Trickstan crawling on his hands and knees onto the rim. He was fighting against the wind and heat, struggling to inch ahead.

He was covered, head to toe, in white cloth. Like a fucking mummy brought to life.

I growled to get his attention, but he ignored me in favor of inching toward the rim where the lava was sputtering out. I prowled forward, slowly so I wouldn't spook him, but he kept his head down as he reached the top. He steadied himself, peering into the volcano, and squared his shoulders. The fucking idiot was about to jump in. I bounded toward him, unsure if I wanted to nudge him into the volcano or save him.

Nah. Terra would've been pissed if I did all this and still killed him. If it wasn't for her though…

Trickstan finally noticed me flying toward him and turned to look over his shoulder.

Nope. He turned his head, but his entire face with covered in the white cloth, so there was no way he saw me. I couldn't figure out how he was breathing.

I dove for him, chomping on to anything I could get my teeth into. He screamed as I bit into his ankle. I used all the strength I had to keep myself and the asshole fairy from his death plunge, twisting my body, to hurl him away from the rim and the lava flow. I still clung to his ankle so he wouldn't do something really stupid like rushing back up and trying a forward one-and-a-half somersault in the pike position into the fucking volcano.

The bandage tasted like ass and my gums instantly stung from having it in my mouth. It wasn't an ordinary white cloth, that much was certain.

He better have had a damn good reason for all of this madness.

Undeterred that a werewolf had his teeth sunk into his ankle, he used his other leg to kick me in the head, nearly snapping my neck in the process.

Motherfucker.

I lost my grip but managed to keep the vile cloth in my teeth. He glanced down. Interpreting it as a win, his muffled laugh went through the cloth on his face.

For a second, and I mean literally one second, I went soft, remembering how he used to annoy me by getting in my hair. I missed that guy.

That was Tristan. Not this guy. Nope, I was battling Trickstan. Betrayer, manipulator, the thorn in my damned side. And he was about to wrestle himself out of my grasp if I let him. I couldn't allow it. There was too much at stake.

I needed hands.

Prepping for the pain that would soon be ripping through my human form, I bore down, hoping to the Mage there were dentists in Aetheria if this went sideways.

I shifted, clenching my jaw together to hold on as best I could as my teeth went from canine to human. Trickstan's muffled voice called to me. "Let go, Ren. I'm chopping the bits to do this."

When I had my hands back, I grabbed the fraying cloth, pulling as I shouted back at him. "*Chomping at the bit*, you Fuckwad. What are you trying to do, kill yourself because you can't remember shit?"

He lay there on the rocky surface of the volcano, not answering me, so I marched over, pulling the cloth from his face so he could see how dumb I thought he was. He stared up at me with blinking blue eyes brimming with so much sincerity it startled me. "Well, yeah."

That was it. I snapped. I was done with his nonsense.

I yanked on the cloth I still had in my hand. Hard. The force of my tug caused him to roll to his side. That wasn't good enough for me though, so I jerked even harder. It sent him rolling.

Down the side of the volcano.

Along the bumpy, rocky surface.

I didn't give any fucks at all as he screamed his way through it.

I just stood there watching and grinning as he unraveled from his cloth like a roll of fucking toilet paper.

Felt about right.

He jerked to a stop after he'd unrolled all the cloth from his body. I had one end in my hand, and he had the other in his. A manic look crossed his face before he yanked the end of the cloth, knocking me off balance. I tried to stay firm, but he'd surprised me and had more strength than I'd realized. I tumbled forward, twisting my body to hit my ass instead of landing cock first.

Wincing, I tucked myself into a ball as I rolled over the rocks. Trickstan was the one laughing now. I could hear him as I zoomed past him on my own forward roll.

It wasn't over.

As soon as the cloth tightened between us, meaning I'd stopped rolling and started wanting to hurl, I pulled, sending him rolling all over again, bumping and cursing me as he plummeted.

I should've stopped it because I was now acting as ridiculous as he was, but the anger simmering inside me had breached the surface and I couldn't stuff it back in. I was mad at him for what he did, at Terra for loving Wells, at Wells for abandoning us, and at myself for allowing my feelings to rule my judgment and actions. I was just fucking angry, and he was the best and closest thing to bear the brunt of it.

We alternated turns, pulling each other down the volcano in a strange and brutal tug-of-war that ended when we tumbled together at Terra's feet.

He scrambled to his feet. "You've got to let me do this."

I grabbed his shoulder, whirling him around to face me. "Magedamn, what are you talking about?" His eyes roamed over my naked body, fixating on my dick. Some things would never change. "If you don't get your eyes up, I'm not giving you the chance to off yourself via volcano. I'll rip your thoughts out now. Talk."

Terra stepped between us, putting her hand on my back. I winced, knowing my back was cut to ribbons. I'd heal soon though. "Yeah. Start at the beginning. What are you doing?"

Trickstan snapped his eyes from my groin to Terra. "Fine. I need to remember what I know, what the key is for, and how I can save everyone, not to mention make you guys like me again. Binding Magic of this magnitude is permanent, so the only way to end it is to end my life."

Sighing, I ran my hands over my hair, missing the last hair tie I gave to Terra a little too much. "Great. You break the Binding spell, but dead people don't have memories."

"They do. They're just in Netheria with them, not here. So, I figured if Wells got Terra back from Netheria, he could get me out the same way. I could come back knowing what to do and everything would be alright."

It was hard to deny the logic in it. I pressed my lips together so hard I was certain they were turning white. He had a lot of faith in Wells, but there was no way Wells would give him his phoenix blood, not after what he'd done. "You didn't think this through, did you? One, Wells isn't here. Two, you didn't know we were following you until I snuck up here, so you would've died in the volcano with no one knowing where you were or how to get you and give you the phoenix blood, even if Wells had agreed to it. You failed."

He squared up to me. There was confidence on his face. It was a stark contrast to when we first encountered him outside of Midsummer. "No, I didn't. I remembered something on the way down."

Terra

Trickstan's chimera friend, Kiko popped in from nowhere, landing in front of Trickstan. "What have you done, Mister? When you asked for a vial of my venom I thought it was to help you with your skin care."

He patted his face, which was tight and glowing if I was honest. "It was, but not exclusively. I had to try."

She snatched the cloth bandages from them, giving them a big whiff, then glowering at Trickstan. "You tried to protect yourself from the Fire magic? Silly man. It wouldn't have worked. You could've died, but I'm guessing that was the point, am I right?" His response was to shrug at her, which made her face scrunch in anger. *I* wouldn't have wanted to be on the receiving end of that death glare.

Ren was still standing there buck-naked, looking as comfortable as he did in his clothes. I averted my eyes from his nice ass to the scratches and blood on his back as he addressed Trickstan. "We all agree it was a stupid stunt, but let's hear if it was worth it. What did you remember?"

Trickstan opened his mouth to reply, but I stopped him. Kiko wasn't affected by Ren's body. Mage knew Trickstan had checked him out more times than either of us could count. Ren was fine with it, but my face was flushing with heat. And it wasn't from embarrassment.

"Can we go somewhere to discuss this? Not out in the open?" The 'and fully clothed' part I kept in my head.

It was troubling how much his body got my attention.

Kiko bowed. "Yes, miss, of course. Follow me to my family's pods."

Trickstan took off behind Kiko. I don't know why, because I should've kept walking behind them, but I paused in step with Ren as he bent to pick up the clothes he'd left on the ground when he shifted. He stepped into his underwear first, then surprised me by looking over his shoulder and giving me the most smoldering look, I'd ever seen him make. It traveled through me like a wave of ice. "You stopped. See something you like?"

"Maybe."

Shit. Did he just flirt with me?

And more importantly, did I flirt back?

Signs point to yes.

What was I doing?

Nothing good, that was for sure.

"I mean, no. Stop messing around. We need to get the info and figure out what to do next. Fox can't be far behind us."

"Mm-hm."

I sailed past him, ignoring his throaty laugh, catching up to Kiko and asking her some bullshit questions so she'd keep my attention.

No clue what her answer was. She may as well be speaking Latin because all I heard was the sound of Ren's zipper and my loud thoughts reminding me Ren was my friend. It must have been watching him slide down the volcano thinking he was about to die. That had to have been what was making me go all weird about him.

Had to be.

We walked around to the far side of the volcano where we found a village, of sorts. There were no big structures, only small egg-shaped buildings that might hold two or three people, max. They were scattered all along the base of the volcano, backing up to a forest of blackened tree stumps. "Is this your home, Kiko?"

"Yes, miss. These pods belong to my family. Most chimeras prefer to live in the Autumnlands because they believe Fire is our fiercest element. My father feels otherwise. I'm very proud to say he designed these pods to be indestructible to Fire magic and they float when the lava flow comes this way. They're quite safe and will protect us from any wayward lava."

"I'm sure they are. Do you use them to cross the Cinders? We saw Trickstan on the Autumnlands side earlier."

"Yes, but don't tell anyone who swears to the square. We'd get in quite a lot of trouble for daring to cross the emperor's strict rules." She changed her voice, doing an impressive imitation of Magnus. "Order is important. The boundaries are there to protect you. Don't you dare not swear on the square or I'll knock you off the chair and put you in despair and not even care."

We all laughed at that as Trickstan opened the door to one of the pods. "You can trust her, Kiko. Mom's the word with her."

I shook my head. "*Mum's* the word."

"That's what I said."

"No, you didn't. Never mind. Just tell us what you remember."

We all entered the pod, which was tough. There was a long bed with pillows on both ends to accommodate two and a standing shower with a curtain that circled it on the opposite side. In the middle was a small cooktop and table surface. It reminded me of one of those tiny houses. The entire back of the pod was windows, but obviously not glass if it was meant to survive the lava. It was cute and cozy, and I wanted to ask a million questions, but Ren had perched on the bed and scooted to make room for me. Trickstan and Kiko sat on the floor in front of it.

I waved at Ren, leaning against the door frame. "I'm good here." He shot me a strange look, but Trickstan started talking so we both focused on him.

"I still don't know about the key or who put the Binding spell on me, but as I was falling down the mountain, thanks to Ren—"

"You're welcome."

"Yes, right. Anyway, a song popped into my head, *Take the Plunge.* Wells needs to listen to the song and follow the directions in it. I'm sure it'll help him with everything he needs."

"This is a memory you have?" I asked, not following the sudden jump to Wells.

Ren huffed, clearly not understanding either. "Why would someone, let's say Magnus, tell you to do something, then put a spell on you that keeps you from remembering it? Makes no sense."

Accurate.

"I'm not sure I was supposed to know about the song. There were five of us going through the Conduit that day. Each of us had a different mission and I think we were bound from knowing anything else, including the whole plan. Something happened that I can't remember, and I never saw the others on your side of the Conduit again. The mission got nailed up from the start."

Ren uttered, "Screwed up," under his breath.

I put my hand on Trickstan's shoulder, just for a second. The misery in his voice had gotten to me. He'd found himself alone in a strange place, not knowing what he was doing there until years and years later.

Just like me.

I wasn't ready to forgive him, but I was starting to see his side of things. "But now you remember the song. Why, if it wasn't your part of your mission or the plan?"

"I think I wasn't supposed to know the song, but my friend Jack who was with me told me. I can't explain it, but Jack's connected to the song, and I can feel it's meant for Wells. Just like I can feel my heart beating in my chest."

"Okay. I may have a way to get the info to Wells, but I need to know everything. Is it a song he can get on Spotify or something he could look up on the internet?"

"What do you call it when you sit in a place and hear music while the singer is singing? A consort?"

"Concert."

"Yeah. Jack is supposed to sing the song at a concert. He's a good singer." Kiko nodded her agreement. "Wells will understand what to do based on the words. He must get to Aetheria. I know I was supposed to send the golems to take the magic, but I had a secondary purpose too. You and Wells. You need to be together in Aetheria. That's all I can remember now. I know it's peanuts, but it's true."

It did sound nuts, but no worse than some of the other things we'd seen and heard. We were way past crazy and moved into the territory of Cuckoo for Cocoa Puffs.

I needed to sleep to speak with Wells. "Okay. I'll give him the message if I can get it there. Both of you need to be patched up after you tumble down a volcano. Would you mind if I let Kiko handle that while take a nap? My sleep is all messed up and I need to… I just need to sleep." I glanced at Ren. He knew why, but his face was set like he wasn't keen on going anywhere.

Kiko jumped up. "Okay miss. No problems. You can have this pod. I'll see to their injuries. When you wake up, feel free to eat or drink what you find here, or come and look for me at the pod farthest from the volcano and I'll get you everything you need. Shoo, shoo, Misters, out you go. Good night, Miss."

I liked that chimera.

She *was* nice and had no problems handling Trickstan, but mostly because she was ushering Ren out of the pod. I couldn't face him. Not with the swirling emotion about him that seemed to come out of nowhere. And not since I was starting to get jittery about seeing Wells in the dreamscape soon.

I shucked my shoes and dove for one end of the bed. I was hoping I'd fall right asleep, but that didn't happen.

Not even squeezing and releasing my muscles or counting sheep worked. I tossed and turned for an hour until I got up and started pacing, hoping something would spring to my mind to make me fall asleep.

I had too much on my mind. It was flip-flopping between mystery songs, pondering Trickstan's betrayal, and two different werewolves, neither of whom I could live without.

The knock on the door wasn't asking for permission. It was announcing that he was coming in. That was Ren for you. He closed the door behind him and pointed to the bed, saying nothing. When I didn't immediately move, he brushed past me and perched on the bed instead. "Come here."

Never in my life had I wanted to move and not move at the same time. "I don't think we—"

"No. Thinking is the fucking problem, Terra. Come. Here."

I took a tentative step in his direction, but my feet didn't seem to want to stop. Before I knew it I was standing right in front of him and looking into his shining emerald eyes. His hands were on my waist, and I'd be Magedamned if I didn't resist when he pulled me down, forcing me to straddle his lap. "What are you doing?"

"I'm tired of waiting, so I'm making the moment happen."

I swallowed down the horde of bees that seemed to be flitting in my throat somehow. Everything inside me was buzzing. "What moment?"

"Stop pretending. I see you. And I know you want to…" He crushed his lips against mine and the rest of his sentence was left unspoken.

He didn't have to say it though. I knew what he meant. I *had* been pretending. Pretending not to rely on him to get me through being apart from Wells, lying to myself about being attracted to him on some level. Pretending not to notice how he looked at me sometimes.

There *was* something there between us. Whether it was based on circumstance or something more, I couldn't say. I couldn't process any of the feelings thundering through me.

I just *felt*.

He was always blunt, and candid, said what he thought with no apologies or regret, but his kiss was unexpectedly tender. The way he moved his mouth against mine was slow, deliberate, haunting. Like he was trying to whisper his way into my heart.

And I let him in, raking my hands through the long strands of his hair, thanking the Mage he was wearing it down all the time now. He moaned at the feel of it, and I gasped against his mouth, surprised at the lump forming in my throat as he deepened the kiss, stroking his tongue along the seam of my mouth.

When his hands slid from my waist over my ass, I was hit with the smell of the outdoors and sunshine and freshness. I recognized it as him now. His troll-fused blood gave off an intoxicating scent when he was turned on. He pulled me closer, and I felt the evidence of that arousal between my legs.

Oh, my Mage. That was Ren's hard dick. And I had made it that way.

Something in me cracked.

And the slow, dripping wrongness seeped through me.

Kissing him was great, but it wasn't the right kind of great. It was the kind of great you settled for before you found the *real* person you wanted to kiss. Maybe for the rest of your life.

I already had that person.

It wasn't Ren.

My senses dulled. Or maybe they were dull to start with and that's how I ended up kissing him and tasting the forbidden sweetness of his lips. I had to stop it, wanted to stop it, but to do so would break his heart, so I let him continue, just a few more seconds. For him. For me too. For the two of us that might have been if the Conduit stayed closed forever.

But we were going to open it again.

When I pulled back from him, I rested my hands on my thighs so I couldn't—wouldn't—touch him. Then everything I felt spilled out of me like a dam had broken. "I'm sorry. I don't know what I was thinking a few minutes ago, but I can't do this. Kissing you was heart-stopping, but you know I…have feelings for Wells." The lump in my throat. This is where it came from. My body knew before my heart or mind.

He grabbed my face, turning my head up so I was looking into his eyes. They were hard. Unbelieving. "But you want me, I feel it."

"Yeah. No. Maybe?" I took a deep breath as I moved his hands from my face. I wanted to explain it to him, so he'd understand and still be my friend. Somewhere inside me though, wondered if that ship had sailed when I didn't stop him immediately. "Look, I love you, Ren. So much, but I can't let this thing with us, whatever it truly is, hurt Wells.

I choked down a sob. "When I think about being without him, I can't function. It consumes me. It's not fair to do this to you, I know that. Not when my endgame is Wells. I'm sorry. I'm so, so sorry I let myself be swept up in you. The last thing I want to do is—"

"Stop. Don't fucking finish that sentence."

I realized I was still straddling his lap, so I jumped up and put my hands on his shoulders, feeling like the biggest Dickhole in Aetheria. "It was wrong to give in to my curiosity and need for Wells by kissing you and I'll never forgive myself, especially if it ruins our friendship."

He laughed. In it was the sound of defeat, the sound of finality. It ate at my soul like a demon possessed. "We're past friendship. You might not see it, but I do. And there's no going back from the line we just fucking crossed. Remember this, Beautiful. I didn't cross it by myself." He stood, brushing past me on his way to the door.

I grabbed his arm, swinging him back to face me. "You're too important to me to lose, so like it or not, Trollboy, we're going to work through this and get back to where we were. I'm not losing you."

"But I've already lost you."

The walls going into the dreamscape seemed to close in as I ambled down the spiral staircase. It was like the tunnel was pushing in on all sides and getting fucking uncomfortable. I'd asked Annigan what the strange dreamscape staircase had been, and they said it was a construct of my mind and I'd have to interpret it myself. What-the-fuck-ever. Didn't care as long as the spiraling stairs took me to Terra.

This time as I emerged, she was already sitting in a huge expanse of trees with turquoise leaves and white bark. It seemed familiar, but I couldn't place it. "Where are we?"

"The garden at the emperor's castle. I guess I fell asleep and got here first. I was thinking about these trees when I first arrived here. I must have conjured them up, though I wasn't trying. I prefer it when we meet at Boulderbrook. Even though my head knows it's the dreamscape version, my heart feels like it's my true home."

Not her Gram's house or her birthplace. My home was her home. I felt that on a soul level, so I closed my eyes and when I opened them she was sitting on my bed. "You mean like this?"

"Exactly. Come sit. I have things to tell you." Her normally expressive eyes were devoid of emotion and a somberness clung to her body as she twisted her hands in her lap. Something was wrong, which sucked considering what I was about to tell her was awful as fuck.

I couldn't do that until I made those juicy lips smile again, so I crossed the room in two strides and took her face in my hands. The rich scent of her overwhelmed me as I pressed my lips to hers, capturing a much-needed kiss that she gave me freely. When I pulled back, she sighed in a way that spoke directly to whatever magic made my heart pump blood and fire in my veins. I could barely speak the words, knowing how they might ruin us. "I have something to tell you too."

Perching on the bed, I twisted to face her. We stared at each other for a few moments, her chewing her bottom lip and me rubbing my jaw until I knew the skin was reddening. I'd accepted this would be hard, but I had no idea how much. We each took a deep breath, then blurted out at the same time, "You first."

It eased some of the tension. She scooted closer and I took her hand, lacing our fingers together and getting momentarily lost in the familiarity of it. I kissed her temple. "Ladies first."

"Okay. I have two things. First, please let me get to the end of this before you explode." She paused long enough for me to nod. My muscles tensed as I tried to control my reaction to whatever this was. "We've found Trickstan. He recalled something he swears could help us all. He's under a powerful Binding spell that he's trying to beat. I think he may be telling the truth and the answers to everything are in his mind. What I'm about to tell you will make no sense, but you have to do it anyway."

I'd agreed not to explode, but everything in me wanted to punch something. Not her, of course, but a substitute for that damn fairy who'd betrayed us. I took some breaths to even myself as I clenched and unclenched my fists and my abs. My asshole. "And you believe him, just like that? You want me to do what he says?"

"Not at first, but yeah, I do now. Even if you don't believe him, if you did this, it would be a test, of sorts. If it doesn't play out, we know he's either wrong or lying."

Trying to relax, I reached out, lifting her chin and grazing my thumb along her jaw. "I'm game to try anything that brings us back together in reality. What do you want me to do?"

"Trickstan said he had a friend named Jack that was supposed to come with him to our world. He doesn't know if he made it, but if he did, his mission was to make sure you listen to a certain song called 'Take the Plunge' at a concert of some kind. You're supposed to follow the lyrics and it'll get you to Aetheria. He didn't know where to find the song or Jack. I figure if you hear it and it makes some kind of sense to you, then we know Trickstan's onto something."

There was an earnest questioning in her expression. She believed and wanted me to do the same. I wasn't sure I could, but I could damn well do a Google search for the song at least. "I'll give it a shot, but don't expect me to trust the fairy again."

"Fair enough. I'm not sure I do either. There's just been so much going on here and I'm tired, Wells." She closed her eyes. "My defenses are weak, and I keep thinking and rethinking and overthinking until I'm turned upside down. I need something to ground me."

I reached out, untucking the vial of Aetherian earth around her neck that signified her birthplace. She hadn't taken it off. I knew it reminded her of Gram. "This isn't working?"

"Don't you realize you're what grounds me now? I still have so much to tell you, but right now, I need you. More than anything. Please."

I pulled her to me and let her rest her head on my chest as I stroked her hair. "You never have to ask, Precious. Whatever you want from me, take it. It's yours."

When she looked up, her eyes were brimming with tears. It knocked my ass for a loop, and I abandoned all thoughts of what I had to tell her about kissing Autumn. All I wanted was to ease her troubled expression and to drown the unquenchable thirst I had for her in the process.

Wasting no more time, I dove for her mouth, kissing her with a fire that burst from me whose only match was the feeling I got when I released my inner wolf. It was raw and greedy, and I knew she would take every bit of me, that she loved every bit of me. Even if she had yet to form those exact words.

I didn't want them in the dreamscape anyway. This wasn't real, despite the feel of it. This was the substitute for what we would have when we were back together, and it would have to do.

She groaned into my mouth, then we tangled together as we worked to rip the clothes from each other as fast as we could. It resulted in a lot of grunting and heaving and at one point I accidentally bit her lip. Hard. She responded by pushing me down on the bed.

The sheets were cool to my back, in stark contrast to the warmth of her skin as she climbed on top of me. I couldn't stop myself from reaching out and tracing her already-hardened nipples with my thumbs.

"If I'd known how much you liked that, I would've used my teeth more creatively before now."

She laughed, taking my lower lip and biting enough to break the tender skin. My cock damn near speared her as the taste of blood on the tip of my tongue washed between our kisses.

Fuck yes, I didn't know where it was coming from, but I was going to enjoy the experience of feral Terra.

I must've lost my mind.

Nope. I'd lost my inhibitions.

I was a woman consumed with a need for the man I…

Without a doubt.

…loved.

I'd known it all along, but I'd resisted admitting—even to myself—that I was in love with Wells, but I'd been stupid. It wasn't about how much of him was in my heart. It was about how much of me was in his. The abrupt shift in thinking woke something in me: a profound sense of self that comes from knowing your heart, mind, body, and soul are all safe.

He was my haven.

I was his.

I wasn't going to tell him in the dreamscape though. That was something best saved for an in-person experience. It needed to be real. Though the hardness he was pressing between my legs as I kissed my way to his vulnerable throat felt as real as all the other times we'd been together. His body, his touch, and the way he devoured my mouth was pulling me in and I was no longer concerned about doing or saying the right thing. I wasn't going to fight this side of me, I was going to let it out like a phoenix being reborn and taking flight.

Cage the Mage, I wanted him. And I think kissing Ren had been the catalyst. It was going to suck to have to explain things to him, but that would come later. "I need you to fuck me, Wells."

Never in my life had I considered uttering this phrase aloud, but there I was grinding against him and begging. He growled, lifting his hips as I nipped at his Adam's apple. "I'm about to do just that, Precious, and I'm not going to stop until you're panting and needing ice for your swollen sore pussy. Is that what you want?"

I raised so I could watch his eyes flash fuchsia. "Yes, please."

His smirk went straight to the most female parts of me and held them captive. "Then you better get ready and hold the fuck on."

Before I could react, he put his hands on my back and flipped us over, bringing the comforter and sheets with us. I couldn't help but notice they weren't the bland cream ones that Autumn had gotten him, but silky, deep purple ones. I didn't know if they were dreamscape-induced or if he'd gotten more, but I didn't care because he'd taken my undies in one hand and jerked them off my body as he plunged his tongue into my mouth to ease the discomfort of the fabric as it ripped into pieces.

Such a considerate act.

It was a strange time to think it, but Wells was very sweet.

This was not about to be sweet sex, however.

I tugged at the waist of his jeans, and he helped me to pull them mostly down. I don't know how he did it, but he managed to squirm out of them completely and press his cock against my core at the same time. All I could do was close my eyes and feel it all.

The man had some skill, that was for certain.

Nine, point nine, nine on the mount, Jim. We'll see if he can match that with his dismount coming up.

"Eyes on me. I want to watch you when I give you what you need."

My eyes popped open, then practically bulged out of my head as he thrust inside me. There was no warning, no warm-up to get me ready, no apologies. Just sheer and utter drive and that's how I wanted it. "Fuck."

I'm not even sure who said it. Maybe both of us. I'd tried to use our phoenix blood mind link to communicate how much I enjoyed the feel of him taking me like that, but it didn't seem to work. He knew anyway. "I've never felt anyone this wet before."

Gripping his ass, I pulled him to me, forcing him to go even further inside. "I've never wanted anyone this much before."

Those were the truest words ever truthed.

Not satisfied it was enough, he shifted, rolling his hips up and pressing his pelvic bone against me. The result was him hitting that sweet spot that made my head spin and my mouth betray me. "Yeah, that's it. Mage, I think I'm going to pass out."

"Not yet. I'm just getting started." To prove his point, he grabbed my left leg, hiking over his hip and giving me a new sensation as he propelled his cock into me over and over at wolf speed. Just when I thought it was going to be the death of me, his hand went between my legs, and he used that same speed to play with my clit.

I swear I vibrated.

Throwing my head back, I raised my hips as best I could to meet him. A feral sound ripped from his throat, and I matched it.

This was beyond sex, way past pleasure. It was transcendent.

I ran my hands down his immaculate chest, letting the smattering of chest hair tickle my fingers until I reached his glistening abs. The sweat decorating his body made it easy for my palms to glide as they explored every ridge and hard muscle, each inch of his taut skin as it flexed and contracted with his gyrations. "I love the feel of you." Leaning up—Mage only knew how—I licked between his pecks, savoring the salty sweetness of his skin. "I love the taste of you."

"Fuck." He pulled out of me long enough to grab both legs and lift them, so my ankles rested on his wide shoulders, then I cried out as he shoved into me again. The angle was even deeper, and I almost lost my mind at the sound of our skin slapping together. "Keep talking."

Eager to do what he wanted, I closed my eyes and focused on him, not just the feel and taste, but all my senses. It was easy to tell him how he affected me. "I go to sleep remembering the sound of your growl, the one you save for me alone. And sometimes when I'm thinking about you, I swear I can smell you in the air. Smoky sandalwood sweetness that makes me ache for you."

He growled again and when he threw his head back, I marveled at how beautiful he truly was. My orgasm came quickly and violently, bolting through me as I screamed his name.

"Magedamn, I love feeling you clench when you come." Once again, he switched his timing, rolling into me and reaching every millimeter of my pussy until I was he was quaking right alongside me. He gripped my ass, pulling me closer as I grabbed the ropy muscles of his arms and held on as we grunted, riding out the storm of feeling and emotion.

When we were both spent and panting, he kissed each of my ankles and then helped me lower my quivering legs. He fell beside me and wrapped us in the twisted sheets as our breathing returned to normal.

Ish.

A perfect ten on the dismount, Jim. Check the record books. This must be a Sexlympic record.

I couldn't stop staring at her. The way the sheets draped over her body, revealing patches of her skin was—this is a word most alpha wolves would not throw out *ever*—sublime. She did that to me: made me want to make me write poetry and sing love ballads at the top of my lungs.

Maybe I would when we were together again.

However, the reality I so desperately craved with her was about to come crashing in and ruin our perfect unison.

I had to tell her about Autumn.

She turned toward me, bringing half the sheets with her. "That was next level, but we need to talk."

The curve of her hip was peeking between the sheets, so I ran my hand over it just so I could feel her. "You first."

She absent-mindedly ran her index finger up and down my chest as she spoke. "No, I went first before. You go."

I didn't want to shatter the perfect peace and I sensed she didn't either. We lay there touching each other, neither one of us speaking. It seemed like we lived a whole lifetime in the moments before we both blurted out what we had to say at the same time.

"I kissed Autumn." "I kissed Ren."

She said something after it, but my brain didn't register it. I was too busy jumping off the bed and bellowing "What?" over and over.

All thoughts of my temporary betrayal kiss with Autumn? They didn't just go out the window, they went out of the camp, the city, the country, fucking outer space.

Surely I'd misheard her. We were both talking at the same time, right? She couldn't have said what I thought. I had to confirm my need for a hearing aid. "You kissed Ren? My best friend, my damned brother. He kissed you? The fuck?"

"Let me explain." In my experience, anytime a person uttered those words, the explanation would never be good enough.

I paced as ran my hands through my hair, trying to process. It made no sense. Why would she? Why would *he*?

Feeling her cool hands on my back, I stopped. She ran around and took my face. She was still wrapped in those purple sheets, like a damned Greek goddess in a toga, but my bedroom had disappeared, and the dreamscape had morphed into the field where the Conduit had led us in Aetheria. The spot where we were separated.

"Wells, give me the courtesy of listening to what I have to say."

Her big, beautiful eyes were boring holes in me. I needed her to fix this gaping ugly scar that had sliced through my heart at her words, so I nodded for her to attempt to explain this away.

"I won't lie to you, now or ever, so I'll admit when he kissed me, a tiny part of me reciprocated. I was curious, lonely, and frustrated about being apart from you, and I just wanted some comfort.

"He's been there for me this whole time and we've shared so much, so I was weak, and I gave in to make myself feel better. I'm going to do my best to earn his forgiveness for not taking it seriously. I didn't mean it, but I know now I was toying with the true feelings he has for me. To me, he was and still is my good friend."

Ren has always kept his deepest thoughts in his head. I figured it was a product of his upbringing. Sure, he'd share things with Gideon, Mace, and me, but since I'd known him, he'd kept his emotions mostly on lockdown.

He'd had plenty of women in his bed, but never had a steady relationship outside of Kelsey, which we all knew was about fucking now and then, nothing else.

I never stopped to think about it. None of us—when we were betas and beyond the fusion—had ever had a long-term relationship, outside of Mace and his was complicated as fuck and over before he wanted it to be.

But Ren was harboring feelings for *my* girl.

As angry as I was about it, I understood it. How could anyone not love her?

How could anyone not love *him*?

He was a damned good friend. Loyal and brutally honest, and though he'd hate it if he knew anyone saw him this way, there was a vulnerability to him that made people want to get close, to protect him like Bash did when they were kids. Ren had a big heart under his rough and tough exterior, one he rarely let anyone see. His charm was his refusal to be charming.

"Wells, please say something."

Right. I needed to respond to this news verbally, not just mucking it around in my brain.

"Do you have feelings for him?" My voice was shaky. Some fucking alpha I was. My emotions were getting away from me. Ironic that I wished to be more like Ren at the moment.

"I won't say the kiss meant nothing, especially because I know it did to him, but believe me when I say this: there is and will never be anything romantic between Ren and me. You may rely on it. I love him, but I'm not in love with him. Even if you broke up with me right now, I'd never be with him or love him like I…"

All the breath rushed from my lungs.

She almost said it. I *knew* she felt it, but I wanted her to admit it to me, to herself—to the fucking universe and beyond—that she loved me.

The anger in me evaporated like a puff of smoke in the wind. It would take some time to wrap my head around Ren, but looking into her eyes, I didn't give any shits about one kiss. Not when I had so much more of her. "Love him like you what?"

Was I goading her? Yep, sure was.

Didn't care.

She chewed her lower lip for a few seconds before she finally responded. "Like I know he wants."

"Ah, Okay."

She slapped my chest. "Stop smirking. You're not mad?"

"I can't say it was my favorite thing to ever come out of those delicious lips of yours, but I'm certain enough of us and our relationship to let it go if you say it was nothing. A heads-up though, I might punch Ren when I see him again, but you're good Precious." I leaned down and took that lower lip in my teeth before kissing her good enough to erase any traces of Ren's mouth on hers.

When I pulled back, she sighed. Out of relief or pleasure, I wasn't sure. Maybe both. Seconds later, she laid into me. "You kissed Autumn? I thought you declared you never would cross that line. What happened because I need to make it clear to you and her and to anyone who might cross your path in the future: you're mine."

Magedamn, there was the feral cat I fell in love with. I wanted to fuck her again. We were running out of time in the dreamscape though.

"I'm yours. Got it. There's more to this though. Let me explain."

Yeah, I heard it myself. *Let me explain.*

She put her hands on her hips as I tried to get it all out in one breath. "You know the mate bond makes me want to be with her, but I'd been doing a good job of keeping her at arm's length. We've had some issues at Boulderbook with the magic crapping out in annoying and unpredictable ways, so she was in my cabin—*while I wasn't there*— and when I came home, she'd taken the ruby necklace from my drawer and was putting it on."

I paused just so I could focus on her face as it scrunched in anger. I wouldn't tell her this, but she was so damned cute when she was mad. "She said she'd heard the jewels whispering to her and she went over to investigate. The ruby was too irresistible, so she put it on. We both tried to get it off, but it won't budge. Just like your bracelet." I took her hand and kissed her palm as she examined her bracelet.

"So, she has one of my Gram's jewels forever now? Great. I'm sure it looks *fantastic* with her hair."

Her sarcasm game was one of my favorite things about her.

"Diggs has dug up—pun intended—some old gnome rumors about a set of jewels going missing from the first Winter Queen's court a long time ago. He's trying to get more info, but neither of us has a lot of time to spend on it.

"She's trying to use the ruby to stir the Conduit open or do other things, but so far it doesn't do much but warm up and enhance her Fire magic a little bit."

I kissed her other palm, so she'd know I didn't give a fuck about Autumn personally. I was interested in the jewels. "I think we should consider why she thought the ruby was speaking to her specifically. I haven't heard a peep out of it since I found them in that tree."

"Well, duh. The ruby would look awful on you. Red is not your color."

Welcome back, cock. Good to see you're paying attention.

She glanced down, probably to bring my manhood back into the conversation herself. Pressing her lips together so the drool would stay in her mouth, she shrugged. "I guess the necklace is a good enough second prize since I get the grand one."

I stepped toward her, ready to give her the grandest prize I could deliver when the ground opened up between us. It was too late to get another round of hot and sweaty sex in. We were being ripped from the dreamscape. It was going to hurt like a bitch.

She yelped as she fell through the hole. I reached out, but she slipped from my hands, and I fell in after her, though she was nowhere to be seen. Flames began to lick the sides of the hole. My face flushed from the heat, but I knew it wouldn't hurt me. This was just like being ripped out before. I was plummeting into a bottomless, flame-fueled pit.

It seemed eternal.

As soon as I had the thought, the flames around me reacted, turning from orange to gold to white as if they were calling my name. My feet hit a hard surface and I found myself in the middle of the spiral staircase with ornate gold scrollwork again.

This was new.

I peered up and down, but I couldn't see where either way led. When I heard my name again, it was louder than a whisper. I didn't know who it was, but I wasn't going to let it get to me. "What do you want?"

The steps retracted and my feet slid down the smooth surface left there. I tried to grip the rails, but it did no good. I just slid down until I was engulfed in darkness, and I heard the voice declare, "You."

F*ailure is a good thing, Renfield. It's how you build resilience.*

Fuck that noise, *"Mom."*

I wasn't resilient. I didn't want to move on from the failed attempt at romance, but I knew I had no choice. I'd built that reality up so much in my head and when it happened, I wasn't prepared for it to end. Now I had the shadow of a memory to take with me the rest of my life because I wasn't going to get another kiss.

I should've known.

I *did* know.

Not even a barrier between the two worlds could keep Terra and Wells apart. And the shit of it was, I was happy they had each other.

I don't know what the fuck that said about me. Probably I'd been twisted my whole life, conditioned to watch others thrive while I skulked in the shadows like the vampire our parents so longed for us to be.

Messed up.

The situation. And me.

And now I'd have to live with acting too soon. I'd ruined one of the most important relationships in my life by sticking my prick into it. I had no idea how I would face her again.

Someone tapped my shoulder. "A pen for your thoughts." Even though there was no room, Trickstan plonked down next to me on the pod steps and shoved an old-fashioned—at least in our world— quill pen at me.

"The phrase is a penny for your thoughts. What the fuck am I supposed to do with a pen?"

"Oh. I thought it was a pen for your thoughts so you could write down what was troubling you and it would make you feel better. That's what I've been doing since I got back here." I threw the pen like a dart, watching it arc, then hit the dirt upright.

I hated it when he made sense with his incorrect phrases.

"What have you written down? A list of the people you betrayed and the shitty things you did to them?"

He frowned, actually looking remorseful. "Not exactly, but I know what I did. Now anyway. I'm trying to make up for it, but you have to understand, I was bound by the spell."

Fuck him and his logic. I still wanted to hate him, especially with the rage churning in my heart—rage I directed inward—but I couldn't. I'd been bound by Mateo at one point, we all had. It was horrific to want to say something and not be physically able to spit the words out.

I didn't tell a soul, but when Wells gave me the okay to tell Terra about my fused troll blood, I puked for hours afterward and had headaches for days on end. The spell Mateo used wasn't that strong because he thought, as our alpha, he had us on lock anyway. Only Wells and his phoenix blood had been strong enough to break completely free of it.

If Trickstan's spell was even half the strength of the one Mateo put on Wells when he realized he was falling for Terra, the fact that he remembered anything was, to use a human word, a miracle.

Magicals didn't believe in miracles. We believed in the four tenets of heart, mind, body, and soul. In that moment as Trickstan blinked at me with those crystal blue eyes, my heart softened. Just a bit.

"The question is, would you do it again? If faced with the same situation, would you betray us to do whatever your mission was in our realm?"

He thought about it for a minute. "What I have in my head is important. I know I scotched part of it, but if I can fix it, everything will be better for all of us. So yep, I think I would do it again, but this time I'd find a way to remember everything."

"I'd give good money for a scotch right now, but it's botch, not scotch."

"I could make some fae froth."

"No." That would be the very last thing I needed now: something to make me remember the pain and humiliation, the look on Terra's face when she pulled away from our hot kiss.

He stood up and offered me his hand, which I took. "This is my official apology." He shook once, then pulled me off the steps. "I don't what happened between you and Babycakes, but whatever it is, she'll forgive you, just like she'll forgive me. Her heart is big and she's not stingy."

"Stingy."

"That's what I said."

"No, you said sting-y, like a bee. The word is stingy, which means someone wants to keep everything to themselves. You're right, Terra's heart is huge."

Huge enough to fit in a brooding alpha wolf and his whole pack, along with a wayward horny fairy, and Mage knows who else. It's what I loved about her.

That fucking word.

I needed to get rid of the idea that I loved her. Just, push it out of my heart and replace it with stone. I had to find the hardness I used to feel when Bash and I escaped the foster home. Cold, calculating, unfeeling. Make a plan, follow the plan, succeed, rinse, repeat.

I needed to become a vampire.

But first, I would be a wolf.

I shucked my shirt, throwing it at Trickstan. He cocked an eyebrow before I said, "Don't go there. I need to run for a few, shake the cobwebs off of my wolf. When I get back, I want to go over everything you remember and everything you know. No detail is too small. Get it all ready and get Terra up too. Tell her it's time to get down to business."

I was going to help him do what he wanted, what we all wanted. I was going to get the magic back and deliver Terra into Wells' open arms. Then I was going to come back to Aetheria, or maybe find a cabin in some remote woods in our world where I could forget I had a heart altogether.

The run did me some good. It didn't shake everything off, but it reminded me I was a feral creature, born to rip apart anyone who threatened me or mine. I'd enjoyed being with Terra, alone, but a part of me would always long for my pack. Which would suck after I went off alone, but Bash could teach me the ways of the lone wolf and my brother would follow me to the ends of the earth, or Aetheria, wherever I went. I could only imagine how he was coping with me being gone.

Lone wolves still needed family.

Wait, I knew exactly how he was coping. It was doing it from the bottom of a bottle. Whiskey, bourbon, scotch, gin. Whatever he could get his hands on. I knew Wells, Mace, and Gideon wouldn't let him spiral out of control, but at the same time, I knew what happened to us as children and how it fucked with his head.

I needed to get back to him.

No more fucking around with feelings or situations I couldn't control.

I dodged between the last outcropping of colorful trees, making my way into the open area at the base of the volcano where Kiko's pods were placed with the Cinders simmering behind them. Searching around for my clothes, I came up empty, so I darted behind the pod with the open door where Trickstan and I had been earlier, meaning to peep in the window before I shifted back into my human form. Or at least, go into one of the vacant pods and grab a towel.

As soon as I rounded the corner, my fur ruffled. There was a person in all black, head to toe, peeking in the window.

I didn't think, I acted, lunging for them and sinking my teeth into their leg. I got a mouthful of fabric at first, but I held on and managed to get flesh in no time, savoring the coppery taste of a job completed. Growling, I pulled the screeching person—female from the sound of her screams—around to the front of the pod, gathering soot and dirt, until we were at the entrance.

Kiko popped into existence mere feet away from us. Trickstan and Terra were both wide-eyed as they raced out of the door. I spat out the intruder's leg as Terra pulled off her hood and gasped. "Jael? What the fuck?"

It had been five days since I'd been ripped from the dreamscape. I'd done two more blood lettings with Fitz and successfully avoided Autumn by spending time in Illusion Hill with Lore as we assessed the damage the lack of magic was having on the town. We even called in Theo, the new alpha of the bear sleuth near Boulderbrook to help take out the wendigos Liam had located. He was going to be a great help with security and control since Ren wasn't around to take charge of that.

Ren.

I wanted to say I was over *the kiss*, especially since I'd told Terra I was cool with it, but if I was honest, I still got a stone in my gut when I thought about him acting on his feelings for *my* girl. As I lay around at night—not sleeping, therefore not connecting with her in the dreamscape—all I could do was wonder if he'd acted on his urges because he was in Aetheria and had no other options or if he would've done it right under my nose if they'd been at Boulderbrook.

It made me want to tear his throat out.

Then I wanted to throw my arms around him and pat him on the back for taking care of her so well.

Fucking complicated.

Just like the mate bond with Autumn.

My life was a tangle of emotional threads that were tightening around my neck like a noose.

The phone rang and I double-checked that my office door was locked one more time before I answered. "Mace, how's it going? Has it started yet?"

There was a lot of noise on Mace's end, which made sense for a person standing in a bar. Bash had sobered up enough to fly him to Columbia for the Joseph H. Mann show. It was a long shot, but they were willing, and I was desperate. "About that. Seems there's been a last-minute substitution. Our rockstar has pulled an Elvis and left the building without singing. The emcee just said someone called Jack Ripper is filling in."

I stood up so fast that my new desk chair went flying behind me, slamming against the open window and tumbling outside.

Order a new desk chair.

"You're sure? The person singing is named Jack. That's the name Terra told me would sing a song I was supposed to follow."

We'd tried to locate this song in every place we could think of but hadn't found it yet. The fact that it might be something Mace ran into only because we were following up on a weird hunch, was more than a coincidence. It sent chills up my spine.

"Yep, I'm sure. He's about to start. Bash is here—" His voice got muffled and I heard him bellowing to someone near him. "Get that fucking drink out of your hand. Water only. I'm not flying home with a drunk pilot. Anyway, Bash will record the whole show and I'll stay on the line so you can listen in real-time."

I turned the volume up as loud as it could go and put it on speaker so I could pace while I listened. At first, all I heard were Mace and Bash arguing, chattering bar sounds, and clinking glasses, but in a matter of minutes, the crowd erupted in applause.

"Good evening, I'm Jack Ripper, filling in for Joseph H. Mann tonight. He's trapped in a magical underground fortress getting blown by a nymph as we speak." The crowd went silent, unsure what to make of the guy's weird joke. "I'm kidding, of course, he has the flu. So, let's get started. First up, I song I wrote a long, long, long time ago. It's based on the advice I'd been given throughout my life. I hope you can find something in here that will help you get where you want to go."

This was it. I didn't know how the fuck everything was lining up, but I didn't give a Magedamn. I grabbed the magical pen Mateo had left. It was made with Etching magic. I said the proper spell over it and set it down on the pad, waiting for it to scrawl the words Jack would sing.

It was all about her right from the start.
That's why it's time to just follow your heart.
To places unknown and places unseen,
To the places we've made inside of our dreams.

The door has been closed but the window lies open,
The path you're searching for is more than just hopin'.
It's the journey we take, not the destination,
It's the price of admission you give without hesitation.

It's time to take the plunge,
Time to drain yourself dry,

The time's past for running, you need to fly.
To throw yourself in with no looking back,
To follow your heart to find the right track,
It's time to take the plunge.

The dreams are so real and the danger is high
If you don't come together, you might even die,
The magic you shared will wither in the sun
If you lose one another, the damage is done.

It's time to take the plunge,
Jump into your task with both feet planted firm,
The fire you give up will be worth the burn,
There's more to this life than you could believe,
If you don't act now, your heart can't be retrieved.
Trust me now. Take the plunge.
Take the plunge.
Take the plunge.
Set the fire with your heart.
Make the path with your blood,
You'll protect what is yours
As you make your word good,
Take the plunge.
Now's the time,
Lives are on the line,
It'll all be fine if you take the plunge.

"Those are the worst lyrics I've ever heard in my life. The crowd is going insane like they liked that nonsense. It's unbelievable!" I was staring at the paper, not even listening to Mace ramble about the song we'd just heard.

The lyrics might not have won him any Grammys, but the meaning in them was crystal clear to me as I read through them again and again. I shouted to Mace that I'd see them when they got back, then hung up. My hand was shaking as I punched the contact I needed to reach. It rang once. "Yeah?"

"Fitz. Meet me at the garage right now. We're doing the final ritual tonight."

I hadn't even considered Jael in the time we'd been in Aetheria. I knew she'd gone through the Conduit before us the day the giant golems came, but she wasn't important enough for us to bother with, not when we had Trickstan to find and an emperor to dethrone. "Again, I say, what the fuck? Why are you here spying on us?"

"I swear on the square."

It was the same response she'd given me the last three times I asked. And for the fourth time, Ren punched her. Blood spewed from her mouth as she hit the ground. "We're not going to get anywhere with her. Her head's too far up her square asshole."

He wasn't wrong. "Yeah, but there has to be a reason why she showed up now. And how did she find us anyway? There's something fishy here."

Ren snorted at my unintended pun. She was a siren, a sea creature. As odd as it was, it gave me a little breath of hope that he sounded so normal. We felt like us again. Then he turned his head so I couldn't catch his eye and I knew I had my work cut out for me. It would take a lot of time for us to be anywhere near normal.

Trickstan waved Bex and Louie over. They'd gone to get food and had come back carrying sacks full. "Bex, can you guard her while we discuss our plans privately?"

Bex nodded once, then pulled Jael up by her hair—yowch—and dragged her away with one hand while she gripped two sacks in the other. The rest of us piled into one of the pods. Trickstan had his notebook open, and a map of the central province laid out on a table. He wasted no time in telling us his plan. "Magnus is looking for me, so I say you take me in right before the Spring Frolic. Kiko, Bex, and Louie can set up ahead of time and we strike then."

Ren rubbed his temples. "Attack how? Do you really think a handful of Magicals can take out the most powerful Magical born, during a public ceremony he is running? You know nothing about launching an attack strike."

"Maybe not, but I know you and Terra are two of the bad-assiest Magicals there are, and I have enough faith in you and my friends to put my life on the line. And I remembered something important when I saw Jael. Want to hear it?"

"We wanted to hear it the second you thought of it, Dimwit. What is it?"

"I was thinking what a two-faced person she was, then I remembered that I had two people put Binding magic on me. Powerful spells, but two different ones. I didn't remember my mission because it was overwritten in my mind. I don't know who did what, but I think I'll start remembering more now. I'm sure I will."

It made sense. If two different people, with potentially opposing missions, gave him Binding magic, it would explain why he can only remember bits and pieces. And it would imply that he wasn't just some random fae I happened to capture one day. It was something set in motion before we knew him.

The whisper came back, like a sudden breeze blowing through the trees. It had become a strange comfort to me on some level. I knew it was saying the truth when it spoke, even if I had no clue who it was or where it came from. Some might say I was dumb to listen to it, but since my heart was feeling hurt over what had happened with Ren, listening to the whisper in my head gave me a sense of relief, in a way. "The key is to take him out when he's not there. Tell Trickstan and he'll understand."

"The whispering voice says you'll understand this: The key to taking him out is to do it when he's not there." I paused. "I hope you get that because I sure don't."

He shook his head. "No, I don't. Sorry."

"Okay, rando disembodied voice. Time to reveal yourself and stop playing games with me. Who are you and what is your goal? I don't know if you realize this, but there are big things—life-dependent things—at stake here. Give me something."

I got nothing from the whisper.

Ren's eyebrow shot up, waiting for confirmation that the voice said something. I shook my head no and he replied, "Concentrate and ask again, huh?"

"Exactly. So, what do we do now? Does Trickstan's plan have any shot of working?"

"Maybe. If you and I haul him back and give him over to the emperor, we'll lose control of what happens to him. He'll take him away and we'll never see him again. Even if he figures out the emperor's big secret flaw in time, he won't be able to communicate it with us, so we'll be blind. Assuming we put Kiko, Bex, and Louie in the crowd for backup that night, we don't have a way to strike. We have a goal and no way to execute it until we know that secret."

Kiko sat up suddenly. "Something's wrong with Bex, Mister." She poofed away and the rest of us shot out of the pod toward Bex and Jael. When we got there, Jael was looking up with terror in her eyes and dirt all over her. "Where am I? How did I get here? Terra? Ren? What's going on?"

Bex dusted off her hands, having been the one to throw Earth magic at her. "She woke up and started shooting Water magic at me, which I countered, covering her in dirt up to her neck. She didn't like that, so she fought her way out and came after me, trying to use her siren magic, which I dodged. Now she's either lying or something is going on with her memory too. She doesn't know where she is or how she got here."

"Well, that doesn't matter, does it? We can take her in with Trickstan and his crew at the same time." We all swung around and found Fox ambling in like he'd been on a Sunday afternoon stroll in the park. He shoved half of a sandwich in his mouth and smiled. "I've been looking for you two, but well done on finding our traitor. We've got one day to prep for the Frolic. Emperor Magnus should be happy to take care of this one publicly."

It was a total one-eighty from his earlier statements. I don't know if he was acting for the benefit of Jael, Trickstan or the rest of the people around us, but it made my hackles rise. Had we been wrong about him? Had Joy? His constant mood swings made no sense. I pulled him by the sleeve, averting my eyes to the swipe of mayo smeared on his chin.

Gross. "What are you doing? I thought we were going to use Trickstan to get rid of the emperor, not turn him in."

He wrenched Trickstan's arm, dragging him away from the group. "We have to make it look good. If we don't turn him in, then Magnus will know what's up. Let's take him in and I'll make sure he's held in a low-security facility. We can break him out whenever he figures out the secret."

I shot Ren a look, muttering under my breath, knowing he could pick up what I said with his wolf hearing. "Unless Magnus kills him first."

Ren didn't bother with a whisper. He marched over to Fox and yelled. "Are you dumb? Why take him in at all if we're going to break him out? We need to stop and get our shit together before we go anywhere."

Hashtag truth.

Fox swung his head around in all directions, then pulled Ren and me close like he was going to share a big secret with us. "They're watching us. We have to act like we want to take Trickstan in or they'll be onto us. Just follow my lead." Again, he started hauling him away.

Ren and I shared another glance. We needed to play it cool with Fox until we knew more about his motives. Maybe he was telling the truth and there were eyes on us. Though I still had reservations about Fox, I fell in line behind him and Ren anyway.

Bex and Louie agreed to come quietly with us. Kiko had popped away, so she was the only one in our group that remained free. Fox led us over to the flying carpets and I let Ren ride with him and Trickstan and I took up another with Bex and Louie.

Aetheria had turned out to be complicated. What I wouldn't give for a night of watching reruns with my Gram. Or hanging out and dancing on the picnic tables with the pack.

Normalcy of some kind.

What we were experiencing was as far from normal as it could get. We were flying—literally and figuratively—blind. We had no plan, no guidance, and no secret had been revealed to Trickstan that would help us. Ren looked over his shoulder as the carpets surged above the clouds. I'd have given anything to communicate in my head with him like I did Wells. I knew, no matter what had happened between us, he would not leave me or act without me, but like this, we didn't even have the means to speak privately. All we had was belief in each other and a whispering voice that had grown annoyingly silent.

I t took Fitz some time to get to the gas station. He had to get some extra supplies and do a little prep. This time, though, it would be just us. No Liam or Annigan or that damn bear Alec to mess things up. I couldn't take the chance.

After I heard the "follow your heart" part of those lyrics, I knew it was what I was supposed to do. It's what the Nameless Queen in Netheria had told Terra the same thing, so I wasn't fucking around anymore. Too many things pointed me in too many directions, clouding my judgment, and making me second-guess myself. My heart was Terra, and I would get to her. We'd work out the rest. End of.

I'd memorized those lyrics, listening to the recording I don't know how many times since Bash had sent it to me. He and Mace had tried to catch Jack and bring him back—at my insistence—but he turned out to be a wily little fucker and hit the back door after his one song. The bar manager had no contact info for him, surprise, surprise. The guy was a ghost, just like Joe Houseman had been. I still didn't understand all the connections.

Mace had suggested I put up one of those murder board things with red string connecting to all the bits and pieces. I hate to admit it, but I considered it. There was a connecting thread between all of this, but I couldn't see it.

If Fitz's Dark Magic spell failed to work, I'd personally go all the red string in Illusion Hill if it would fix just one thing in this clusterfuck of sucky situations.

A loud rumble behind the gas station drew my attention. Fitz had pulled up in a truck and backed into the bay as best as he could. He jumped out and whipped the blue tarp off what was in the back, and I have to admit, I gasped. "Planning on napping in your coffin while I bleed to death, huh?"

"Haha. Very funny, wolf. I love vampire humor. No, I sleep in a regular bed just like you, but this coffin belongs to my ancestors, so you better keep your claws to yourself when you're inside it, no matter how bad it gets in there. No scratching the wood."

I wasn't claustrophobic, but I wasn't going to make any promises about my claws or any other part of me if I was going to be stuffed into that ancient thing after my heart stopped beating. Feels like a thing he might have warned me about, but in his defense, I didn't ask for specifics. "Let's do this. As many cuts as possible this time. We're in a time crunch."

I wasted no time stripping, and he strung me up like normal. As soon as the blood started to gush down my legs and into the chalice, he pulled out all the supplies he needed, including a wooden stake and an even bigger chalice. "I thought you were a vampire, not a slayer."

I'd imagine Mace would've come up with the clever Buffy nickname for him, but I'd never even heard of Buffy the Vampire Slayer until Terra had given me a season-by-season discourse one night when my teeth got a little more bitey than I'd planned.

After we were finished banging, of course.

She'd even joked about the time Mateo had a real vamp bite her for his sick fusion experiments. I loved how she simply moved on from traumatic things. She had to deal with it and once she did, it was nothing but a laugh to her. So fucking strong.

"Nope. The stake's for me. Just let me work. It's not going to take you long to drain with that many cuts."

I was glad to hear that. Truth be told, my head was already starting to swoon anyway. So, I kept my mouth shut while he sliced his wrist with his fangs and let his blood drip into the larger chalice. He said a spell over his blood and stirred it with the stake. Smoke began to waft from the cup.

Next, he reached into his jacket pocket and pulled out a small Ziploc bag of gray powder, and added it to the mixture, glancing up at me. "Ancient ashes from The Cinders in Aetheria. Legend says the Mage created vampires with these ashes and they hold special Magical properties that seek out Dark Magic."

"Seems a little too important to carry around in a baggie."

"I swiped them from my family's stash the last time I was in California. I was in a rush, so I had to use what I had on me. Quiet while I do the next part of the spell."

I tried to focus as he added the ashes, but my eyes were swimming around the bay, unable to fixate on anything. He muttered some more words and then a white flash in flared his direction, but that was it.

Bile began to rise in my throat. I was close to dying. It felt way more real than the other times I'd bitten the dust, so to speak, but it was what I wanted. I had to do one thing before I completely succumbed. "Listen, Fitz. There's something you don't know about me. Once I die, I'm going to come back alive. Don't let it freak you out."

"Of course, you are. That's the point of the Dark Magic spell. You sacrifice your life first, but the next thing I add will bring you back again. Don't worry."

"No, Asshole, I'm not worried. I've got phoenix blood, so I can't die. I guess technically I do, but my phoenix blood will kick in and I'll be reborn. I just thought you should know. I'm trusting you to keep it on the down-low." I guess he was in the circle of trust now.

He paused his stirring. I think. Hard to tell through fluttering eyelids. "You forget I'm draining all that blood out of you, so don't rely on it. You need to give up your life for the spell to work anyway. Too late to back out now though.

"You're nearly there. When your blood is drained, I'll place you in the coffin and close the lid. You'll hear the voice of Augustus the First, the original vampire who developed Dark Magic and was cast into The Cinders for it. He'll tell you what to do. Follow the directions. If you wake up after, knock on the coffin lid four times and I'll pull you out and give you some of your blood back. If I don't hear the knock in a few hours, I'll know you didn't make it through the process. Good luck, friend."

It was hard to believe I considered him a friend, but when I added up all he was doing for me and what we'd shared in the dreamscape, he was. He had to be, or I might very well be strolling into my real and permanent death in a matter of seconds. "Have you personally seen anyone not make it through this spell?"

His voice was an echo as I started to wilt under the loss of blood and Magic. "Yeah, but I think my dumbass brother fucked that one up. I know what I'm doing."

Mage, I hoped so.

I assumed my death would be a sudden dramatic pulse of darkness, light, something, but it was slow, creeping inside me as the last drop of blood dripped into the chalice. I tried to take another breath, but there was no air to suck in. Though I tried to control it, real panic set in. I tried to push some fire from my fingertips, but nothing happened.

Everything faded into a crawl and the last conscious thought I had was of Terra's eyes the first time I touched her elbow. The slight widening of her pupils spread down to her mouth as it twitched despite herself.

I think—no, I know I fell for her that moment. Everything that came after it was me making her fall for me.

REN

We were running out of time, and I was tired of playing catch-up, only to feel like we got no answers. Something had been off about Fox from the start. I know Terra trusted Joy and I backed her up on it. Joy's motivations were pure and very clear.

However, we were soaring back into the enemy's camp without real intel and no plan. It was time to take the bull by the horns and see what Fox really thought. At least we'd have some answers by the time the carpet hit the shitting pavement in the central province.

I could prep as long as I knew what to prep for. It was the key to keeping Terra safe. Trickstan too. I didn't want to see him killed for some half-baked idea rolling around his brain.

You don't know what you don't know, Renfield.

It was up to me to get more info.

"How long have you been fucking the empress, Fox?"

He spat out the banana he was eating. Probably fell on some schmuck's head below us. "Pardon?"

Trickstan's eyes went wide. "She's my sister. I don't want to hear about her—what was the word Mace uses—sexcapades."

"Too bad." I punched Fox on the shoulder in that dude's way, hoping to get him talking. "I want to know your story and we've got some time to kill, so spill it."

He wiped his hands on his pants, not even trying to hide his nervousness. "Um, a while, I guess."

"You guess? No specifics? How did you get your job to guard her and how did that turn into smashing behind the most powerful man in Aetheria's back?"

If I had to pin down a word for his expression. It would've been shocked. "Um, I'd been assigned guard duty for the emperor since I was of age. I wanted to do something important, so I applied and got accepted. I suppose I stood out to the emperor as a worthy guard, so he put me on her detail as soon as she moved into the palace, so twenty years or so, maybe more."

Trickstan slid his head between us. "That's no time for us. Fae have the best genetics and longest life pans."

I shook my head. "Lifespan. So, Fox, you've been working with her since before the Conduit closed then. When did you start banging?"

Was it crude to talk this way about Joy? Yes, but I had a purpose for it. I could only imagine how hard Terra would have smacked my head for it if she'd heard me.

"Not long after." He leaned back on his hands, his head searching the clouds above us. "The emperor's job takes him away so often. At first, she'd beg him to stay home, but he never did. I was just there, and she was lonely, I guess. Whatever the reason it happened, She's the most gorgeous fae in Aetheria and she makes me feel...joyful."

I glanced at Trickstan to see if that sounded right. He shrugged. "And when did you two launch the plot to overthrow the emperor? Was that your idea or hers?"

He slowly turned, swiveling all the way around and glowering at me like he was angry about the question. Interesting. I continued my line of questioning. "You know we're with you, but I have to ask, why are you taking Trickstan straight to the emperor instead of sheltering him until he remembers the secret that will help take him out. Gotta say, from a security standpoint, your story's feeling a little shaky."

"It's not shaky. It's sound. I'm just acting like I'm taking him in. I won't actually do it. When we get there, I'll stash him somewhere safe so the emperor can't get to him."

"Feels like I was safer where I was," Trickstan huffed.

"I agree. You're not being honest with us. The question is, are you double-crossing us or Joy or both?"

"I would never hurt Joy! I told you; I love her. She thinks...she just doesn't understand what we're doing. Thinking is not her thing, but she'll see once our plan falls into place."

Trickstan jumped to his feet. "There is no way Joy would be into someone who thought she wasn't bright. I call full shit!"

Once again, Trickstan had hit the target by saying the wrong thing. "Yeah, me too. The question is, what are we going to do about it?"

He didn't hesitate. I'll give him that. He just launched himself at Fox, throwing him back on the flying mat and starting to pummel him with his fists. The mat swiveled and we all came close to tumbling off.

From behind us, I heard Terra yelp. "What's happening?"

I couldn't answer her because Fox managed to slide closer to the edge of the mat. He pressed up on his heels, then flipped Trickstan over his head and off the mat altogether. I reached out for them, managing to grab one of Fox's feet, but Trickstan tumbled off, screaming like a little girl.

I hauled Fox up—didn't want to, but it seemed like it was best until we knew everything—and whipped my head, searching for Trickstan as he fell.

"No worries, Mister. I got him." Kiko popped into existence, scooping a grateful Trickstan in her arms, tsk-tsking him, then disappeared again.

Thank the Mage's balls.

That was close.

I turned to Terra, my breath heaving from my chest. She had the same look of terror I knew I had on my face too. That fae fucker had wormed himself back into our hearts. At least a little bit. I nodded that we were okay, and she relaxed just as the carpets soared down below the clouds.

Fox was quiet—too quiet—as we rode the rest of the way into the castle. The wheels were turning in his head, and it made him look like a guilty man. The trouble was I didn't know exactly what he was guilty of. As the carpet landed, I gripped him by the back of his sweaty neck. "Nervous much?"

He went stiff as a board, then despite my steel grip, he slumped forward onto the ground. I stood there looking at him, perplexed. "What did you do to him?" Terra asked.

"I guess I made him so nervous he passed out."

She poked my ribs, and the motion went straight to my cock, despite my best efforts to nip it in the bud. "You have that effect sometimes."

"True."

We shared a laugh, and everything seemed normal, just for a moment.

Then Fox woke up. "What happened? How did I get here?"

I woke—was that the right word—gasping. It was impossible to tell how long I was out in the coffin, but it seemed like less than a second. I was hit with the immediate wrongness of the state I was in.

Numb.

I felt nothing, even when I twitched my fingers against the fabric lining the coffin, my sense of touch was absent. I opened my mouth and tried to speak but I had no idea if I did or not because I heard nothing.

No smell either, which was disconcerting for a werewolf predator.

Sucking in a breath that went nowhere, I thought I should try to calm my heartbeat, but I didn't have one of those either.

Death was troubling.

Then I heard the whisper of a voice and things got worse.

"I must say, this is a rather unexpected event. In all the millennia I have been summoned for this ritual, you're my first werewolf and an alpha at that. How delightful. I think I'll enjoy playing with you before we complete the ritual."

"You don't scare me vamp." My words echoed through my head since I couldn't speak. It made me think of Terra and the bond we shared through the phoenix blood I gifted her.

"No? Pity. We'll see how brave you are momentarily."

"Get on with it. I have somewhere to be. What do I do?"

"So impatient. First, you must tell me what you want, then I'll tell you what it will cost you. It's simple really."

I longed to take a deep breath, but I couldn't. I managed to raise my hand and run it over my jaw, though I couldn't feel it.

What I wanted wasn't a simple question at all.

I wanted a lot of things. Terra, for one, but I also wanted Magic flowing again, and a way to break the mate bond that wouldn't end with Autumn and I being unable to love anyone again. I wanted my pack safe, my life back, I wanted the emperor who had been the one to close the Conduit in the first place to suffer and die for all he'd caused.

And I could've gone for a burger if I was being honest. I was famished.

"Cat got your tongue, alpha wolf?"

In my head, I laughed. "Yep, a feral cat with kissable lips and quick wit and a heart of fucking gold."

"She sounds wonderful. Can I meet her?"

"No"

"Tell me more about her, then. What's her name? Where did she come from? Is she lupine like you or something else? I do get dreadfully bored waiting to be summoned. Regale me with stories of your woman."

"She's..." Nope. Not going to share anything about her with this Dark Magic fool. Nice try. "She's great. That's all you need to know. Can we get on with this?"

"I'm merely waiting for you to tell me what you want. I can see you're grappling. Here's a word of advice: the bigger the ask, the greater the cost."

I groped around for a way to roll everything I wanted into one firm statement that didn't sound like a run-on sentence. There was no way he was going to accept 'I want to get to Aetheria to get Terra and Ren back and kill the emperor and fix everything there so that magic is flowing back to our world again, and I want my pack to be safe and back doing what they do best, and I want Autumn to find a great man to love her like she deserves so I can be with Terra guilt-free with no consequences to any of us.'

To go along with all the things I wanted, I had just as much advice and words of wisdom to weed through. Starting with what my mom said my Dad wanted me to know more than anything—

Your wolf is a beast, a necessary part of who you are, but it's your job to be a bigger man. Putting the needs of others before your own shows how big your heart is.

Follow your heart, even though it will be difficult at times.

It was all about her right from the start.

That's why it's time to just follow your heart.

—and going all the way to what Terra once told me.

Your heart is the best part about you, Wells.

She *was* my heart. Without her, none of the other things I had to do or consider mattered. I might've been judged badly by the pack—the fucking world—one day, but I knew what my decision was. "I want a way to get to Aetheria from here. I need to take some people with me too."

As soon as I thought about it, I knew it was the right decision. I didn't get an easy sense of peace about it though; I got a tingle in a numb body that made me want to claw my way out of the coffin without knowing what else to do beyond that.

I felt like I could do it like I could get to her on sheer willpower alone.

"My, my, that's not a simple ask at all, is it? The Conduit is closed from Aetheria—permanently, mind you. There is no other way to simply stroll in and say howdy, is there?"

"I know that motherfucker. It's why I'm here. You know what I want. What do I do next?"

I was starting to feel antsy, partly because I'd sensed I'd been in the coffin for a while, mostly because he was pissing me off by being so courteous, yet not fulfilling his part of the spell. "Wait. Are you stalling? Trying to keep me talking until the hour is up?"

I expected blowback from him, but that's not what happened. "Guilty as charged. You seem interesting and if I can keep you here past the hour, you'll be mine. Your body will be burned and once that happens, your soul will soar to The Cinders. We can have chats every day."

"Not happening. If you don't tell me now, I'm going to tear this fucking coffin apart, melt all the chalices and make sure no one in that family can summon you again. Then it'll be you and me for all eternity and if you think for one second I will chat with you in all that time, you're a bigger idiot than you seem."

Meant every word.

He sighed audibly in my head. "Fine. You're no fun. There is a way for you, and your buddies, to get to Aetheria. The rest of the spell will be completed when I reach out through the netherworld and touch the blood smear on your forehead. Don't be alarmed."

A shiver raced down my spine when a cold, lifeless finger touched my head. Logic dictated that he wasn't in the coffin with me, but Dark Magic held powers I knew nothing about it, so the part of my brain that was awake and functioning freaked the fuck out about it. I managed to shift my head, which made him laugh. "Oh, I guess you don't want this as badly as your words claim."

Shit.

Fine.

Okay. "Do it."

I held still as he took his time fingering my forehead. When he finished whatever it was, he cackled in my head. "Well, now I understand everything. You're not truly worried because you believe your phoenix-infused blood will bring you back to life. I'm bereft to inform you that isn't the case. Since you cannot sacrifice your life——not truly—then the only way for the spell to work is for you to sacrifice what gives you the ability to live again: your phoenix blood. Say it and it'll be done."

"You want me to say that I sacrifice my phoenix blood? It's not possible. It replicates constantly and you can't separate it like a centrifuge." Mateo had made Arlo try it. It didn't work.

"You cannot, but I can. What is it that the moron child who messed up the last ritual and gave me the dullest soul I've ever known say? I'm the OG vampire. I can most certainly take your phoenix and it would barely be an inconvenience to me. Is she that pulls you to Aetheria worth your phoenix blood or does your affection have limits, like most? You can always find another woman. I taste one laced in your blood."

I shuddered at that. Even in death, I couldn't get rid of Autumn.

Of course, Terra was worth my blood, but I didn't know who I was without my phoenix. It was almost as much a part of me as my wolf. There was no consciousness to it like the wolf, but it was a steady beating force thrumming in my blood. It formed me, shaped the man I became into someone I was proud of. It was a part of my soul. The thought of him peeling it out of me made my stomach roil and claws itch to come out and fight him for merely thinking it.

Yet.

"She's not just another woman. She's everything. Go ahead. Take my phoenix."

Fox was staring up at Ren, pale and confused. Ren wasn't buying his innocent act. "Don't be a dumbass. We caught you. You're faking confusion to get out of my questions. And you flipped Trickstan right off the flying mat."

"What? I wouldn't." He scrambled to his feet, taking in the scene. More of Magnus' guards were heading toward us, Joy in tow. Ren pulled me close, mumbling in my ear so only I could hear him. "See how he acts with her. He's lying and I don't think he's on our side, or hers."

I glanced at Fox. He might have been a liar, but it was hard to fake the tone of his skin and the nervous shake of his hands as he stuck them into his pockets. "I don't know. Maybe Trickstan's memory loss is catching. First Jael claims she doesn't know what's going on, then Fox. Could be something to it."

"Maybe. Stay on guard, no matter what happens."

Of course, I would. Always was. Just like he'd taught me.

When Joy was feet away, she cast her eyes on Fox. Deep concern echoed through her. He nodded in her direction. It was a slight tilt of his head, respectful and guardy-like, but the soft glow in his gaze was evident. He loved her.

Joy smiled. "Terra, Ren, you're back. How was the hunting trip for my wayward brother, Trickstan? Did you catch the scoundrel?" Her voice was clipped, rehearsed, loud enough so that all the guards could hear her denounce him. I knew better though.

"That's an excellent question, my Darling wife. Did you get him?"

We hadn't even seen him walking from the other direction, yet there he was, Emperor Magnus, strolling in, bustling past his guards to give Joy a peck on the cheek. Her nose scrunched, but she managed to school her face before he pulled away. He looked down at her with loving eyes. He might be an overbearing assdick who was responsible for a lot of catastrophic things, but it was clear he had true feelings for her. It irked me.

Fox saluted him, then bowed in apology. "Almost, Sir. We had him, but he escaped, somehow." He whipped his head to Ren, begging him with his eyes to fill in the blanks he couldn't.

He could've been faking it, but it didn't appear like he knew what he'd done. Ren rolled his eyes. "His chimera friend took him from us. What now, Emp?"

Fox was quick to step in again. "We can go back to her home and likely find him there." Joy's sigh of relief turned sour at the end of his suggestion.

What was he playing at? He didn't have to tell Magnus we knew where they'd been. He could've just said he escaped.

"I have a better suggestion," the emperor bellowed. "Joy, was just on her way to prepare for the ceremony tomorrow. Why don't you take your new friend with you? I'll do a debrief with her wolf companion and Fox. We can all meet at the Highfall Bridge at sundown tomorrow to enjoy the festivities together."

Ren and I shared a look. He didn't want to leave me, but the better move for him would be to go with Magnus and Fox, to see what happened when Joy wasn't around. I didn't want to be separated either, but nodded my agreement anyway, linking my arm with Joy's. It's not like we could refuse the emperor. I put on my best girly-girl voice. "I admit, I need a bath and some rest after our adventure. It sounds nice."

The emperor pulled Ren and Fox in line with him, chattering as he escorted them into the castle along with several guards. Joy wasted no time, dragging me around to the far side of the castle. After a short walk, we came to a huge gate made of wood and bone that read Winterlands.

We stepped under the arch, and it was like all the pictures I'd seen of Disneyworld as visitors moved between one world and another. The temperature immediately dropped, though that didn't bother me much. The earth beneath my feet hummed, waking up my gnome blood. I couldn't help it; I stopped and shoved my hand beneath the surface of the soil. Joy didn't seem to care. She might not have gotten it, but she appeared to understand it was a gnome thing. Though I was far from just a gnome.

A surge of warmth washed through me. Yes, the dirt was cool to touch, but it was so ancient, so rich, so unbelievable. It reminded me of the soil at Boulderbrook.

Everything I did, was doing, was hoping to do was for them. With the commotion of our trip back to the castle with Trickstan, I'd put Wells and home and what happened with Ren on the back burner of my mind. I needed to focus on the work left to do. "Where are we headed?"

"Willowvale, a town close to the border, a sort of second home to the Queen of the Winterlands. Being Empress comes with some perks, one of which is permission to enter the dryad territory. Normally, they don't let others in. They're very sheltered."

I supposed that made sense considering dryads were spirits born inside trees. They were Earth creatures, like gnomes, and could take human form if they wanted, but if my Gram was correct, it was only on rare occasions they did so.

When male dryads come out to play, their wood is already primed to go. It happens so rarely, be sure to document it if you get one in human form in your bed. Don't write it on paper though. They hate that. It's their skin and all.

"Tell me what happened. I need to know if Trickstan is safe."

"I assume so. His chimera friend must have been following us in stealth mode. She caught him and poofed him away when Fox threw him off the flying carpet. Joy, I know it might hurt to hear it, but I saw the whole struggle. Fox flipped him off the mat on purpose. He would've fallen to his death if Kiko hadn't been there."

She stopped in her tracks. "I don't believe that. He would never…"

"I'm sorry. He did. How much do you know about Fox? Are you certain he's on your side and not the emperor's?"

"Positive. He loves me, really loves me, not like Magnus who merely wants to possess something pretty. I don't know what's going on, but I have the most faith in him that I've ever had in anyone. He must've had a plan or known Kiko was there. Something."

I hoped for her that he did, but I had so many suspicions. "He did mention not remembering the incident, so there could be something wrong with him, his mind. Maybe."

345

She nodded. We walked the rest of the trip in silence. The trees around us were bare, Winterlands and all. It was nice, and another reminder of home. I got lost in my thoughts until we ended up at a beautiful cottage-looking palace. It was nestled among a huge grove of trees. All kinds were growing there. The vibe was serene, ancient, calm. Definitely Willowvale.

A dozen people filed out of the front door, bustling and bowing to Joy, declaring her Empress and all the stuff that went with the title. We were offered warm drinks and food before we even set foot inside.

The interior of the cabin reminded me so much of the Boulderbrook lodge, that I choked on emotion. There was an overlook rail with doors behind it, just like Wells' office. The chandelier that hung in the middle, however, wasn't made of antlers, but of bones and gold. My steps faltered. Joy rushed over. "Something wrong?"

"No, it's just this cabin reminds me so much of Boulderbrook, my home, it took my breath away. The architecture is so similar and even the wood is the same shade. It's an exact copy."

"Yes, well, the question is which is the copy, and which is the original? Aetherians have been copying things from your world as long as you've been copying things from ours. When the Conduit was open for all to roam freely as they liked, there were bound to be similarities. I wish I'd been born at that time because it must have been so much fun to learn and discover things about humans and them about us. It's a shame things had to change."

"Why did they change? It's a question I've had for a while. Why did Magnus close the Conduit, and then send a golem army through it over twenty years later? Maybe if we understood why, we could fix it."

She crossed over to the fluffy gray couch in front of the fireplace and settled in the corner. I sat beside her, my body grateful for the plush seat. I'd had a rough few…days, weeks, months? It was hard to determine at that point.

"Magnus is the most powerful fae to ever been born. His Magic is unheard of. That's how he got to be emperor and how he convinced the fae kings and queens of the court to agree to the closure. I don't even know the extent of his Magic. He got it in his head that the Magicals on your side were stealing magic to turn humans into Magicals.

"He feared an uprising of abominations, as he called them, coming to Aetheria and taking what was rightfully given to us by the Mage. He closed the Conduit so he could prepare his golem invasion, hoping to take over your world and become the emperor in both places."

He wasn't entirely wrong about using magic to create other Magicals. Mateo had done it, only not with humans. Still. It didn't make sense to be so jealous and possessive about Magic unless…

"Magic is running out everywhere, isn't it? Not just in our world."

She shrugged. "Appears so. The story our ancestors told is that the Mage left an unending supply for us when he left our realm. It was his design for it to be everlasting. Nobody knows exactly what happened to it, but the fact remains, the amount of Magic is finite."

Well, that was a kick in the pants.

It was hard to wrap my head around that little nugget of news.

The crackling and warmth of the fire in the fireplace seeped into my body as I mulled over what she had said. I couldn't help it. My bones rattled in fear of what lay ahead for all of us, but I yawned.

Joy went into business mode before my eyes, jumping up and calling over the servants. "Please fix us each a tray of fruits and bread, warm cider, and water. Show my friend to the copper suite. I'll stay in the adjoining gold suite tonight."

The servants raced into action and Joy pulled me behind her as she trudged up the stairs. "There's a bathroom with a huge soaking tub between our rooms. You sleep, I'll bathe, so the tub will be cleaned and free when you wake up. Tomorrow we'll do our prep. You're going to love the process. It'll take your mind off what I just told you."

I doubted it, but most of what she'd said sounded great, so I thanked her and headed to the door with the copper doorframe. My body wanted to sleep, but I wanted something more than sleep too.

I needed him. Especially now that I knew the diminishing magic problem wasn't contained to just our realm. That thought tumbled in my mind as I was led into my room.

The entire thing was decked out with copper accents. Even the bed was covered in a shimmery copper duvet that changed into teal and purple depending on the angle of the light. I flopped down on it, just as a servant came in and set a tray on the table beside me. "If you need anything else, ma'am, ring the bell here. We'll hear it."

She pointed to the copper bell, closed the coppery drapes, and backed out of the room.

Sleep.

Well, after I scarfed down the best croissant adjacent pastry I'd ever eaten and shucked my shoes as I did so. I laid back on the soft shiny bed and took a deep breath, praying to the long-gone Mage that sleep would come quickly.

I was expecting the same thing I'd gotten the other times in the dreamscape—a bright white room with no features until one of us thought something into being, but that wasn't the case. The atmosphere was dark, dank even. There was no air and the only light in the space was a sliver of moonlight in the corner of the room streaming through a small window. I took a step toward it and stumped my toe on something wooden. And hard. No, I didn't just stump it, I whacked the crap out of it. "Shit, that hurt. Damn it to motherfucking Netheria."

"Do you kiss your boyfriend with that dirty mouth?"

"Yeah, he likes it."

"You better believe I do. Come here."

I took a tentative step, trying to walk around whatever was on the floor that had tried to take out my pinkie toe, but all I got was more wood. It was so dark in the room and the object seemed to be long and endless, like a barrier. "Where are you?"

There was a snap of fingers. The moonlight flared a little brighter and I was able to adjust my night vision. "Here. Waiting for you."

Wells was sitting on a chair under the window. I dashed right over, turning around before I got to him. I almost swallowed my tongue in shock. "Is that a coffin? You don't have some twisted vampire kink you never revealed, do you?"

"No, I do have a gnome, slash, golem, slash phoenix blood kink I need to fully explore though. Interested in helping me?" I couldn't stop staring at the open casket. It just drew my gaze away from where I wanted to look. Like a magnet. Wells growled. "Never mind that. Look at me."

That did it.

The growl always did.

Now that I knew what it was, I was able to maneuver around the coffin and get to Wells. He wrapped his hands around me, fisting the t-shirt—his t-shirt—I found myself in. He buried his head in the crook of my neck, breathing in. "I needed this. To smell you, touch you. You're the lifeboat that keeps me from drowning every day. Right now, I'm going under."

Sweet as it was, and something that got my heart revved in a certain direction, I put my hand in his hair, yanking him back. He smirked because he liked it. "What's wrong Wells? If you say nothing, I will make a punching bag out of your balls. Talk."

Probably not the right thing to say because it only made him look more predatory. His grip went from my shirt to my waist. He jerked me toward him, his eyes roaming over my body as he licked his lips. "Fine. It's something, but I don't want to talk about it right now. It's okay, I swear. I just want to feel you." He ran his tongue over my neck then nipped at my ear, growling as he bit down. Shivers exploded in my nether regions. "I want to taste you, to hear you purr my name, Precious. The rest can wait. I'll see you soon enough."

I snapped to attention, taking a huge—and admittedly difficult—step away from him. "What do you mean? What have you done, Wells?"

"What I had to. Come here and let me have you or I might not make it through this. Don't ask what. I'll share everything in time. Just come be with me so I can breathe." When I took the step toward him, he sighed in relief. The next thing I knew, the creaky wooden chair he'd been sitting in morphed into a more comfortable lounge chair. He threw me into it and the back reclined a long way, making me yelp in surprise.

I'd experienced his desire for me many times. He was a predator, took what he wanted when he wanted it, and I had no problem with it. Loved it, actually. He was always very giving and tender during the right times and pleasantly, I'll just say zealous, when the time was right.

Never had I experienced such a desperation in him.

It made it hard to concentrate as he pulled me toward him, pushing my ass halfway up the seat back and throwing my feet on the armrests. So, we were doing this acrobat-style, weren't we?

Lowering himself between my legs with a growl and a nip on my pulsing clit. "Mage, Wells. Ah, that's…"

He raised his head. "What do you want? I know. Let me give it to you just like you like." I mean, who's going to say no to that? Not me. My Gram raised no dummy.

My head rested against the wall as he lowered himself again, licking and moaning as he worked his fingers inside me. With the first twist of his hand, my ass bucked off the chair, but he pressed me back down by placing a hand on my stomach and sucking my whole clit into his mouth at once. I sunk deeper into the chair, unable to find the right position to meet the onslaught of what he was doing with his mouth.

He was relentless in a way I didn't know was possible. Yeah, I loved it, but I could already tell I wasn't going to last long under this amazing assault. I grabbed his hair, pulling him up and biting my lip as his eyes flared deep amethyst. Mage, I had missed that flash that was uniquely him. "Not that I don't appreciate this—" He cut off my sentence by angling his fingers. He'd been holding off that move, but he pulled it out to make a point. One I would agree with every damn day of the week.

I sucked in a breath as goosebumps erupted on my flesh. My every sensation was overwhelmed by him: the scent of his skin, the slickness of his tongue, the sound of that simmering growl that burst out of him every so often. Even though I was doing my best to hold off my orgasm and make him slow down, he ramped up by adding a second and then a third finger. I twitched. He smirked.

It was like he was trying to stuff every little thing he could throw at me into one burst of lust and light. It was amazing, but...

Reply hazy.

I opened my mouth to stop him, but it was too late. He used his free hand to grab mine as he lifted from his knees. "Say my name when you come. I want to hear everything you feel for me, for us, for this, in your voice. Please."

I didn't have a choice in it. I moaned his name, over and over. Not because he demanded it of me—yes, hot—but because I demanded it of myself. I wanted him to feel what I felt. To know what I knew. What I hadn't said.

She was a dream, a vision, a spectacle as she came for me. All I could do was stare at her, my heart pounding, pulse racing, body aching to drive myself inside of her. So, she'd never let go of me.

I would hang on to her for my entire life.

As long as it lasted.

I only had one left.

She didn't seem to notice anything different between us. Thankfully the dreamscape didn't require the use of our phoenix blood connection. If she'd known—when she found out—she'd have...opinions on it.

Too fucking bad. I loved her and I made the choice I made for her. Damn the consequences. We had a connection that went beyond the phoenix blood.

She lifted her head, biting that lower lip, and released a breath of satisfaction that went straight to my dick. "Come up here."

Didn't have to tell me twice. I climbed over her, settling against her warm wet —and fucking satisfied, thank you very much—pussy, eager to drive into her. She raised my head by putting her finger under my chin. "No. Higher."

I had to laugh. "I'd crush you. We can switch positions for the next part."

She squeezed the hand that I was still holding, folding it back just a little. Did it hurt? Nah, but I could tell she meant business. "Do it."

"You know how I like it when you're bossy."

"Yes, so get up here or I'm going to have to do something drastic."

Mage, that loaded statement left me wanting and hard. Curiosity, and sheer horniness, driving me, I inched up her body, raking my pecs over her tits, brushing against her still-hard nipples. She licked my chest as I moved higher and pressed my knees on either side of her head. The chair leaned a little, but I threw a hand on the wall to keep it from going completely horizontal.

As I had with her, she left the sensual foreplay at the door and gripped my ass with one hand, guiding my throbbing hard cock — expertly, I might add—into her soft and eager mouth. The groan that left my throat was embarrassing. "Fuck, Precious."

How she managed to smile around the head of my dick will remain a mystery, but she did. Then she went to town, drawing me in with a slurpy suck and popping that thing out of her mouth again.

The sound of it made me mad with lust for her.

I pumped into her mouth, deeper and deeper as she widened for me. When she took the base of my shaft in her hand and began to twist as she went up and down made me see stars. I slammed my other hand against the wall, lifting my hips and angling toward the back of her throat.

Remarkable.

Sweat began to trickle down my chest as we worked together. She was going to ruin me. "You know, if you keep devouring my dick like this, it means you're mine."

She popped it out, running her tongue along the head, down the shaft, and back up again. "I was yours a long time before I ever put the Big, Bad, Wolf in my mouth and you know it."

"Tell me."

"I'm yours."

"Again."

"Yours, Wells. Only yours."

I knew what she meant by that, but I didn't give two fucks about Ren and whatever little thing had gone down between them. It simply didn't matter.

She paused, a gleam in her eye, then went back to business, sucking me in, stroke and stroke and stroke again. My hips kept up with her tongue, driving in deep enough to make her eyes well up. I wiped the tears from each corner, intending to pull away and give her jaw a break, but she held on fast, gripping my ass to drive my hard and slick cock down her throat.

It slammed through me as if I'd been hit by lightning. A force so electric and sharp, I didn't feel it building or have time to warn her. I came so hard, right down the back of her throat and she never stopped. Not once. Not until I was spent and huffing, lying slack against the wall as she drained every drop of my soul from me.

Everything I had left.

It was all hers.

A clap resounded behind us. We both jumped. I was going to rip Annigan apart. I envisioned clothes on us both and whirled around to greet them with my fist.

It wasn't Annigan.

It was a hooded dark figure with orange glowing cinders for eyes.

"Augustus."

"Well, of course. Who else would it be? Nice finish, by the way. It takes a real woman to do that so effectively. It was...entertaining."

I flew toward him. "You leave her out of this, motherfucker." I expected my body to connect with his but collided with nothing but a shadow and a laugh.

"Wells, who is this dickwipe?"

"He was just leaving."

"No, you know I can't do that. We haven't finished our bargain. I'm just waiting for you to wake up from your slumber to seal the deal. Better hurry. Tick tick. It's been fifty-eight minutes, give or take."

Cold dread shot through me. If I didn't get out of the dreamscape, consequently the coffin, in time. This would be the very last time I'd ever see her.

"I've got to go. Now."

"But, I have things to share with you. We need to talk about Trickstan and the emperor and—"

"I'm sorry. We've got to wake up. I'll explain soon. Look for me." Frantic, I glanced around for something that would wake me up. Having no other option in the room, I dove into the coffin and shut the lid with a bang.

The dreamscape faded and I opened my eyes, finding myself in the actual coffin. Annoyed and no longer willing to play the nice guy, I banged four times on the lid. "Tell me what I need to do asshole. Now."

"Fine. You'll need to make yourself an Eternal Flame with the ashes from The Cinders. The ones your man used in this spell. Anyone

357

who comes with you must use their Fire magic to create the blaze, and their blood to pay the price of travel. This will not get you back home. That'll be your problem to solve at a later date." He paused. "Unless you want to do this again for the return trip. Warning, doing this a second time gives me your eternal soul as if it had been taken out by a Ripper. A vampire has to be paid for his troubles, know."

My hands clenched. Never had I wanted to punch someone so badly in my life. "That's it? Just make our own Eternal Flame and walk into it? I thought the Eternal Flame, Neverending Wind, and all the others were in specific places."

Augustus sighed audibly in my head. "They don't teach the young ones like they should these days. I am the Eternal Flame. The Mage used me, my punishment, as the catalyst. Yes, there are places in your world primed to activate when you know the correct spell, but if you have ashes from The Cinders, you have a part of me with you and can conjure the Eternal Flame when you want.

"Be advised, it's going to hurt, and your Fire magic will not protect your belongings or clothing. Have fun. It's been nice getting to know you. And watch you get off with your girl."

The lid creaked open, and I swear I almost punched a very concerned-looking Fitz in the face just for being there. It wasn't his fault though, so I restrained myself. He helped me out of the coffin, and I was overwhelmed with a sense of loss.

My phoenix blood was gone.

I was chilly, weak, and shakier than an alpha should be.

More than that, it seemed like I'd lost someone very important. Like when my dad died. I was only three and even though I barely remember his face, his absence was always a tangible thing, like I could hold it in my hands if I wanted to, but I never tried because the idea was always just too big to carry.

I scrubbed my hand over my chest, longing for that warmth I'd held for as long as I could remember, like a phantom limb clinging to my soul. I would make the loss of my phoenix mean something.

Something had been wrong in the dreamscape, including but not limited to the appearance of that Augustus person-thing-entity. I needed more info to fully label him. It. I intended to get that information too, as soon as I had the chance to go back to sleep.

It would be a while before that happened though. The rip out of the dreamscape had been more violent than the others too. I moaned and cried a little for hours due to the burning pain and misery I was in. I finally was able to doze off though, and I'd woken up to more delicious pastries by my bed. The bath I crawled into was shorter than I wanted it to be, but Joy was antsy because I'd slept in and half the day had been wasted, in her words.

I was feeling more like myself now that we were outside in the nippy breeze taking the short walk to the place with the dresses.

I expected a shop or storefront or maybe a fashion-filled trunk to be brought out for us to view.

Ha. Nope.

From a distance, it appeared to be a standard willow tree, huge, leaves flowing in the breeze. As we approached though, I had to blink a few times to make sure I was seeing it correctly.

Instead of leaves, there were strips of cloth growing from the tree branches. Most of them were white or off-white, but they were of different widths and weights. Some of them sparkled and others had slight patterns on them. Diamonds were nestled among the branches like lights on a Christmas tree.

I was awestruck at the simple beauty. Joy? She ran over like a giddy child getting an ice cream cone. "This is the one and only tailor tree in Aetheria. There's a dryad soul inside who's dedicated her life to keep this tree growing. It's like a religion to them. Only the most noble dryads are allowed to sacrifice their human forms to keep a tree living." She lovingly stroked the trunk of the tree. "Hello, Elanie. I've brought my friend Terra with me today. Make us look gorgeous, okay?"

The fabric in the branches swayed, gently floating around her in a hug, then whisked around me before returning to normal. "Um, hi Elanie. Looking forward to getting a fancy new dress, I guess."

Actually. I preferred my jeans and Wells' hoodie and as soon as that thought flew into my head, I swear the tree—Elanie—laughed. It was more of a tinkling rustle than an actual giggle, but it was clear.

Mind-reading fabric trees. Why not?

"So, what's the procedure here? Do we pick a fabric and Elanie whips up our dresses for us?"

"No. I want you to experience this like I did the first time, with no idea what was happening. It'll be fun. Take off everything but your undies. It's fine. No one is around except for the dryads in the trees."

Yeah, that didn't help ease my nerves about undressing out in the open. *At* all. But Joy stood there with her hands on her hips waiting and I knew I had to channel the inner werewolf I didn't have and strip down.

Joy pulled me around to the other side of the tree, ducking around and between the floating wisps of fabric. There was a hollow in the tree, just big enough for my hand. I raised an eyebrow at Joy. She huffed. "Put your hand in the hollow. There will be a small prick—she'll need your blood—but it isn't bad. As the blood is drawn, you need to think about how you want to dress. Simple commands are best. I plan to think of the word 'elegant,' but you could choose sexy, demure, fun, loud, trendy, whatever you want, then step a few feet away. Elanie will pull what she needs from you and dress you. Relax, it's fun."

I wasn't sure fun started with the word 'prick' unless it was a different kind entirely, but whatever. I stuck my left hand into the hollow. About a dozen different descriptive words were going through my mind at the time. Not sexy, not elegant, for sure. I closed my eyes and tried to focus and the one clear idea I had was wearing a dress Wells would like on me.

Joy lied. The prick hurt like hellfire, but I endured, stepping away and holding out my arms, mimicking what Joy was showing me to do.

The tailor tree began to hum as the fabric whipped softly in the breeze, shifting and moving. The neutral whites burst into colors, more than I could identify. Suddenly it was a cacophony of color and movement and the silky feel of the fabric as it slid across my skin.

I had to open my eyes at that point.

The fabric twisting around me had a slight shimmer to it, not as much as some, but it wasn't flat. As it slid over my body, it went from white to cream to warm yellow, flicking through just about every color there was before settling into a deep plum purple that was nearly black.

I *had* been thinking of Wells. Of course, it was purple.

The fabric snaked up my torso, slid over my shoulder, and settled over my body in a matter of seconds. When it was finished, I was draped in plum over one shoulder, across my breasts, then over the opposite hip, leaving a pretty big swath of skin exposed between my breasts and hips. The skirt fell just at floor length, and it was roomy enough to even have a pocket on the side where a shiny diamond was holding the entire thing in place.

"My Mage, Terra, you look stunning."

The dress made me feel like some Greek warrior goddess from the old human stories. Sure, if I raised my arms, onlookers would get a bit of under-boob and there was a lot of stomach showing, the dress was secure enough for me to move around in—I tried it to be certain. I knew in an instant that Wells would definitely approve. I even had a quick fantasy of him ripping off the diamond with his claws.

Needed to focus though.

Joy gave me an approving clap and I stood back while the tailor tree bathed her in a golden silk gown with a gold choker collar. It skimmed her body tightly and ended with a three-foot train that shimmered when she walked. Elegant was correct.

"Magnus is going to have a fit when he sees you. Fox too."

She blushed at Fox's name. She certainly believed in Fox and his feelings for her. I just wish I knew if we could trust him or not.

Also wish I knew what shoes I was supposed to wear with my new dress. "So, do we go barefoot?"

S pencer paced in front of the Conduit, the place I'd chosen to walk through fire to our possible deaths. "I'm not one to second guess my alpha or my friend, but are you sure about this? I want them back too, but this is nuts, to put it mildly."

"I know, but I'm doing it anyway."

Gideon slapped my back. "We all are." Mace nodded beside him. Walking through fire for me. I'd expect nothing less from the men and friends they were. "Here, give me the extra clothes you brought." I handed my jeans and hoodie over to him and he started stuffing all our clothes into a silver duffle bag. Once he zipped it closed and threw it over his shoulder he wiggled his eyebrows. "Fireproof. Since the creepy old vamp in Wells' mind said we'd lose our clothes on this adventure."

Spencer shook her head. "Shit, Gideon. Good call, but this doesn't instill me with confidence."

"Just take care of the pack and the camp, Spence. I'm leaving everything in your hands. You've got the Conduit key to release the magic. Do it as little as possible, but enough to get by. Lore will be coming to help with that, and Diggs is here to help you too. Keep your eyes on Micah and just hold on until we get back, capiche?" I pulled her in for a big hug and Mace dragged us all together into a huge lump of limbs.

Autumn was somewhere behind us. I could feel her heart beating, but she didn't join the group hug. When I'd told her what I was doing, she insisted on coming with me. I didn't even bother trying to talk her out of it. I didn't know what us being in two different worlds would do to the mate bond. She knew where she stood. She was more like a passenger on the journey than a participant. Still, leaving her behind seemed wrong.

Leaving my pack though went against every cell in my body. Ever since I'd become alpha, a role I seemed to have been born for, the burden of caring for the pack was like second nature to me. It wasn't a burden at all, though. It was a privilege. I knew what it must look like to them: that I was abandoning them for a woman who wasn't even my true mate. It was up to me to show them why I made the choice. She wasn't just some woman I deeply loved. She was the answer. I was surer of that than of anything. I had to follow my heart and get to her. "Let's do this."

I poured what was left of The Cinders ash on the ground in front of the Conduit. It seemed like a fitting place to meet Eternal Flame. The smell of the ash burned my nose, taking me back to the coffin I'd been stuffed into the day before. My body went rigid at the acrid taste it made in my mouth. Ancient assholes stink.

Slicing my palm first, I handed the knife over to Gideon, who did the same. Mace followed, then Autumn stepped up, marring her hand with the blade. Together we let our blood drip into the ash. When it began to bubble and smoke, we knew there was no turning back.

My Fire magic came as soon as I summoned it from within me, but it was weaker without the phoenix fire. I missed the silver flames and the power I felt when I used it. I hadn't told any of them it was gone. I couldn't bring myself to form the words.

As far as they knew, I'd played Augustus by being able to be reborn. I'd tell them eventually, but it I didn't want them overly concerned about me as we traipsed into the unknown. Thank the Mage's right ass cheek they didn't seem to notice the fire blazing from my fingertips was simple Fire magic and nothing more.

The others brought their magic to the surface and before any of us could prep for what was coming, a huge fireball erupted, engulfing us with intense heat and flickering flames.

As Fire elementals, it shouldn't have burned us, but Augustus, the Ass, had warned me it wasn't going to be pleasant.

Our clothes shredded as the flames beat against our bodies. It was torture trying not to run, but even if we had, I don't think we would've been able to get out of there. I needed to focus, but the fiery pins and needles plucking my skin were making me dizzy.

"Shit," Mace screamed. "I mean, I know I'm hot, but—"

The rest of his words were swallowed by a massive crack of caustic smoke billowing around us. My feet, our feet, lifted off the ground. I launched sideways, grabbing onto any of them I could catch, connecting with Gideon's arm. He gripped me back and I grunted into the flames. "Hold on to each other."

Autumn wrapped her arm around my waist, and I had to assume Mace had latched on to the other two, as our bodies ascended at the same time. Or maybe we descended. It was hard to tell because it was impossible to open our eyes in the heat, the smoke, and the flame.

Sucking in a breath as best I could, I ground my jaw together. I wasn't sure about the passage of time, but it felt like we were in the spiraling vortex of heat for hours.

Days.

My feet hit with a thud and the next moment the smoke dissipated. The fire was out, and we were standing in a rocky cavern, all naked and shaking. "We've got to get away from that," Gideon shouted.

I swung around and saw what he was referring to. A not-so-slow ribbon of smoldering lava was heading toward our bare feet.

From pretty much every direction.

It was like a little pocket of earth had been created for us to land, but it was shrinking in size with every second we lingered.

"Thanks for the landing, Augustus, you asshole. Could've let us out first." I didn't know if he could hear me, but it felt good to scream at him anyway. I did a quick survey. "We have to shift, use your wolf to scale the walls of the cave. There's sky up there through that crevice. Make it fast and get to safety any way you can."

Gideon and Mace immediately shifted and took off. Gideon even managed to drag the fireproof bag in his teeth with Mace's help. Autumn stepped toward me instead of doing what I asked. "Are you okay? Something seems off with you."

I growled at her, trying to force her into submission. "Not the damn time, Autumn. Get out." She hesitated a few more seconds, fiddling with the ruby pendant around her neck before finally shifting, the ruby still clinging to her neck. I waited for her to make the first few bounds up the rocky crags, and then I called my wolf to the surface, howling as I scrambled up the slick rocks too. They were hot enough to burn my paws on the ascent.

When I hit the top and shimmied through the crack my lungs filled with fresh air. I sucked in as much as I could, then made sure the others were okay. We were on the top of a small volcano, for lack of a better word. The lava from where we came from was spilling out over the rocks, creating a river, of sorts.

The Cinders. Final resting place of Augustus, the Ass. If I had any saliva and my human mouth at the time, I would've spit in it.

I put it on my To-Do list.

Spit in The Cinders.

Nope. *Piss in The Cinders.* He did creep on Terra sucking my cock, so spit wasn't enough for him.

Gideon and Mace were already scaling their way down the narrow sloping rocks, dragging the bag, so I shoved Autumn's wolf ass— literally— in their direction to make her move. I took up the rear.

It didn't take long to make it down into an odd camp of egg-shaped trailers that were perched at the base of the volcano.

I took two steps toward them and froze.

She'd been there.

R en too.

Maybe I was going loco, but I would've sworn I caught the scent of Trickstan as well. It was unsettling to think of him being anywhere near Terra and Ren. I knew they'd had contact and Terra had said there was more to his betrayal, but I didn't much give a shit on that. He's the one that got us into this hellscape. End of.

Gideon had shifted back to human form and thrown on his clothes. Mace and Autumn followed suit as Gideon scanned the perimeter. "Do you smell them?"

Still in wolf form, I nodded, lurching into the first trailer I saw, searching for anything that would tell me where they'd gone. Their scent was too weak, so it had been hours, maybe a day since they'd been there, but we were already on the trail within minutes of arriving. If we hurried, we might be able to follow them.

I lost the trail soon after I found it. My gut burned with the need to find them. When I let loose a mournful howl, Autumn jumped. She came over to scratch behind my ears, but I nipped at her hand. I didn't break the skin, but she got the message: leave me the fuck alone.

Gideon stepped in between us. "Following their scent isn't working. Let's go back to where we know they were and look for clues. Maybe something they left behind will tell us where they went."

"Good idea, Scooby. Race you to the containers," Mace said as he sped off with his wolf speed. Gideon took off after him and I didn't even look in Autumn's direction to know what she did.

The closer I got to Terra, the further away I wanted her, which meant I was being an ass and I knew it. Didn't care.

Gideon came out of one of the eggs, holding a piece of paper. "There's a map here. A town called Mystia is circled. I don't quite get it, but apparently, there's a McDonald's there, only someone turned this golden arch graphic into huge tits."

Mace jerked the map from his hand. "I don't know about Terra, but Ren *is* fond of boobies. Couldn't hurt to check it out if we've got no other leads."

I paced back and forth, growling, angry at myself for being so close, yet so far.

Mace was right. We had no other choice but to give it a shot. Aetheria was a huge place. I don't know what I'd been thinking. I should've been more specific with Augustus. It was yet another alpha fail to add to my ever-growing list.

I yelped at them, bounding out of the camp. The three of them were still in human form, but they used their speed to get to Mystia. I knew it was best for me to stay in wolf form. Mace and Gideon would understand. Probably Autumn too. So, for a few hours I focused on the trail in front of me, letting my mind go primal and pushing all my feelings down as far as they'd go.

When we got to the outskirts of Mystia, I shifted so I could dress and as I hitched my jeans up by the belt loops, Mace let out a cackle.

"Tell me I'm dreaming. There is *not* a McBrothel right there across the street. Wait, tell me there is."

Autumn toyed with the ruby around her neck. "My aunt told me about this. Fae brothels have been around for millennia. Nobody is hung up on sex or stereotypes in Aetheria. When travel between our world and Aetheria became common, the fae were fascinated with human culture, so most of their brothels turned into humanized establishments. I guess it's sort of flattering. Anyway, I bet it would be a good place to find out what's going on."

Mace ran his hand through his curls. "On it."

He started to cross the street, but I pulled him back by the arm. "No way. You'll get lost in there and we'll never see you again. Gideon or I should go."

Autumn shook her head. "Neither of you should go. Look at the both of you. The women—and probably men too—will be falling all over themselves to get you in bed. I'll do it." She didn't even look back before trouncing across the street. She said a few words to the half-dressed female clown who pointed to the door. Autumn went straight in without looking back.

The ten minutes she was gone, I tried my very best not to take my anger out on Gideon. Autumn had implied he was attractive, and our mate bond woke up like an angry beast in the night. Jealously ripped through me and I wanted to hurt him for the audacity of turning her eye. It made me want to punch myself even harder.

When she strolled out of the brothel, my body went rigid at the sight of her. Gone were the jeans and sweater she'd had on. In their place, a flowing orange dress that hugged her curves and opened down the middle, revealing her perfectly round tits. I had to close my eyes to keep from pouncing on her as she approached us.

"Wow, that's a look," Mace breathed. I shoved my hands into my pockets in response.

"Here's the deal. There's a big festival tonight for the Spring Equinox. There's a dress code, hence the look. The ladies I spoke with said that the emperor and empress will be in attendance and if we want to find our friends, to look there. It'll be a free-for-all party, but the emperor insists everyone in Aetheria celebrate. Now, off with your clothes."

A growl cleaved from my throat. I had to get the mate bond under control. "Why?"

"Because what you're wearing will make you stand out. If you want to blend in to find them, we've all got to look the part. The workers inside are more than happy to trade our human fashions for suitable attire tonight, but none of you are going in there. Give me your clothes and I'll make the trades. It's almost sundown so we don't have time to lose."

Mace groaned about losing his best band t-shirt from some group I'd never heard of, but we handed over our clothes and went inside an alleyway while we were bare-assed on the street.

Autumn came back with some pants for us—no shirts for males was the custom unless she was playing us—and I considered backing out when I saw the ones she handed me.

I had no problem with pink, but these were bubblegum-colored and wide-legged with a built-in belt that was more like a sash. They hugged my ass too tight and made me feel as conspicuous as I could be.

Mace's neon green, which he loved, was worse though. Gideon got the pale blue pants, so he was the clear winner of the wardrobe situation. We looked ridiculous, but when a crowd of people walked past the alley in the same kind of pants, it appeared we'd blend right in.

Mage help us.

Autumn jumped out of the alley, following the crowd of people over to a place where we ended up on flying carpets.

Yep.

Mace was all about it, but I couldn't sit back and enjoy the ride. No, I was getting closer. I could feel it, though we had no blood connection anymore, and I had no reason to believe we'd be able to find them in a huge crowd, or even if they'd be there. It was intuition, a deep-seated physical manifestation in me. I would see her soon.

Our carpets let us off in the center part of Aetheria, based on the map. People were milling around everywhere. The mood was fun and festive, people were drinking, and laughing, all discussing who would be the big entertainment the emperor would provide for the night, guessing who they'd hook up with. I saw it and heard it all, but it was just white noise in my head.

Until I heard her laugh.

Hers.

It was like the wind picked it up and delivered it to my ears alone.

I swung around, my eyes scanning the crowd, past all the revelry and celebration, through the wispy trees, and into the garden behind the castle.

My heart stopped.

She was wearing a deep purple dress that draped around her body in the most sensual way. It reminded me of the way the sheets twisted around her when we got lost in between them.

Her stomach was exposed on one side, revealing a silky bronze patch of skin that beckoned my tongue like nothing had before. And her hair—Magedamn—her hair was piled up on her head in ringlets that begged to be played with and torn apart by my hands.

I had to get to her.

Didn't even stop to explain myself to the others. I just bolted as fast as I could, blurring past people and carts and trees and every little crumb of a thing between us until I got to her.

Her gasp was everything. And the way she said my name was even more than that. "Wells?"

Guards dressed in white pointed rods at me. I didn't care. To me, there was no one else around. We were back in the dreamscape in our little cozy bubble where existence was just us.

I fell to my knees before her, grabbing her by the waist and pulling her to me, pressing my nose, my mouth, and my face to her body, and breathing her in. "I'm here, Precious." She dug her hands into my hair as her quiet sobs reached my ears. "I'm never leaving your side again."

A voice from behind us dared to burst into our bubble. "I'm not so sure about that."

Wells didn't even have time to see who'd said it. He sprang to his feet, lunging at Magnus with his wolf speed.

Of course, the emperor's guards were quick to protect him. Wells got blasted with Fire, Wind, Water, and Earth Magic at once, knocking him back into the nearest tree. Turquoise leaves rained down on his head as he scrambled to his feet, preparing to strike again, even though his first attempt was thwarted.

"Wells, wait!" I shouted, running across and getting in front of him to protect him from the next assault. The feel of his hands as they wrapped around my waist ignited the phoenix blood inside me. I flushed with heat and desire and warmth, protection. It had felt real in the dreamscape, but that was nothing compared to this. This was palpable, but I couldn't let that distract me though.

If I didn't diffuse the situation, he would be carted away like Ren had been. I had no idea where Magnus had taken him and Fox. I couldn't let that happen to Wells too. "This is Emperor Magnus. There's been a mistake, Emperor. He didn't mean any harm. He wouldn't have come at you if he'd known who you were."

A low growl came from behind me, but I stepped back, right onto Wells' toes to get him to shut it off. "We came across this wolf in Mystia. He'd been ill, lost from his pack. Ren didn't want to leave him stranded so he let him travel with us for a while. I guess he got attached to me. He's harmless, I promise. Just a little out of his mind. He didn't even realize it was the Spring Frolic until we told him. I'll take care of this. Just give me a second."

Magnus narrowed his gaze on Wells like he was trying to get an internal read on him. I had to tighten my shoulders to keep from shaking. There's no way Magnus could've known who he was, that he'd come from our world. Somehow. I had a feeling that the story was complicated and while I was dying to hear it, I couldn't risk Magnus learning any of it.

I didn't allow him time to interrogate. I just grabbed Wells by the hand and dragged him away from the garden, out into the crowd that was starting to swell around us.

I knew there would be some guards following us, so I had to make them buy my story. When I pulled him to a stop, I purposely put my hands on his hard chest—gulping at the familiar feel of his pecs against my palms—and pushed him back a few feet. I said nothing out loud but sent a message in my head.

"I've never wanted to kiss you more than right now, but we've got to be cool until I figure out what Magnus did with Ren and Trickstan. Can you do that?"

He blinked a few times like he couldn't believe he was seeing me. At his sides, his hands clenched and unclenched until he reached out for me, dragging me against his chest.

Wait.

I pulled away again. "Did you not hear me in your head?" I whispered. "Why isn't the phoenix connection working?"

He stalled for a few seconds, rubbing his jaw before snapping out of it and curling his hands in the fabric at my waist. "It's nothing. I just can't believe I made it to you. It's been a lifetime of waiting to get here."

Sensing the overbearing white presence creeping in on us from all sides, I swallowed and did my best to school my voice so it didn't give away everything I felt for him to the guards who were currently sucking at stealth mode. "Right. Well, I'm glad you found us again, but I need to get back to my friend, Joy now. Emperor Magnus wanted to speak to Ren earlier. I'm sure he'll be back soon, and you can have a chat. I hope so anyway. Did *you* find your pack? Are they here with you?"

Meaning: Ren and I were separated by force, and I don't know where he is. I hope you brought the cavalry with you.

He narrowed his eyes as he read between the lines. "Yeah, a few from my pack came with me: Jase, Gabriel, and October."

I was able to release a slow steady breath. Wells had caught on and he'd made a good call with his fake names. The longer I'd been apart from Ren, the more nervous I'd become that Magnus was unraveling our plot to get rid of him. I'd been milliseconds away from asking Magnus where the crap Ren was when Wells appeared.

If Magnus sensed there were more of us from the other side here, it would be a problem. He was all about control and suppression, so he'd kill us or use us if we were exposed. Our best hope was to chill and wait until we could all meet up together and get a true read on everything. Had to play it cool until then.

Cage the Mage, I couldn't believe I was close enough to Wells to touch him and I couldn't.

Knowing Autumn had tagged along wasn't the best news of the century.

Of course, he would've brought his fated mate with him. Even though I knew—*knew*—he loved me and would never give in to their bond, it still ate at my soul that she was involved in his life.

Didn't have time to chase that particular rabbit though.

I patted his shoulder, like the good *acquaintance* I was. "I'm glad you found your pack. I can't wait to see them. Why don't you take a look around the central province? There are some cool buildings to explore on the edge of the Springlands. Might enjoy the architecture. Or maybe the castle would be a good place to start."

To find Ren.

He nodded, and then his eyes skated over my body in a way that gave me chills. "Good idea. I'll get on it, but can I ask for at least one dance with you later? You look like a precious jewel, if I'm allowed to say that."

Arm's length, Terra. We're acting here. Do not accidentally rip his pants off and get on your knees in the middle of the crowd.

"Of course, you are. Thanks. You don't look so bad yourself. Love your pink pants. They'd look better with polka dots though."

Right there. His eyes should have flared at that.

They didn't.

He *did* laugh though.

"I'll get on that tour now. Just remember, you owe me a dance." He pulled me in for a big hug and I melted into him as if we were molded into one person. His whisper was full of raspy hotness that made my knees buckle. "I'll send the others, but I'm keeping my eyes on you. You may rely on it."

I had to laugh. Magic 8-Ball speak was like my love language.

The whispering voice in my head cut through his throaty laugh though. *"You have to find me tonight. If you don't, outlook not so good."*

I rubbed the back of my neck and let out a snort, annoyed at the interruption. And the vague whisper. "I don't even know who you are, stupid disembodied voice. How can I find you?" Wells lifted an eyebrow. "The sporadic whispering voice I keep hearing wants me to find it but not telling me how to do it. I've got enough shit with Magnus so, if it doesn't give me actionable intel soon, I'm going to ignore it. Or maybe go ballistic from trying."

"Actionable intel? You sound like Ren."

At the mention of his name, we both stilled. "Wells, I'm—"

"Nope. Not discussing that now. Just go do what you have to do. I'll find you later." He squeezed my hands and disappeared into the crowd.

Great. I had him, then he slipped away again.

The voice in my head was stronger this time. "I can only send short bursts, so listen. I need you, Wells, Trickstan, and Autumn to find me. Come tonight. We won't get another chance. This is all the magic I can spare. You have to —"

The urgency of the whisper wasn't lost on me. I was already on edge about Ren and Trickstan, then for Wells to show up out of nowhere, looking all hot but acting all different. It was like the grandfather clock in my Gram's house was ticking away to our doom.

I closed my eyes and wrapped my hand around the vial of earth at my neck. Well, more accurately, tucked in between my boobs so as not to mess with the neckline of my dress, according to Joy. "Gram, if ever I needed you, it's now."

Silence.

Then a faint whisper of light from my bracelet.

I took it as a good sign.

Or a goodbye.

I'd soon see.

Trickstan

K nowing I was about to splat onto the ground put a lot of my life into perspective.

Yes, I was ashamed of hurting my friends, of leaving my sister in the crutches of a bad man, of being too dumb to figure out what memories I was missing. All of it. For a second as the ground loomed at me, I welcomed my end. It was fitting to be splattered all over the ground like a mud puddle for people to walk over for years to come.

Here likes Trickstan…

Tristan?

Neither sounded right to me.

"Hold on to my neck, Mister. Stop fighting me and I'll get us to safety."

Kiko. What a friend.

I should've been like her.

I nestled into her arms as a blast of Water magic hit us. We plummeted again and there was a big pop, and I was lost in darkness.

I woke to the sound of Kiko popping in and out of existence. I raised, finding myself lying on a bed of dry leaves with the stench of the Boiling Swamp in the air. "Who shot that Water at us?"

"Imperial guards. They must have been waiting for you to arrive. Magnus didn't want to take any chances of you getting away."

"Hm. So, you brought us to the Autumnlands?"

"Yes, I figured it was the last place the emperor would look for us. He doesn't come here other than to do his evil bidding." She mimicked his puffed-out chest. "I swear on the square that I don't care if you kick my derriere. I'll treat you all unfair if you dare to reject the square."

She was very good at impersonating him and had chosen a safe spot for us to land. True, he'd brought me to the very spot to put the Binding spell on me, he didn't know that I knew that. If he knew I knew it, I'd know it, but I didn't, so it was safe to assume he didn't know I knew.

I tried to take a deep breath to get my bearings, but that was hard with the odor in the air. Because I was standing in the same place as when it happened, memories started slapping around my head like jolts of electricity. It was like they were tickling my brain and trying to get out.

He'd been so kind to Joy—to me—at first anyway. He'd showered her with affection and brought me in like I was his family. He gave me a home and a position of status as he rose to emperor above the kings and queens of Court, and I was…happy.

Tickle.

"You understand, there'll be a few casualties in the war for magic."

Poke.

"I can trust you to keep your sister out of this, right? She doesn't need to bother her pretty little head with the specifics on how we get all the magic back."

Smack.

"We're family now. You'll get more than anyone who helps me if you just let me guide your actions a bit. The spell won't be strong, and you'll only be gone away a few years. I love you like the brother I never had; I'd never use a spell that would hurt you in any way. I swear on the square. It's going to change our lives and when I'm in total control, you and your sister will want for nothing."

"And the humans on the other side?" I'd asked.

"Gone. Nuisances like bugs under our feet to be squashed. The new world I'm creating will be nothing but fae, the way the Mage intended."

I doubted that was true. The Mage had created so many other amazing Magicals. Still, I didn't see through his lies. "Should we not keep the humans around, maybe let them have their world and we live in ours? Seems cruel to wipe them out."

"It's not cruel, it's kind. Once they see our strength, our might, knowing they can't touch us will be catastrophic to them. They'll either rebel and we'll have to kill them, or they'll submit and be useless to us. It's for the best to take them out. You'll see. I have a plan. I just need you on the other side to stop those meant to stop me."

At the time I'd assumed he meant humans.

I knew better now. Terra was created as a defense against Magnus.

It was so confusing to think of him warmly, then flop to his vicious plan. It was like he was two different people.

Wait a second.

Wait just a Magedamned second.

Two people.

Not one.

Shit.

"Kiko, you've got to get me to Terra right now."

"Are you sure? That doesn't seem safe."

"It doesn't matter. I know what I forgot, what I was Bound to forget. If I don't warn her, none of them will make it through tonight, including us. We have to go now."

I'd shifted from human to wolf back to human again, pacing in both forms. Growling in both forms.

Losing my fucking mind in both forms.

"For the love of the Mage, will you stay human and sit down? Wearing a hole in the floor isn't going to get us out of here any quicker."

I sneered at Fox, bearing my teeth as I stepped back into my pants. "It makes me feel better."

"Well, it makes me feel worse. Just stop it."

We were locked in the turret of Emperor Magnus' castle. I knew I had good hair, but the Rapunzel routine was too damn much. There was some kind of Magical barrier in place—elf spell work most likely— and even though we could see and hear everything due to the open-air windows, we were bound so our voices couldn't be heard.

I screamed myself hoarse before I realized it. That meant we were probably hidden from view too. We weren't that far up in the grand scheme of things. Maybe four to five stories in our modern terms. We could see and hear, but we were invisible.

There were a couple of chairs—that wouldn't go through the barrier— and some cream-colored drapes tied over the windows we couldn't use. It might have made a cool lookout or sitting room at one point, but it was clear as glass that it was a prison now.

The only good thing about the situation—and good was exaggerating it—was that I was now certain Fox was on our side. He'd been thrown in this room just like I had. "One more time, what do you remember?"

He stood up, daring to walk at me like he was going to hit me, but he swerved at the last minute and went over to the edge to lean out the window again. "I remember you and Terra coming out of an underground door near Midsummer, telling her where to get food at the open market and saying I'd meet you there. The next thing I knew I was flipping Trickstan off a mat. That's it." He paused to move to another window, craning his neck to see as far as he could. "I don't see her yet. She should be getting ready to announce the music. If he's done something with her—"

"Look, as much as I know it sucks to hear it, another man is in love with your woman. He won't hurt her. At least you know she'll be safe with him for now."

I couldn't say the same for Terra.

The thought of Magnus getting anywhere near her made my muscles tense. I *had* to get out of here. And to get out, I had to know everything.

"Have you ever experienced memory loss like that before?"

He turned away from the curtain, huffing in my direction. "A couple of times. Once when I was first assigned to the emperor. It was at night in my room, nothing serious. I just suddenly realized I'd taken out all my belongings, papers, books, and treasures from home, and strewn them all over the place. No idea why. The other time I recall was the first day I was placed on Joy's detail. She was so warm and welcoming, but I could barely speak to her because I was already in love with her. I kept my head down and before I knew it, the day was over, and I was back in my room. I don't think it's happened again until now. Do you think I'm sick?"

I ran my hands through my hair, then yanked one of the curtain ties and used it to pull my hair back. A wave of sadness washed through me, but I didn't have time to dwell on the phantom feeling of Terra's hands in my hair. "No, I don't think you're sick, I think you've been used somehow. Maybe it's a Binding spell, maybe not. We've got to get out of here to find out."

I paced the perimeter of the turret, glancing down to search for something, someone who could help us. Terra was down there somewhere if I could just get to her.

The figure I saw wasn't Terra though.

I rubbed my eyes, just to be certain.

Wells.

He was walking with eyes focused on something ahead of him, predatory, like the alpha he was. And while my heart flipped knowing my friend was here, that feeling quickly turned into a lead stone sinking in my gut.

If he was here, then Terra was nothing but a memory to me.

Terra

There was a dais set up in front of the castle. I was somehow a guest of honor at the shindig, so I was seated beside Joy. Magnus had walked to the front to introduce the music. As soon as the crowd noticed him stepping forward, all the noise stopped. He stood there in his white pants, chest puffing out, reveling at being the center of attention.

It was likely his sole reason for everything.

I kept my eyes peeled on Wells. He was leaning—oh, how I missed that sexy lean—against a tree with pink leaves that matched his pants. Sly. It had been easy for me to spot him that way. He was sporting Gesture Two like everything around him was cool as ice.

I knew better by the way his body was tense with uncoiled power just below the surface.

He was going to move if Magnus did anything suspect. While my first thought of him going beast on the emperor was 'oh hell to the fucking yes,' I had to be smart about it. If we had no way to open the Conduit or some other suitable plan for Magic, letting Wells rip him to pieces wouldn't do us any good.

We had to find his secrets, the source of his power first.

Then I'd let Wells go all cage-match on him.

A girl can have her fantasies, right?

"Thank you, Aetheria for coming out to celebrate the Spring Equinox. It's my joy and privilege to bring Aetheria's finest musicians to the stage to entertain you tonight. I see most of us have begun to enjoy the ample libations provided by my darling wife and me." He took a glass from the podium and raised it toward Joy. She smiled and did the royal wave to the crowd.

"Please, have as much as you like. Now, once the show begins, feel free to give in to all those Spring urges we all enjoy during this season, no matter our homeland or species. But do remember that consent is an important part of the celebration. Guards will be filtering through the central province to make sure we're all behaving as good, square citizens. Mind you, if you end up on the wrong side of the barriers, you'll be stuck until the Summer Solstice, so choose your locations wisely."

The crowd laughed. I didn't find the joke in it, but thanks for the heads-up, Mags. We were about to experience a drunken orgy.

Nope. No way and forgettaboutit.

"Let us take a moment to pause and remember how we came to be in this place of prosperity, free from the shackles of human interference on the other side of the Conduit."

I stiffened in my seat as the entire crowd—save for Wells—took a knee, murmuring "I swear on the square."

Could Mags not hear how half-hearted that was? I guess he didn't care. He had them right where he wanted them. They were beholden to him and none of them had any power at all.

After a few moments of eerie silence where he and Wells had a stare-off most adolescent boys would've died for, he clapped his hands.

They all stood up and he announced with no fanfare whatsoever, "Allow me to introduce Chord and Coda. May the festivities begin."

The crowd erupted in cheers as two men with what I can only describe as fluffy, swoopy hair took the stage carrying streamlined hollow cellos with two additional necks on them. They were shirtless like all the men in attendance and the second they sat down in the chairs; they unfurled wings covered in feathers.

They began their song, each of them playing their cello like normal on the middle neck. It was nice, then they ramped it up, using their wings to pluck the other necks, and the sound was like nothing I'd ever heard. It was rich, intense, and mesmerizing in the most sensual way. I mean if I was going to pick a soundtrack for an orgy, I'd probably choose this music. I had hard suspicions Mace would back me up on that.

Joy leaned over. "They're cockatrices. When they're in their shifted forms, they can't play a lick, but halfway between cockatrice and human, it sounds like this. Amazing, right?"

It was beautiful. Though, I was sad to recall I never heard Gram say a thing about cockatrices. It seemed like a gimme for her.

Magnus strolled over to Joy, holding his hand out to her, but glaring at me. "You won't mind if I share a dance with my wife?"

I put on my cheesiest, fakest grin. "Not at all. Could you tell me where Ren is first? I'd like to dance too."

He was quick to answer, leaning over to deliver his lines right in my face. "Oh, he said he'd prefer to hash out a new plan to capture Trickstan with Fox. They opted to stay behind instead of celebrating with us. I tried to persuade him, but I assume you realize how stubborn he is. He said to send his apologies for not attending the festival. I'm sure you'll find him in a day or two after everything here dies down." He turned to Joy, pulling her out of her seat. "Now, come along, Dear."

I wasn't a werewolf, but I could smell the lie in his tone. On top of that, Ren would never apologize for anything. Not even standing me up at a party. Nope, Magnus wasn't even trying hard to hide anything anymore. He knew Ren and I were helping Trickstan, and he had some scheme to deal with it. I could only hope and pray to the Mage he hadn't done something drastic to Ren already.

I tracked Magnus and Joy off the dais. As they made their way down, the crowd automatically parted for them. The cockatrice duo switched from an upbeat kind of melody to something slower. As soon as they hit what was standing in for the dance floor—a section of cobblestone covered with a thick layer of sand—Magnus began groping Joy's breasts, looking over to me as he did so.

Did not want to witness that, so I scanned away, pinning my eyes on Wells. He kicked off the tree and gave me a Gesture One with the familiar tilt of his head.

Everything around me zoomed into perfect focus. I sailed off the dais and went careening into his arms. His smirk was around level eleven on a scale of one to five when he wrapped his hands around me, slowly inching across my back. His voice in my ear made my blood sing. "I haven't forgiven you for saying I was out of my mind earlier. You're going to have to make it up to me."

I leaned against him, breathing in the manly scent of smoke and sandalwood, letting it course through my body and ease my mind. "Aren't you at least a bit out of your mind though?

"For you, I am, yeah."

"Then there's nothing to make up."

He lifted my chin, forcing me to step back and look up into his eyes. There was a whole world there. I knew it well and I wanted to explore it all the same. "I suppose not."

It was such a perfect moment, so long in coming, that I would've sworn the sand beneath my feet heated up. That was probably just the lust in my body soaring to catastrophic heights because I was finally with him again.

There was too much to say and to do, but everything was a tangled jumble of intensity in my head. Nothing would come out. My limbs wouldn't move. I just stared at his gorgeous face and thanked the Mage silently for bringing us back together.

He wasn't at a loss for action. He flipped me around, pressing my back against his chest. As his hands snaked their way across my bared belly and he began to move against me, I was taken back to the night at Boulderbrook when we'd danced on the table. When I'd thrown myself at him and kissed him like I'd wanted to since the beginning. I didn't need the fae froth this time though. The memory appeared in my head on its own.

Damn, could he still move his hips? Well enough that the tell-tale burn in my stomach raged to life. A tremor rocked through me, and I had to grip his hands to keep myself upright. Pushing against his chest, I leaned my head back, encouraging him to take his hands lower with an arch of my hips.

The tremor turned into a rumble. I didn't even care who was around us to feel it. I mean, we were at an orgy. Would it be so far of a stretch for us to...do things?

Just when I thought I would burst into flames, he leaned down and pressed a trail of soft kisses along my neck, inching his way up until he had my earlobe in his teeth. I tensed, waiting—aching—for the sting of his teeth, but it didn't come.

Instead, he chuckled. "The things I'm going to do to you…"

Mother of the Mage, the rest of that sentence.

"Like what?"

"I'll start by tearing this dress from your hot body. Don't get me wrong, I like it, but I want what's underneath it." He reached down low, gathering the hem of the dress in his hands, then bringing it slowly up my flesh. My legs were entirely exposed, but I didn't care. The feel of his warm hands on me was way more important.

"And then?"

"Once I get you naked, I'm going to make you so wet that you beg for me to fuck you, but I won't."

"That seems needlessly cruel."

"Maybe, but it'll be worth it."

"If you say so."

"I do."

This tango between us was more than just a dance. It was an acceptance, an apology, a promise and a prayer all rolled into one.

He dropped the dress and I hummed at the familiar feel as he sank his hands into my hair, loosening the curls so he could play with them. "I cannot wait to get my cock inside that soft, wet pussy of yours. I'm getting harder thinking about how tight you grip me when I'm inside you."

This was dangerous. We needed to stay focused, but I was having trouble remembering just why. "Wells. Please."

I meant please stop. He heard please continue.

"More? Okay. If you think I'm going to stop at one or two times, you're mistaken. I'm going to rail you until your eyes roll to the back of your head and you're hoarse from screaming my name. Sound good?"

"Yes. Yep. Uh-huh. Affirmative."

I was so into what he was saying, what he was doing with his voice, his words, his hands, and his tongue, it was like we were dancing in an earthquake. Somewhere in the back of my mind, I realized I might be losing control of my Earth magic because I was so turned on. It had happened before. I took a deep breath to calm my hormones.

Simmer down, Terra. We'll get to the sexytimes soon.

Wells pulled my hair, forcing me to look back up at him. He pressed his lips to mine and even though we were sideways and upside down, an explosion went off in my heart. Kissing him was like the beginning and end of everything. There was no way to separate us, no way for anything to get inside our bond. When he pulled back, colorful leaves from the trees around rained down on the two of us. He laughed. "Nice job with the ambiance. Now, I want to hear every little juicy, dirty, scandalous thing in your head. Tell me what you want, Precious."

"Ren."

Wells stopped moving. His hands, his cock that was pressed against my back, his lips against my neck. He didn't growl or scream or shove me away. Everything in him just…turned to stone. I cursed myself for the bad timing, but it wasn't me doing it.

I grabbed his face and directed it toward the ground in front of me. "No. Look." Ren's name was scrawled into the sand that covered the cobblestones around us. "That was not there when we started dancing and I didn't do it," I told him. We both whipped our heads, searching the crowd for him, but he was nowhere. "Where are you, Troll Boy?"

The ground shifted, it was slight, but enough for me to tell he was using his Earth magic to make this happen. His name vanished and *SOS* and *castle* appeared in its place. Wells growled. "He's in the castle."

He started marching in that direction, but I grabbed his elbow. "Hold on. It's a huge place and the guards aren't going to just let us waltz in there and bring him out."

"I'm not waltzing in. I'm breaking the fucking door down." The determination on his face to get to his friend, his brother, despite what had gone on between us made me swoon even more. He whistled, then followed with a short howl. It went mostly unnoticed because the music and the party itself were ramping up to a fever pitch already.

Before I could blink, I was lifted off the ground from behind. My legs went flying as I was swirled in a circle several times.

It wasn't hard to figure out what was happening. "Mace, I missed you too, but put me down before I take someone's eye out!" It took a few more seconds for him to drop me, but when he did, I found myself sandwiched between him and Gideon in a hug. I would've loved to sit around and catch up, but the ground shook again.

Mace bent down. "Did that sand just arrange itself into a dick? Some party you're having here."

Gideon smacked the back of his head. "No, it's a replica of the turret on the top of that castle."

"That must be where Ren is being held. Let's go." I turned around, ready to storm the castle, and bumped right into Autumn.

There was a second where I wasn't sure exactly what was going to go down. They'd both been waylaid by Terra sprinting off in search of Ren and were standing there blinking at each other, neither of the two knowing what to say.

Make that three of us.

How the fuck did I resolve this for either of them? Or myself?

No damn clue. The facts were still the facts. Autumn was my fated mate. Terra was the one I loved.

Terra finally broke the tension. "I'm sorry. I didn't see you standing there. I'm just anxious to go make sure Ren's alright." She glanced over her shoulder at me, gauging my response.

Who was I to be offended by her need to get to him? I shared it.

Autumn shook her head, her auburn hair caressing her bare shoulders as she gripped the necklace between her fingers. "It's fine. I should be the one apologizing. I didn't know the ruby necklace would get stuck. Sorry."

"No big deal. It's not mine anyway. Keep it."

Gideon, thank the Mage's crusty ball sac, stepped between them. "Weren't we launching a rescue?"

That snapped them out of it. Terra took off toward the castle while the rest of us fell in line behind her. Something told me that she,

Autumn, and I would have more than enough time in the future to work out our dynamics.

I checked out the turret and there was no sign of anyone that I could tell, but Magnus seemed to be a crafty bastard. Who knew what magic he possessed and how he used it?

Terra led us over to the far side of the castle. She motioned for us to stay behind the shrubbery while she and Autumn approached the two guards standing point at the door. "Excuse me, do you mind if we go in and use the powder room? I'm staying with Joy, you know."

The guards took more than a few seconds to ogle the goods on both of them. My blood boiled with the urge to rip out their throats, but Mace and Gideon stepped around me, beating me to the punch by sneaking behind the guards when they were distracted by tits and cutting off their air supply.

We bolted in and up three flights of stairs. Knowing we needed to go higher, Terra paused. "I don't know how to get up there. There's got to be a door somewhere right?"

We checked every room, nook, and cranny and found no other way to get to the turret from where we were. I growled, my frustration getting the better of me. "Mage, this thing is made of sand, we should just claw it down."

"Interesting idea," Terra muttered as she placed her hand on the sandy wall.

I was awestruck when the sand began to shift and fold under her fingertips. "Maybe wait until we're out of here before you bring it down on our heads, Precious."

"I'm not bringing it down, I'm communicating. Just like Ren did."

A single break in the sand inched up the wall, splintering and winding until it passed under the ceiling. All the while, her amethyst bracelet glowed. "We're here, Ren. Tell us how to get up there."

It took a few minutes we probably didn't have, but finally a single scroll of sand came rippling down the wall. It veered right and crawled over our heads, down the long hall, halting at a corner where a sconce was burning. An arrow appeared next, pointing to a tiny dent in the sand along the wall. If you weren't looking for it, there's no way anyone would've seen it.

Terra strolled right up to it and put her hand there. The sand disintegrated at her touch, making a door for us to go through. Mace barreled past her, shouting, "Renny!" at the top of his lungs. We all fucking missed that bastard so much.

Gideon shrugged. "So much for the stealth approach." He took off a step behind Mace. Terra followed him and I took up the rear, completely forgetting that Autumn was lingering behind us until she touched my back. "Maybe I should play lookout. I'll shout if anyone comes near."

"Good thinking." I nodded and bounded into the darkness, finding a staircase. The others were way ahead of me, so I used my speed to get caught up to them. My heart was racing more than I wanted it to. I was as anxious to get Ren out of there and to safety as the rest of him, but the lingering unfinished business of Terra between us split me in two.

I still wasn't pissed about it, but I'd have been lying if I said I wanted to watch Terra hug the life out of him like I knew she was about to do.

Light streamed down the stairs as Mace hit the solid door at the top, busting it in with brute wolf strength. One by one, we clamored into the turret. Ren was standing at the far side, a shot of flames in his hand. When he realized it was us, they extinguished. A smile—about as big as I'd ever seen him make—stretched across his face as his gaze bounced over each one of us. When he landed on Terra, it faded.

She either didn't notice or didn't care because she shot over, throwing her arms around him. He stood there with his hands at his side, looking over her shoulder at me with a mix of apology and remorse. His pain was unmistakable.

This was the moment when I would discover what was in the depths of my heart and soul.

As I crossed the floor, I had no idea what I would do when I got to them. None. My head was a blank slate of possibilities, scenario after scenario running through at lightning speed.

He tracked me as I walked toward them, his eyes questioning. When I got there, I took his arms and placed them around Terra's waist—forced him to do what I knew he wanted. What he needed. I threw my arms around them both, pressing them together and enveloping them both with all the love I had for them.

Ren tensed and Terra's body went limp as the relief I knew she felt flooded through her. Stepping back, I allowed them a couple more seconds of hug time. When that was done and she moved away, I made a fist and punched him in the jaw.

I never said I was noble. He *did* kiss my girl. He didn't fall for her on purpose. I knew he'd probably done a million things to try and stop it, but none of that mattered in the end. Her heart was mine. We all knew it, all accepted it. He'd get over her, in time. And she'd never let him forgo their friendship over it. She was too stubborn for that.

Before Ren had even righted himself from the force of my blow, he started laughing. A real, genuine laugh and I had missed that damn sound. I took him in my arms again, slapping his back as he grunted, "What was that for?"

Was he serious or did I knock his brain a little too hard? "You kissed my girl. I'm happy to see you, but I couldn't just let it go."

He looked over at Terra, his face scrunching up in confusion like he'd already forgotten what he'd done. He shook it off quickly though. "Your girl. Yeah. Sorry."

My hackles went up. I hadn't hit him that hard. I was about to ask if he was okay when Mace had gotten his fill of waiting. He piled on Ren's back, rubbing his head. "Your hair's down. I never thought I'd see the day."

Ren bucked him off, then turned around to hug him too. "I like it down."

He, in fact, did not like it down. I glanced at Terra, who had given him the side-eye. She'd noticed too. "It's my fault. I took his hair ties, but we don't have time for idle discussions about fashion. We need to get out of here."

"Great idea," Gideon said. He gave Ren a quick bro squeeze, then took a few steps toward the door. He didn't even get a foot through before Autumn came flying in rolling across the floor like she'd been thrown.

REN

Autumn took a tumble as she rolled. She'd been thrown into the room with force by the guards.

My guards.

No, not mine, his. Emperor Magnus. A bubble of laughter got caught in my throat at the sight of the wolves' wide eyes.

I told myself to wait just a Magedamn minute.

Why did I think the guards were mine? And why would I laugh about Autumn getting caught?

That was the second time it had happened in the past five minutes. First I'd forgotten that Terra and I weren't together, then I'd thought the guards were mine.

Something wasn't right.

The faces in the room around me were familiar yet felt so distant I couldn't remember one thing about them. It made my mouth dry with fear. I should've known them.

I scanned the room, noting everyone I saw, as panic clawed at my insides. Wells: he was my alpha, my brother in almost every sense of the word, Terra's real boyfriend and guiding beacon of life who showed me what family meant. Gideon: smart, charming, a steady force of nature who taught me about stability. Mace: funniest asshole ever, gave dumb nicknames, total fuckboy, taught me about being comfortable with who

I was, and that joy was never far below the surface, even in the darkest of times.

Then there was Autumn, who was somehow Wells' mate, and Fox, my trusted guard and newest enemy. Unfiltered rage shot through my body. He dared to sleep with my wife. I was going to murder him.

The fuck was happening to me?

I shook my head, trying to get my bearings and lose the wicked feelings racing through me.

It won't work. I've taken over. All you can do is go along for the ride while I take out your entire crew with your own hands.

Magnus.

In my head.

Whispering threats.

But how?

This is how much power I have. I can enter the body of anyone whose blood I've collected. I can manipulate people and events, and bend things to my divine will, all while maintaining a bit of my soul in my own body. It's my gift, my legacy. I know you think you can take me down, but that's not possible.

This must have been what happened with Fox and Jael, and possibly Trickstan too. He'd taken over and they had no recollection of what had happened when he was in their bodies. Just like them, when I swore to the square, he collected my blood. And now he was in my body about to do something awful. I could feel his malicious intent rising inside me as if it were mine. For a nanosecond, I wanted to murder everyone around me. My friends. Terra.

I couldn't let him take over completely. I wouldn't. I'd throw myself off the turret if it meant he'd use my hands to harm anyone I cared about.

As Wells and Terra discussed options on what to do next, I inched over to the edge of the turret and glanced over the side. If I kept my wolf subdued when I jumped, it would kill me. And maybe that would trigger something and take Magnus out with me.

Don't you dare, wolf. Don't you fucking dare. It will take nothing for me to subdue you into cooperation.

I focused on his voice, hoping I could relay my thoughts to him in the same way he did me. *"If you don't get out of my body and my head right now, I'll do it. If you have any way to read my mind you know it's not an idle threat. You can't control me completely or you would have by now."*

I wasn't bluffing. If it meant protecting Terra and my brothers, I would give my life. No hesitation.

I admit, you're stronger than most I commandeer, but I can make you do what I want. All I need is a little boost of Fire magic to override your wolf.

For a controlling asshole, he was stupid. He'd revealed that he used the person's elemental magic to control them. What he didn't know was I had more than Fire within me, thanks to the fusion. If I could use my Earth magic, maybe I could keep enough of myself to defeat him; To cause a chain reaction and kill him.

I placed my hands on the sand ledge, drawing on my Earth magic, pulling what I could from the sand. His anger—confusion—bloomed. It was like it woke a monster inside me who was trying to claw its way out. My vision grayed, but I managed to get one boot on the ledge before everything around me went black.

"Ren, what are you doing? Get down!"

At my panicked words, Wells used his speed to get over to Ren, wrestling down from the ledge to keep him from jumping. "The fuck, man?"

He shrugged. "Sorry. I was just looking to see if there was a way down." Ren apologizing? Had to be a first. "I don't think there is. We'll have to find a way through the door."

"Which is what I was just saying," Wells growled. "Brute force is the only way. Between all of us, I bet we can take any guards that come our way." Mace put his hands on his head, looking unsure. "Do you disagree, Mace?"

"Yeah, no. I'm with you, but before we go, I think I need to mention something important, but I don't know how some of you are going to take it. I may get my ass kicked for it."

I motioned for him to talk. "Out with it."

"Okay. Don't shoot the messenger. You know that birthmark on your wrist, Terra?"

"Yes?"

He took a side step toward Gideon, almost bumping into him. "Autumn has one just like it between her tits," he blurted in one breath.

For a few seconds none of us said or did anything. I'd noted her breasts were exposed with the halter dress she was wearing, but it wasn't like I was peeping her cleavage all night. That was Mace's jam.

Wells stepped over and we both framed Autumn. Her hands flew up to her chest, seeing how everyone was staring. I pulled her hand down and flipped over my own, revealing my wrist to her.

Mace was right. It was the exact same mark.

There was no way that was a coincidence. Especially when I considered how the ruby necklace had spoken to her as the amethyst bracelet had me.

Her face went ashen. "What does this mean?"

Ren rushed over. "You're a golem too?" he snarled.

"What are you talking about?" She was addressing Ren but looking straight at me. "Golem?"

"Long story, short. I'm a golem, but I have gnome DNA too, so I can do most gnomey things. So far—even though it was a bitch to discover it—the golem news hasn't interfered much with my life."

It was weird to boil it down to a few sentences, but it had become something that was just a small part of who I was, I didn't give it much thought.

Autumn didn't look comforted at all with my revelation. I knew how that felt and while we did have an antagonistic relationship thanks to our feelings for Wells, I wouldn't wish that hollow feeling I had when I learned about myself on anyone. "We're assuming the squiggle birthmark is the maker's mark, but I don't know who created me. Um, us, I guess. I'm hoping the answer to that will become apparent in Aetheria since we were made from Aetherian soil."

Everything I said to make her feel better seemed to do the opposite. She slumped over into the closest arms. Ren's. He caught her, but the look on his face was murderous. Wells saw it too. He moved to snatch Autumn from me just as Ren growled. "I can return you to Aetherian soil just as quickly as you were made."

Ren's hands erupted in Fire magic, but Wells had gotten Autumn away, basically throwing her at Gideon.

He took Ren's blast of Fire, which did nothing but skate over the surface of his skin as he combined his own orange flames with it. I was surprised he didn't use his silver phoenix flame, but I guessed he was only trying to deflect the magic, not hurt Ren with it.

"Ren, why are you trying to hurt Autumn?" I shouted, but he didn't get a chance to reply because Wells clocked him in the jaw with his alpha strength and he hit the floor with a thud.

"Something's wrong with Ren, but we don't have time to figure out what it is. I had no other choice but to incapacitate him for now. One problem at a time."

Right. We had to get out first, then figure out what was going on with Ren, and then deal with Autumn's potential golemness. It was a lot.

Help is coming, but I have to go silent until you get to me.

Oh yeah. We had to figure out who the voice in my mind was too.

Our list was getting pretty damn long.

"The voice in my head says help is coming, but I don't know who or what or when or how. And apparently, it's going dark until we find it, which makes no fucking sense because he won't tell me exactly where he is."

Was my voice a little loud and screechy? Yes. Didn't care.

Before anyone had a chance to ask any follow-up questions, Kiko popped into the room with Trickstan. The second his feet touched the floor, he started spewing words faster than I thought possible. "I remembered what Magnus can do. It's bad, Babycakes. Real bad.

He has more power than any other Magical ever born. He can use magic to jump bodies, control people, and make them do things. We're all in danger, including you, Fox." He strolled over to the fae. "He found out about you and Joy. He'll murder you and torture her for her betraying him.

"And Terra, I don't know everything yet, but your purpose is to take him out. That's why you were made." He turned his head slowly to Autumn. "I don't want you to get up in harms about this, but I think you're a golem too. Just like Terra."

I grunted. "Up in arms, not harms, though I guess that applies really. But yeah, we just figured that one out."

"Good, but if we don't get out of here and underground in the next few minutes, Magnus will kill all of us but you two. If you, Wells, Autumn, and I get separated, we can't do what we need to do. It's all over."

Autumn finally snapped out of it. "What are we meant to do?"

Trickstan sighed. "I'm not sure, but I know where we need to go. We have to get to the Forge. Now."

Wells hoisted Ren off the floor, handing him over to Gideon. "The rest of us will fight off the guards. You carry him."

Gideon nodded, but Kiko shook her head. "No need, Mister. I've got the guards."

She popped away, then came back within a matter of minutes. She opened the door for us. "You go where you need to go. I'll make sure Joy is okay."

Fox shook his head. "Not without me, you aren't." He raced down the stairs and if I was a betting person, I'd bet he'd arrive at Joy's location before Kiko popped there.

Trickstan hugged his friend, then bounded out the door. We all filed in behind him. The guards were lying on the floor, their necks snapped. "Remind me not to cross Kiko in the future."

"She's good to have on your side. I am too, if you'll let me." Trickstan glanced over his shoulder at me, questioning with those crystal blue eyes of his. He seemed so much like *my* Tristan, that I was overcome with emotion for him. He'd betrayed us, but it was clear now he had no options. He'd been bound by Magic and not done it on purpose.

Before I could respond to him, Wells stepped in front of me. "We can discuss that later. Where are we going?"

Trickstan started walking again. "Underground. Way underground."

We stood on the threshold of the castle's side door. I did a quick scan and frowned. "There are guards everywhere and we're not exactly stealthy like Kiko. We need to split up to avoid being spotted." I was seconds away from telling Terra I wasn't splitting from her. Never fucking again. She pressed her lips together in the way she did when she was thinking.

"If we had a distraction, we could get away." Her eyes were shining with mischief as she turned to Trickstan. The playful arch of her eyebrow made my dick twitch. "Joy said she hated this sandcastle prison."

"What are you thinking, Precious? You look like a sneaky little fuckbunny right now" I murmured in her ear, lingering so I could breathe in her luscious scent as I nipped her ear.

She shrugged. "I need to know where Joy is now."

Trickstan nodded. He didn't even bother taking off his clothes before he made himself small, flying over the castle to survey the crowd. I guess he'd gotten his magic back since he'd returned to Aetheria.

He returned moments later, lighting Terra's shoulder. "She's on the dais talking to some people. Didn't see Magnus anywhere. He could be on his way to the turret as we talk."

"As we *speak*. And that's right where I want him." She pressed her hands on either side of the doorframe. Her bracelet glowed as Earth magic flowed through her fingertips. I motioned for the rest of the group to step outside with my head.

The group of us watched in fucking awe as a crack appeared over the door and sprawled its way up the side of the castle, branching into two, then four, then more. It took only a couple of minutes for the structure to start rumbling and shaking in the wake of her magic.

She was phenomenal.

The cracks snaked around the side, arching up to the turret. As it started to crumble into dust, Mace used his wolf speed to dart around to the other side. I heard him shout over the crowd. "What's happening up there?" before he sped back to us.

There was a moment of eerie silence as the crowd gazed up.

Then there was screaming.

All hell broke loose.

Satisfied that she'd started the process, Terra grinned. "I think that's enough to distract them for a while."

Damn right, it was.

The sandy turret disintegrated before our eyes, crumbling and sliding down. Gideon hoisted Ren over his shoulder and sent a hot blast of Water magic toward the top, wetting the top of the castle and making it slope even further.

It was time to go.

I nodded for Trickstan to get in front and show us the way. The others filed in line, and I took up the rear, glancing over my shoulder periodically and finding no guards following us. Everyone was freaking the fuck out about the castle falling in on itself to worry about us. Thank the Mage's long schlong.

We entered the square building, quickly taking out the four guards left in there. It had been quick work. Gideon even got one with his Fire and Water magic combined while Ren was still out on his shoulder.

Terra suddenly gripped my bicep. "Can you hear him? He's talking to us."

I cocked my head. "Who?"

"Andras. The phoenix whose blood we have. Why aren't you speaking in your head with him? He's so excited to meet you." She was pointing up to some cages at the top of the room. A burst of silver fire shot out from one of them, then a bunch of squawking.

The pain and excitement at seeing the creature who'd saved my life overwhelmed me, but I couldn't hear a damn thing in my head. I didn't know how to break that to her. Or him. "Wells, what did you do to get here? Why can't you hear us?"

Ignoring her questions for the moment, I snatched Trickstan out of the air, not even stopping to make sure I wasn't grabbing him by the nuts. "Where do we go now?"

He screeched. Oops. Got the nuts I guess. "Down on the middle platform. All the way."

Terra side-eyed me as she walked over to the center gold circle and positioned us in place around her. Instinctively, I wrapped my arms around her, resting my chin on the top of her head. She squeezed. "Don't think you're getting out of that conversation but hold me tighter."

Autumn shifted uncomfortably, inching closer to Mace, who put his arm around her. "Sorry, I was checking out your tits. In my defense, they're pretty nice."

A slight smirk appeared on her face, as she hooked her thumb at me. "Tell him that."

"He doesn't have to."

Terra pinched my ass—not in the playful way— just as Ren lifted his head and called out to her. "Terra?"

It was a big quadrafuck of mess, the four of us. But none of it mattered at the moment.

The platform jerked as it came to a stop in a huge, cavernous room made of rock with five identical pathways. We stepped off and Trickstan flew over to one of them. Terra pulled my sleeve. "The door over there is where they took us to swear on the square."

"And the other one is where they go to take the phoenix blood and perform the spells to convert all the magic Magnus steals into power for himself," Trickstan spat. "We're going in this door."

"What's in there?" Terra whispered.

"No idea. I just know it's the right place to go. Call it superstition."

Gideon laughed. "I think you mean intuition. I hope so anyway." He set Ren down on his own feet since he'd woken up.

He ran his hands through his hair. "The fuck happened?"

Mace slapped his back. "Your body was snatched by Magnus. He tried to make you kill us, but Wells knocked you out to stop you."

He shot his gaze in my direction, and I shrugged. "Not going to lie. It felt pretty good to hit you again, but are you okay?"

"I think. I just don't remember anything after Magnus took Fox and me to the castle earlier. How did you guys get to Aetheria? Where are we?"

"How do we know it's him now?" Gideon questioned. "He could be faking amnesia to see where we're going."

Trickstan flew up to Ren, practically landing on his nose. "Ask him something from a long time ago. Magnus has access to memories, but he doesn't have time to look at everything, especially when he's trying to make you do something. Something from childhood would work."

I glanced at Mace and Gideon. Ren had shared a lot of things with us, but rarely talked about what he and Bash had gone through before they left the vampire foster home.

Terra stepped over to him. "Sorry for this but name the vampire elders in order."

He frowned but answered anyway. "Augustus I, Cyria, Fantasia, Augustus II, Davina, Leopold, Benedict, Augustus III, Alessandro, Virgil, Leonardo, Helene, Samanthia, Crystal, Benton, Samuel."

At the mention of Augustus I, I frowned too. That slimy asshole was still lingering in my mind any time I thought about what I'd given up getting to Aetheria. But one look at Terra and the feeling faded. "I think it's him." When I noticed how he looked at her, I knew she was right.

Feeling comfortable that Ren was himself and we weren't followed, I stepped in front of the group, wanting to take the lead into the unknown. I would protect them all with my life—the only one I had left—if I had to do so.

I took one step and a torch on the wall flared to life with gold flames. Behind me, the gasps filled the stale air. No one had been in this door in years.

Another flame across the room blazed up and I lost my breath as the light filtered out the darkness.

It was the spiral staircase from the dreamscape. Exactly. Down to the swirling coil scrollwork between the balusters. "I have no idea how this thing got in my head, but this is the staircase I would see when I went into the dreamscape. Annigan told me it was a construct of my mind to help my subconscious travel from the waking world to the dreamscape. I've never seen it before though."

I took a tentative step onto the staircase. As I did so, torches came to life all the way down as far as I could see. Terra gripped my waist and took a step after me. The group of us started the lengthy trek down the stairs.

We descended in silence for a long while. Everyone was up in their heads about one thing or another, I guess. I kept pushing, descending step after step, trying to search my mind for memories that just wouldn't surface.

Finally, Autumn cried for us to stop. I paused and turned around to see why. She had crouched down and was running her fingers over the gold scrollwork. "Terra, look at this."

We all immediately saw what she was talking about. I was too preoccupied before, but the scrolls were exactly like their birthmark squiggles.

My pulse raced as Terra bent down to look for herself. How could I protect either one of them if we had no idea what all of this meant? "Trickstan, care to shed some light on this?"

"There's plenty of light with the torches. Can't you see it? Their birthmarks are right there on the stairs."

"No, idiot. I'm asking if you know *why* their birthmarks are there on the stairs?"

"Oh. Nope. Sorry. All I know is to keep going. I'm certain all our questions will be answered when we get to the bottom of these stairs. All of them."

I didn't need to hear anymore. I was more anxious than ever to get down these familiar stairs. I huffed, swatted him out of the way, and started to pick up the pace, keeping slow enough that Terra could follow along without getting behind.

About an hour or so later, we'd made it into yet another cavernous room. Only this one was lined in silver like someone had painted the walls with sterling. There was a torch of silver flames burning on each of the four walls.

I grieved at the sight. I missed my phoenix fire.

Autumn grunted. "Remember what I said about silver being anti-magic? This room was lined in silver to prevent magic from working here. I'd bet my life on it, but I can't imagine why."

Good question. Even though the room was massive, the walls seemed to close in on me, like a tomb. It reminded me of being in the coffin with Augustus, but there was something else snagging at the back of my brain. I got a sour taste in my mouth as I scoped out my surroundings.

Familiar and unknown at the same time.

420

Mace went over to one of the walls. "What are these grooves? Decoration for an empty room or something else?" He ran a finger over one of four tracks in the wall. They weren't bigger than a couple of inches and had been carved into the silver "They're dusty."

A whooshing sound echoed, bouncing over the silver as a strong gust of Wind magic swirled around us. Mace had Wind, but all he'd done was swipe the groove with his finger. "Did you release your magic?"

"No. I was just doing a glove test. I swear I didn't make that happen."

Something had.

My gut lurched with anticipation and dread. I'd seen this before. No, I'd felt it.

Terra joined him. "Four channels in the walls, four kinds of elemental Magic. Maybe we need to wake the other ones up." She ran her fingers over one line, but nothing happened. When she hit the second one though, dust from the floor flew up and entered the groove she'd touched. Earth magic came to life like the Wind.

She was onto something.

Gideon went over to use his Water magic, but Autumn stopped him. "Wait. Wells, you need to come see this."

She'd walked around to the back side of the spiral stairs. It was darker there because the flames weren't big, but she was crouched down touching something on the concrete floor. When I made it over to her, she stood to get out of the way.

Something in my mind flashed like lightning. A strong sense of déjà vu overwhelmed me.

I had been here.

Right under the stairs.

Terra appeared at my side, holding onto my shoulders as I bent down.

There were two sets of handprints left in the concrete. One large, one small. Two names were etched above them. Darian and Wells. Payne was written underneath.

Terra gasped.

I couldn't gasp. I couldn't breathe. Or blink.

Placing my hand in the larger handprint, I had to choke down the sob that threatened to come out. I hardly remembered my father, but I always got the warmest feeling of love when I thought of him.

He'd left his handprint.

So had I.

I moved my hand, tracing the tiny one I'd left in the past, needing to connect to it in a way I didn't fully get. As I did, the space between the two hands shimmered and a small circle appeared. Of course, circles meant magic, but I was at a loss for what it all meant. "I don't understand."

Terra kissed my cheek. "I don't either, but maybe we need to activate all the magic to get answers."

I stood. Nodded. Squared my shoulders. No time for sentimentality or confusion. My pack, my friends, needed me strong, not breaking down over the memories of a father I never really knew.

I nodded at Gideon. He touched one of the grooves and released Water. Autumn touched the last one and it lit on fire.

We were standing in an empty silver room at the bottom of a staircase I'd seen in my head, watching all four magics swirling around the perimeter of the room. I could feel the ghost of my father's handprint grazing my hand.

"Thank Me, you're finally here."

We all jumped at the voice echoing across the silver surfaces.

Terra swung around. "Wait, you all heard that?"

Ren, who'd been silent for a long time, stepped over to her, adopting a protective stance that I both hated and loved him for. "Is that the voice you've been hearing in your mind?"

"Yes. Thank the Mage everyone else heard it too this time."

"Don't thank me yet. I need the key."

Terra pulled a weird key out of her bag. "Um, I've got it. What do we do?"

The voice laughed. "Put it in the keyhole. Over between the handprints. Each of you must put a different prong in and turn one revolution. Terra, Autumn, Trickstan, and Wells. No particular order, just whatever feels right to you."

Terra walked back over the handprints and handed the key to me. "You should go first. This is your legacy."

I'll be damned if a lump didn't form in my throat, but I swallowed a few times and took the key, sticking the first prong in the hole and then turning, before I handed it back to her. As the single most important person in my life, she should be second. "You next."

She kept her fingers around the prong I'd used so she'd pick a different one, then stuck it in and turned, handing it to Autumn. "I thought I'd feel something."

Autumn did her turn as Trickstan enlarged. Ren reached inside Terra's bag and handed him a pair of pants to put on. Once he was dressed, he inserted the key and turned.

We all held our breath.

.

Terra

The room began to hum as the magic in the four grooves grew. Before long we had a raging tornado of Earth, Wind, Fire, and Water above our heads. Just when I thought we'd go deaf with the roaring sound, it stopped, falling to the floor.

We all ducked to escape it and when we recovered, a large black glass ball was sitting in the middle of the room.

A.

Large.

Black.

Glass

Ball.

"Are you kidding me right now? This looks like my Gram's 8-Ball."

The voice, now we could determine was coming from within the—I just went ahead and called it like I saw it—imitation Magic 8-Ball laughed. "Um, my sources say no?"

"What is this? I need to know what this is. Trickstan?"

I turned to him, and he was staring at the ball, motionless except for the rapid blinking of his big blue eyes. "Oh," he muttered. "Oh, oh, this dings a bell."

Ren smacked the back of his head. "Rings. Now tell us everything you know, or I will end you."

Trickstan walked over to the ball and placed his hands on the glass. "I think it's better if I show you." At his touch, the glass began to swirl. All the black faded until there was nothing left but a clear ball.

Inside said ball?

A man with long salt and pepper dreadlocks, wearing an old mustard yellow shirt and holey jeans, barefoot, mind you, was standing in the middle of the ball playing the violin.

Gideon cleared his throat. "Missouri Joe Houseman?"

I scoffed. "What do you mean? This is the guy who owned my Gram's house?" Gideon nodded. "I don't understand."

The guy, Missouri Joe Houseman, kept on playing, dancing around in a circle like he was oblivious to the fact he was encapsulated in a glass fish bowl, and we were all there staring at him.

I rapped on the glass, but he didn't respond.

Wells stepped up, and let's just say he wrapped harder than I did. Nothing.

We all turned to Trickstan, who shrugged.

Finally, when Missouri Joe Houseman was finished with his tune, he turned back around and bowed. "Apologies. It's been so long since I've had an audience. Did you like my song? I wrote it."

I forced a fake laugh, irritated to the core. "Sure. It was great. I'd love your autograph."

Missouri Joe Houseman, apparently, was not well-versed in sarcasm. He walked over to the glass and used his finger to scrawl the autograph I'd requested with etching magic.

There in sparkling gold was the same squiggle as my birthmark and Autumn's.

He had been our maker.

And I immediately realized the squiggle wasn't a squiggle or a coil, or a decorative scroll.

It was an M.

"You're the Mage. Like, *the* Mage."

"In the flesh. You can call me Mage or I'm fine with Missouri Joe. Now you all need to get in here before Magnus finds you. We've got a lot of work to do to defeat him."

My brain spiraled like the staircase at my back.

It was impossible.

The Mage had died and left Aetheria millennia ago.

Or so they said.

He'd made us.

And Wells and his father had had something to do with it.

And he wanted us to come in the glass bowl.

I couldn't process any of the zillions of thoughts sparking around my brain. Everything just went blank. Then I had one solitary thought in my head: Gram was right.

The Mage had a beard.

The story's not over yet! Look for the fourth and final book in the Diminishing Magic series coming in Spring 2024. Until then…

enjoy my paranormal Christmas Why Choose story,

Fixin' Vixen.

Fixin' Vixen Chapter 1

Vixen

Santa was a real dumbass if he thought his little trick was going to work. You couldn't just stuff Christmas spirit into someone like you were Gordon Ramsey making holiday turkey. No. Christmas spirit was born of love and magic and both of those had been obliterated in my heart roughly six seconds after I found my boyfriend of two years recently 'fixed' nose between the thighs of his ex.

Fucking Clari—

Sorry. She'd rebranded when he did. Lost a couple of letters.

Fucking *Clare*.

I hoisted my bag over my shoulder and trudged toward the Holidays Inn. No, not that one. The one at the South Pole, designed for magical species, with small idyllic cabins, huge evergreen trees, and a picturesque setting that looked like it was ripped out of every Hallmark Christmas movie ever made. It wouldn't have surprised me if Santa had some boring, but handsome man who just happened to be here to run these cabins for his dear old ailing auntie locked and loaded for me to fall in love with behind these doors.

The joke was on Santa. I was finished with romance for a while. Maybe forever.

Heartbreak would do that to a girl. Er, reindeer shifter.

When I reached the porch, I stomped all the snow off my boots that I could and took a deep breath. Even after shifting back to my human form, my body ached from the long flight from North to South. I craved a gallon of alcohol and a nice warm bed to wallow in.

At least I would get those here on my little forced vacation. I just had to get through the long weekend. I'd play nice, plaster on a fake smile, and "chillax" as Santa put it. I'd bide my time until I was allowed back at the North Pole again. Because I'd be damned if I let that asshole Rudy ruin my place on the fleet. I was Vixen. *The* Vixen and I'd been one of the leaders of the fleet for centuries. Way before he ever showed up.

Christmas was a couple of weeks away and Santa was going to ground me if I didn't have an attitude adjustment, so adjust my attitude, I would. At least externally. Though if you asked me, Rudy was the one who needed to change.

Or maybe die.

The wooden door squeaked as I opened it and the second my toes stepped over the threshold of the cabin facility's main lobby, warmth penetrated my bones, and the ache of flying melted. This place wasn't going to make my heart ache go away, but at least my body felt better thanks to whatever magic was laced within the walls. I pulled off my hat and my curly red mane tumbled down over my shoulders.

Rudy had said my hair was what drew him away from Clare at first. He'd run his fingers through it every chance he got. I should've known then. It should've hit me like a blinking red warning light. He pursued me before they broke up. I didn't act on it until after they'd called it quits, but the old saying was true: once a cheater, always a cheater. He had only her short brown pixie cut to play with now. Sucker.

I shook my head to dislodge the spiral I was taking. I did not need to think about him anymore. He will go down in history as the worst boyfriend, the most despicable reindeer, the embarrassment of Santa's fleet. He had to. The pain in my heart demanded it.

I slid out of my coat and trudged over to the counter, passing several people who were sitting by the huge fireplace chatting and sipping drinks. A man caught my eye on the way over. He was dressed in a black suit, though his red tie had been loosened around his collar. He seemed very out of place for that kind of establishment. His dark hair was slicked in a carefully controlled way that made his cheekbones even sharper. A fleeting thought of what he would look like with bed head swirled in my mind, but I tucked that away in the darkest recesses where it belonged.

The way he was poised in the chair closest to the door said he was all about refinement and control. He wasn't relaxed, but he didn't look uncomfortable either. His back was straight, jaw tight, and his cold-as-ice eyes seemed to drink me in. The coolest shiver spread through me; goosebumps erupted over my spine.

I looked away, unable to hold his gaze for very long. Something about him was magnetic, but I didn't need any warning bells this time. He was the lethal kind of gorgeous that signaled trouble. It practically drizzled from him like melting icicles dripping on the snow.

I dropped my bag on the floor and picked up the—Santa help me—set of jingle bells lying on the counter, ringing them to call someone over to check me in. A woman's voice called from beyond a swinging door. "Ho, ho! I'll be just a minute. Make yourself at home!"

Leaning against the counter, I turned to face the fireplace. A man was drinking a beer sitting next to a young girl, probably around eleven or twelve. He stared at her numbly while her thumbs flew over the phone in her hand. She sighed and looked up. "OK Boomer, the Wi-Fi in this place sucks. You hauled my ass all the way here in the middle of a crisis and then cut me off from the world so I couldn't keep up with what was going on. SMH. Dad of the damn year."

The man frowned. "Language, Cherish." She huffed at him and went back to flicking her phone. "I told you this trip was to help us become closer. We can't do that if you don't try too. Love is a two-way street."

Cherish kept one hand on her phone and twirled her long black braids with the other, never even looking up. "I'll get that printed on a t-shirt." Then she raised her voice to punctuate her point. "If we ever get out of this hellhole!"

I couldn't help but laugh. She was my kind of kid, and I instantly felt a connection to her and her brazen sassiness. Her father's dark eyes fell as he took another long sip of beer. I could read the anguish on his face. It made me feel for him. He was trying to connect with her. However, I knew from experience that sometimes trying wasn't enough.

"Ho ho, here I am! Come let's get you all checked in and decked out, shall we?" I turned and found a woman striding through the swinging doors backward, carrying a tray of cookies. Her hair was a piled-up mess of salt and pepper curls tied with a huge red velvet bow and two literal candy canes hung from her ears. It looked like Christmas had exploded all over her.

At the North Pole, we liked to call them Festivers. They're the ones who start listening to Christmas music on Halloween and leave their tree up until Valentine's Day. They're so full of Christmas spirit, it erupts out of them like volcanoes all the time.

I shuddered. They were the worst. And I swore if she tried to put me in an ugly Christmas sweater with kittens on it, I would've bolted. Flown right back to the North Pole.

"Hello there. I'm Holly." Of course, she was. "I'm assuming you're Vixen. It's quite an honor to have such an esteemed member of Santa's fleet here with us this week! Please, have a cookie."

I took a cookie because it had Rudy's face on it. I bit into it with extreme force, chomping and chewing out my frustrations at the asshole reindeer. It would probably give me indigestion later, but I didn't care. It felt good to grind him between my teeth. "Thank you, but can we keep the reindeer shifter thing on the DL? I'm trying to be lowkey here if that's okay with you. Just a little chillaxing time to myself." I cringed at the words coming out of my mouth. Who still said chillax? That would be Santa.

She tapped her finger on the side of her nose. "Of course. Mum's the word." She rummaged around behind the counter and produced a key. "You're in cabin twelve. I'll just check you in under the name Vicki Klaus with a K." She winked, thinking she was being so stealthy, and handed me the key. "We have drinks here in the lobby at five each evening. Breakfast is from seven to nine, lunch from twelve to one, dinner from six to eight. The Wi-Fi doesn't always work," she said in a hushed tone as she glanced at Cherish. "But the password is Jolly with a capital J, twelve, twenty-five. Anything else you need, just jingle the bells in your cabin and one of my staff or I will come running. Santa gives us a little magic to use here and there."

I didn't plan to jingle the bells. I'd planned on a three-day drunk that ended with me flying back North to claim my spot on the team. I fiddled with the collar around my neck, a touchstone, and symbol that Santa hadn't given up on me completely.

Okay big guy, I'll play your little game.

Get FIXIN' VIXEN by scanning the QR code.

It automatically gets you on the Nice list.

(But wait, there's more. Keep turning…)

ACKNOWLEDGEMENTS & A NOTE FROM THE AUTHOR

This one was tough, y'all. I put these characters through some things and I failed to account for the idea that I had to go through it with them. The angst, the angst! Luckily, I made it through to the other side and I hope you did too. There's a little more story to tell for Terra, Wells, and the Boulderbrook pack. The final book in the series will answer all the questions and hopefully end in a way that makes you smile.

I want to thank you readers first & foremost for coming along with me on this journey to fulfill my biggest dream. (I've given up on making it as a Broadway star. Some dreams will never be...) I appreciate every review, every kind word, and every social media post or shoutout. It's tough being an indie author these days, but the readers make it worth the effort. So, thank you. If I could give you the moon and all the gold in Aetheria, I would.

I couldn't have made it through this book without you, Mandy O'Dell. Thank you for all the opinions, ideas, kicks in the pants, and general brain-sharing. I'm published because of you and I won't ever forget it!

Shoutout to our property manager, Betty, for allowing us to move from the loft with the spiral staircase to the one-story loft across the hall. Y'all, those stairs were killing my back. But they served as great inspiration in my latest turning lemons into lemonade feat. (Did I almost fall down them once? Yep, but it scared me so much that I dreamed about them. *lightbulb*)

Special love to those who follow me and interact on TikTok, the person who invented Diet Coke, and my cats Poe and Raven, all of whom have helped me in various ways on my journey through this book. As always, big love for my family who continue to support me and listen like they're interested when I ramble on about my books and characters.

Also: Sorry McDonald's. I love your nugs.

Sign up for my monthly newsletter for behind the scenes looks, teasers, writing updates, current reads and more.

I hope to be able to get my act together enough to update all my socials on the daily. I'm trying. It would help if I had someone to talk to there. (Hint, hint. Nudge, nudge.)

Follow me for general shenanigans on these sites.

@CatCollinsBooks everywhere

Thanks for reading.

Please consider leaving a review on Amazon. It helps indie authors like me gain more traction in their algorithms. Most of us don't have the big bucks to pay for reviews and advertising like the big publishing houses do for their authors. So, I'd appreciate the reviews on Amazon and wherever else you might leave them.

Don't forget to follow me there too!

Scan the QR to be whisked away to the review page magically.

ABOUT THE AUTHOR

Cat Collins is the #1 bestselling author in her home. No really, her husband wrote a training manual for work once. Sold one copy to his boss. She writes what she likes to read: swoony alphas, witty dialogue, and steamy scenes that make your heart (and various other parts) flutter.

Her Diminishing Magic series has garnered praise from reviewers and a 5-star Readers' Favorite review for its hilarious banter, sexual tension between characters, and turns you never see coming. Described as a "twisty bundle of fun," and a "rollercoaster ride you won't want to get off," the series includes elemental magic, wolf shifters, and a main character who's full of sass.

A reading interventionist by day, reader and binge-watcher by night, Cat lives in the Southern US with her aforementioned husband, two kids and two cats, one of whom likes to edit as Cat is writing by jumping on the keyboard unexpectedly. Any stray typos must certainly be the work of Poe.